MISTRESS
OF
BEES

I0582831

BERNIE MOJZES

DRAGONWELL PUBLISHING

Design by Dragonwell Publishing

Published by Dragonwell Publishing, Dragonwell, LLC
www.dragonwellpublishing.com

ISBN

978-1-940076-84-3 (Paperback)
978-1-940076-86-7 (EPub)

PRAISE FOR *MISTRESS OF BEES*

"*Mistress of Bees* collects the adventures of Lady Maris Goselin, who is introduced to us as if we're about to read a collection of tales suitable for children. But Lady Maris has no intention of bowdlerizing her own bawdy retellings. In presenting the unvarnished truth, she reveals herself as a perpetually lustful, ill-tempered, immodest, and sly practitioner of bee magic. Here she takes on human villains and mad conjurers, a magic-user with a rat in her hair, a dead cat, a race of goblins, and even, now and again, conjured creatures from other worlds. Bernie Mojzes serves up one rollicking adventure after another in the entertaining and *true* recollections of Lady Maris."

—Gregory Frost, author of *Rhymer* and *The Secret House*

"The perfect blend of magic, adventure, humor, and heart. Each interlinked story builds upon the last, creating a rich and full tapestry of a living, breathing world."

—A. C. Wise, author of *Wendy Darling* and *Hooked*

"A page-turning collection of stories of a well-developed, complicated character trying to survive in a difficult world full of magic and intrigue!"

—Michael Ventrella, author of *Fortannis* series

TABLE OF CONTENTS

THE KNOWN NATIONS
OF FORTANNIS

THE
BILE
DENS

CUULANNIS

MOORGRAVE

THE
PLAINS
OF
RAGE

AMISARA

FALKIRK

ICENIA

DUCHY
OF
ASHBURY

THE
CONTESTED
LANDS

ASHBURY

IMLADAR

THE
VACARRAN
ISLES

BAY OF VACARRA

LEMPUR

THESSI

THE
SARR LANDS

THE GREAT DESERT

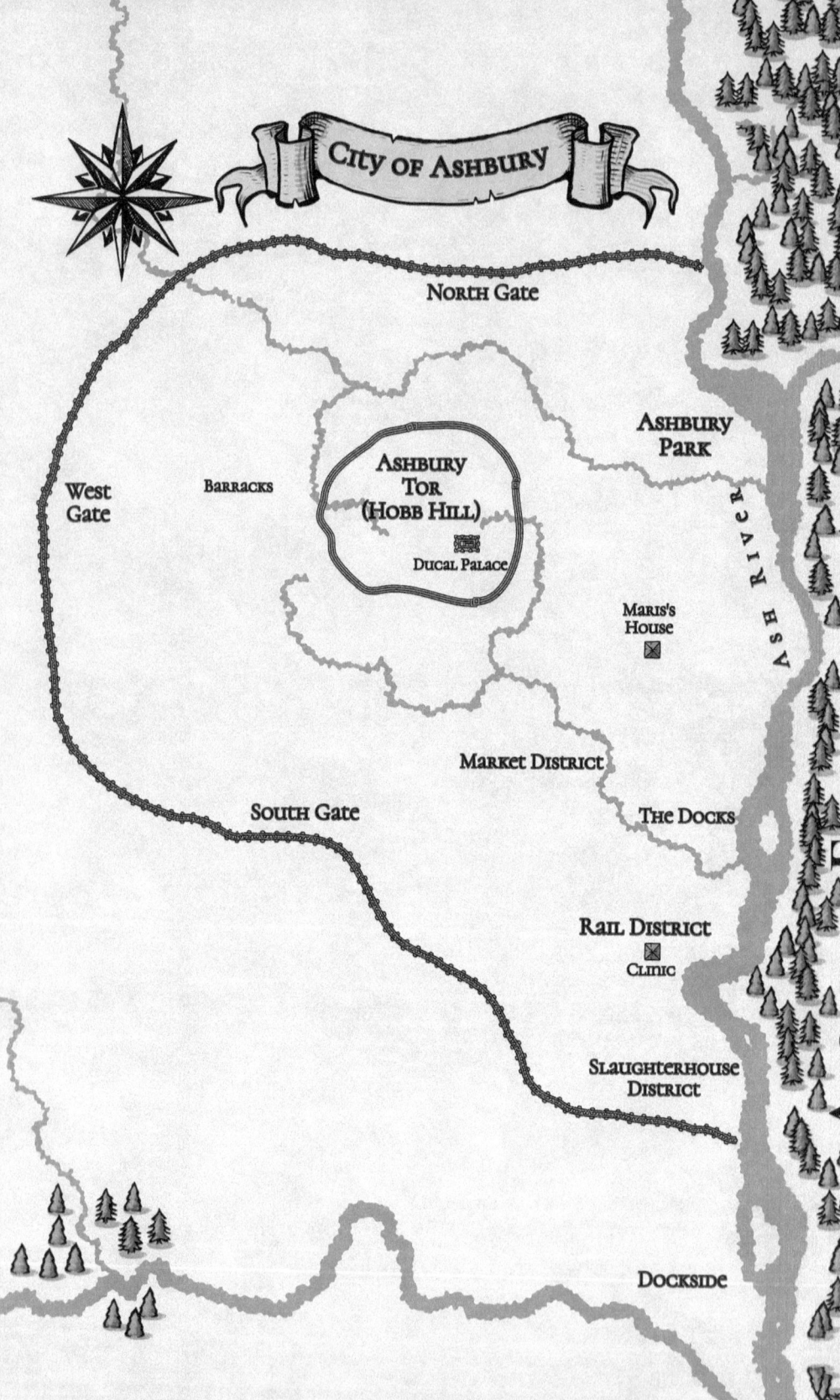

INTRODUCTION

L ike every Amisaran child, I was raised on Maris Goselin stories. I think my favorite was *Maris Goselin and the Lost City of Clouds*, with its vertiginous escapades and lofty ideals, but I loved them all. What child hasn't reenacted scenes from *Maris Goselin and the Mud Men* on a rainy day? Or *Maris Goselin & the Valley of Ice*, in the winter months? I must admit it came as quite a surprise to me to learn that it is only within the last few years that this hunger has infected her home city of Ashbury.

As happens with every figure who shuns the limelight, these Amisaran stories grew to proportions implausible, improbable, and mythic. In Ashbury, where she remained a very real and present force, the stories surrounding Maris Goselin were whispered in the dark, and those who remembered her did so with fear and unease, as she preferred.

It was with shock and wonder when, one difficult day barely a year ago as I write this, I was handed the most precious gift Lady Maris Goselin could have given me: all of her original manuscripts.

Since that time, I have devoted myself to devouring every page written in her hand over the long course of her life—whether they be episodes from her life or designs for spells, shopping lists or detailed descriptions of the identification and preparation of certain poisonous herbs—until I felt I could recite them word for word.

Maris was no stranger to the printed word, having published everything from spell books for the disabled to subversive political treatises, from erotic fantasies to unflinching memoirs, from suppressed histories to medical diagnostic handbooks to gaming manuals of the purest escapist fantasy.

What you hold in your hands is a mere fragment of the person who took to herself the name Maris Goselin, but a deeply personal fragment which I hope will reveal the true depth and flawed complexity of the person behind the myths and the stories. But for one piece (offered here by Sollaman Jonthansen—a dear friend, and one of the rare few whom I would trust to tell a tale true and without embellishment), the words are her own, with only the lightest of editorial touches for purposes of spelling or clarity. I hope that in reading these glimpses into her life, you—and the world—will learn to see Maris a little bit closer to the way I do.

—Frida Marisdottr, 10 Julo, 488AA

BAD DEBTS

This is all Justino Frankwell's fault. He came to me asking if I could write up the story of what happened in Ashbury Park last summer. The Midsummer Day's Massacre, he calls it. He wanted to serialize the tale in the *Ashbury Gazette*, which I guess he can do, since he owns it.

Do I want to talk about it? No. But having become unemployable due to last year's events, the money was enticing, and I quickly wrote up exactly what occurred. Next morning, Frankwell sent a courier to call me into his office, where he demonstrably lit my manuscript on fire and dropped it page by page into his trash bin. What can I say? I've seen people spend money on stupider things than magic smoke-free trash bins.

"Anybody can write a history," he said, "but nobody wants to *read* history. People want to know about Lady Maris Goselin, and how she got tangled up in all this mess. They want to know what she was thinking, what she was doing, and most importantly, what she was feeling. They want to know about *you*."

"Yeah, right," I said, unconvinced.

"And that bard friend of yours, what was his name?" he said, almost as an afterthought. "Spring something. They want to know about you and that Spring fellow."

And Spring. Of course. Bastard.

If I hadn't already spent part of the advance, I might have stormed out. I might even have altered his décor on the way. But I've done more distasteful things in my life to put food on the table, and to have a table to put it on, so here it is: the story of me, my ex-boyfriend, and his girlfriend, saving the world, for all the thanks we got.

With feelings.

A hot Midsummer Day in Ashbury Park. Perfect for a midday concert in the park, and pretty much the opposite of what you'd expect for necromancy and mass murder, but imagine how boring life would be without little surprises.

I wasn't there for the concert. In fact, it was the last place I wanted to be. Posters advertising the return of Ashbury's most famous bard were plastered all over the city, and I never knew when I might turn the corner and be confronted with his face. What I really wanted was to crawl into bed for a year and not come out until the concert was over and all the posters torn down or plastered over. But if I did that, I wouldn't have a bed—or a roof over it—for very long. I was at my former lover's concert for the same reason I'm writing these words: money. I was being paid to witness the handoff of an illegal object of power from one wizard of dubious ethics to another, and report back the identity of the recipient to my employer. And, if someone tried to interfere with that transaction, to make sure they failed.

I'd sent my bees foraging around the park and buzzing through the audience, and picked a spot for myself under a tree a bit up the hill overlooking the stage—well out of the writhing, sweating crowd and, not coincidentally, with a good view of the entire stretch of the Ash River as it passed through the park. The stage had been built against the backdrop of the river, just above the flood line, and constructed to project sound out across the park grounds. No expense spared. The air hung thick and still, damper than Duchess Dara's nethers at a formal tea, and everyone knows how she loves tea. And formality. The merciless sun glared through the haze.

None of that deterred the eager throngs crowding the stage to see the triumphant return of Ashbury's favorite son.

It set my teeth on edge.

Spring had filled out over the years. Broad shoulders and strong arms. Scandalously tight trousers that nobody seemed to mind. It was odd that the ruggedly handsome man on the stage was the same scrawny street urchin I'd last seen when we'd fled Ashbury together. The same boy who'd walked away and left me alone in the wilderness. Irony, thy name is Fame; the soldiers that used to drive us away if he gathered too large a crowd now guarded the stage built in his honor and watched for pickpockets in the audience.

Spring had always performed alone when I knew him, just him singing and playing his lute. Now he had an entourage: a Selunari guitarist with a braided beard, garbed almost entirely in what appeared to be brightly colored scarves knotted together, and a grey-furred Sarr in an off-white robe perched in the midst of a dizzying variety of drums and percussion. Both displayed a finesse and professionalism that still eluded Spring. Yet it was *his* name on the billing, *his* face on the posters. *His* trousers the crowd mooned over. It was easier to stoke my rage than address the quivering in my chest.

He had no right coming back to *my* city, just because it was safe for him now. Coward.

I tore my eyes away from the stage. This was a bad idea. I never should have taken this job, but now that I had, I had an obligation to see it through. I scoured the crowd for my quarry: one Helmar Q'agit, dabbler in petty magics and pettier crimes. He was due to meet the buyer at precisely noon by the river's edge.

Four sharp clacks of the drumsticks counted out the beat, drawing my eyes back to the stage just in time to see the trio launch into their first song. Well, not the whole trio. Spring strutted and posed at the front of the stage while the Selunari strummed strong chords on his guitar. The Sarr pounded exotic southern rhythms on the drums while the tail-held tambourine wove an intricate counter-rhythm, dancing and twitching like a charmed snake.

Then Spring reached into a case behind him and raised his lute to his chest. I gritted my teeth. He still had it. The lute I'd gotten for him. Gotten? Stolen. The lute that ruined everything. His fingers found the strings, and sound and light and sensation washed over the audience.

The adoring crowd swayed in time with the music (and the tail), and I felt my own hips moving to the throbbing rhythm of the drums before I knew I was dancing.

Maybe later I'd get Spring to introduce me to the Sarr, clearly the talent in the band. In the meantime, I had a job to do. Ignoring the stage and the music and Spring's voice as best I could, I scoured the park for any sight of Q'agit.

The shadows had grown short when one of my bees informed me that the target of my vigil had arrived. It took several minutes to identify *which* of the bees was feeding me fractured images of the man's pallid face. Q'agit waded into the writhing chaos that was the audience on the northwest corner of the field, crossing diagonally past the stage toward the southeast, where a sandy beach dipped down into the river. I settled in to watch, fanning myself with my skirts. If only it wasn't so blazing hot. Sweat beaded on my neck and thighs and gathered under my arms and breasts. What was wrong with these people? Proper Evil happened at night, midnight on a full moon on the darkest day of the year, not at high noon on Midsummer Day. Hadn't they read the handbook?

On the stage, Spring shifted into another song. An older piece. Unaccompanied.

My breath caught.

All these years, and I still knew all the words. Bastard. He had no right to sing that song, not here, where I could hear it. Not anywhere. And why today, when I couldn't avoid him?

I considered sending some of my bees to swarm the stage and let him know what I thought of him coming back to my city. What I thought of him singing a song he'd written for *me* to anyone else. Ever.

After what seemed like an eternity of misery, he finished the song and launched straight into another, the entire band joining in. Simple and anthemic, it lacked even the most basic musical component: melody. The audience loved it, dancing and raising their fists in the air.

I was
Born in Icenia.
Born in Icenia...

The crowd chanted the moronic refrain every time it returned.

A bee bumped my nose. And bumped my nose again. I was paying attention to the wrong thing, the hive was telling me, and had lost sight of Q'agit. If something happened to him before the handoff, I wasn't getting paid. And I liked getting paid.

Cursing Spring under my breath, I took out my spyglass and scanned the crowd for Q'agit's ostentatious robes. Ah, there he was.

He'd made it quite a bit farther than I'd expected. But something seemed wrong. Rather than weaving through the surging crowd, he shoved through impatiently, pushing much larger men aside with unexpected ease, heading directly for the riverbank. No, not impatiently. Mechanically. He broke free of the audience and headed toward the river. His diminutive figure was oddly distended, hunched, as if he wore a pack of some sort on his back under his robe. Was this where he was carrying the package?

I shook my head. Something wasn't right. Even the bees knew it, but I didn't have enough information to act yet. Gathering power to myself, I expanded my surveillance. I sent bees to the shoreline to search for the buyer. No one there looked particularly suspicious.

But then, if you're going to engage in illegal necromancy in broad daylight, why look suspicious?

It was high noon; the sun was directly overhead. Q'agit reached the river and waded into the water, ignoring everyone on the beach. He pushed past naked children splashing in the shallows with their mothers, past the young men who flirted with the mothers whose husbands danced in front of the stage with younger girls. He continued until the water reached his ribs, then lifted both arms and cast his head back.

The hump on his back swelled. His robe split, and shadows spilled out.

And then I was running, down the hillside to the river, stupid skirts gathered up around my waist, any thought of discretion forgotten. Around Q'agit the water roiled, liquid tentacles rising from the once-placid shallows, dancing with the shadows that burst from his back.

The screams started.

I reached for magic as I ran, catching the gossamer threads in my fingers and gathering them close, twisting and tying and knotting to shape them to my will. The Earth moved under my feet, the sod rolling before me to speed my descent. The wind gathered me in her arms and propelled me forward over the crowd, over the bathers in the water and the people on the shore, caught in the creature's coils. Water rose up at my command, caught me and spun me to face my quarry.

Responding to my distress, my bees swarmed Q'agit, sinking stingers into his body. He ignored them, and me, dead eyes staring through me as the shadows spilling from his split body melted into the liquid tentacles. Two monsters—one an elemental called up the river from the deepest depths of this world, the other something much worse from far beyond—intertwined and merged.

I understood then: Q'agit wasn't the courier. He was the package.

And I was the stooge that guarded his delivery.

How do you kill someone who is already dead? Did it even matter anymore? His body shrank visibly as the night poured out of him. Whatever had been inside his shell had escaped, infiltrating the shimmering waters of the elemental with its shadowy void, turning it into something inky and viscous and ravenous.

I stared as people thrashed in the monster's grip. What could I do? Waist-deep in the river, the prevalent form of power available was tied by its nature to water, and there was no way I could use that to fight the elemental force of water itself. There was air, but that was a flighty and insubstantial power, unless you have the time to build its strength. But time was in short supply—already, a woman near me held with her head under the water went limp. Air magic it was.

I wove a spell to whip the air into a frenzy, forming small whirlwinds to cut through the watery tendrils where they emerged from the surface, stripping them to a fine mist. It took less than a minute to sever a fully grown tentacle. Detached, the limb immediately lost its form and splashed back into the river.

But a minute is a long time, plenty of time for the thing to crush whatever was in its grasp. In the meantime, more tentacles than I was destroying emerged from the depths. Several dozen were reaching toward the audience, and toward the stage. Toward Spring.

A tentacle swung in front of me, holding a squalling toddler. I tried bringing my whirlwind to bear closer to the victim, where the tendrils were thinner and quicker to cut. Maybe.... No. The monster squeezed the child until he popped, spraying me with viscera.

Nothing I could do would save those caught in the monster's grasp, I realized.

In another moment, dozens more would be snared, maybe hundreds.

Something bumped up against me. A woman's body, caught in the current. She was young, still just a girl, too young to be a mother, and far too young to die.

No. A feeling as dangerous as the creature I faced rose within me. I could not save these people, but this stopped here.

I reached into the sky, twining hot threads of power that had travelled unimaginable distances into my fingers, and pulled down fire, stolen from the very sun itself.

It was only for a second or two, but that was enough. The stench of hot river muck and burnt flesh—both human and otherwise—filled the air. What was left of poor Q'agit collapsed in on itself. Boiling tendrils dropped their charred victims and retreated into the river's depths. The tentacles reaching out toward the stage boiled away at their root and dissolved into droplets. I had stopped the monster.

But I hadn't killed it.

Bodies bobbed in the water, swirled and bumped around me, and slowly drifted downstream. Someone screamed my name, my old name, over and over. I remember staring at the carnage and thinking how easy it would be to let exhaustion take me, to sink under the wavelets and let the current bear me into oblivion, where I'd never have to hear that name or any other ever again.

Then something twisted around my feet and pulled me under. It lifted me up and slammed me against the surface of the water with enough force to drive scalding hot river water up my nose and into my lungs. Coiling around me from head to foot, it started to squeeze.

Staring into the liquid ink, I saw stars that reached forever, and beyond that, a hideous void that watched, and saw, and stared back into me.

It whispered to me, its voice like viscous sandpaper tongues across my skin, vile and delicious.

It was only a few moments.

It was only for eternity.

It ended too soon.

I woke gasping and clawing for air. A familiar face hovered somewhere; panicked, I reached for it, came in contact with it far too soon.

"Ow!" Spring's voice, surprised and hurt.

I'd heard that tone before. It had enraged me then. This time, flavored with the scent of scorched flesh and river muck, it had a different effect. I turned my head and vomited, water and mud and bits of the morning's sausage. I swatted away helpful hands as I pushed myself away from the offended earth.

The world spun, too close and bright and claustrophobic. Too *present*. I fell back to my hands and knees and pressed my head against the resentful soil until the whispers quieted. I'd saved some lives—the people on the stage and in front of it—but at what cost?

Guards were fishing corpses from the Ash, hooking them with spears and halberd spikes. Boats in the marina upstream remained moored—nobody was braving deeper waters. Those bodies out of reach caught in the current and drifted downstream. There were more than I could bear to count. Yes, the creature would have killed them all. But it hadn't.

I had.

When I could finally sit up, I tried to wipe my face with my sleeve, only to discover I had none. My skirts clung wet and translucent against my legs, but of my blouse there was no sign. I was too weary for either shame or modesty.

"It's burned off," I said.

"I know." Spring touched a handkerchief to my face. "It'll grow back."

"Yes," I said. Then I realized what he'd said. "What?"

He stroked my head, and his hand felt cool against my scalp. "Your hair. It will grow back. Remember that time...?" His hand fell to my hip.

I remembered. Wildly drunk, we'd taken turns daring each other with a straight razor I'd acquired until not a single hair remained on either of our bodies. The hair had grown back. Something else I'd given away that night had not, and I resented Spring for tying that magical experience to this. I slapped his hand away.

"I'm going to bed your drummer. I want you to introduce me to him."

Spring gave a surprised laugh. "Kilanh is female."

"Even better."

His laugh faltered. "You can't. She's involved." A touch of color spotted his cheeks, and I knew the nature of her involvement.

The Sarr's face floated in the wavering haze that was the world behind Spring's back. From the look she gave him, and from the irritated sound of the tambourine as her tail twitched, I also knew that her understanding of her involvement was different from his.

My turn to laugh, even if it tasted a bit of bile, and sounded of it, too. "Good."

"I just saved your life!" His strong fingers gripped my chin and directed my gaze into his. Once upon a time that's all it would have taken, a touch and a look. "I went out there into that, that boiling river, and I pulled you out. I breathed air back into your lungs. From my lips to yours." His thumb traced my lower lip.

"You did me no favors." The whispers rose in my mind, and I willed them into sullen silence. I pushed both Spring and the whispers away, and ran.

I had been unfair to Spring.

He had been brave, risking waters that no others would dare, to save my miserable life. He had been gallant. Self-sacrificing. He had been the boy I'd fallen in love with as a child, before everything changed.

I didn't care. I had more important things on my mind.

I assessed the damage. Those parts of my body that had been beneath the surface of the water when I seized a piece of the sun—everything below my midriff—were unscathed. Above that, I had been scoured clean. Every hair was gone, not just on my head. Eyebrows, eyelashes, armpits, everything. My skin was pink and fresh, as if the outer layer had been burnt away without affecting anything beneath. A bit tender, yes, but not permanently harmed.

I changed into more accustomed garb—leggings and a baggy white shirt over a loosely tied black leather corset, and soft leather boots that reached to my knees, all of which served to conceal all manner of useful and lethal tricks. A wide belt supported my visible blade, a small-sword that rarely saw use.

I ran soft and tender fingers, callouses burned away, over my smooth scalp. My client had some explaining to do. A trip to the wig-maker would be but a short detour, and I fully intended to present that invoice for reimbursement. But before I departed, I took a few moments to tend the hive in the thatched roof of my home. My friends were agitated and upset. How many had died? Not even the queen knew. I apologized, letting her feel my sorrow, and opening myself to her loss, but it was too soon. It would be some time before she trusted me again, and I retreated as the bees rose to swarm between me and the hive.

It wasn't an entirely wasted effort, though. I discovered quickly enough on the roof as the midsummer sun beat down against my unprotected scalp that I would need to set aside my dislike of such frippery and condescend to cover my head. I chose a wide brimmed cavalier hat of black felt, with a red band and an extravagant feather. Discrete? Hardly. But the time for that had passed. Let them stare.

I had been angry. Furious. With Spring — for saving me, and for ruining it in the next breath. With my client, for his criminally negligent failure to provide me with critical information that might have kept this transaction from going so horribly wrong. But mostly at myself, for not having the decency to die after the carnage I'd wrought. Too many broken promises, my own being the worst of them.

That was before I visited E. Klug, Wigmaker. Afterwards, I was just scared.

Three women's hair had gone into that wig, harvested at the sanitarium on Hastings Street. Mr. Klug did not tell me this; it was something the women themselves made known, through senses left open as an unwelcome residue from my encounter with the thing in the river. Two of the women raved in my head, tortured and frightened and manic, the moment the wig touched my flesh. I flinched at their touch. But it was the third presence that terrified me—still and silent and present as death. I flung the wig away from me and fled the shop in horror.

I kicked my client's door open when I heard the butler unlatch it. It was a testament to his buttling that his eyes betrayed only the smallest trace of surprise, none of which reflected in the rest of his face. He would have had my fullest recommendation wherever he might seek an appointment, should a recommendation from one such as I bear any weight.

"Lady Goselin," he said, "the household is not at present prepared to entertain."

"Bugger that," I said. "I need to see him."

"That would not be possible at the present, madam. Should you wish to pay respects, a notice shall be posted—"

I pushed past into the house, hand on the hilt of my blade. "Where is the bastard? I'll kill him if he hasn't got a bloody good..." And then the butler's words registered. "...Respects?"

He bowed. "Yes, Lady."

"He's dead."

"Regrettably."

"When?"

"Perhaps noon, madam. He had retired to his chambers shortly after breakfast with instructions to notify him an hour prior to tea."

"And he was...?"

"Yes, madam."

"Show me the body."

He stiffened. "That would hardly be proper."

"I am hardly proper," I said. "Now show me the fucking body."

The butler's concern was not ill conceived. My client lay naked and spread-eagled in the middle of an occult form—which I shall not describe even in the most general terms, for fear that some misguided fool shall inevitably attempt to replicate it—engraved in the hardwood floor. The rug that normally covered the floor was loosely rolled to the side.

My client's face was blue. There were marks on his bloated body, as if of ropes. But I knew better. He had not died of strangulation, but of drowning, even if the only liquids present were those voided by his corpse. The stench that rose from him was of river muck, with which I'd recently become intimately familiar.

Other than the corpse, and the symbol in the floor, there was nothing in my client's chamber to answer my thwarted questions.

"Please, madam." The butler spoke from the doorway, as if he didn't dare cross the threshold.

"Yes, of course." As I exited the room, I removed my hat and handed it to him. "At noon today, I had a full head of hair, and eyebrows. At noon today, several dozen people, women and children, played on the riverbank in Ashbury Park. A few moments later, they were dead, and my hair was gone. Your employer may be dead, but he still owes me an accounting, and you, sir, have been volunteered to give it."

He actually blanched. "It is not my place to meddle in...."

"A good butler sees all, and witnesses nothing. You, sir, are an excellent butler, and right now, if you wish your master avenged, you will remember *everything* that you have seen."

When I left my client's residence late that night, my fear was undiminished, but my anger had returned, cold and deadly. With what I had learned, I knew exactly what I would find within the cluttered confines of Helmar Q'agit's pathetic shop. Not even my reputation of professional discretion was enough to keep my client's identity—and the nature of his crime—confidential. It is only out of my respect for that butler, and his hope of someday securing a new position, that I keep that confidence.

I searched Q'agit's hovel in the dark. I needed no light; the whispers in my head told me where to find what I sought, though the effort strained my sanity. The object of my search spoke only emptiness and longing. It was a human skull, deeply etched with intricate patterns radiating from a single, obscene form—the same form that defiled my client's floor.

I sat cross-legged on the floor so that I could look into the black pits of those empty eyes. And I understood.

His name was Corey. A boy, an innocent: he had never drawn blood in battle, nor from between a woman's thighs. Never even slaughtered a chicken, or tasted flesh. He had been purchased as an infant and raised in isolation to this purpose, of which, even in death, he was unaware.

All he wanted was to be touched.

I, Maris Goselin...

No. Let us use the name with which I grew up, the name Spring had called across the boiling waters: Gosling. I, who have been pickpocket and harlot, camp follower and mercenary, wizard and murderer—I who have fucked and fought and stolen and slain my way from the streets into an odd sort of semi-respectability—I would be this boy's deliverance.

Behind those empty eyes, behind that hungry ghost, something infinitely more hungry waited. I would lie if I said that death was not to be feared. But the thing that gazed back at me was not death. It had come from somewhere beyond that grey realm, found a way into Corey's mind, and through this dead boy's hunger, it had infiltrated our world.

I had much to prepare. I wrapped Corey's skull in a black velvet tablecloth (Q'agit owned no other sort) and took it home.

"Death," I said, not waiting for Spring to invite me into his hotel room, "is not the enemy." This was something of which I was now certain, having spent two nearly sleepless days and nights devouring every word in the esoteric tomes and parchments that the butler had delivered to my home, and listening to the mad whispers of the ghosts of those who had written them. I slipped my lockpick into my corset as I stepped around the spluttering and indignant bard. Behind him, Kilanh snatched up the bed linens to cover herself. "Death is as much a victim in this as Life is." Gripping the back of Kilanh's neck, I leaned up until my lips met hers.

Face to face, she was taller than I expected. She smelled exquisite. She tasted of Spring. For a moment she melted against me, fingers twining in my shirt as her tongue met mine. Then she pushed me away with a drummer's strength.

"When this is done," I said, running my fingers improperly through sweat-damp fur down her back to the sensitive spot above her tail. She breathed in through needle teeth and arched against my hand. "Spring will tell you where I live."

Kilanh glanced at Spring.

Debt differs not merely in quantity, but in quality. No amount of money can ever truly pay the debt of a life taken. Likewise, Spring could save my life twenty times over without making a down payment for his betrayal. He looked away, and down, and would not meet Kilanh's eyes, or mine, but the dark tide that washed within me gave me ears to hear what was not said—that he still held a hope of reclaiming me, after all these years, and even now of having us both. Kilanh's inner voice spoke only what we all knew: with three words I could take her lover from her forever.

But she wasn't the one I needed to hurt. I pushed those thoughts aside.

"Assuming we survive that long." I plopped down on the disheveled mattress. "Get some clothes on, you two. We need to talk, and I can't afford the distractions right now."

Later, when Spring stepped outside to relieve his bladder, Kilanh confronted me.

"Whatever has been between you and Spring must stay between the two of you. I will not be your pawn, or his penance. I will not bed you."

"You will."

Her tail twitched. "I have seen what you can do, but I promise you, if you try to force me, I *will* kill you."

"When you come to me," I said, knowing the words as truth as they spilled from my lips, "it will be of your own free will. The only thing I'm unclear on is why."

The best conditions for countering an intricately worked summoning is the opposite of its own optimal conditions. But we couldn't wait until the winter solstice. By that time, the thing that I had fought in the river would have established itself irreversibly, entwining life and death inextricably in its shadowy tentacles. What exactly that meant for this world remains unclear to me, but it had only been two weeks, and already there were rumors of odd illnesses in people who lived or worked near the river's banks, of sores and tumors and unexpected growths, and of unquiet graves. No, there was no time to wait. We would just have to hope that a dreary, rain-soaked midnight would be enough. At least a full moon hid behind those clouds.

Spring would put on a concert. Not the energetic, crowd-pleasing songs he'd played before, but songs that touched deeper emotions. There would be no audience, none to hear but those who were there to help. He would play alone. And he would play to me.

The butler volunteered to assist—both to atone for his master's crimes and to avenge the bastard's death—but instead, I gave him his master's books and detailed instructions of who to contact if we failed. We wouldn't be around for a second attempt, and even I'm not so self-centered that I'd wish that fate shared with the world. Instead, I spoke with a gentleman who still owed me for some discrete services. Both Spring and I asked Kilanh to stay away, but she insisted.

"If I can't help on the stage, then I can help in some other way."

And her assistance was, in fact, quite valuable.

I'd spent the two weeks reading and rereading every book and note on the subject that both my client and Q'agit had in their possession. My client had attempted to cheat death by inviting something beyond both life and death into himself, with no regard to what that might do to the rest of the world. Whether the spell had failed because of a lack of power to pull it off, or because of my interference, or because of the water elemental's involvement, I didn't know. Another possibility remained: that he had just bollocksed up the spell in the casting. It was, after all, not the sort of spell you got to practice. Had he just miscast a perfectly sound spell? Or was the spell misconstructed from the start? Whatever the failure was, it hadn't failed well enough, and some remnant of that ravenous power remained in our world.

The plan was actually fairly straightforward—it was only the execution that would be difficult. We needed to replicate the occult form that had been on my client's floor, and that was etched into dead Corey's skull, large enough to encompass the area of the original spell's effect, from the stage out onto the river. At midnight, with Corey's help, I would repeat my client's spell, with some omissions, modifications, and reversals. I would draw the darkness into myself, and this time, instead of fighting it, I would embrace it. I would take it in and feed it back to the Thing that still lived behind Corey's empty eye sockets. Then I would destroy the skull, and we would destroy the occult form. Simple, right?

Etching a line into a hardwood floor is one thing. It's a little tougher to paint moving water. It was Kilanh who came up with the idea of using rope and buoys. A handful of people in boats would maintain the shape, and destroy it when it was time. Other people, she suggested, could be on shore waiting to pull things on the ground apart when the time was right.

People from a surprisingly wide swath of society provided materials and support: paint, rope, buoys, boats, people to handle the boats. Lords and criminals worked side by side, abandoning temporarily the artificial distinction between their livelihoods. My gentleman friend called on his gentleperson friends. It's funny how the need—or at least the desire—for discrete services multiplies as one accumulates wealth and influence. And every discrete service comes bundled with the potential of a future favor in exchange for continued discretion.

I didn't doubt their discretion in this case: nobody is stupid enough to admit to participation in the most powerful act of illegal necromancy that Ashbury has seen in a century or more. Nobody but me, that is.

Other than the possibility that the casting might fail and all of us end up dead or worse, my biggest concern was that someone might retain enough memory of the pattern to replicate the casting. I'd already burnt Q'agit's hovel to the ground and elicited a heartfelt promise from the butler to destroy the defaced flooring in his master's house after we succeeded, as well as all the books and notes. But what of those participating in the ritual themselves?

It was Kilanh—again—who provided a solution; each person, herself included, would wear a mask, a full-head covering of thick, black leather, with blinders incorporated to obfuscate vision. It would be impossible for any one person to see more than the small portion of the pattern they were responsible for. The mask would be fastened around the neck, and locked. Spring would hold the keys. Kilanh knew of a shop that sold such masks and could customize them to our needs. I'd had no idea there was a market for such things. It wasn't foolproof, but my threat to murder anyone who took their mask off early should discourage fools.

I spent several days poring over maps of Ashbury Park, drawing the obscene pattern over them until I felt I could recognize if some piece was incorrectly placed. I walked the length and breadth of the now-abandoned park, taking measurements, placing markers, checking and rechecking my measurements. There would be very little room for error.

After the rope was measured, cut and spliced, and I had burned the appropriate inscriptions upon its length, a large carriage arrived to deliver the supplies down to the deserted riverside, where Spring's musician friends were making hasty repairs to the stage. Kilanh and I helped Spring prepare for his concert. Almost like old times. As we restrung and tuned his instruments, Kilanh and Spring discussed the set list. He would play for half an hour, helping us focus the energy we needed for the spell. He would begin his last song at midnight. That one, he said, was a new song. No one had heard it yet, not even Kilanh.

"Wait," I said, looking around at the guitars and lutes and mandolins scattered around the stage. "Where's your lute? You were playing it when..." My voice choked; all these years and I still couldn't talk about what happened. What drove us apart. I took a breath. "The magic one."

Spring shot an odd look at Kilanh, and she glared at the floor. "It got smashed," Spring said. "When the river thing attacked."

Good.

"I'm sorry," I said, instead. I tried to sound sincere. I failed, and Kilanh abruptly stood and walked off the stage and into the rain, tail twitching her anger.

Spring chose songs I had not heard for a lifetime. Simple songs, imperfect and juvenile. Songs he wrote for me, played for me, before he ever performed to an audience. Songs of love and yearning, songs of the taste of a lover's flesh. Of *my* flesh.

Before I ruined everything.

Out on the river, the boats found their positions, anchoring the ropes into the necessary form. A handful of others watched over the rope on the riverbank. Kilanh was closest to me, and then Spring, on the stage. Everyone had strict instructions to stay outside the form we had created.

Of course, if I failed, that would not protect them, but they didn't need to know that.

I sat, alone, at the river's edge, listening to Spring sing. No, not alone. I had Corey with me. I had set him next to me on the grassy riverbank. Waves of loneliness emanated from him, washing over me and mingling with emotions I had killed years ago. Had *thought* I had killed. Fucking Spring. Why did he have to be here, now? How many years had it been since he'd walked away, leaving me alone? And then he just wanders into town, and back into the middle of my life. And then he has the nerve to be *nice* to me? To just *presume* I still cared?

I started to shove the feelings back to where they belonged before remembering that they were exactly what I needed to make this work.

It was almost midnight. Spring finished a song and set down his mandolin. He picked up a lute I hadn't seen on the stage when I'd been up there earlier, and tuned the two strings. I stared at him. It was the old broken lute I'd given him when we were children, living on the street. His first instrument. He still had it. Bastard. He had no right keeping *anything* of that time.

"Stupid, clumsy bastard should be playing that magic lute right now," I grumbled, perhaps a little too loudly.

Kilanh stepped over the rope, into the pattern. She walked up to me and slapped me across the face.

"He broke that lute saving your miserable life. Normal weapons had no effect on that creature. When he saw you in the water, he broke away from me and beat that thing off you with the only magical object around."

Spring had started his final song, soft and sweet, and written for a two-stringed lute. The new song. It sang of love and loss, of the impossibility of redemption. It sang of him, and of me, and, though he didn't realize it yet, of Kilanh. She knew it, though.

"I hate you," she told me.

"I hate you too," I said. It was only half a lie. "Run, if you want to live."

It was midnight. She ran.

I gathered power in my hands, and the darkness flowed.

I cannot tell you what happened within the confines of that fragile pattern. There are others who might, if they even know what they saw. I have not asked, and they have not said. I know only what happened within me, and within Corey.

I performed the ritual.

I know the monster came, not because I saw it, but because I felt it. I took it, fed it my longing, my hurt, my desire, my stupid desperate yearning. I fed it Spring's song. I fed it Corey's innocent lust. I called it, invited it in.

Everything, just as planned.

It was unutterably horrifying.

It was even better than the first time.

Long moments after it was done, after the darkness had fed on itself and I had laid poor Corey's ghost to rest, crushing his skull to powder with a stone pulled from the river's edge, my body shuddered and clenched.

It was Kilanh this time, not Spring, who pulled me from the water.

"Let me drown," I said, too weak to struggle. It had taken all my remaining strength to throw myself into the river. "Please."

I couldn't read the look on her feline face.

"I'm not done with you yet," she said.

And that, dear readers, is where the story should have ended. And as far as the Midsummer Day Massacre goes, it was.

She came to me, as I had predicted in a moment of spite and arrogance, the following day. The voices of the dead and tortured and mad had faded with poor Corey's departure, and with them the hideous knowledge they imposed, but even so I knew it was Kilanh. I willed her to leave, to let this last act go unplayed, and I buried myself deeper in the pit of my bed. But she banged at the door long enough to concern the bees. They filtered down from the rafters in ever increasing numbers, a gathering swarm, until I forced myself to my feet and across the floor. I unlatched the door and let it swing open.

She stared at me. "Did you sleep like that?"

"Sleep?" I turned and walked away, through the living area to my bed. I crawled back under the covers.

"You look like death," she said, following. "And smell even worse."

I didn't respond, and she went away, for a time. When she returned, it was to order me out of bed. She had drawn water from the well, heated it on the stove, and filled the tub. Her hands were confident as she stripped my clothing and washed me, and also as she dried me. And when I was clean and dry, she stepped close, and her fingers found the place my body refused to let stay dry, the one trace of life left in a body I had so strongly willed dead.

"Kilanh," I said.

She purred, her body vibrating against my back. "I like the way you say my name."

"Did I say it wrong?"

"No. And that's rare, with humans. Say it again."

I don't know which it was that began to melt the dark ice that had eaten my heart, her insistent fingers or her softly spoken words. "Kilanh," I said again, pronouncing the *h* as a half-syllable in the manner of her tribe. Her lips touched my neck. "Kilanh, I'm afraid. I've never...."

She waited for me to finish, and when I didn't, said, "With a Sarr?"

"With another woman, I'd meant. But really, either." My breath caught. "I don't know what to do."

She didn't laugh. Instead, she turned me to face her, brought my face up to look into hers, and said, "I'll teach you."

The next morning, she dressed quickly and efficiently, while I lay in bed, my belly and thighs still quivering.

"Thank you," I said.

"Hm." She buckled a belt around her waist and slipped her sandals on, then picked her bag up from my dresser. "So, all debts paid in full?"

"Stars, yes."

"Good." She strode quickly to the door. I jumped to my feet and ran after her on unsteady legs, caught her as she stepped to the street.

"Kilanh!"

She turned slowly, then stepped toward me. "How do you feel?"

"I...."

Her lips grazed my neck, and she ran her hands down my body. Her fingers touched an inappropriate spot, and my hips arched toward her, inviting. On the street, neighbors and strangers stopped to stare, as if they'd never seen a naked, bald-headed woman with a Sarr's fingers pressed between her legs before.

"I feel alive," I said. "I wasn't sure I'd ever feel alive again, but I feel alive. You saved me, in more ways than one."

She stepped back, away from me and into the street. "Good. You deserve to feel alive."

"Wait! When will I see you again?"

"You won't," she said. "Spring left town last night. I'm meeting him on the road. We're not coming back to Ashbury, and you won't see either of us again. You deserve to feel alive, but you don't deserve him. Or me." She turned and walked away, down the street and out of my life, taking the only man I've ever loved with her. A dozen paces away, she paused long enough to call over her shoulder.

"Unless I need to call in a debt!"

She did not hurry away, and I lingered in my doorway, watching as she disappeared into the bustle of an Ashbury morning.

Sensing my tears, the bees came, first a few, then hundreds and thousands, covering my body and leading me gently inside, and buzzing me to sleep.

EMBARRASSING RELATIONS

MARIS

What is it about Ashbury Park? I mean, really. There's a whole city out there to be crazy in. But especially in summer, Ashbury Park is the place to be seen. And the place to be seen being crazy.

There are buskers, of course: street musicians of varying quality (mostly awful, but I may be biased), puppeteers and actors, magicians and shell game tricksters, dancers and snake charmers, and mimes. And then there are the nutters, each one using the broken stage and the acoustics of the venue to educate the masses in their own inimitable truths. The treasury was conspiring against the people. The nobility was conspiring against the treasury. A mysterious international cabal secretly controlled the world, transmitting details of their nefarious plots directly into the nutter's head through a beam of pink moonlight. The combinations were as endless as the nutters, and often better entertainment than the buskers.

It would be both foolish and rude to forget the people who work the park professionally. The sellers of ill-gained goods and illicit substances. The working women and men who trade in flesh. And the pickpockets.

That last would be me. Ever since my misadventures last Midsummer Day, everyone—friends, enemies, and (most importantly) clients—avoided me. They'd seen what I had done, and what I could do. I couldn't blame them. *I'd* stay away from me too, if I could. Not that I could have claimed any friends to start with, so maybe *that* part wasn't much of a loss. Regardless, with no customers for my peculiar brand of consulting, I fell back on childhood skills.

When you work the park, you learn to tune out the lunatic ravings of the mad, expounded from the stage. I couldn't tell you what the nutter of the day was blathering on about, but his command of the crowd's attention would have made Duke Aramis envious. The crowd's reaction, on the other hand, would have had the Duke's personal guard calling for reinforcements.

The nutter shouted disparaging and nonsensical words at his audience, calling individuals out by name for personal abuse. The crowd, in turn, hurled insults at him. Some threw rotten fruit. One hedge wizard set up impromptu shop next to a fresh fruit stand, casting rotting spells on tomatoes and peaches, and selling them to the enraged mob. Both vendors were making a killing. As was I.

Really, it's a perfect environment for folks like me. Strong emotions focus attention on whatever arouses said emotion, dulling peripheral perception. Standard misdirection. One person punches the mark on the right arm; the other slips the shiny, jeweled bracelet off the left. It works even better when the partner isn't aware of his, her, or its role.

And with the help of my watchdog bee friends, I was even less likely to get caught.

It had been a good day, with a fine take. I couldn't be sure until I counted it all, but I estimated by the weight on my hips, in my boots, tucked into my blouse, and a dozen other discrete locations, I might very well have met my monthly quota early. I'd decided to call it a day when one last opportunity presented itself. A fat wallet in a loose pocket. It seemed a crime not to take it.

A bee buzzed my head in warning. I looked around, but no one was paying attention to me.

I had just liberated said wallet from its negligent prison when I felt an oppressive attention focus on me. I looked up. The crazy man on the stage was staring at me, finger aimed at my forehead.

"You!" he said. "Muh... Guh..." His mouth twisted in confusion; his mad eyes bored into mine. "You! Ambiguously named harlot! Thief!

Whore! Wanton slut who hath engaged in unnatural congress with things foul beyond imagining! Throw yourself upon Cheom's finite mercy and beg forgiveness, that your immortal soul may find solace between Cheom's loving molars, and final rest in Cheom's Most Holy Gastric Juices!"

An oddly accurate accounting of my life, coming from a complete stranger. Except for the part that was utter and incomprehensible nonsense. Still, nobody tells *me* who I can congress with. I mean, I *only* congressed with all those tentacles for the sake of Duke and Duchy, and, well, to save every living thing in the world (*including* the people living in the Duchy and the Duke himself, so I suppose the "Duke and Duchy" line isn't *technically* a lie). Anyway, it wasn't like I was looking to do it again anytime soon. Still, it was the principle of the thing. If I wanted to congress with tentacles, it was *my* sanity at stake, not anyone else's.

I formulated my counter-argument. I opened my mouth to shout it at the nutter on the stage when the guy standing in front of me said, "Hey, is that my wallet?"

A novice move, on my part. Distracted in the middle of a pickpocketing, I was holding the wallet in front of me like I was buying fruit or something. "Uh," I said. Most eloquently, too, if I say so myself.

The recent owner of said wallet was unimpressed. "That's my wallet!" he reiterated, reaching for me. "Somebody grab her!"

Instinct kicked in. I stepped back, slipping from his grasp. Into someone else's, but that hardly mattered. I flipped the wallet open and shook out coins and bills. I twisted a quick-and-dirty confusion spell around the handful of money. And then I flung the whole thing into the air.

Hands that had been grabbing at me now reached for flying coins and fluttering paper—mostly illusory—that rained down upon us. I'd be lucky if the ad-hoc spell lasted more than a minute, but that was more than enough time. I ducked into the maelstrom of greed, and then out, and when I was sure that no one was on my trail, I made my way home.

BRIAN

Oh great Cheom, thank you for delivering me from your unbelieving enemies.

Your hand is firm and your voice is clear, even in this dark land. Strengthen my arm and sharpen my faith, that I may protect your favored one from the Great Deceiver.

My prayer of thanksgiving and reaffirmation of purpose finished, I peered around the great tree Cheom provided to protect me from the chaos gripping my congregation. The city guards were there now, wading through my gentle followers with spears and truncheons, as if mere steel could extinguish a harlot's sorcery.

I crawled through the burnt undergrowth lining the riverbank. It was fitting I was on my knees in ashes; the better to beg Cheom's forgiveness for underestimating the dark forces arrayed about me. I was foolish to think that in evil-shrouded Ashbury I could reveal Cheom's truth with impunity. My poor followers! How Cheom smiled on them as they made their simple food offerings in gratitude for having their sins brought into the light. Then she appeared—that…that craven cutpurse, that ill-bred Adulteress of Ashbury. I knew not her face, but Cheom revealed her through her sins, and I smote her with righteous judgment. It was for naught. The depth of her cunning caught me unawares. Now I pay for my ignorance, as does my flock. Would that I had my beloved mace and shield! Those guards would fall like ninepins.

The Whore of Ashbury. I will remember you, sorceress, and I pray that my divine master's will shall permit me to cleanse your heart as I will cleanse this city of evil.

MARIS

I suppose I can blame it on distraction. I wasn't upset about being caught, and the escape was far from narrow. Getting caught is only a problem if you fail to handle the situation with grace, and there's no point getting upset about it. You just study the way things panned out, and work out a few more techniques to make sure things go better next time.

No, it was the nutter who disturbed me. Something about his eyes, that intense focus. And the *contempt*. I was used to the contempt of my neighbors, but that was a respectful sort of contempt, given my reputation. This was different.

That was no excuse for ignoring the slightly sweet, vaguely narcotic scent of incense in my home, for dismissing my friends' erratic behavior. Agitated but unfocused, they buzzed aimlessly and hung from the draperies. Two bees collided in front of my nose. One settled on my forehead while the other spun away. It was a reason, but not an excuse.

One more thing to examine and file away for future use.

Oblivious to the obvious, I tugged off my boots and dumped the loot on my bed. I stripped off my blouse and shook it; copper and silver rained, paper fluttered. No gold, but I didn't need to maintain an estate, just cover living expenses until I sorted out a new career. I dropped my belt and considered spending some quality time rolling around with the fruit of my nearly honest labor. I figured if I ran into the nutter again, it would give us something to talk about.

I was just starting to ease my trousers down my hips when the visitors my bees had tried to warn me of stepped from the shadows of the other room.

Two of the city guard. And a knight.

I think I squeaked. The bee on my forehead lost her footing and slid down my face, coming to rest on the tip of my nose. Her abdomen pulsed with menace. I felt my eyes cross, focusing on her.

"Lady Goselin," said the knight. He sneered the title, as if he knew my background. He probably did. For weeks, the broadsheets had spared no detail, however indelicate, of my time of notoriety, and printed every rumor about me, however unlikely. He nodded, the most minute bow propriety required.

I, on the other hand, had no idea who this fool was. Newly knighted, I assumed, and still flush with self-importance. I tried to think of an explanation for my ill-gotten loot, but I found myself feeling slightly fuzzy around the brain. Maybe it was something in the air. There was, of course, no good explanation for the day's plunder, and they'd surely attempt to cast me in chains. Which could be fun, under the right circumstances, but probably not these. I was, after all, Maris Goselin, the mage who called down the sun. If I was to be punished, it would be harsh and permanent enough to preclude any possibility of retribution.

On the third hand, I had them outnumbered. I reached behind me until I found something sharp. A cloak pin. It would be enough to kill these three. Or rather, to kill one of the guards, at which point I would have a sword, and the other two would fall. But who knew how many others waited in the wings? I did have a reputation, after all. They would be fools to seek to take me alone.

A comforting hint of fear flashed across the knight's eyes before he reestablished his mask of bland distaste. He managed to make his voice sound bored. He even almost managed to keep his eyes from drifting from my chest to the pin.

"Please, Lady Goselin, I should hate to inform the Duke of your demise, given his regrettable need for someone of your...expertise."

I let a smile play across my lips. "You want to hire me."

The knight's jaw twitched. "The Duke, Lady. It is the Duke who wishes to hire you, not I. I would banish you from the city, if it were in my power."

I laughed. The boy would never have that power, even if he lived long and lucky enough to become King. Which was unlikely.

He had the sense to redden. "The Duke says you have a reputation for discretion." Hesitantly, he stepped close enough to whisper. "What he desires of you, the Duchess must never hear of it."

Oh. That.

It had been years since I'd been paid for sex. More like the other way around, of late. But money is money. I shrugged. "Sure. Why not?"

Duke Aramis kept me waiting.

Of course, I'd kept him waiting as well. I'd spent entirely too long deciding what to wear. The problem was, I was unsure of his preferences. My usual garb was perfect for "You've been a naughty, naughty Duke," but not so much if he expected, "O! Thou art so manly, Sire!" In the end, I compromised: damsel enough in an off-white peasant skirt, which boasted intricate blue embroidery that I'm sure the person I stole it from had spent many hours on. I complemented it with a matching blouse coupled with a severe, black leather corset. The entire ensemble was designed to hide any number of lethal tricks, in case they were needed. I decided against a wig to cover my near-shorn head. If he wanted a girl with long, flowing locks, he knew better than to ask for me.

The knight, who wisely kept his name to himself, escorted me into the palace through a discrete entrance that I pretended I didn't know about. Pity. I'd hoped I might learn a new way in. But maybe I already knew them all.

He led me to a room deep in the west wing, if I had my bearings right, and told me the Duke would be with me presently. Then he and the guards left.

The door locked behind them.

Either this was an elaborate (if futile) way to trap me, or they didn't trust me not to steal the silverware. Which, now that I'd thought of it, seemed too good of a challenge not to take up at some point in the future.

Time passed. No Duke.

I paced.

I assessed the furnishings:

- Several chairs, both hardwood and cushioned;

- A sofa that matched the cushioned chairs;

- A desk, with nothing terribly interesting either in or atop it;

- Two lovely carpets, of Lempurian origin—possibly the most valuable objects in this room;

- A bookshelf full of histories of the realm (largely glorifying and therefore fictitious) and a number of official-looking ledgers;

- Art, in the form of paintings scattered as haphazardly across the walls as if a temperamental chef with a broken roux had selected their placement.

The only things showing any sign of wear were the desk and the chair behind it. Obviously not a room oft frequented by visitors. It certainly had made no impression on me as a child, when Spring and I challenged each other to explore the palace and nick small and interesting items (my coup had been the young Marquess Aramis's abandoned love sonnets to the girl he later married, fetched crumpled from the waste bin—we'd had to get some men at a pub to read them to us, since neither of us knew how, then).

But let's talk about the art, if you can call it that. Maybe we should just call them paintings. Awful things, grim caricatures of the family, rendered over the years as if each succeeding artist strove to demonstrate less skill than the last. Of course, abominable art littered the walls throughout the palace; the fact that these particular paintings were sequestered in this remote office spoke volumes. I couldn't bear to look at them for more than a second or two. Frankly, the ink blotter on the desk had greater aesthetic appeal.

More time passed. And it's not like my time was valuable anymore, but I do tend to bore easily.

The sofa was badly stuffed and uncomfortable. I opted for the desk. It resonated with the acts that had surely been performed upon it at one point or another—the bestowal of deeds, the stripping of riches, the enforcement of arcane laws. It seemed good enough for my purposes.

When the Duke finally appeared, he entered the room with little fanfare, only the calm self-assurance he habitually wrapped himself in.

"Lady Goselin," he said, "you'll forgive my...." He stared, mouth gaping. "*What* are you doing?" He stepped forward, then dashed back to the door and slammed it shut. He fumbled the key in the lock until it clicked, and then turned around. "What are you *doing?*"

"You took so long that I started without you. Your Dukeness."

"Started what?" he spluttered with incredulity. "What did you think you were here for?"

"Um." I batted my eyelashes at him from atop the desk. "A matter of greatest discretion, a personal service for the Duke that the Duchess must never hear of. Quote unquote."

"Really." He cleared his throat. "I require your services in one of your *other* professional capacities. I'll be needing my desk." He walked to the bookshelf, where he pulled out one of the ledgers.

"Then it's a good thing I finished without you." I removed myself from His Dukeness's desk and straightened my skirts.

He set the book down, flipped through until he found the page he wanted, and then retrieved quill and ink. Dipping the quill, he drew a line through one of the entries.

"Shortest knighthood in the history of the realm," he muttered. "Now, to the matter at hand."

I curtsied and held my hand out to him. He took it and kissed it. Did he linger perhaps a bit much, breathing my perfume? All for the good of the realm, I'm sure.

"The matter at hand," I prompted.

"Yes, yes. Of course." He dropped my fingers like they had suddenly grown fangs. "Well, here it is. We've received word that my brother-in-law is coming to visit. He is expected to arrive tomorrow."

I grinned. "That's wonderful! It's so nice when families stay close. Will there be a feast? Can I come?" It isn't every day a person of my standing has a Duke as a captive audience. Financially speaking, it's important to maximize the scorn early so that they value you properly when you get the job done.

"No, you may not..."

Oh," I pouted. "I love your feasts, makes me feel like our tax money is being put to good use."

Aramis's nostril's flared with annoyance. "There's not going to be a feast. In fact, if you do your job properly, Dara won't ever find out he's even near the city. You'll intercept him before he arrives and divert him. I don't care how you do it. Just don't harm him. Keep him away from my city, get him heading somewhere else, *anywhere* else, and above all make sure nobody in Ashbury sees or hears anything about him."

"Why?"

"What?" His forehead wrinkled in confusion. I guess dukes don't get asked that question much.

"Why do you want him gone?"

"I hardly see how that is any of your concern."

I leaned in and spoke softly to ensure his full attention. "There is very little in my line of business to be proud of, Aramis, but one thing I am proud of is my ability to learn from my mistakes. And I learned one Midsummer Day that I should always have a clear understanding of my clients' interests and intents. Not that clients are lining up at my door anymore, but this is not negotiable. Oh, and I hope you don't mind if I call you Aramis, I find formal titles just make me raise my fees."

"Point taken." The Duke nodded, then sighed and looked away. "He's.... Deverran has always been a bit eccentric, and it has only gotten worse as he's grown older. Hearing voices, seeing things that aren't there. Healers have been unable to help, and once he reached his majority, they couldn't keep him locked up in the tower anymore.

Lately, though, he appears to have lost all sense of reality. He's insisted people call him *Brian*, of all the ridiculous names, and that is the most sensible thing he's said. He's an embarrassment to the family, and I'd like to spare Dara the anguish."

"And the pay?"

"Sufficient to ensure you won't be tempted to blackmail me."

I shook my head. "You know perfectly well I have never blackmailed anyone. I've done many unsavory things in my life, but the one thing I bring to the table is discretion. I even have runes tattooed on my body that prevent me from divulging sensitive information under coercion." So maybe that's not actually what the tattoo did. Nobody else needed to know that. "So what's the pay?"

He sighed again. "Do the job, and then tell me what it's worth."

"You're very trusting. I want this carpet."

Aramis snorted in laughter. "I could buy ten of you for a year for what that's worth. Be serious."

I shrugged. "It's just the right size for my cottage. It would really tie the room together."

He harumphed at that. I'd never heard an actual harumph before. But he was right. I'd bill him what the job was worth. Pity. Rich people understand the value of riches, but not so much the value of *money*, at least, not in the ordinary person's sense of money, and they either overpay dramatically or underbid even more dramatically. In either case, you know who you're dealing with right up front. I'd encountered Duke Aramis in the course of prior jobs, but had never worked for him directly. Hopefully, his reputation of honorability was more than propaganda.

"So, how do I find this 'Brian'?"

"He's traveling from Woodwash, down the West River Road. You can intercept him there, if you get on the road at dawn."

"And how will I recognize him?"

The Duke pointed at one of the abominable portraits on the wall. "That's him. Five years ago, but he hasn't changed that much."

He hadn't. I'd seen that face before. Of course, the artist's fetid portraiture skills had failed to capture the burning intensity in the eyes, or anything really of interest. The painting gave the impression that the artist was falling down drunk while painting a model who was distracted by a swarm of butterflies. Even so, there was no mistaking the nutter from Ashbury Park.

"Hmm," I said. "Just a hunch, mind you, but you may need to change your plans."

BRIAN

The waning light made manifest the Deceiver's festering malignancy. His fortress brooded over the town like a bloated troll over a litter of kittens, savoring their helplessness before it feeds.

Despair not, Ashbury! Your protector is here. Though you are overrun with every perversion conceived by minds mortal or otherwise, I will stem the evil tide threatening to drown you. I shall strike at the very font of malfeasance: the lair of the Deceiver himself.

From a public house porch I studied the entrance to the keep. I thought that amongst the lowlife there I could study my adversary's defenses unmolested, but upon my arrival the proprietor attempted to turn me out, as if my presence disturbed the drunkards in their cups. "Get moving," he said. "My customers don't like the smell of you."

"I assure you, sir," I replied, using more courtesy than was his due, "I'll not tarry long." I pressed a coin into his greedy fingers. Cheom provides.

I looked into his eyes. "Rubin Shatterlip," I whispered. "Return to your kegs and beg forgiveness from Cheom. Pray your wife does not discover why your barmaids work so happily for money so mean, lest you are punished in this life as well as the next."

Shatterlip cursed under his breath. He did not recognize my master's name, but he discerned my intent and left me at a bench by the rail.

I watched the comings and goings of the guards whilst the shadows grew long. In my younger days I would have stormed the gate, accompanied by my companions of old. Though they were but heathens, they made manifest Cheom's irresistible will. Now my only companion is divine inspiration. Still, the clippings of Cheom's toenails are sharper than a thousand swords. I shall prevail.

But how can one so unworthy harbor such hopes? For the second time that day, Cheom's firm hand boxed the ears of my spirit. Wallowing in the sucking mud of my pride, I failed to realize I was being ambushed by a cocotte in a corset.

"Buy a girl a drink, stranger?"

T'was the Whore of Ashbury. She was dressed differently than when she ruined my earlier sermon, but her heart appeared the same. Her transgressions hovered about her as bees swarmed a hive. In fact, there was an insect or two, probably attracted by the attar of carnality surrounding her. Of all the unfortunates who unknowingly hungered for Cheom's guidance, this trollop's need was the greatest, but I had no time to help her now.

"Be gone, woman," I sneered. "My business is with the Deceiver, not with you."

The seductress smiled at me. "I thought maybe you stopped here to stiffen your nerve before you storm the castle..."

MARIS

"...Unless there's something else you care to stiffen."

Yes, I know. Don't taunt the wildlife. But sometimes it's so hard to resist.

Deverran's reaction was, I suppose, predictable. He roared to his feet, knocking his mug of small beer from the rail. I caught it, mid-fall. Only a little splashed out, and I handed the mug to him before he managed to utter the vitriol that he was clearly formulating.

"I jest, good sir," I said, pulling a chair from another table so I could sit. There was enough room on the bench, but I suspected the poor man would suffer a case of fits if I were to accidentally brush against him. "Though perhaps in ill taste. My most sincere apologies." I raised my arm to signal the barmaid for ale.

"Spare me your empty apologies, harlot, and leave me be. Evil is afoot, and there are serious matters I must attend, if Ashbury is not to be crushed under the Deceiver's oppressive heel."

Afoot? Deceiver's oppressive heel? Really? I had seen puppet shows with better dialog.

"I know, I know." Hands up, palms out: the universal sign of non-aggression. "I'm not very good at 'sincere.' That's probably why I'm still single. Still, I suspect our missions may coincide more than you think."

Deverran scowled and swallowed the last of his small beer, just as my ale arrived. He ungraciously consented to a refill.

"What do you know of my mission?" he asked. "How could a woman fallen so deep see the workings of the mighty one as you creep at the bottom of the pit? What could you know of the infinite wisdom and power that has put me, Brian, unworthy as I am, into *this* place, *this* body, *this* godless, heathen world?"

His voice rose as he spoke, growing louder as he devolved into nonsense. Spittle flecked his beard as he spat out the word 'godless.' Whatever he thought it meant, it caused him even more anguish than he let on. I stopped him before he got us ejected.

"Almost nothing," I admitted. "As far as I can tell, you're speaking gibberish. But still, I've been watching you all afternoon, and I'm pretty sure we have a goal in common."

That shut him up. Almost.

"What goal?"

"You're trying to get into the palace, unseen and unaccosted by the guard. I'm being paid to get you into the castle, unseen and unaccosted by the guards."

He was immediately suspicious. "To what end? To be slain? That you might lead me into some darkened alley and stab me in the back?"

"How can I stab you in the back if I'm leading... No, never mind. Let's put it this way. If I wanted you dead, I had plenty of opportunities. I could, for instance, have poisoned your beer." I smiled. "Or just cut your throat from behind as you stared out the window at the palace."

"You would have been seen."

I looked around at the tavern's patrons. Only Deverran...No, I must remember to call him Brian... Only Brian was drinking small beer. The others had put away significant amounts of strong ale and brandy and were beyond noticing such trivialities.

Brian followed my gaze. "I take your point."

"May I speak honestly?"

Brian's eyes narrowed. "It matters not. Your foul lies shall be laid bare to the light of Cheom's all-seeing Truth."

"I'll take that as a yes." I swallowed more of my ale than I planned, as I was trying to decide how best to say this. "I think you're insane, but whether you are or not doesn't matter. What does matter is that I'm certain that you are not evil or malevolent. Also, my bees don't distrust you, and they've always had better judgment than I have, at least when it comes to men. So I am confident that I would harm no one—including yourself—by assisting you in gaining discrete access to the palace."

Brian exhaled through his nose as he studied me. Finally, he spoke. "Viper-tongued tart! Your speech reveals the depths of your blindness, and yet you speak only truth. I accept your offer. Come, let us go."

And with that, Brian stood, turned his back on me, and strode out of the tavern.

Me, I still had half a mug of ale to finish, which gave me plenty of time to think about what one could do with a forked tongue.

Like I said, I know ways into the palace. Into much of the old city, actually. Spring and I played a game as kids to see who could find the most interesting secret passageways. He was good at discovering them, not so good at remembering them. Me? I remember everything. So it was a simple—if dirty—matter to get Brian into the tunnel system that linked many of the older buildings in Ashbury.

These tunnels predated the current aristocracy. They had been hidden, and never rediscovered, when the city changed hands, long ago. Perhaps several rounds of Lords and Ladies had been deposed and replaced since the tunnels had been lost. I don't know; there's no documentation. Some had collapsed over time, and all had degraded, filled with rat feces and, of course, rats.

Brian stared bleakly into the tunnel I'd revealed as if he had expected nothing less from me. Maybe it was just the way the dying light hit him, but for a moment, he looked every bit the lost young man the Duke had described, the weight of the world on his almost-handsome features. Deverran was a big man, though soft, and I recalled with distaste the fact that rather than finding him the help he needed, his family had simply locked him away to avoid embarrassment. I had a sense that whoever or whatever "Brian" was, he felt cramped in Deverran's body.

I sighed. "I said I'd get you there safely. I didn't say anything about clean."

"Tis only vermin, rotting in their own putrescence," Brian snarled. "There is no hope for them. But even one as lowly as you can aspire to take up the loofah of Cheom's mercy and scrub the grime of wickedness from your much-handled skin. Cheom will hear your supplication. Join me in prayer, harlot."

Brian began chanting. "Oh mighty Cheom, delve deeply into the compost of this woman's heart and plant your seeds of...."

It seemed too much effort to get him to stop talking, and it appeared to make him happy. So I ignored him, nodding and pretending to listen, making the occasional appreciative utterance—"ah, I see," or "of course," or even "mmm-hmm." It wasn't much unlike any other conversation with a man. But over time I started getting curious. Whatever madness had taken him, it inspired him to construct a worldview that was, on the one hand, internally consistent, yet so alien as to be literally unthinkable.

"So... so this Cheom of yours is a person, but also a... what did you call it? God? And there are other gods that aren't gods?"

"False gods!" he intoned, his voice echoing down the tunnel. "Don't be fooled by cheap imitations! I am here as Champion, to glorify Cheom's name above all those other so-called gods."

"You realize that you're just spelling 'dog' backwards?"

"Dog? The flying purple pachyderms of Cheom will unfurl their tongues to strangle your blasphemy! Hark! Hear the fluttering wings!"

I put my finger to my lips to silence him. We'd arrived, and it wouldn't do to have him giving away all my secrets.

I pointed to a spot on the wall. "Push there."

He did, grunting with the effort. The stones didn't move. They weren't supposed to, I just needed to distract Brian so I could touch the actual secret spots in the correct order to release the locking mechanism. Then the wall opened easily.

We crept out of the tunnel, and I slid the massive stone back into place. All these hundreds of years later, and the heavy stone still moved smoothly and silently, closing without a visible seam. You can't get that kind of workmanship nowadays. I was certain Brian would never be able to find it again.

We dusted ourselves as best we could, picking the cobwebs out of our hair. I slapped webs and dirt off Brian's back, and he jumped.

"Just getting the dirt off you, is all." I turned around. "Can you get my back?"

Brian grudgingly complied, calling me a temptress in the process.

He muttered under his breath, "May the brazier of Cheom's mercy burn away these unclean thoughts." Like his thoughts were my fault.

Once again reasonably presentable, we made our way up the servant's stairs to the second floor, where I knew we would find the Duke. Soon, my business here would be done. Brian would be the Duke's problem, the Duchess' dignity would be saved, and I'd never have to hear about inverted dogs again.

When I told Aramis that Deverran was already in Ashbury, he told me to bring his brother-in-law to the room in which he had interviewed me. He would keep the path clear for us, and meet us there. Imagine my surprise when we turned a corner in the hallway and there he was, flanked by two guards.

"Oh," I said. "Hullo."

The Duke's eyes narrowed. "Who are you?"

Odd. There was nothing of the honorable, if annoying, man I knew in those eyes. Instead, they held anger, suspicion. Even the way he moved was different—none of his familiar bumbling confidence was evident. Instead, he stood poised, ready to act. My mind raced, trying to come up with something to buy us time to sort out what was going on.

It wasn't to be.

"Deceiver!" Brian screamed, launching himself forward. "What have you done with our sister?"

Brian's fist connected with the Duke's nose. Aramis fell back with a terrified shriek, clutching at his face. Blood seeped between his fingers, dripping onto his chest and running down his hands to stain his sleeve cuffs. For a short moment, I tried to think of a way to break the tension and salvage the situation, maybe something witty, or practical advice for getting blood stains out of silk and lace.

"Guards!" the Duke bellowed. "Capture the intruders, or kill them!" The guards advanced, drawing their swords.

At that point, I knew exactly what to say.

"Run."

And I did. I made it down the hall, turned to avoid the guards rushing up the stairs, and headed for another stairwell. Behind me, I heard Brian shouting, and then he fell silent. I hoped he'd been captured, not killed. I couldn't help him now, but I would come back for him. I led him into this. I owed him that much.

I rounded a corner, heading toward another secret passage I knew of, my mind one step too far ahead of where I was. Stupid. A sudden pain stabbed through my body and I found myself veering abruptly to the right and into the wall.

I stared at the wicked spear point protruding from under my ribs. Where had that come from? The haft of the spear jutted from beneath my right arm, held by a man in ill-fitting livery, who stepped out of the darkness of a doorway that I should have noticed. I was helpless to prevent the spearman from twisting me the rest of the way around until I was facing the way I'd come. With a sharp movement, he jammed the spear point into the wooden doorframe, pinning me like an entomologist's specimen.

My vision turned red and black with pain as things inside me ripped, clearing just in time to see a mailed fist swinging toward my face.

BRIAN

The ground was hot. I struggled to regain my feet. My legs wobbled under me as I stumbled to the opening in the wall surrounding the arena floor. My adversary watched me leave; I could feel his eyes staring holes into the tattered flesh on my back. I could not bear to turn to face him.

I climbed the long flight of stairs leading to the landing far above. Each step was agony. On both sides, faceless spectators hurled insults. In a way, their taunts were more painful than the blows I still felt in my bones.

Finally, I arrived at the feet of my master. I lowered my head in shame, lacking the courage to fall to my knees for the pain it would bring.

"I have failed you, my master," I choked. "I am unworthy."

Cheom smiled sweetly. Glowing brown hair cascaded over elegant shoulders, as fine and smooth as polished marble. "You are my champion." Cheom's grey eyes flashed like summer lightning. "Return to your task. You are not yet defeated."

MARIS

Pain. A pool of blood, growing tacky. Dirty straw. Dim light, just enough to cast the shadows of bars across the floor.

I was too weak to move. Too weak to even turn my head to see what condition I was in.

I didn't need to. From the septic odor, I knew. My insides had been ruptured, and were leaking onto the floor.

I was dying.

Carefully, gently, moving just my fingers because I didn't have the breath to make a sound, I constructed a healing spell. I had to be careful—spells required effort, and if I expended too much energy too quickly, I would pass out before I could repair myself.

If that happened, I would not wake up again.

And when I did pass out, I wasn't sure if I had healed enough to survive. But then, I'm here, writing this, so clearly I did.

When I woke, it was to the sound of Brian's voice. The bastards were torturing him; I could hear the pain. But he gave nothing away, as far as I could tell. It was hard to know, really. He was making even less sense than usual. Something about arenas and adversaries.

I was still bleeding, still wounded, but not so much that I was in imminent danger of dying. I worked another healing spell, making sure that all my innards were back together and working again, shoring up the muscle walls. Just in case I might need to use them. And, you know, to stop the hurting. Soon enough, I would need more, to fight the fever that a gut wound inevitably brought. But that could wait. First, I needed to escape.

The problem was that I was in a cell in Ashbury castle.

People don't escape these cells. The bars, the walls and floors and ceilings, are all hardened against magic, both magic applied against them and magic crossing their borders in either direction. The locks are designed to require two people to turn two keys simultaneously, preventing release by a rogue guard. Some of the cells in the Ashbury dungeons had even been constructed within an anti-magic field, completely blocking magic from working inside them. Fortunately for me, this wasn't one of those.

The other observation was that I had been stripped, and lay naked on a floor strewn with straw, now sodden and tacky with my blood. Apparently, even though the new, improved Duke had no idea who I was, his men had had the presence of mind to search me. They took no chances that they might miss any of the dozens of little surprises I kept hidden away in case of emergency.

Which begged the question of why I was still alive in the first place. If they'd gone to the effort of putting a hole in me, why didn't they just finish the job? Maybe not all of the guards were as enthused by the Duke's newfound inclination toward evil as one who'd speared me. It's always a pleasant surprise when people balk at violence when given the opportunity for cruelty. Or maybe the Duke had simply announced his intention to interrogate me, which might make them hesitate to cut my throat. But then, why not at least bind my wounds? None of it made any sense: not my current circumstances, not the change in the Duke's personality, not Deverran/Brian, not any of it, from start to finish.

It didn't matter. As long as I was alive, I'd manage to find a way out. As long as... I grinned with sudden insight. Sometimes being alive is overrated.

I gathered some straw and worked it into the blood that pooled under my body. I drew on the blood's tendency to congeal and used it to hold the straw together, creating a thin shell of straw shaped to my body, just a tiny bit larger. If I lay under it, face down, it would mask the rise and fall of my chest as I breathed. It was no effort to look pale as death; I'd lost enough blood to do that naturally. I dipped a couple more pieces of straw in my blood, magically reinforced their internal structures until they were stiff and unyielding. They would break, striking something as dense as skin, but they wouldn't bend. Used against something as soft as an eyeball, on the other hand, was an entirely different story.

Brian had grown silent, and I heard a grumbling voice as its owner made his way out of the dungeons. The Duke.

Something was very wrong. I'd never had much respect for the Duke, or any of the arrogant bastards who claim themselves worthy to lead us, but even I recognized that he wasn't a bad sort. Torturing a prisoner, even one who had punched him in the face, was very, very much out of character.

Louder voices echoed from down the hall.

"Edwin," said one, "I'd heard you had come to some dishonor, but I hardly expected to see you here!"

"I can scarce believe it myself, Ned."

I recognized this voice. I'd heard it first in my home, just this morning. At least, I hoped it was just this morning; I'd been unconscious for some time.

"I keep thinking I'm dreaming," the ex-knight said. "I keep thinking I'll wake up in my bed, next to my wife, and I'll come to work, and I'll still be a knight."

"What did you do?"

"I don't know. The Duke summoned me, and when I arrived, he asked why I was there. And then he looked in his book and said, 'I see your knighthood has been rescinded. Can't have a man like *that* in the ranks.' Like it was a joke. Next thing I know, here I am. It's got to be some sort of hazing thing for the new knight, hasn't it? Claps on the back and a mug of ale and a *jolly well done old fellow* when it's all over?"

"I don't know, Edwin," said the other voice. "Things are changing, I think. You've heard the Duke interrogating that nutter from the park, and there's a woman two cells down, dying. Ned here fetched a healer to tend her, and the Duke himself sent him away. From the look on the Duke's face, it's lucky Ned isn't in the next cell."

As those two spoke, I heard footsteps approaching. And then Ned's voice.

"Bugger," he said. "I think she's dead."

More footsteps. "How can you tell?"

"She's not breathing, for one. The whole cell reeks of death."

"Pity. She saved the city last summer, you know. She's one of the good ones."

"Was." Ned fumbled with his key ring. "And I know. I was there."

As I listened to the two guards opening the door to my cell, I regretted what I was about to do. Neither deserved to die, or be blinded. But it wasn't like I had a choice. Not if I wanted to escape. Kill them before they have a chance to cry out. Get Brian. Get us out. Taking prisoners was a luxury I couldn't afford.

I had a piece of reinforced straw in each hand.

I felt Ned's hand on my shoulder, turning me over. My hand flashed out.

I saw his face. Concern and sorrow, shifting abruptly to terror.

I stopped my hand. The straw was an inch from his eye, maybe less. I tossed it aside and let myself sink back to the floor with a groan.

"Why'd you have to be two of the good ones?"

BRIAN

"Ow-oh-oooooo" Someone slapped my face.

T'was the Whore of Ashbury. It appears she had been beaten, as I was. Cheom must be sorely disappointed in me, for I was still in chains and this harlot, although bloodied and dressed in but a filthy, oversized shirt, was free. But perhaps not; two men-at-arms stood outside the cell, with another prisoner.

"Brian" she urged quietly, "Time to wake up. We're getting out of here."

"No." Shaking my head was an effort. "The Deceiver's guards are right behind you."

The Whore sighed. "They're going to help us. They're the good guys. If the voices in your head—I mean, your buddy Cheom—supposedly knows everything, he's got to know that." She used the guards' keys to lose my chains and dragged me stumbling to the doorway.

The guards, although now complicit in my escape, regarded me with suspicion, and the prisoner scowled at me with open disdain.

"Edwin Manon," I said. "Former knight of Ashbury, though you have fallen from your lofty, if ill-chosen station, the balance of your deeds pleases Cheom. Fear not! Pledge your steel to the mighty one, now and forever."

The Former Sir Edwin looked at the harlot. "What's he talking about, Lady Goselin? If he causes trouble, it will mean our heads."

"He's right," the guard called Buckminster said. "We can tell the others you are dead and take you as far as Potter's Field, but a supposedly dead prisoner speaking nonsense will fool no one."

"I can keep him quiet," the Whore said, no doubt imagining most wicked deeds to achieve this purpose. "Just try not to pay too much attention to him."

"No," I said, "heed me. There will be no peace whilst the Deceiver bears the ducal signet. His downfall is preordained, but before that comes to pass I must do Cheom's will and protect the Duke and the Duchess."

"That includes punching the Duke in the face?" the so-called Lady Goselin asked. "Maybe we should leave you here... No, your jabbering will give us away."

"I will not leave until the Duke and the Duchess are saved," I assured the carnal one. "It is Cheom's will."

The Whore looked at me. She was planning some trickery, but every trickster is always tricked in the end. "Then we'll just hide here until Cheom's will comes to pass, whatever that means," she said, placing her trust for once in Cheom's divine wisdom. "Your plan is sheer bloody brilliance."

"There is no place to hide," the shorter one, Ned-Too-Fond-of-Ladies'-Buttocks, said.

"Do you still use the cistern room at the end of the corridor over there?" the harlot asked, pointing.

"Yes," said the Former Sir Edwin, "but we will surely be found there, if we do not drown first."

The Whore of Ashbury, ever the seducer, placed a muddy and bloodstained hand on the tall man's arm. "Trust me, handsome, we'll be fine."

MARIS

The thing about buying an old house is that there are always surprises. Termites in the rafters, cracks in the foundation, false walls where the former owner hid her husband's body. Palaces are just like that, except that they've been around for centuries, and they get wrecked and rebuilt by generations of invaders, and who knows what-all got built over?

A bored little girl with a love for secret tunnels and way too much curiosity for her own good, is who.

Behind the cistern is a maintenance hall. At the end of the hall, where the light from the sconces fails, there's a clever little series of buttons set into the stone, camouflaged to blend in. Push them in the right order and the wall slides away, and stairs descend into darkness. A perfect place for us to hide until we figured out our next move.

Except this time, when the passage opened, it wasn't dark. A dim light flickered from far below.

"Something's wrong," I said. "Nobody knows about that sub-dungeon. Nobody but me. But someone's been down there. Recently."

"How recently?" asked Ned.

"They might still be down there."

"This is bad." Buckminster took a step back. "We'll get caught. They'll kill us. They'll torture us first, and then kill us, to death."

"Did you really just say that?" I asked.

"We have to put you back in your cells," he said. "Right now."

Brian, who had started to sag, spent from rigors of his interrogation and his still-bleeding wounds, roused himself. "We shall not flee from danger, nor shirk our appointed task. With Cheom to guide us, we shall face insurmountable odds, and we shall surmount!"

Ex-Sir Edwin was not to be outdone. He seized a torch from the wall, assuming an *en guarde* and brandishing it with flaming flourish. "We shall be victorious! The bards shall sing the praises of—"

"Are you coming?" I asked, from halfway down the stairs.

"Oh. Right. Of course."

Both Brian and Edwin muscled past Ned, who had already started down the stairs after me. Buckminster bravely offered to guard the rear.

It had been some time since I'd been down here, and I'd forgotten just how far these stairs descended. Brian's burst of strength was ebbing fast, and even though he clearly had some command of magic, he refused to heal himself, claiming that his suffering was penance, and served the greater glory of Cheom. I'd always thought that Penance was a clan of dancing pirates, but that might just be an old husband's tale. Regardless, after my own near-death experience, I didn't dare waste what little energy I had left to heal him myself.

The cold air rising from the dungeons below blew up the thin cotton shirt that Edwin had loaned me. He was a big enough man that the garment served well for purposes of modesty, but didn't do much to cut the chill. Also, the sleeves kept slipping over my hands, no matter how many times I rolled them up.

The stairs only *seemed* endless. Once we reached the bottom, and I managed to shush Edwin and get Brian to quiet his constant monologue to a soft muttering under his breath, we followed the hallway toward the source of the light.

It came from inside a cell, dancing across the darkness through the bars of the cell door.

I suppose it shouldn't have surprised me, but it did. I had already come to the conclusion that Brian wasn't just some projection of Deverran's tortured mind—Brian was a possessing spirit, from

45

Cheom knew where, as Brian might have said. I assumed that the same had happened to the Duke.

I was wrong.

The Duke—Aramis—stood up from the straw pallet where he and his wife sat. He approached the door and grasped the bars.

"Lady Goselin," he said, acid in his voice. "Why is it that every time I see you, you're half-undressed?"

I won't repeat what the Duchess said.

BRIAN

Whilst the Duke and the Whore explained away the Duchess's assumption of past peccadilloes, I pondered the problem of penetrating the prison portal. Normally, I would have called upon Cheom's power to unlock the cell, but I was too weak to wield it. Fortunately goodman Edwin had taken up Cheom's cause. Brandishing his torch like a beacon of righteousness, he marched down the corridor until he came upon a long unused cell and kicked an iron bar from one of the rotting wooden doors.

"What are you doing?" the spuriously titled Lady Goselin cried in a hoarse whisper. The two guards were horror-struck to see Sir Edwin (I call him such for he deserves knighthood) approach with the stout bar in hand, his eyes blazing. What a magnificent sight! While the craven guards recoiled and the Whore sputtered her frustration, Edwin brought the bar down upon the lock like Cheom's irresistible wrath.

The lock rang as if under a smith's hammer.

"You will summon every guard in the palace!" the Whore cried.

Sir Edwin marked her not. He pushed the door open and stepped into the cell.

I shouldered by the guards and rushed in after him, eager to be near my ward. But she recognized me not.

"Deverran?" the Duchess said.

"Tis Brian." I bowed.

"Brian?" (The Duke).

"My Duke!" said Sir Edwin, "how have I wronged you?"

"Sir Edwin?" (The Duke, again).

"Praise Cheom!"

"Cheom?" the Duchess wailed. "Oh, Deverran, what has happened to you?"

"It's Brian," I reminded my Lady.

"Will everyone just shut up?" said the Whore. "This is no time for playing catch-up. I need to think."

"Wrong, woman," said an icy voice from the corridor.

The malignant likeness of the Duke stood in the doorway. The Deceiver had brought several of the Duke's once loyal guards, now doubtless the victims of vile enchantment. Ned and Buckminster were pinned to the wall, helpless. "Now that you are all here, this is the perfect time to catch up."

MARIS

I turned slowly at the sound of the voice.

"'Woman'?" I stepped back, putting Edwin and Brian between me and the enemy. "Please, I prefer 'wench.' You know, between friends."

The false Duke had four armed guards, all of them looking quite capable of splitting any of us open, and he himself brandished a wickedly pointed rapier. On our side, Edwin had an iron bar. Ned and Buckminster were neutralized, held at sword-point by two of the guards. I was unarmed, wounded, and exhausted. Brian was injured badly enough that I wasn't even sure how he managed to remain standing. The Duke and Duchess? I hardly expected them to fight for themselves, though the Duke's face was bruised and his nostrils blood-encrusted, as if he'd recently engaged in fisticuffs. If I was even marginally in better condition, I wouldn't be worried, but as it was, we were hopelessly outmatched.

Clearly I was on the wrong side.

"Friends?" The false Duke laughed, and worsened our odds. His rapier slid forward, and Edwin slid to his knees, pierced through the throat. "Hardly."

There would be no negotiating out of this.

I looked down at the blood spraying from Edwin's neck. My fingers worked out of sight to surreptitiously pull together a small healing spell.

"Fool." I stepped forward and smacked Edwin in the back of the head, hoping it would be enough to keep him alive. The effort drained me, and my knees weakened, but they didn't buckle. I took the iron bar from his slack grip.

"What do you know of me?" I asked, stepping forward to block the entrance to the cell. Behind me, Brian moved to Edwin's side. I hoped that his refusal to use his magic to heal himself didn't extend to others.

"Other than that you broke into my palace and attacked me? What else do I need to know?" The false Duke thrust the rapier at my throat.

I smacked it aside and jabbed the end of the bar into his solar plexus. He grunted, but his gambeson absorbed most of the blow. Still, my point.

"My name is Maris Goselin," I said. "I called down the sun. I closed the hole in the world." I tapped the tip of the rapier with my bar, then struck at his elbow. Not fast enough. I connected with his forearm instead.

He let the impact swing the blade around, slashing at my neck. I blocked, stepped in, and jammed the butt end at his face. He leaned back, enough to save his teeth, but his lip blossomed.

And then two of the guards hacked at me. I blocked one. Sidestepped the other. And caught the false Duke's blade in my chest.

"Call down the sun, then, Maris Goselin." He braced his foot against my belly and pulled his blade free in a spray of blood. "Close the hole in your heart, if you can."

Being fatally stabbed sucks. Being fatally stabbed twice in one day sucks a lot more. I fell backward. I don't remember hitting the ground, only being on it, and looking up, seeing the false Duke in front of me, the real Duke behind me. Both of them bled from the mouth.

I understood, then. Whatever spell lay on the false Duke to give him Aramis's appearance linked them. They were reflections of each other now, in more than just appearance, and the success of the subterfuge depended on the good health of the real Duke.

Pity I couldn't catch my breath to say it.

There was no blackness, just a slow fade as I bled out on the floor.

Then I was back in the cell, trying to shake the fog out of my head and the taste of bile out of my mouth. Someone had healed me enough to keep me alive. Brian? Perhaps. Edwin lay near me. He struggled to his hands and knees, and then collapsed.

I blinked. Non-time passed. The Duke stood in front of Edwin and me, swinging the iron bar aggressively. Next to him, the Duchess wielded a broken sword. One of the false Duke's men lay unconscious. Another tried to stab past Aramis at Edwin and me, but the Duke and Duchess were holding him off.

I didn't see Ned and Buckminster from where I lay. I hoped they were still alive. The two men who'd been guarding them were now menacing Brian, who shielded himself with a straw mattress while alternately chanting and verbally abusing his attackers.

The false Duke watched impatiently.

"Kill that raving moron," he said. "Now. Or I'll spit you and do it myself."

The two men glanced at each other, and then charged.

"No!" Dara cried, flinging herself at them. She cut down the one nearest her. The other swung at her neck.

Had her sword been whole, her parry would have worked. As it was, it was the false Duke's desperate lunge that blocked the strike, diverting his guard's blade so that it only took a lock of her hair, rather than her neck.

"Idiot," he said, just before he thrust his point through his own man's throat. And then he turned his blade on the Duchess, neatly piercing her sword hand, and then punching her in the stomach with the pommel of his sword. She sat down hard.

The false Duke looked up at the ceiling. "Sorry, love," he said. And smirked.

He turned his rapier against Brian. It punched through the straw pallet that had served so well against wider blades. I saw Brian grimace with pain. The false Duke pulled the blade back to strike again.

I grabbed the real Duke's ankle and bit—hard— into the back of his leg. Blood filled my mouth.

Both Dukes screamed and stumbled.

I saw a glint of realization in Brian's eyes. He understood the magical link between the two Dukes. But it was probably too late. My maneuver only bought a momentary reprieve; whoever this imposter was, he was an excellent swordsman. In a few moments, he'd regain his balance, and then Brian and Edwin and I would all be dead.

Everything now depended entirely on Brian's mad, unpredictable magic.

BRIAN

After watching the harlot's animalistic attack on the Deceiver, I understood why Cheom had chosen her to aid me. My enemy's weakness had been revealed. I sidestepped the Deceiver, placing the true Duke betwixt that devil and myself. If those nearby thought Cheom's man had lost his nerve I would have to disabuse them of that fallacy later. Time was of the essence now.

I grasped the Duke's shoulders from behind and looked past him into the eyes of the Deceiver.

"Treblonicus!" I shouted. "Prepare to return to the abyss from which you have slithered. And know that your foul mate shall be joining you presently."

Some theorize that infernal creatures can be controlled by those who use their true names. For a moment, I hoped this would be the case. But the Deceiver balked for only a moment, clearly surprised that his subterfuge was so easily penetrated. At least he delayed his strike, not that it made much difference.

"Bah," he spat. "I don't know what abyss you're talking about, madman, but I'll gladly throw your corpse over the nearest cliff when all this is done."

"No!" I shouted, close by the Duke's ear. "I am bound by oath to shed no blood, but I shall not permit you to rape Ashbury, allowing your hell-spawned brethren to exchange the sulfurous pits of Cheom's punishment for the fair fields of this blessed realm."

"You cannot stop us," the Deceiver replied. "You are unarmed, and you won't draw blood. You used the last of your strength prolonging that woman's inevitable death. What are you going to do, poke me to death with a spoon?" He laughed as he raised his blade, preparing to strike at my face over the Duke's shoulder.

"Tis true, I cannot draw blood. Fortunately, you have no such compunctions," I said, pushing the true Duke forward onto the Deceiver's blade, then stepped back as the stiletto point of the Deceiver's rapier emerged from the Duke's back.

The two of them fell together in a heap.

The Duchess rushed to the aid of her husband, rolling his limp body onto his back and caressing his face. There would be no such comfort for the Deceiver.

He grimaced in disbelief. "You murdered your own brother-in-law… You're too weak to save him. My torture saw to that."

"You tortured Deverran," I said. "I am still whole."

The Deceiver managed a weak laugh. "If you save him, you save me."

"Cheom awaits you both. One will be turned away to return here. My master will hold the other in bondage. Forever."

"You crazy bastard," the somewhat sanctified harlot said, from where she lay half-dead upon the cold stone floor. "I don't know what things are like where you come from, but around here, coming back from the dead is a bad thing. If you can save him, do it."

"Save the Duke, Brian." Cheom's love strengthened goodman Edwin's limbs, and he rose to his feet, even though his wound still bled. He kicked the Deceiver's blade away, rolled the dying devil onto his face, and then tore a strip from the Deceiver's shirt with which to bind his arms. "I'll take care of the impostor."

The Duke gasped; the end was nigh. The Duchess wailed in grief.

"Be strong, my Lady," I said, placing Deverran's bloodied hands on the Duke's scarlet chest. "Cheom will return your husband to you. Pray to Cheom. Your time of courage is near."

Cheom's healing love spread from my fingers, seeping through the Duke's broken body, replenishing blood, closing wounds. The Duke groaned and stirred under my hands as Deverran's strength failed. I was dimly aware as my consciousness faded that Maris Goselin had struggled to her knees, and grasped the iron bar that the Duke had dropped.

"You heard what that bastard said," she said. "There's a false Duchess too, and she's still out there. She'll be coming for us." The vixen swung the bar against the back of the Duchess' head, sending her to sprawl limply across her husband's half-conscious body. "Sorry 'bout that, m'Lady."

My adversary was being led away in chains. His destination was too terrible to contemplate. I turned to the stairs leading from the arena floor to the seat of Cheom's glory. As my eyes rose to the top of that stairway I silently thanked Deverran for his role in Cheom's victory. Without his flesh and blood to carry

me I would have failed. But Cheom provides. Now I could look unashamedly upon the glowing face of my master. Would Deverran remember me? I will remember him. And I will remember Maris Goselin, the Whore of Ashbury. She cavorted with chaos, and yet Cheom chose her to aid me. Perhaps, one day, I will be permitted to illumine Maris Goselin's dark heart with Cheom's grace. Or perhaps that task shall fall to another. Whatever comes to pass, Cheom's will shall be done.

MARIS

The thing is, poor Deverran never knew how he saved the day. When he woke up, all he could talk about were the purple, flying hippos, and a disturbing feeling of all-encompassing well-being. Better him than me, I say. I like being grumpy and disaffected.

But, all's well that ends well. Once I regained my strength, and had a chance to concentrate without being attacked, it wasn't too difficult to pick apart the doppelganger spell. The thing was so tenuous and treacherous that it was hard to imagine anyone being stupid enough to seriously attempt it. Maybe it would be a reasonable spell for a short period of time. Maybe. (I filed that away for future reference.) But this? To rule a country disguised as someone else? How many years did they think they could sustain this? That was madness on a scale that dwarfed Deverran's and Brian's combined. Last time I saw either of the purported usurpers, they were in a cell—not my old cell, but one with magic-proof runes.

Ned and Buckminster suffered concussions and bruised egos, but were otherwise unharmed. Sir Edwin is a Sir again, and nearly as insufferable as he was before, at least in public. But in private, he's more thoughtful, and he's taken to reading his way through my library in his spare time, instead of whatever it was he used to do, much to his wife's annoyance. I think there's hope for the boy, yet.

Duke Aramis has been properly grateful, financially, at least, something for which the pockets of the people of Ashbury Park rejoice. And I was right. The carpet really does tie the room together.

Duchess Dara, on the other hand, can hold a grudge. I'm okay with that; it makes it all the more fun when I show up unannounced at her gala events.

EMBARRASSING RELATIONS

As for Brian, well, everyone is convinced that Brian was not some possessing spirit. That was he not a visitor from some terrifying other world where vastly powerful entities used people as willing pawns in their incomprehensible games. Everyone is convinced that Brian was just Deverran's poor, fevered brain trying to find a way to be effective.

Everyone, that is, but me.

THE HOLE IN VORAK'S PEAK

Power is a funny thing. People think of it as a thing in itself, like, um. Well, like, someone who isn't me might say, "I have the power to return the animate dead to their natural state if they come within thirty feet of me," or "I have the power to send ten thousand troops to lay waste to your western borders," and think that this is something absolute. Something that they have found or earned or was theirs by birthright, that has been subsumed and made an integral part of their essential nature. That powers are things to collect, like Lempurian tribal masks, or those disgustingly cute porcelain bunnies that all the jewelry shops were selling a few years back, and the more powers you collect, the more powerful you are.

But this is to fundamentally misunderstand the nature of power. Power isn't a thing to collect. It's a relationship. Or a complex web of relationships, really. It's where, and how, we meet, and how we treat each other when we do.

In the end, it doesn't matter how powerful you are. There's always something that can bring you down. And the power that can save you? It isn't necessarily yours.

This is the story of how Lady Maris Goselin, humble author of these words, started down the path that led her to reformulate her theory of power.

And before you comment on the bunnies, they were a gift. So don't even start.

Once upon a time—before I became the crazy old witch in the crazy witch house that throws harmless but embarrassing hexes at the children stupid enough to steal from her fig tree, before I began publishing obscure goblin histories, before certain friends and I started a health clinic in the worst neighborhood in Ashbury, even before my neighbors moved away complaining of the growing bee infestation (and I tore down their homes to create my garden)—a woman unexpectedly knocked on my door. I say unexpected not because I'd already established somewhat of a reputation as a cantankerous bitch and the neighbors knew better than to drop by for a friendly visit, and not because I'd established quite another reputation (mostly, but not entirely, unsubstantiated) for dabbling in less-than-savory arts that left my client list decidedly sparse, and not even because it was barely dawn, and it is common knowledge that one approaches me before noon at one's own peril.

No, it was who it was that made it particularly unexpected: Laura Telesi, spouse of one Sir Edwin Manon, who had acquitted himself quite well, for a knight, upon our initial acquaintance, and proved himself an invaluable ally on more than one occasion since. He was also one of the few people in Ashbury whom I could say still treated me with unfeigned friendship without having to be paid for the service. Sir Edwin was, in fact, one of the only people whose company I actually looked forward to. On the other hand, his wife (who, you'll remember, was knocking at my door) had expressed some rather strong emotions, in rather strong language, about the quantity and quality of time her husband spent in my company.

For point of clarity, when I say "knocked at," I really mean, "slammed my door knocker violently and repeatedly against the strike plate like she was trying to drive it completely through the heavy oak."

Me? It had been a good night, and while I was slightly hungover, I had for once neglected to drink so much that I failed to remember the anonymous young gentleman I had met at The Wyrmwood Tavern the night before. He had been seeking employment for the evening.

His professional services rendered that night had been more than satisfactory, and the morning's encore had generated an afterglow that lingered even as he dressed and slipped out into the pre-dawn twilight.

Bard of the Night, his card proclaimed, a winking allusion less subtle and less clever than he thought. He'd given a name that I'd promptly forgotten. It was likely as real as the sweet lies he whispered in my ear.

Regardless. There was afterglow. There was basking. There was a half-waking dream of a different voice whispering those words, perhaps even meaning them, and pretending I didn't recognize the face I saw when I closed my eyes and let my fingers wander. There was pleasure, building. There was a persistent hammering at the door. Obnoxiously persistent.

Moment ruined, I threw a robe on. It's possible I tied it. It's also possible I didn't. I don't remember. I opened the door a crack, with a curse on my lips. I didn't get to utter it. The person on the other side (Laura Tilesi, wife of my very close friend, Sir Edwin, in case you weren't paying attention) pushed hard against the door. I stepped backward to avoid getting hit in the face. Or maybe the door hit me in the face and I stumbled backward. Ultimately, same effect: a wide-open door, with Laura on one side and me on the other, and whatever extraordinarily witty remark I'd been about to say completely forgotten.

"Edwin's missing," Laura snarled in greeting. She pushed past me out of the rain.

Did I mention it was raining?

It was raining. Had been for days, which never helps my mood, except on that particular morning, when there had been not only afterglowing and basking &etc., but also listening to the rain on the thatch roof above, and on the cobblestones outside my window, the drowsy buzz of the bees in the rafters as they woke to another lazy day, whilst afterglowing and basking &etc., and it had been kind of nice, until the aforementioned disturbance.

"Well, he's not here," I said. "Haven't seen him for..." Truth was, I wasn't sure when I'd last seen him. She seemed to misread my hesitation.

Did I mention that Laura was convinced that I was sleeping with her husband? No idea where she'd gotten that idea, as we'd both assured her that he'd never demonstrated more than the slightest interest.

Laura stood in the foyer of my one-room house, dripping all over the floorboards and scowling at my emphatically non-innocent-looking bed, a tangle of twisted and sweat-stained sheets, which, I realized, would need a good washing before I entertained any other guests, even if they *were* being paid.

"He's not in there," I said, "or under there, but you're welcome to look."

Laura spun and slapped me, fast enough that she actually made contact. Her nostrils flared with anger.

"If I thought he was here with you, I wouldn't be here. He's *missing*. And...." her voice caught for a moment. "And I need your help to save him."

There were two survivors of the ill-fated mission that Sir Edwin had led into the Contested Lands, both of them baggage handlers or wet nurses or something—I think the knights call them "squires." Neither of them could tell us what the mission was, or where in the contested lands they had been heading to, because they'd never known. Not the sharpest bricks in the wall, as they say, but then, I guess that was lucky; if they'd known anything more, they'd probably have never made it home.

They'd been set upon as they skirted Vorak's Peak. The attackers had struck from the skies, or burst from the ground—the reports were confused and the survivors beset with more than a little battlefield trauma. It's not that they didn't try, but listening to their accounts was like witnessing a descent into madness. Neither of the stories matched up, and it was clear from what they recounted that before the attack itself, others in their party were also experiencing entirely different events from either survivor. Something had interfered with their perception of the attack, and it was beyond my abilities to penetrate that fog. No amount of digging would find the truth behind the illusion, because the magic that befuddled the squires' memories was no longer active; that truth of what had happened had never been experienced in the first place.

One thing that struck us in both squire's tales was that nobody in the military or the government seemed in the least bit interested in investigating their stories, or finding out what had happened to the missing expedition. They'd been checked by a healer, and then sent home to "take a well-earned breather." Two weeks had passed, and neither had been called to duty. Laura, also, had received no notice that her husband was missing.

(Maybe you're thinking, two weeks and I didn't even notice my best (only?) friend was missing? I never said I was *good* at being a friend.)

The other thing that struck us was that in neither account was there any indication of bloodshed. Fantastical battles of gnashing teeth and choking vines and giant, scaly, feathered wings, talons sharp as swords and all that, yes. But when they'd found themselves alone on the mountain pass, neither of them remembered seeing any blood.

That, Laura insisted, meant that Edwin was still alive.

I was less optimistic.

Laura had encountered obstruction and obfuscation when she tried to get more information from the military, before she'd come to me. (She'd tried everything she could think of before coming to me.) Not surprising, I figured. No commander wants bereaved spouses interfering with sensitive operations. I, Lady Maris Goselin, who called down the sun, and saved Ashbury on multiple other occasions (and was, coincidentally, well-known as Duke Aramis's secret unofficial special investigator), wouldn't encounter the same resistance.

Except I did.

I worked my way up the chain of command, and got nothing. I requested an audience with Duke Aramis, which was declined. That evening, after I broke into the palace and stole into his private chambers, I explained the foolishness of his position.

The Duke rubbed his jaw as I rubbed my knuckles.

"I could have you executed," he said, fundamentally misunderstanding the power relationship between us.

I corrected him, and he rubbed his left eye, which would purple nicely, I was certain.

"My friend is missing," I said. "You're going to tell me everything you know about that."

"I can't."

I lifted my fist.

"I *can't*."

But he tried. He got out half a word—"It's"—before the convulsions struck. He dropped to the floor, his limbs spasming. And then I saw it, the spell, black and ochre and puce-colored threads of magical power which had lain dormant within now extruded tendrils of force that wrapped around him, around his throat, tying his tongue, stabbing into nerve clusters. It was immensely strong and hideously complex, and I saw no means to unravel it. I couldn't imagine the pain that trying to speak was causing him. He kept trying, anyway. "Evil" he said, and blood began to seep from his pores. "Blackb—" was interrupted with gush of blood and bile.

"Stop," I said, wiping it out of my eyes. Blood was everywhere—on my face and all over my clothes. "For Cheom's sake, stop. I don't want to know."

Aramis spit out a mouthful of blood. "Heh. Cheom. Heh, heh. Now there's a name I haven't heard in a long time." By the time he finished chuckling, the spasms had almost completely subsided. He looked bad, but not in a brink-of-death way.

Duchess Dara found us that way: him lying on the floor in a pool of his own blood, and me trying to mop it up with what turned out to be a very expensive dress she'd had made especially for that evening's orchestral gala.

She took one look at us, and said, "Get out, before he tries to say anything else."

Laura was waiting for the news at my home, curled up in my one comfy chair, reading a book by candlelight. It was an idyllic scene, if you ignored the title of the book, "Hamilton's Cryptozoology"—my go-to text when preparing to battle monsters.

I was in no mood for idyllic scenes. I used a bit more force than was strictly necessary to unlock and throw the door open, and to simultaneously light all the lanterns in the house. Laura leapt to her feet, wide-eyed and panicked, but she'd had the forethought to draw her knife. Which is more credit than I'd have given her, aristocratic lady of leisure that she was.

"What did—?" She stopped and stared.

"Don't worry," I said, pulling the bloody tunic over my head. "None of its mine."

"Who—?"

"The Duke."

"You killed him?" There was perhaps less shock and disbelief in her voice than I would have preferred.

"Stop asking stupid questions and go fetch some water. I'll tell you everything, if I can. But only after I'm clean." Because I wasn't yet sure if I'd be able to speak of what I'd learned. If things went badly, I wanted to be able to tell how much blood was mine, and not Aramis's. Besides, this was all her fault, and there was no way I was going to let her lounge her lazy high-bred ass in my comfy chair while I did all the work.

The neighborhood well was at the end of the street, a hole covered with a wooden cap, bolted to stones embedded in the street to keep curious children and drunken idiots like me from tumbling in. A metal pipe protruded and bent into a faucet about waist high. Surely even a useless society woman like Laura could figure out how the pump worked. She grabbed a bucket, but stopped in the doorway.

"It's pissing down rain," she said. "Why don't you just stand in it?"

The idea of joining forces with a jealous woman to save her husband had seemed both unappealing and unavoidable. I'd imagined hours of sullen silences punctuated by angry recriminations about my ethical failings. But if we were going to spend our time together bickering stupidly and taking jabs at each other, maybe it wouldn't be so bad.

"I will, but it won't be enough. And you'll need to wash my clothes, if you want my help, so take two buckets."

When she got back (with two buckets of water), I'd stripped out of everything that had the Duke's blood on it, which turned out to be everything, and was stoking the fire for the stove. She stood in the doorway, looking at me. Judging. I sensed it before I saw it.

I've never been a pretty girl. More like a mouse. My hair had been flat and dull, and the most uninteresting shade of brown imaginable. I was skinny and boyish and more likely to punch when startled than to scream. And my face... the best thing I can say is that it was unmemorable. Growing into a woman didn't really change anything. My hips widened a little, but not much. My breasts, well, you can see them if you're looking from the right angle. My hair? Lost it in the fire of the sun, and I decided to keep it cropped short or shorter. If there's anything that's changed, it's internal. It's in the eyes. It's a place I worked hard to get to. A place that lets me make my own rules, live my own life, and never, ever, look to someone else for assistance, or approval, or love. A mouse, maybe, but a mouse with teeth.

I remember feeling Laura's judgmental eyes on me—Laura, who was all the things I'd never been: stunningly beautiful, curvaceous in all the ways that men write sonnets and love songs and dirty limericks about, with lustrous black hair that hung below her waist, and smooth, olive skin over cheekbones that shamed the artwork of the greatest sculptors of the realm—and thinking, *I don't need anyone's assistance, or approval, or love, especially yours.*

Also thinking:

> *There once was a girl from Alegas*
> *Whose body was shaped like an hour-glass*
> *Said, "She don't need a corset*
> *to fill out that doublet,*
> *But what shall I do with that...*

Well, we all know where that's going.

Laura poured one of the buckets into the pot on the stove, and the other into the washtub in which I'd thrown my clothes.

"Baking soda?" she asked.

I nodded toward the cupboard where I kept my soap. It wasn't the first time I'd had a bloodstain to deal with. Hers either, apparently. Still, I stubbornly refused to acknowledge her competencies. I could do jealousy as well as any rich girl, maybe even better: I could do it without even realizing it.

She poured some into the washtub and stirred, then reached for the buckets. "Gonna need more water," she said.

"Blackbourne," Laura said, pointing to a piece of the Contested Lands closest to the City of Ashbury. Vorak's Peak lay directly between the city of Ashbury and Blackbourne. "He must have been trying to say

Blackbourne. Though what sort of evil might be lurking there, I couldn't say. I've never even heard rumors. But why are we able to talk about it when nobody else can?"

"Edwin never told you anything about his mission, did he? Yeah, me neither. My guess is that whoever ambushed the company was powerful enough to cast a spell that sought out everyone in the world who had any knowledge of it and bound them to silence. The binding is ongoing, but the seeking was single event. Since neither of us knew anything at the time, we're not caught in the spell."

"Makes sense. So, what do we do?"

"First light, we get a mule, and a cart. We'll leave at noon, when the rain breaks."

"A mule... How do you know the rain will break at noon?" Laura shook her head. "And shouldn't we be getting reinforcements? You know people, mercenaries, that sort. You move in those circles. You can talk to them."

"That sort?"

"You're being deliberately obtuse. You know exactly what I'm talking about. The sort of people who put more value on money than on life. I'll pay for it."

"Oh. You mean aristocrats and the petit bourgeois. You don't have enough money to hire them—or me, for that matter. No, they won't help us. Besides, we don't want to bring more people into this. The more people are involved, the more likely we'll be detected and suffer the same fate as Edwin. This isn't the kind of fight that's going to be won on a battlefield. And besides, I already have all the reinforcements we need. That's why we need the mule and the cart."

"I'm trusting your judgment." Laura's tone of voice said exactly the opposite. "But if we're going to be hiking around the mountains of Blackbourne for a week or two, I'm not doing it in *these* shoes. I'm going home to pack. See you in the morning."

The reinforcements were not happy with having their hives messed with, and they were definitely not happy with the hostility Laura was showing toward me. It took a fair amount of convincing to keep her from being stung, especially when she started swatting at them.

On the other hand, they liked the idea of having a chance to explore new fields. The queens discussed and let me know which of the hives situated in my roof would be coming with me.

I don't like moving the hives any more than the bees like being moved, but I also dislike being without their eyes. Which means, mostly I don't leave the city, and when I do, I'm nervous and on edge until I get back to my bees. This time, I needed to leave the city, *and* I needed their eyes. So, I carefully cut the hive out of the rafters beneath the thatched roof, and Laura and I *very* carefully carried it down the ladder and placed it gently into a hive box. The queen did a commendable job of keeping the hive calm, and we managed it with no casualties. Afterward, Laura poured a glass of wine, hands shaking so much that she spilled almost as much as she got into the glass, and downed it in one long swallow.

"I don't like bees," she said, and poured another glass.

When the rain stopped (around noon, as the bees had foretold), we loaded the box into the cart and took our leave of the city. Well, not quite. There was a brief stop at Laura and Edwin's home to pick up her traveling pack. Which happened to be an unreasonably-large-and-heavy trunk that filled half the remaining space on the cart.

"What?" she said. "I only packed the necessities."

She opened the trunk and pulled a pair of walking boots from under a pile of sweaters. They were dark brown leather, luxuriously polished, with grooved leather soles for traction. They laced up the sides to her knees, and they looked amazing on her. Both sensible and fashionable. I imagined her tumbling off a cliff.

Once we were outside the city proper, the bees set out to forage. It had rained too long, and they were eager to get back to work. The roads were mud, with muddy ruts and patches of deeper mud, scattered with massive pits of mud, all of which slowed our progress. It wasn't long before we were both splattered to the waist. Gustavio, the mule, took it all with a bit more good humor than either of us. Which isn't to say that he wasn't as grumpy as you'd expect a mule dragging a cart through the mud to be. Just that Laura and I weren't taking it as well.

(I did take some satisfaction in watching her scrape the mud from inside her fabulous boots that evening. Not that I didn't have to do the same. Still.)

On the second day, we came across a beekeeper's stand on the side of the road at the outskirts of a village. I bought jars of honey, three cases worth, and twice as many empty jars, at a price the merchant was happy to accept. It wasn't enough to just hope to not be noticed as we walked into the trap that had ensnared Edwin and his squad. We needed to *be* something else, something non-threatening. Like traveling honey merchants.

Who am I kidding? There's no way I could pass for a merchant, of honey or anything else. Too mean-looking. And too mean, in general. So, Laura was the merchant, and I her less-than-reputable bodyguard and hired hand. Between villages, I taught her how to move amongst the bees, and how to keep her breathing even. I trained her first to suppress her instinctual reactions when a bee landed on her hand or nose, or in her hair, and eventually to not flinch at all. She learned faster than I expected, and on the sixth day out, when the bees unexpectedly swarmed out over her hand and up her arm, she remained calm, stepped back from the hive, raised her arm, and said, "Some assistance, please?"

I was, very briefly, both proud and impressed. Quickly replaced with annoyance and, yes, again, jealousy. I tamped that down when I realized the bees were getting agitated. The last thing I wanted was for a few dozen bees to give their lives fighting against an ally, however amusing it might be.

By mid-day of the second day, the weather had turned sunny and hot. The puddles dried, but the moisture hung in the air. Our clothes stuck to our skin, and Laura wove her hair into a braid for comfort. The plants loved the weather, of course, and so did the bees. We pressed miserably on.

On the good side, business was booming. Laura would just flash her smile and people gathered like... well, never mind. They'd hover around for a chance to trade a few words, for the brief brush of flesh as money exchanged hands. Laura basked in the attention. If I hadn't already despised the woman, I certainly would have started. On the other hand, we sold so much honey we had to restock, and if we weren't paying as much to restock as we were selling for, I'd have had to call it a wildly successful venture.

Mid-morning of the eighth day, as we drew close to the pass through the mountains, skirting Vorak's Peak, some of the bees saw hints of the beginning of the trap: faint lines of magic draped across the road, where the pass twisted along the side of the mountain. To the left, the mountain rose in an unassailable cliff; to the right, a sheer drop to a fast-running river. Hardly treacherous, though. Someone, long ago, had carved away the cliff face wherever the pass narrowed, so that two wagons could cross in opposite directions without danger to either.

The vision afforded me by my bees is limited, of course, by the bee's attention span, which is, if you'll pardon the pun, flighty at best. A lot of time looking at flowers, and what time is spent looking at impressions left by magical doings is further limited by their fuzzy, fractured perceptions. But as far as I could tell, the first sign of intentional magic on this road was a warning system, and not the trap itself. I'd know more when I could see it in person, but by then it might be too late.

"We might be too late to save Edwin—"

"—and the rest of his team," I interjected, because despite the time spent bonding over handling the bees, the basic unresolved tension remained between us, and as long as that remained, I was determined to use it to poke her when I could. "Sorry," I said. "You were saying?"

"I don't remember," she said. "Also, I hate you."

We continued on.

The magic, when we reached it, turned out to be what I'd suspected—an early warning system that did something, though I wasn't sure exactly what, when we crossed it. We weren't immediately attacked, though, which was a good sign. But there was no indication that anyone else had been attacked there either, so maybe not as good a sign as all that.

On the third hand, we'd had a good week of rain, so maybe there was nothing to be deduced.

"Let's take a break for lunch," I suggested. I put a hand on Laura's arm to stave off any debate. "Gustavio isn't used to hills."

Gustavio watched us with mild amusement and flicked his tail. We found some shade against the cliff wall and unhitched the cart. Laura fed and watered Gustavio while I broke out our own rations. We sat with our backs against the cliff and ate in silence, and as we ate, I surreptitiously inspected the magic arrayed at our feet.

It was definitely a communications mechanism, and one not nearly as complex as the magic that tongue-tied Duke Aramis. It drew nominal power from somewhere within the mountain, so the spell likely needed minimal effort to maintain. As far as I could tell, it did nothing but collect information and pass it on. The transmission threads ran up the cliff face to some place higher on the mountain. If we were lucky enough to appear to pose no threat, that would be where we would need to go.

I hinted to the bees that they might find some tasty mountain wildflowers up there.

We finished eating, and moved on.

The site of the attack that had claimed Edwin and his compatriots was a little less than two miles up the road. No indication of violence, per se, but a field bag, torn open now and emptied of provisions, had been left by the side of the road.

At first glance I saw no obvious magic here—no *active* magic—but when I looked carefully, yes, the signs were there. Shredded remnants of spells that clung to the gravel, and to the rock of the cliff face, where it appeared that something with claws sharp enough to gouge into rock had climbed. But there was more than that. Something distinctly magical lay buried a few inches in the gravel. Something familiar.

I kicked the gravel away, and there it lay, golden and glittering.

Edwin never went anywhere without it. When worn, it made his armor appear shinier than it was, and cleaner. It erased the wrinkles in his cloak and the stains in his trousers. It even made him seem to smell better, he claimed, though I'd always found his scent to be one of his more appealing traits. It was given to him by a wealthy and grateful client of mine, for his assistance in a case I'd solved, which had required the two of us to go crawling through the sewer only moments before making an appearance at my client's son's wedding. I was never sure whether the gift was out of gratitude, or a joke. Edwin didn't care which it was. He called it his Medallion of Fastidiousness. I called it his Medallion of Insufferable Ego Inflation.

I motioned Laura over.

She dropped to her knees beside the pendant and scooped it into her hands. When she looked up, there were tears in her eyes.

"My poor Edwin. He'd never let this go, not while he lived."

I crouched next to her. "He buried it, intentionally. So that we could find it. You know what that means, right? It means he knew he couldn't fight what was happening, but that I... that *we* could." Oops. I continued quickly. "It means that he knew he was going to be taken alive, and wanted us to be able to find him. And we *will* find him."

"You're just trying to make me feel better. He's dead, and you know it."

"You hate me," I said. "I know, and I don't care. I have no compulsion to be the better person. I have no interest in making you feel better. I'm just interested in saving my friend. And that's what we're going to do."

I'd expected that our ultimate destination was Blackbourne, but whatever had taken Edwin wasn't there now. It was here, on Vorak's Peak. Before the light shifted and the bees started back toward the hive, they had traced the strand of magic up the side of the mountain to a cave almost entirely obscured by delicious flowering wild raspberries.

The problem, of course, was that I'd cleverly failed to plan for a mountain climbing expedition. I could probably manage it by myself, with the help of a little spellcraft, but this didn't help Laura get up the mountain (or help a rescued Edwin *down* the mountain). And there was no guarantee that a little spellcraft wouldn't attract the attention of whatever lurked above.

Laura listened to me complain about my lack of foresight for several minutes before opening her travel trunk and dumping her pile of sweaters and blouses into the cart. She handed me a spool of rope and a pouch of metal spikes—pitons, she called them—before divesting herself of her skirt and boots, donning, instead, well-knit hose and soft leather shoes that were flexible enough to grip a foothold as reliably as with a bare foot.

"You've done this before," I said. I was incredulous, and grateful, and annoyed, and I think I might have managed to keep all that out of my voice.

"It's a hobby. My uncle took us climbing in Trollsgate when I was young. I've climbed the Palisades of Cuulanis. Vorak's Peak is a foothill." She wiggled her toes. "Sorry, I didn't know your size. But I got you a harness."

The harness was a stupid-looking and uncomfortable contraption built of rope and leather that wrapped around the waist, crisscrossed under the crotch and squeezed one's buttocks together tightly. It was adorned with metal loops, and looked like nothing so much as a torture device.

"I'm not wearing that," I said. Incorrectly, as it turns out. Laura is, apparently, one of the few people more stubborn than I am.

We parked the cart against the cliff face and tethered Gustavio with enough lead that he could move around, but not enough to accidentally fall into the ravine. We put out enough food and water for several days. I didn't worry too much about thieves—if I was alive, the bees would keep people away, and if I wasn't, well, both Gustavio and the hive would be worth more to them alive than dead.

I took off my boots and hung them from my belt. Laura handed me a permeable bag of white powder that came off on my hands and made them oddly dry, but better able to grip the rock. Resin, Laura called it, and she hung a small sack of it from her belt. I followed suit.

And then we climbed.

I have to admit, I don't think I'd have made it, even with the rope and resin, without Laura's help. When my hands cramped at an inopportune time, Laura climbed over to me and attached a safety line to my harness.

"Feet against the wall, and then let go," she said, "I've got you. Take a few to rest your hands."

"You hate me. Now you want me to trust you?"

"I need you," she said, "now. Trust me less on the way down."

I asked the bees to look into the cave ahead of us, and they kindly consented. Dozens filtered through the caverns, following the various twists and turns and forks. Beyond the immediate range of light filtering through the raspberry bushes, it became pitch black, and the bees grew upset. They traveled in a pack, communicating to each other when they would encounter an obstacle, until between them, they—and I—had a reasonably good spatial concept of the cavern.

Outside the cave, Laura and I rested with our backs against the mountain. She picked raspberries, and I drew what the bees showed me, so that I could share it with Laura.

The cavern ended abruptly: a cold stone wall, and a pit. The bees flew down into the pit, a hole that seemed not too much bigger than could be negotiated by a man in armor. Toward the bottom of the pit they noticed light, coming from above and slightly deeper into the mountain. Following that light, they came out into a brightly lit passage. The light, I could tell, was magical in nature, and not simply because of the lack of torches.

Happily buzzing, the bees continued their explorations.

Several hours later, I had a map, and I had some good news, though it wasn't *entirely* good.

"He's alive," I told Laura. "We've seen him. They're all alive. Our people, and others in a dozen different uniforms."

"Alive?" She sounded stricken.

It was then that I realized that she had never expected to rescue him. She had expected to avenge him, or die trying.

"Don't worry," I said, "he could still be permanently damaged. It appears that whatever took him is using its prisoners as energy sources. So, he's breathing. But he's not doing anything else. Is that better?"

She cursed me then, roundly and thoroughly, until a bee bumped her nose, and she realized that others had gathered around her face.

She took a deep breath to gather herself. "What's the plan?"

"You mean, how do we fight an immensely powerful entity with unknown abilities?" I shrugged. "No idea. The things I can think of is, sneak in and see if I can figure out a way to disrupt its energy source, without killing them. And if that fails, I try to distract it while you put a knife in its back."

"Does it have a back?"

"Literally? I don't know. But everything's got a figurative back."

She nodded, and checked her knife. "Then let's finish this."

Despite having the bees' sense of the cave, or perhaps due to our overconfidence in my interpretation of their senses, we did not come through the cavern unscathed. The ceiling was lower than I'd anticipated, and they'd either failed to notice or neglected to inform me of minor inconveniences, like rocky spikes hanging from the roof and protruding from the floor. Laura cursed loudly, once, in shock, and then more softly, if more colorfully, at great length. She was taller than me, a fact that the bees were oblivious to, and bumped the top of her head on the roof. Ducking instinctually, she smashed her face into an inconvenient stalactite.

"I think I broke my nose," she complained. "I'm bleeding."

I'm pretty sure I said something sarcastic and insensitive in response, a mere moment before I encountered a stalagmite, which would have surely unmanned me, had I been so equipped, and the rest of my insult was lost to my own stream of whispered invective.

"Do you have a spell to make light?" Laura asked.

"Of course. Do we want to bet that this creature won't detect it?"

Laura harrumphed, which has a decidedly different timbre as performed by a woman with a potentially broken nose, and we proceeded more cautiously. Ultimately, we reached the pit the bees had warned us of. Laura tied something to a rope and lowered it until it struck rock, and then estimated the depth by arm-lengths of rope. We opted not to jump down. Laura felt around until she found a stalagmite she trusted, and looped the rope around that. She went down first, and then whispered for me to follow. Sure enough, once we crawled beneath a rocky ledge, we could see light filtering from above. Laura boosted me up, and I was able to pull myself into brightness. Laura was able to climb without my assistance.

The corridor we found ourselves in was no more natural than the light that filled it. The walls were smooth, as if some great worm had burrowed through it, dissolving all it touched. A handful of bees flitted about, disturbed not only by the lack of flowers, but by their inability to discern the direction of the sun. Still, they infiltrated deep into the mountain. Ahead was the first chamber of victims. I slipped quietly into it. Laura followed.

They were arrayed in rows, lying on cots fashioned of branches and interwoven highland grasses. It looked infinitely more comfortable than what the poor of Ashbury sleep on every night, but I was certain to someone like Laura, the conditions were abominable.

I began to examine one of the victims. She was a soldier. I didn't recognize the crest on her uniform, or the insignia.

Laura scowled at the woman and shook her head in disbelief. "Lavistani, archer corps. That's.... that's not possible."

I almost asked why, but the last thing I needed was a history lecture to show how inadequate I was. Besides, the answer was already right in front of me. The uniform looked old, old enough to be rotting on her body. The woman, on the other hand, looked hardly a day over twenty-five, her skin smooth and unblemished, save for a long-healed scar on her forehead. Her breathing was regular and unlabored. She seemed healthy and well fed, but her body had lost all muscle tone. I wondered, if she woke, would she be capable of sitting up?

Magic permeated her body, of course, both sustaining her and feeding off her. A thick cable of raw magical power dropped from the back of her neck and disappeared into the rock floor below her cot. I looked for a way to unravel the spell without killing her.

"He's not here," Laura said, looking around.

"No," I said. "He's deeper. These are the older chambers. He'll be in the most recent."

"Then let's go."

I shook my head. "You want me experimenting on Edwin? Or near him?"

Laura snorted her derision, which in her case caused red bubbles to pop from her nose and set her bleeding again. Blood dripped on the floor. She dabbed her face angrily with her sleeve.

"Fine. You hide here with the Lavistani. I'm going to find him."

I didn't watch her leave. I was busy tracing tendrils of magic, looking for a thread to pull.

My education is far from systematic, but I remembered reading or hearing something about Lavista, and I struggled to remember what it was. Sadly, I failed in that, and what I relate here comes from subsequent research. The city-state of Lavista had never wielded influence beyond its own borders, but had successfully carved out a civilization in the midst of the barbarian lands. Their farmland was fertile and the hillside the city was built against was rich in metal ores. Their warriors were not many, but they were brave and skilled, and better armed than the tribes that surrounded them.

It was a song, I remember now. A traveling bard who specialized in obscure and suppressed history offered a private performance. Yes, I have a thing for bards, at least those with clever tongues and fingers.

Lavista's fortunes changed overnight, during a war that was so trivial to modern historians as to have no name. Faced with overwhelming force, Lavista dispatched a small, well-trained force of archers to flank the enemy's lines and surgically excise the enemy's command structure. Those archers disappeared somewhere in the mountains. Lavista fell that day, razed to the ground, an event of such import that most histories describe it thus: *Meanwhile, the barbarian lands to the west suffered centuries of constant warfare.* It is a testament to Laura's education that she was able to recognize the crest on the soldier's uniforms.

The spell binding the young woman was complex, yes, but that was only part of the challenge. It had been constructed under an entirely alien logic: not that of any of the legitimate human schools I had encountered, nor of the necromantic disciplines. It exhibited none of the brute force of chaos magic, nor any hint of the improvisational elements of my own style of spell weaving. Perhaps with time, I could have worked out the logic of it, gained an understanding of its inner workings and the interdependencies of the forces at play within the victim's body. Perhaps not fully. Perhaps not even enough to predict what would happen to her when I unraveled the spell.

Ultimately, it came to a choice: experiment on these people, and see what happened, or experiment on Edwin. Which was no choice at all.

I laid my hands on the Lavistani woman, seeking a finger-hold on a thread of magic I could use as a way in.

I found it.

Her eyes opened, and her mouth. She screamed, silently; only air pushed through long-unused vocal chords.

It was enough.

The air grew electric with the creature's attention. Inhuman feet slapped the stone floor. Its shape darkened the doorway, shadowy and indistinct, with enough similarity to human form to make it truly monstrous. It stood on two legs and braced itself against the doorframe with two arms, but those limbs seemed to have too many joints, and the hands, too many fingers. Its face was a long thin shadow, eyes high on its forehead, and everything below the eyes featureless. More than that, I can't say. It seemed as if my eyes slid away from anything I tried too hard to focus on.

The creature made no sound, but I heard its scream of rage through my entire body, like the memory of shattering stone. *Leave me alone!*

No, not while it held Edwin. I threw everything I could get my hands on at it—deep power gathered from the mountain's strength, from the flowing springs within it, and the fire that raged below it. From the plants that grew on its slopes and the sun that warmed them. Anything and everything that I could steal from the lines of force around me. Fire leapt from my hands, and lightning. A cloud of corrosive gases. A hail of ice and stone. I would tear this whole mountain down if I needed to.

It wasn't enough. Or rather, it was too much. My power fed the creature, made it stronger. It took everything I gave it, absorbed it all into itself, and then sent a blast of force back at me. I flew backward, flipping up and over one of the cots and its occupant, and slammed painfully against the floor.

I was lying there, trying to come up with a plan that didn't involve feeding it more power to use against me, when I saw movement behind the creature. Laura, still operating on the original plan.

Groaning, I picked myself up, and began to prep another spell. It didn't much matter which spell; the purpose was to keep the creature's attention on me, while Laura put a knife in its back.

And it worked, to an extent. The creature didn't seem to notice Laura moving quietly into striking distance. It also didn't seem to notice the blade shattering against its back, or the burst of energy that flared behind it, or Laura dropping to floor, where she sprawled, motionless. As if she was too insignificant to acknowledge. The creature's eyes stayed on me. Its purplish red pupils filled almost the entire eye, like a dog's. It never blinked. I was unable to look away, the strength seeping from my body, gathering at the base of my skull and draining from me there.

I didn't need eyes in the back of my head to know that what I'd seen in the other victims was happening to me. That in a very short period of time, I too would be laid on a cot, helpless and paralyzed, as my strength fed the creature.

I staggered to my feet. I tried to pull my blade, despite seeing what had happened to Laura, but my arms were so heavy. I managed to take one step before sinking back to my knees.

The creature caught me before I fell, lifting me in its cold arms. I pushed against it. Or maybe I dreamed I pushed against it. My body obstinately refused to do what I demanded of it, and I lay draped across its arms like an overdramatic actor in a Baconian tragedy, unmoving, for all that I raged within.

And then I was falling, as the creature slapped at its face.

From where I fell, I couldn't see what happened next, but I didn't need to. The familiar and comforting buzz that filled my home every day grew to a terrifying roar as the bees swarmed. The sound echoed in the cavern, amplified. Half the hive crawled over the creature as it twisted and slapped and raged, and eventually, cried.

I felt the magic that was draining my strength vanish, and I was once again able to move. When I looked at the other victims, the thick ropes of energy-draining magic had dwindled to mere strings. The creature itself looked smaller, though I thought at the time that it was only a visual effect as it cringed in upon itself under the onslaught of the bees.

I wasted no time, and tried not to think about what might happen to the victims as I tore the remaining strands away from their bodies. They were awake now, but didn't move. They hadn't moved for so long their bodies had forgotten how. All they could do was whimper.

I could now see the threads of power feeding the creature, extending out through the walls to victims in other chambers, and severed them in batches at the source.

The creature was truly diminished now; reduced to the size of a cat, it cowered in a corner under a cloud of bees.

No! Stay away! I won't go back. I'll never go back!

Go back where? I didn't care. The bees were still attacking it, and it grew smaller, from feline to rodent-sized. And the bees were falling to the floor, dying, as their stingers tore from their bodies after delivering their poison. Hundreds of them. Thousands. More. I experienced each tiny death, and realized that I was crying.

Enough.

I tore strips of cloth from the helpless bodies of the creature's prisoners and wove them into a sack. As I did, I took strength from the stones around me, and laced those strands of magic into the fabric. When it was done, I scooped the struggling creature into the bag, and then swung it against the cave wall until it stopped struggling. And a few dozen times more, just to be sure.

Dying bees covered the floor. I couldn't take a step without crushing a dozen or more. I swept them aside as best I could as I made my way to the doorway. The air was thick with angry bees flying in and out of the room and filling the corridor. Almost the entire hive had come to my rescue, and the toll had been horrendous. I told them that the danger had passed, but that they might want to watch the sack for movement.

Laura lay in the corridor, just outside the room. The red bubbles in her nostrils showed she was breathing, which meant that she was likely not in danger, which meant I could ignore her. Instead, I ran deeper into the mountain, to the room the bees had shown me held Edwin.

I found him sitting up, rubbing the back of his neck. He saw me.

"Maris! I knew you'd find us. I knew you'd save me."

And he was on his feet, and I did not stop him from wrapping me in his arms. And I did not stop him from cupping my chin in his hand, or from bringing his lips to mine. When had I fallen in love? I hadn't realized I was capable of it, not any more.

I don't know if the kiss lasted mere seconds, or went on for minutes, or at what point I moved from standing to perched on his cot, with my legs locked behind his thighs. Whichever it was, it was too long.

There were others in the room, of course. Edwin's company, and a company from Blackbourne. I'd noticed them peripherally. They were unimportant.

One of Edwin's company cleared her throat.

"Sir Edwin? Your wife..."

"Laura?" And then, "Laura!"

I don't know how long she'd been standing in the doorway, or how much she'd seen. Enough, from her look. Edwin's fingers untangled from my shirt (when had they gotten into my shirt?), and he pushed me away like I'd suddenly revealed myself as a viper.

Laura looked like she was going to slap him. I was sure she was going to slap him.

"Laura, I'm sorry—"

She didn't slap him. He dropped to his knees, clutching his groin. Me, she punched in the face. I tasted blood. She grabbed my collar and raised her fist again.

"One I'll give you," I said, "as a thank you for helping me save my...friend. Just one."

She breathed her rage through gritted teeth, and I plotted my moves: deflect the punch; trap the hand that held my collar; turn the hand over to expose the elbow; strike the elbow while turning my body to create a ledge for her to fall over. Thoroughly enjoy the snap of the elbow, and the satisfying crunch of face meeting floor.

She lowered her fist, denying me that satisfaction.

"Stay away from us," she said. "Just stay away."

Edwin's company followed Laura and Edwin out of the room. Some of them muttered words of thanks, or of consolation. None of them looked me in the eye. The Blackbourne troops followed, questions on their faces that they knew well enough not to ask. And then I was alone.

Of the oldest prisoners, a handful died, their bodies too weak from over two hundred years of inactivity to keep their hearts beating. The others did not, but were unable to rise from their beds.

Laura and two of the Blackbourne troops were skilled climbers, though the Blackbourners had been inactive for too long to fully trust their bodies. But between the three of them, they were able to guide Edwin's company in lowering the others down the cliff face to the road.

The Blackbourne troops went down first, and then assisted bringing down the others. Two of them went with one of the Ashbury knights to the nearest town to get help. Other than sending the bees to guard the hive, I stayed out of the way.

Eventually, they were all gone. Laura was the last one down. I watched from the mouth of the cave, and I could tell that she was debating pulling the rope down with her. After her feet touched the ground, she looked up at me, hand still on the rope. Edwin touched her shoulder, and she slapped his hand away, but she left the rope where it was.

I moved back into the cave. I'd stay until people came with wagons and carted those who could not walk back to civilization. Besides, right now, I still had one more task ahead of me.

The woven sack containing the monster lay motionless where I'd dropped it. I crouched beside it.

"Well, it's just you and me here, now," I said.

No response from the sack. I poked it.

"You still alive?"

I am undone, it said. Again, in my head. It sounded frail and scared. *They will come for me, and you will not be able to stop them. They will come for me, and I am too weak to run. They will come for me, and wield me again against the world.*

They? "Who is 'they'? Wield you how?"

I opened the sack. Upended it and shook. The creature tumbled out. Its shadow-dark flesh was angry, covered with thousands upon thousands of bee stings. The hive had been forty thousand bees strong when we left Ashbury. More than half of them had died.

You are not strong enough to resist them. I have hidden for centuries. Why have you done this to me?

"You took my friend. I don't have many of those." I knocked it off its feet, and pressed a finger against its stinger-festooned chest. *"Who are you hiding from?"*

Eventually, it told me.

There are those who run the world, loose networks of wealth and privilege that maintain the social order, for good and for ill. I knew them well—it was by catering to their more dubious desires that I had crawled my way out of poverty. And then there are those who run those networks, a deeper network of shadowy figures that manipulate the manipulators. I have skirted the periphery of that world, on occasion. An insidious web of dangerous people, but for all that they work toward their own interests, their interests require a stable world.

There is another network, older, deeper, darker. One that profits from chaos and upheaval and destruction, and wields its strength to bring about these conditions. There was a time when wars raged across the continent. And then, those wars slowly ground to a halt, and the madness that drove them faded. How many centuries ago was that? That is how long this creature had been hiding.

But now, we had broken the creature's power, and too many knew of it to cover up. I couldn't leave it here, not alive.

Power is a funny thing. A creature with the power to manipulate people across vast distances, brought down by bees and the intersection of three people unable to come to terms with their own relationships.

Could I have bound the creature to my will? Wielded it for my own purposes? Maybe. But that's not the kind of relationship I wanted to get into. There are better kinds of relationships.

It's thirty years on now, near enough, and the people who sought the creature finally visited my home.

There were four of them in my house, and another two keeping watch. When I arrived home, they'd torn the thatch from my roof and thrown my bees into confusion, and had cast some sort of disintegration spell on my floorboards and irreparably destroyed my priceless Lempurian carpet. They smashed the other two porcelain bunnies from that set. They tore my house apart by the timbers in an attempt to reveal all my secrets.

But secrets don't live in houses, do they? At least, not for long.

I killed the bastards, of course, all but one to tell the tale. Did I do that by myself? Or did I have help?

The creature is long, long gone, its nest in the rafters of my cottage abandoned and filled with honeycomb. But the fight was strange enough that I suspect it left behind a few surprises, triggered when its ancient nemesis threatened me.

Yes, you read right. I brought it home with me, hid it from view, and, with the help of the bees, taught it. Taught it to feed its strength from the forces generated from the land and the water and the air, instead of people. Taught it how to cultivate consensual relationships with the living things around it. Taught it how not to be alone, even though I hadn't entirely learned how to do that myself.

And when it had learned enough, it left, and one of the queens chose to go with it. Where? I have no idea. It can go anywhere now. And those who would seek to wield it against the world? They will never, ever find it.

I, on the other hand, know exactly where *they* are, now. And by the time anyone reads this, I, too, will be long gone. Hunting.

And it might look like I'm alone, but I know I won't be.

THE MYSTERY OF THE DEAD CAT
IN THE DARKNESS

Normally, finding a dead cat is a bad thing, especially when it's nailed to your front door. But there are worse things.

Being poor, unemployable, and shunned by society, for one.

Being suddenly but discretely wealthy, but still unemployable and shunned by society, for another.

Falling in love—or at least lust—with a married man whose spouse has been unambiguously clear that you're not even worthy of being a threat to their relationship, and ruining a perfectly good friendship in the process, for a third.

I suppose it was fortunate that one of my jobs earned me enough money that I'd never need to work again, if my needs were reasonable, because it's not like clients were lining up at my door.

Except for the cat. And that didn't really count as "lining up." More like just hanging around.

Which is exactly what my own life consisted of at that point. Hanging around and waiting for something to happen to break through the daily monotony of dining (alone) in Ashbury's finest restaurants and then drinking myself stupid until it was late enough to go to sleep.

Can there be anything worse than boredom?

I examined the cat. It wasn't terribly large, but showed no signs of being feral; its coat was glossy and well groomed, a calico, and it wore a worked leather collar with a bell. An iron spike had been driven through its chest and into my oak door. Blood stained and matted the fur beneath the wound and discolored the wood below.

Very curious, and I decided I'd begin my investigation immediately upon recovering from my hangover the following afternoon. In the meantime, it wouldn't do to have a cat hanging from my door. What would my neighbors say? They already hated and feared me. I would, I decided, put it in a canvas sack and store it in the root cellar until the morning.

I reached for the cat.

And learned exactly what is worse than boredom.

As I carefully tugged the dead cat off the nail, it hissed and spat and raked a sharp claw across my cheek. I dropped it and jumped back, gracefully catching my heel on a cobblestone, and sprawled on my back.

The last I saw of the dead cat, it was racing into an alley.

There was no way I'd be able to catch it, so I went inside, poured myself a glass of brandy, and collapsed on the bed. And I don't remember much else.

I awoke with the expected pounding hangover and a face full of bees. Which, in hindsight, should have been a clue that something was wrong. But at that moment, my dizzyingly intense headache exterminated all rational thought, and the bees were only an annoying and dangerous impediment to getting my face over a briefly empty chamber pot.

I managed to scoop them away with no loss of life, and afterward, spent the remainder of the day sheltering in the quietest, darkest, coolest place in my humble abode, with cool compresses against both the back of my neck and my forehead.

The sun had crept low enough that his insufferable gaze intruded through my windows into even the darkest depths of my home, my hangover refuge, when something crashed against my door with the force of a stone giant's fist. I pressed my wrists against my ears to block the sound and rolled over.

The sound came again, a thunderous hammering that felt like sharp iron spikes driven into my skull.

"Go away," I said. Perhaps. I'm not certain that I actually moved my mouth. This was the worst hangover I'd ever had. My head pounded, and felt like it had been stuffed with cotton, stretching my skin painfully. My face hurt. My kidneys hurt. *Everything* hurt.

I managed to reach the door before the timbers splintered, throwing it open with what I hoped was a suitably impressive display of force.

"If you touch my house again," I said, "I will kill you, and everyone in your family."

"I should hope not," said Sir Edwin. "Laura would be rather put out by being killed."

I tried to get my eyes open enough to see him. It was at that moment that the air filled with swarming bees. Clearly come to protect me in my moment of distress. I remember hoping they wouldn't hurt Edwin too badly. And then I remember realizing that, no, I didn't actually care, as long as he went away.

"What are you doing here?"

"I followed the bees, now, didn't I?" Edwin sounded pleased with himself. I couldn't tell if he was preening; I still couldn't get my eyes open properly.

And I still might have killed him, but the bees corroborated his story, so I settled for just thinking bad thoughts. The bad thoughts swirled around my head like bats caught in a sudden storm. In fact, everything was swirling around, both inside and out of my head.

"You look terrible," Edwin said.

I considered telling him to fuck off, but decided to collapse instead. Worst hangover ever.

Where Edwin managed to find a whole bathtub's worth of ice in the middle of summer (and what it cost him), I still don't know. I also didn't know where he dredged up the sorry excuse for a healer whose countenance hovered over my face when I awoke. She was an antique, a septuagenarian at the very least, with a single tooth protruding at an unlikely angle from her wrinkled face. Her hair clearly hadn't seen blade or comb since she was a child; there were twigs and leaves caught up in the matted tangles, and between blinks of my eyes, a brown-whiskered face shoved strands of white hair out of its way to peer down at me with beady little rodent eyes from atop her head.

The sight sent shivers through my body. No, it wasn't that. It was the fact that I was sitting in a tub of ice water.

I tried to get up, but the healer put a withered hand against my chest, and with her mighty, twig-like arm, pushed me back down.

"Need to get your temperature down," the crone said. The rat in her hair nodded in agreement. "So stay put until I say otherwise."

Given that the monumental effort needed to lift my body was far beyond what little strength I had—most of which had left me after my first attempt to stand—my nodded assent was unnecessary. Still, it seemed only polite.

She raised an eyebrow at that, but accepted my promise. I watched her shuffle away, and then things got a bit hazy.

Next thing I knew, strong hands were gripping me under my arms and hauling me out of the tub. I considered threatening my assailant's life, but it seemed too much trouble. Far easier to just let him lay me atop my kitchen table and towel me dry.

I blinked my eyes, trying to get them to focus. When they did, I realized it was Edwin. His hands felt hot on my skin through the towel, and then even hotter when he held my wrists fast and leaned his body across my thighs, effectively restraining me. I tested it. I'm pretty sure if I was in full health, I could have squirmed away, but as it was, I was helpless. Then again, maybe helpless with Edwin lying atop me wasn't so bad. Or wouldn't be so bad if I didn't hurt so much.

"If only your wife could see us now," I said. "I'm sure she'll want to hear all about this little adventure. Especially since she's barely forgiven you for the last time."

The crone hobbled up and scowled into my face. She grabbed hold of my short-cropped hair and tugged a bit harder than necessary to hold my head immobile, and then she jabbed a knobby finger into my cheek.

The pain was indescribable. I tried my best to describe it with my screams, but I'm sure I did an inadequate job.

The crone, on the other hand, seemed unimpressed with my vocabulary, and continued to poke and prod at my cheek. Why? What was wrong with my cheek? I struggled to remember. Had I been in a bar fight? Entirely possible, but it didn't feel right. The old woman leaned in close and sniffed. She pinched and squeezed, and I learned that what I'd earlier thought was pain was really just mild discomfort.

"Oh," Edwin said. "I forgot to make introductions. Lady Maris Goselin, I'd like you to meet Laura's grandmother, Larissa."

I have an unfailing ability to impress new acquaintances. Usually negatively.

"Ah. Um." It was difficult to speak between screams, but I did my best. "It's a pleasure to meet you."

"The scratch has gone septic," Larissa said. "You're going to die."

A wound gone septic is not necessarily a death sentence, especially not with the miracle of modern magic. Even before proper curative spells were perfected, there were healing balms and charms that could draw the poison from all but the worst infections, and in extreme cases, there were surgeries to excise or amputate the affected area.

Larissa, it turned out, was no minor hedge witch, despite her some-what hedge-like appearance. She was professor emeritus at the Royal College of Healing Arts. Which explained her bedside manner.

She had performed all the greater healings while I lay unconscious, and all it had done was slow the progression of the illness. It's only her knowledge of ancient and discredited techniques—old wives' remedies that had been "proven" by the medical authorities to have no beneficial effects, such as ice to reduce fever, and herbal medicines that worked only on a physiological basis—that had brought me to anything resembling a state of coherence.

"This was no accident," she said, poking my cheek again. Maybe to remind me that it was there. Or maybe just to hear me whimper. "It's a magical affliction, but unlike any spell I've ever seen. So far nothing that I know has worked to counter it. Do you have any enemies who might want to do you harm?"

Edwin kindly laughed out loud, since I was feeling too weak to do it myself. "Only half of Ashbury," he said. "Including your grand-daughter."

"Used to be three quarters. I've been slacking." I closed my eyes and tried to focus myself enough to visualize the spell within me. The in-sides of my eyelids pulsed black and grey, with blotches of red where the sunlight hit. The random shapes coalesced suddenly into a form: a cat, dangling... And I remembered.

"It was a cat scratch," I said, and before Edwin could reprimand me for letting it go so long, continued: "It happened last night."

"Powerful magic," Larissa said. "Where's the cat?"

"It's dead."

"That's probably a good thing. I'd like to examine it."

I shook my head, and got so dizzy I almost threw up. It took a couple deep breaths before I could speak again. "Can't. It ran off."

Larissa understood before Edwin did.

I ignored Edwin's babbling and turned my attention to the magic that infected my cheek, and more. It had gotten into the bone, I could tell. No. Farther. I could see it: sickly green and yellow tendrils of magic, red, and black—the color of pus, of infection, of fever, of necrosis—twisted and tangled around and through my body, permeating my flesh and bones, burrowing its way into my lungs and other organs.

"I recognize this," I said. "But the only person I've ever seen use magic like this is in the deepest cell under the Duke's castle. Edwin knows who I'm talking about."

Two years earlier, I had, with the help of an insane man named Brian, two guards named Ned and Buckminster, and our very own Sir Edwin, defeated a plot in which an evil mage with the uninspired name of Luk sought to make himself a doppelganger of the Duke, and his partner into the Duchess. This bore the signature of his mad magic.

"You need to convince him to remove the spell," Larissa said. "Or kill him. That should dissipate it."

"Can you get me into the dungeons?" I asked Edwin. "You might have to carry me."

He shook his head. "It's not him. That villain died last month, of a fever."

A fever. Like mine? That seemed too coincidental to be a coincidence.

"Then I need to see his lover. Partner."

She'd been as mad and broken as Luk, glaring daggers at me throughout the trial that put Luk in the dungeons, even though I was the one who reminded Duke Aramis about due process. Luk was lucky to escape an executioner's blade long enough to see trial; the girl could have served a lighter sentence, if she hadn't insisted on staying with her man.

"What was her name? Melissa something?"

"Malena," Edwin said. "Malena Bane. And you can't. She's gone. The Duke decided that she was just a pawn, and harmless. After Luk died, he set her free."

To say I spoke freely of the Duke's naiveté is, perhaps, an understatement. By the time I had finished my monologue, several bottles of not-inexpensive wine lay smashed on the floor and my bees swarmed through the house in a confused rage. Edwin cowered within my wardrobe. Larissa did not. She stood and waited, lips pursed, until I came into range, and then slapped me.

I'd like to think that in the heat of the moment, she simply forgot the magically festering wound on my cheek. That she would have realized it would have been kinder to disembowel me with a rusty scythe, and done so.

It took everything I had to calm the bees. Not because I cared at that moment what happened to Larissa, but because I love my bees, and didn't want any unnecessary deaths. Larissa may have deserved to be stung by a thousand bees, but she wasn't a threat to anything more than my dignity, and those bees didn't deserve to die from my anger.

"Screw it," I said. "I can see how this spell is put together. I can pull it apart."

"No, you mustn't!" For the first time, genuine concern flashed across Larissa's face. Or perhaps it was fear.

"I've taken apart spells like this before," I said. "You just have to find the right thread and the whole thing unravels."

Nothing Larissa—or anyone else—told me could dissuade me from tearing this wretched spell off me. I stood in front of my mirror and examined the spell.

"It's a trap."

Ah. There it was. I needed to reach into the festering wound to find the thread. It was blindingly painful. Larissa jostled my arm.

"Didn't you hear me? It's a trap. The spell that's making you sick is just a container for another spell. Pull it apart, and you'll loose this sickness as a plague over all of Ashbury. Save yourself and you kill us all."

Malena Bane had been escorted to the city gates and told not to come back. Though nobody reported having seen her since, clearly she'd ignored that advice, just as she'd previously ignored the rules that said you can't imprison people and take their place, and then start torturing and killing everyone who might have a problem with that.

In a city the size of Ashbury, finding her at all would be feat; finding her quickly was nearer to an impossibility. Unless you were me. I had a hundred thousand pairs of eyes at my disposal. The only problem was that they were only good during the day, and I'd wasted away the daylight almost dying. If Larissa's ministrations could keep me alive another twenty-four hours, I had no doubt my bees could find Malena Bane.

But while Malena wasn't the least of my problems, she also wasn't the worst of them. Somewhere out there was a dead cat, and whatever was going on with me was tied closely to that creature. I could feel the ghost of the thread of malignant energy tethering us together. And so, with a strip of willow bark between my teeth—which almost overpowered the taste of the other foul concoctions Larissa required me to gag down—and a flask of sweet cream in my pocket, I set off into the dark of night.

Edwin tried to accompany me, but I knew his presence would only distract. For this, I needed to be alone.

This was no systematic search. Nor was it random. I opened my eyes only as much as needed to keep from tumbling over curbs or stepping in front of carriage horses. Instead, I felt for that wisp of death that linked me to the cat and followed, through streets and alleys, behind heaps of trash and down drainage tunnels. Over fences, or under them, or through them if need be. I tried to conserve my strength as much as possible.

Once, I was accosted by four roughs in the alley behind a tavern where the dead cat had hidden. One of them joked about wanting to get into my purse, in a way that made it clear that it wasn't my purse that was on his mind, but when he grabbed me and felt the heat of my fever, he released me quickly. Nobody wants to play with plague.

I held on to him, pulling him close to stare into his eyes.

"Come on, then," I said. "Come die with me."

He pushed me away roughly. But not before I learned his face. If I lived through this, I would come back here some night.

Big *if*. The tussle took more from me than I expected. I crawled away, following the dead cat's trail. I heard the men's jeers only vaguely; they didn't matter, as long as they didn't stop me.

What mattered was the cat, and the cat wasn't far away. I found her at the end of the alley, hiding behind a broken water barrel. She looked worse than I remembered, some of her fur coming out in patches; whatever affliction I suffered was but an echo of the rot and decay that ravaged the poor beast.

I despaired then. I wasn't suffering from some illness that would eventually kill me; I was suffering from decay itself. How do you cure that? In my misery, I saw only two ways to save myself: find some way to bring a dead cat back to life, or unravel the spell and loose death and decay on the whole city.

The cat cowered away from me, ready to run. I knew I'd be hard-pressed to catch it when in the best of health. In the shape I was in now...? Even the dead could outrun me.

I put a small bowl down and poured in some cream, pushed the bowl close to the barrel and stepped back. I spoke gentle nonsense to the creature. The cat took nearly twenty minutes to approach the bowl, and another five before she dared to taste it. It was nearly dawn when she consented to let me pet her. She was cold to the touch.

She arched her ragged body against my hand and vibrated. It should have been a purr, but the air escaped through the hole in her chest with a moist, rumbling hiss.

When I stood, she twined between my legs, smearing the cream that leaked from her body onto my clothes.

"Come on, then," I told her, "let's go home."

The cobblestones were warming under the morning sun when we arrived at my door, and my friends were humming and buzzing happily as they emerged from the hives on my roof and prepared to embark on their daily rounds. The effects of willow bark had worn off, and I ached as my fever spiked. The dead cat followed on unsteady legs, keeping as much to the shadows as she could.

My front door was ruined. The heavy, iron spike was still jammed in the splintered wood, and the cat's viscera still stained the surface. It was dried and had started to peel. Worse, it had started to stink.

I worked the spike free, further damaging the wood. I was about to toss it into the street when I saw the dead cat cowering away, its back arched and hackles raised. That meant something, though my fevered mind couldn't think what it might be. I wrapped the spike in a handkerchief and shoved it into my belt pouch. Once it was out of sight, the cat relaxed and rubbed her cold body against my legs.

When I pushed the door open, she ran inside. I heard hissing, and Edwin's startled shout, and a sudden rearrangement of furniture. Inside, I found Edwin standing on a chair, looking as pale as I felt, blade pointed at the dead cat. I scooped her up and rubbed behind her ears. She purred, and leaked pinkish cream on my shirt.

"That's an abomination," Larissa said, making a warding gesture. Her rat, which had been—I think—helping her sort twigs out of a bowl of dried herbs, squeaked and ran up her arm to hide in her hair. "A necromantic abomination. You could be jailed for this. We all could be."

"I think I'll call her Thana," I said, placing the dead cat on my bed.

"You're delirious," Larissa said. "You need to get some sleep, and let me tend to you. And while you sleep, I'll do what I can to banish this *thing* back to the grave, where it belongs. You'll feel better when you're rested."

I certainly couldn't feel worse. And I wanted nothing more than to lie down. It was a struggle just to care whether I ever woke up again. But I couldn't afford to do that. Not yet.

"No graves, no banishing. Help me get to the roof." The ladder was more than I could manage by myself.

Larissa crossed her arms, and Edwin shook his head. The rat poked his little face out of Larissa's hair and shook his head as well.

"Edwin. Just five minutes to talk to my bees. Then I'll rest."

"Five minutes?" He shifted on his chair.

I nodded. "And then rest. I promise."

I dreamed in hexagons. Fragmentary images in yellow and blue and violet, and colors deeper than violet that I have never seen with my own eyes. Hundreds of faces, thousands, as my bees searched the city.

Edwin woke me a few hours past noon.

"Something's wrong with the bees," he said. "They're angry."

They weren't. They were excited. They'd found what I'd asked them to find—that singular, special flower that the Duke in his wisdom had deemed "harmless"—and they had begun to swarm into my home, eager to lead me to it.

"They found her," I said. "I need to go."

I collected what I needed: dagger, sword, a poisoned knife.... I tried to think what else I might need, but my mind was foggy, and my strength started to fail me before I'd even finished dressing.

Larissa handed me a glass of greenish-brown liquid; I swallowed it without asking what it was. She gave me a couple of small leaves, each about the size of my thumb, to chew. My mouth went numb almost immediately, which would normally have bothered me, but at the moment, it only meant that I wouldn't have to taste the willow bark she gave me next.

I felt somewhat more energetic, almost like I wasn't dying.

Larissa gave me more of the leaves. "They provide energy, but any sense of well-being they give is false. Use them when you need them," she said. "Not before."

"Yes, ma'am." I put them into my belt pouch, next to the iron spike.

I scooped up Thana, wrapped in a towel to shield her from the light, and Edwin and I went out into the glare of the afternoon sun, following the bees.

Freedom had not treated Malena Bane kindly. She had found refuge in a crowded tenement in the Rail District.

"Where are we?" Edwin glanced around nervously, like a shipwrecked sailor in a foreign and hostile land. His hand strayed to the hilt of his sword, and stayed there.

"Ferris Street," I said. There was no sign, of course. The Rail District lay just south of the Docks, adjacent to the slaughterhouses, and derived its name from the rails that ran live animals from the docks and dead ones back. Once the slaughterhouses built their own docks to bypass the rail tax, there wasn't much left but the people here. When I was still just a girl, the Duke—the *former* duke—vowed to clean up the city. Guards swept through and arrested hundreds of whores and pickpockets, drunks and gamblers. They put cobbles down atop the mud and whitewashed the walls. They put up signs for streets, and for the few businesses they hadn't closed down.

A week later, Rail District struck back. They hammered the metal of the signs into weapons and used the cobbles to smash in the bars of the prison in Ashbury's largest jailbreak in history, before setting the building to the torch.

So now, the streets are mud again, and there no signs, and you won't find that prison break in any of the books.

Sir Edwin wrinkled his aristocratic nose. Possibly against the odor. Possibly against more. "This is unbelievable. In *Ashbury*! This squalor is an affront to decency. It should be razed to the ground."

I didn't have the energy to argue. The effects of the mouth-numbing leaves were starting to wear off.

"However, it *is* fitting that our quarry is to be found surrounded by the worst dregs of humanity."

"I grew up here," I said.

"What?" Edwin stopped in his tracks. "Here? In one of these...? I hesitate to call them buildings."

"No." I pointed down an alleyway. "Down there. There's shade in the summer, and there's always a trash heap. Enough to keep a fire going in the winter, and attract rats for food."

"I don't understand."

I spun to face him, anger overcoming the sudden dizziness. "You have no idea how hard it is to change your position in life. Look at you. No matter how stupidly *you* live your life, you haven't managed to become destitute. The people here work hard, when they can find work, and harder when they can't. They do the kind of work that would kill you, at the docks, or in the slaughterhouses, shoveling coal or shit or breaking rock to turn it into the cobbles that pave your pristine streets, and what do they get for it? They get old and sick, and they die, and then they get blamed for not working hard enough to live a good life. Do you have any idea what your friend *Lady* Maris Goselin did to get out of that trap?"

I pushed him, and tried to pretend that I hadn't actually forced myself to take a step back. Thana hissed in her towel.

"Go home, *Sir* Edwin, where it's *safe*." I braced myself, and pushed him again, and this time he was the one that stepped back.

"Maris, I'm sorry. I wasn't thinking." He reached for me, but I slapped his hand away.

"Don't touch me!" And now, finally, my friends clued in to my anger and swarmed up between us, forcing the bastard back, away, and down the street, before I called them back.

The confrontation with Edwin had exhausted me. I fished more leaves from my pouch and jammed them into my mouth, leaned against a sun-warmed brick wall until I felt their effects percolate through my body. Larissa was wrong—what they gave was not a sense of wellbeing, false of otherwise, unless perhaps I was just beyond that. It was a sense of power, of intensity. Of strength that I knew came from burning away what little life remained to me. I chewed a few more, just to be safe.

The bees had shown me her window, on the third floor of a grimy tenement. If I was healthy, it would have been no trouble to scale the wall, where I could peer through the soot-stained glass to determine what kind of trap I was walking into.. There was no shortage of handholds where the pointing between the bricks had crumbled. I wasn't healthy, though, and I had to settle for the stairs. That was hard enough.

The lock on her door gave its secrets without difficulty, despite my jittery hands. Thana tried to trip me as I pushed the door open, and slipped through the crack before I could.

Malena Bane sat on her filthy mattress, facing me. She had never been pretty, except for the one brief, shining moment when she had looked like the Duchess, but now, she was gaunt. Her bones showed through her hollow cheeks, and her clothes hung off her emaciated frame. There was nothing that hinted of food in her room, and I wondered when she had last eaten.

Suddenly, I no longer wanted to kill her.

"You're more resourceful than I expected," she said. "But it won't help you. If there's one thing I learned from you, it was to prepare for the unexpected."

I refocused my eyes and let myself see the threads of her magic. They wound around me like poisoned brambles, and coiled around her like dense armor, a net that would catch and deflect anything foreign. Any blade I struck her with would shatter. My bare hands would suffer a similar fate, and my magic would slide off her like water on wax. In time, I could pick apart her defensive spells. But time is what I didn't have; I would be dead before the sun set, unless I gave in to the temptation to save myself and condemn the city to my fate.

I closed the door, and sat next to her on the bed. Fleas hopped away from me. Thana jumped into my lap.

"You were always the real wizard," I said. "Not him."

"Luk," she said. Grief and loss welled up, drowning the hatred and madness in her eyes.

I wondered what she'd have made of the smirk on Luk' lips when he struck the Duchess, knowing that every blow would be reflected on Malena's body. Would it surprise her if I told her? Would she even be able to hear it?

I'd been with a man like Luk, a soldier whose love promised a life without whoring, back when that's how I made my living. A man whose persistent, cruel mockery made me almost believe, the first time he hit me, and every time after that, that I surely deserved it.

No, not almost. It wasn't until I realized that he was going to kill me that I knew I didn't.

Instead of dying, I jammed a knife in his neck and watched him bleed out.

A hundred moments like this were what separated my life from Malena Bane's. And thousands of moments of pure chance, pure dumb luck.

Nothing I could say now would change her course. The madness had settled too deeply into her mind, so deeply entwined with her magic that I couldn't tell which had given rise to which. But I had to try.

"I can help you," I said. "I know where you've been. I know how hard it is. It doesn't have to be this way."

Her face tightened and she stood, spinning to face me with a knife drawn. "What do you know? How could you *possibly* imagine what my life has been like?"

She threw down the blade.

"You don't get to die quickly. I'm going to watch you die like Luk died. I'll hold you in my arms like I held him. I'll cradle you as you scream in pain because a little scratch went unattended, and the magic-proof cell *you* put us in *kept me from healing him*. And when you're gone, I'll find the guards who watched without helping, and the judge, and the jury, and everyone else, and I will not stop until they are all dead."

"I understand," I said, because I did.

And I flung Thana into Malena Bane's face.

Malena's defenses protected her from foreign assault. But the dead cat was *her* magic. Thana's claws dug into Malena's flesh, distracting her for the few seconds I needed to find the iron spike, also imbued with Malena's magic, and jam it into the poor girl's throat.

It felt like I was killing myself.

Thana ran under the bed as Malena fell back onto the mattress. She clutched at her throat. Her mouth worked, but no sound came out.

I knelt at her side, and brushed the hair from her eyes.

"I'm sorry," I said. "For everything. We can end this now, together." I placed her knife into her hand, and helped her press the tip against my ribs, aimed at my heart.

Her lips moved. *Closer*, they said.

I leaned in, and the blade moved up to my throat, and then to my cheek. She drew a line of red across my face, under my eye, parallel to the festering wound left by Thana's claws.

I kissed her forehead, and when she was gone, I closed her eyes.

The fever was already fading, and the infected cat scratch was cooling, but I felt worse than when I climbed the tenement stairs. I fetched Thana's cold, stiff corpse from under the bed and clutched her close, rocking softly next to Malena's body.

The door creaked as it opened.

Edwin, of course. Nobody else in the Rail District smelled of such fine perfumes.

"It's over, then," he said. "You didn't need me."

Of course I did. He was the only friend I had left, the only one I hadn't already driven away, or abandoned, but I'd poisoned even that. Only his knightly sense of duty brought him back.

"Give Larissa my thanks," I said. "I'll pay for her services promptly."

He put a hand on my shoulder. "Let's get you home."

I flinched away. "I can't. Not now. Not yet."

He crouched next to me, put a hand on my forehead, tilted my head into the grimy light to examine my wounds. Then he nodded.

"When you're ready, then," he said.

I listened to his footsteps down the stairs, until he was gone.

The problem was, I wasn't sure where home was, anymore. I had run so hard and fast and far to get away from this place that I lost who I was, and thought myself the better for it. It was only when I was alone with Malena that I realized I hadn't been angry with Edwin. I'd only lashed out at him because I couldn't bear to lay the blame where it belonged.

Edwin gave voice to the words I had been thinking. *The worst dregs of humanity.* Of *course* it was his fault.

I needed to find who I was, if I was ever to be whole.

I sat with Malena and Thana through the night, remembering pieces of my life I had worked hard to erase.

And in the morning when I stumbled into my house, my friends were waiting.

Malena Bane's real name was Kiema, according to those who remembered her, and that's what we put on her grave, and on the sign Edwin painted over the door: *Kiema Memorial Clinic & Shelter.*

When Larissa came to see the building I'd bought on Ferris Street, she declared it a disgrace. Barely adequate. Her nose wrinkled in disgust at the rodent droppings and the boldness of the cockroaches—which is odd for someone with a rat living in her hair—but her eyes shone with the challenge of it.

"It's a crazy idea," she said. "It's not going to make the Rail District a paradise."

I shrugged and gestured toward the door. "If you're having second thoughts, I can find other healers."

"Hrmph." Larissa jabbed a finger at my still-tender cheek—scarred not from Thana's claws but from Malena's knife, her final gift, which I had refused to let Larissa heal. "To work for someone as stubborn and pig-headed as you are? Doubtful." Her rat stared at me from the back of her hair, chittering in agreement, as she went to inspect what would become the examination rooms.

For once, I didn't try to stifle the grin on my face.

"Well, there's something I'm not used to seeing," said Edwin, who was coming down the stairs from the second floor, wiping his grimy hands on his trousers. A tool belt hung from his waist, in place of his sword. It looked good on him, though I doubted he'd recognize that as a compliment. He laughed at my gestured response.

"How's it look upstairs?" I asked.

"It'll need some changes to make it defensible. Nothing major."

"But it'll work?"

"Laura says it will. She's the expert."

Had I known before that Edwin's wife volunteered in the women's home where she and her mother had once spent three months in hiding? Had I bothered to learn *anything* about her other than how to annoy her?

I've made a career of knowing everything about everybody that can be used against them, or against someone else. How to push buttons. How to push people away. I still marvel at how much I *didn't* see.

Maybe it was about time I started.

THE CONSISTENCY OF SMALL MINDS

It ended in tears, as you might have suspected.
   This is how it started.

The child was a heap of rags huddled against the cold in the doorway of the clinic, almost invisible in the dark, the outline of a small body under a pile of tattered cloth. Alive or dead, I wasn't sure. In the Rail District, either was distinctly possible, especially after a cold night in front of the door of the *Kiema Memorial Clinic*. I nudged the body with my foot, and it gave. Alive, then, or only recently dead.

"Hey." I nudged it again. "You have to move."

That elicited a response. The heap shifted, resolved into a diminutive, black-swathed figure, grumbled, and ultimately shuffled out of the doorway. It turned to watch me. I could just barely see the glint of eyes under the layers of fabric.

I kept one eye on it as I unlocked the clinic door. I knew better than to turn my back on a street urchin. You don't grow up fast on the streets, but you think you do. I certainly did. This one stood barely tit-high on me, but I'd already killed my first man when I was that age.

Still, it had been a cold November, with worse to come, if the weather witches could be trusted.

"Clinic's not open yet," I said, breath misting in the pre-dawn chill. "Healer won't be in until after sun up, but you're welcome to come in out of the cold, if you want."

The figure didn't answer, but shuffled in and sat in one of the waiting room chairs where I'd indicated, watching patiently as I lit lanterns and stoked flames in the coal-burning stoves, readying the clinic for what the new day would bring.

Not too very long ago you wouldn't have caught me waking before the bees unless my life depended on it. Funny how things change when you start caring whether someone *else's* life might depend on it.

Running the very first free house of healing in the supposedly great city of Ashbury is not a trivial matter, even with the help of my very close friend Sir Edwin, his wife Laura, and Laura's grandmother Larissa (who, it must be said, still didn't approve of me). Don't get me wrong. It's rewarding work, helping the sick and injured, but far more demanding than merely saving the world every time the rich and/or powerful decide to destroy it. Especially the morning after a bar brawl that grew big enough for the city guard to intervene. The brawlers had used fists and sticks. The city guard countered with swords and spears. We'd worked late into the night healing those who'd lived, and when it was done, we'd been too exhausted to tidy up properly.

Being an actual knight had its benefits. Edwin had scheduled an investigatory hearing against the captain of the guard that morning. That not only meant that we were one person short for the morning shift—leaving me alone to sweep and mop and boil bandages and restock herbs and salves—but that I would need to produce detailed documentation by afternoon, in the unlikely case anyone in the Duke's court cared enough about Rail District denizens to let the case proceed.

By the time I sat at my desk, a dim glow was just beginning to filter through the dirty, barred windows, and I'd completely forgotten that I wasn't alone.

I'm not sure what clued me in: a shift in the light, the soft susurrus of fabric dragging along the floor, a breath. Regardless, I found myself standing, chair tipping behind me, letter opener in my hand held defensively in front of me.

The slight figure stood motionless in the middle of my office. Then, slowly, it began to unwrap the filthy, grey rags from around its head.

The first clue of my visitor's identity came in a hint of green flesh, and then a long, crooked nose under beady, glistening eyes. The next loop of fabric came away, confirming my suspicions in a shock of orange hair.

I did not lower my improvised weapon. I had never before seen a goblin, not in person, but we had been in an informal war with them since the founding of Ashbury. Their defeat at the Battle of Ashbury Fields was immortalized in tapestries and paintings cluttering the ducal palace, as well as in the national anthem: "Ashbury Fields Forever." After their defeat, the goblins had taken to the wild places, the forests and mountains and deserts, raiding and killing where they could.

A medical clinic in the poorest neighborhood in Ashbury seemed an improbable target for such an attack, however.

"You're far from home, goblin," I said.

The goblin glanced out the soot-stained window, where across the river and atop Ashbury Tor, the ramparts of the ducal palace gleamed alabaster in the morning light. An inexplicable smile creased its hideous features.

"Not so far," it said.

The goblin was not unarmed, it turned out, once it finished extracting itself from the dirty rags. This was no surprise—the treacherous creatures may be the butt of a thousand jokes, but no less dangerous for all that. More surprising was that, far from the nigh-bestial rags and furs the bards love to dress goblins in, this one wore a threadbare but lovingly patched uniform. The insignia was faded, but where it had become unrecognizable, it had been re-embroidered.

It—he—hadn't drawn his short sword. He glanced meaningfully at the letter opener I still brandished and narrowed his piggy eyes.

"My name Karl. I not here to harm no one."

"Why, then? What could possibly be worth sneaking into the biggest, most well-defended city within a thousand miles, where every single knight is duty bound to slay you on sight?"

The goblin glanced toward the front door, through which I could hear the sounds of a city starting to wake. He took a deep breath, exhaled, then, with a shudder, reached into a sack that had been bundled with his rags. He pulled out a skull, small and misshapen, and held it into the light.

"You Lady Maris Goselin, call down sun against evil. Now, more evil come. Take our children. Need you."

The skull was covered in patterns, intricate and mad and—I could feel even from a distance—subtly flawed. And wholly, horribly, familiar.

I had given up the kind of magic needed to deal with this kind of threat when I opened the clinic. Now, I used my skills to stitch flesh and mend bone, under Larissa's stern tutelage. Magic that wove and knitted, rather than surging and roaring and singing seductive anthems of power in one's closest, most secret ear. I could not—would not—go back to that. But I couldn't turn away, either. Not from this.

I put down the letter opener.

"It's a trap," Edwin declared, later that day. The hearing had gone badly, and he was in a foul mood.

"Don't be an ass," said Larissa, Dame Emeritus of the Royal College of Healing Arts, the clinic's chief healer, and Edwin's grandmother-in-law, inexplicably taking my side.

"If the goblins lure Maris—"

I shook my head. "It's not a trap. If someone wanted to lure me into danger, there would be easier ways than hiring a goblin to infiltrate Ashbury's defenses while carrying around evidence of necromancy."

"Roccam's Razor would indicate that there's no need to imply some third party to hire the goblins. Goblins are quite fiendish enough to hatch this nefarious plot themselves, and we should take immediate action to eliminate the threat." Edwin gripped the hilt of his sword.

"I right here, you know," said Karl. "I hear everything you say."

"This is a house of healing," Larissa snapped. "*I'm* the only one allowed to shed blood here."

"Yeah!" Karl had put Larissa between himself and Edwin, but at the mention of blood shedding, he stepped sideways to stand behind me. I shifted so I could keep one eye on him. I mean, I knew it wasn't a trap, but there's no point taking unnecessary chances.

I pointed at the defaced skull, sitting on an examination table. "*That* is not the work of goblins. That is the work of someone *preying* on goblins."

"Then let the goblins deal with it." Edwin glanced at our unexpected visitor. "What does it concern us if someone is killing off our enemies? If anything, we should be looking for this guy to give him a medal."

I didn't need to see the goblin to feel the anger and hatred coming off him, intense like a physical thing. I couldn't blame him one bit. Despite the stories of horrors perpetrated by the goblins on innocent victims, to casually joke about the murder of their children was unconscionable.

"Get out," I said. "I was hoping you'd run things here while I was gone, but right now you need to be very far away from me and everything I care about."

Edwin puffed up defensively. "I—"

"*Now!*"

When Edwin stormed out of the clinic, Larissa shook her head and patted me on the shoulder.

"Don't worry, dear. We'll find a way to manage."

The goblin glanced between the two of us.

"I sorry," he said.

"Oh, shut up."

I knew one thing the moment I laid eyes on the skull: this was my fault, at least partially. Something I had left undone, years earlier, too broken after my victory over an evil that threatened to consume all life on Fortannis to follow up on loose threads.

My younger self made her living catering to some of the baser needs of society, and had a deep understanding of the value of a reputation for discretion. When Lord Gastonbury—my client—cast the spell that cost so many their lives, I made the decision then to keep his involvement silent in an attempt to salvage my career. He was dead, after all, and couldn't possibly cause any more trouble.

Now one of those loose threads was murdering goblin children in an attempt to recreate the spell I had broken. Exactly what that thread had unraveled remained to be seen, but I knew where to start my inquiry: the domicile of the late Lord Gastonbury, the architect of the spell that nearly destroyed the world. I had entrusted Gastonbury's butler, Rudyard, with Gastonbury's effects as a desperate backup should I fail. I had made a quick judgment of Rudyard as a man of servile efficiency and little else, and I never stopped to think what kind of person chooses to work for someone like Gastonbury. Given that I had until earlier that day worked for Gastonbury myself, that wasn't the sort of question I'd have wanted answered.

The Gastonbury estate had remained in the family, that much I knew. While I had not given particular attention to the property or its inhabitants, I did have a bad habit of keeping an ear out for any gossip on the rich and powerful that could be turned to my advantage, and I would have heard of any sale. So what had happened? Had some family member taken up the late Lord Gastonbury's scheme for immortality? Had Rudyard sold the artifacts to some generous buyer? I couldn't imagine he would be stupid enough to try it himself—that way surely led to madness. Just a few days of working with those spells had left me shattered for the better part of a year, and I have experience in handling immensely powerful forces.

The sudden memory of that spell left me trembling. What I had dealt with was only the final product of generations of experiments; it had never occurred to me to consider how many had been sacrificed to get there.

At least this time it wasn't *human* children, I thought, though I wasn't so crass as to actually say that in front of the goblin.

When a city has lived long enough, it begins to cannibalize itself—wiping old spaces clear and building anew. Or, in the case of Ashbury, just covering the old with dirt and rock to form the foundations for new buildings. There is, consequently, a labyrinth of tunnels that lies beneath the oldest—and richest—neighborhoods of Ashbury, hollowed out along the ancient, buried streets by time, and smugglers, and who knows what else. As children, my friend Spring and I had stumbled upon them, and we wandered them all, discovering secret doorways that opened into the basements of some of the wealthiest households of Ashbury, if we could solve the puzzles that unlocked them. As far as I could tell, we were the only ones who knew about them—certainly there had been no tracks in the dust other than ours, no evidence of recent use by anything other than rats, bats, centipedes, and spiders.

Once we learned our way around, we never went hungry again, and I was later able to parlay my ability to access just about any place in the old city to some significant advantage. Like now, when I could easily use the tunnels to visit Gastonbury Towers in Oldtown, high on Ashbury Tor, not far from the palace, and take a surreptitious look around before confronting Rudyard about the atrocities. There was only one problem, though. I wasn't about to give up one of my trade secrets to anyone, *especially* a goblin, who, for all I knew, might return with a raiding party to strike at the heart of the city. And Karl simply refused to stay behind.

The ensuing argument earned me yet another scolding from Larissa, and I eventually yielded. We would take the high road, so to speak, escorting the goblin along the city streets wrapped in his dirty beggar's rags. If need be, I'd tell people he was a leper whose tongue had fallen off. Hopefully Karl could remember to keep his mouth shut, so his unmistakable grammar wouldn't give him away.

We made it out of the Rail District without incident. From there, it would become increasingly more difficult as we moved into ever-more-affluent communities—the streets shifting from mud to gravel to cobbled stone—until we reached Oldtown.

Unfortunately, Oldtown boasted elaborate defenses to prevent access by undesirable elements, by which they meant anyone who wasn't a resident by birth, or a guest or employee of someone who was. There were walls and fences and armed guards, none of which would have been a problem for me, if I hadn't had Karl in tow. But Karl's disguise would never stand up to scrutiny.

"Where we go now?" Karl asked, as we made our way more and more conspicuously up the hill in the center of town.

The Ducal Palace stood at its summit; Oldtown sat at the palace's southern border. I pointed up the hill.

"That building there, with the marble columns and the decorative spire, is Gastonbury Tower. I'm still working on how to get past the guards."

"Tell her, or no tell her?" the goblin grumbled under his breath.

I shushed him. Despite the fact that almost nobody in the city had personally encountered a goblin, his squeaky voice and horrendous language skills were certain to give him away to anyone who'd ever heard a stupid goblin joke. And everyone's heard a stupid goblin joke. *How many goblins does it take to light a candle? You hear the one about the goblin who thought he was a donkey? So these three goblins walk into a bear and order a pint of ale...*

Yeah, so that last one always makes me chuckle. Get it? Bear? Never mind. When I stopped giggling to myself, Karl was gone.

Shit.

There were enough people in the street that I couldn't let myself look as frantic as I felt. I strolled casually around the area, keeping an eye out for a small figure in dark rags, but the little bugger was nowhere to be seen, until—

"Psst! Maris Goselin!"

I peered into a shadow I was certain I'd inspected before, behind a gargoyle-encrusted column that guarded an alley between two stone mansions, and there he was, waving.

"This way," he said, when I came closer. He disappeared into a shadow within the shadow.

Which wasn't possible. *I* knew about this entrance to the tunnels, of course, but, well, I've already told you, *nobody else* knew about the tunnels. How had a goblin, a *foreigner*, stumbled onto it?

I slipped into the darkness after the goblin. He tugged me in and closed the hidden doorway behind me.

"This way," he said again, leading me in the darkness through tunnels I knew like the back of my hand, unerringly toward the house with the marble columns and ostentatious spire.

After an interminable time in which Karl led me through tunnels that *he should not know exist*, we stopped.

"We here," he said.

And he was right. Above us was the ladder that would take us to the tunnel that connected the basements of six of the wealthiest residents of Ashbury, including the domicile of the late Lord Gastonbury. Its rungs were pitted by time, and covered with grit and rodent droppings, but far less corroded than one would expect, given their age.

Karl hopped several times before he was able to catch the bottom rung with his fingers. I heard him scrabble in the darkness until he found his footing, after which he moved nearly silently. I was able to just reach over my head to do the same, and made a point of getting my footing more elegantly than he had. It doesn't do to be out-stealthed by a goblin.

Eventually, we reached the right portal and entered Lord Gaston-bury's mansion.

"How do you know about these tunnels?" I asked, now that I could see Karl's expression when he answered. We say as much with our bodies as we do with our tongues, and this was important enough a question that I wanted to hear everything he had to say, both verbally and visually.

I half expected him to look away, to close into himself, to lie. Instead he rolled his eyes.

"What they teach in school these days?"

"Um..."

Karl gestured around us. "This Hob Hill," he said. "Me hobgoblin. This my people's home, before the barbarians come."

It shouldn't have surprised me. People ignore what they don't want to think about. I grew up in the part of Ashbury the world likes to forget exists, like something that you'd scrape off the heel of your boot and pretend the stink doesn't follow you into the house. There was a time I could play dress-up and almost pass in Society. *Lady* Maris Goselin, with her hair elaborately coiffed and silken skirts hiding daggers and lock picks. Handkerchiefs so lacy that they were useless for blowing your nose.

I lost my hair when I called down the sun, and I've kept it short and ragged in memory of those who died that day. There's a scar pucker-ing my cheek from just below my left eye almost to my lips, given to me by a woman who trod a very similar path to mine, but took one wrong step too many.

The world writes itself into our flesh, Larissa had told me once, when I asked why she didn't use her magic to give herself youthful, wrinkle-free skin and perky teenaged breasts, the way so many healers these days do. *Each wrinkle and furrow and scar is a line in the book of us*, she said. She had touched the still-hot scab on my face, which I had not allowed her to heal. *You understand this, even if you don't know it yet.*

This had been the goblin's land, before the Great Goblin Wars drove them into the wastelands, and we built our great city of Ashbury upon the rubble of their hovels. That's the story that's told in the history books, that's woven into the tapestries that line the palace walls. It's the tale the bards sing and the children play-act.

But Spring and I had seen things below the city, places that the city above hadn't quite crushed: elegant architecture, filigree stonework, ancient and alien. Old buildings too sturdy to easily destroy.

Do I really need to spell out who the barbarians were, and whose was the great civilization that was destroyed?

I didn't think so.

Karl and I spent the rest of the day searching Lord Gastonbury's house. By nightfall, we knew what we needed. An archeology of the evidence would undoubtedly reveal far more about Rudyard's descent into madness, but that wasn't what we were looking for.

I won't waste your time with a step-by-step account of our search. Just the most pertinent details, gleaned from the remains, and from the incoherent notes we found scribbled onto any surface available—paper, walls, furniture, flesh:

- The butler, Rudyard: He had remained in the house for quite some time after his master's abrupt demise, but had departed—estimating from the condition of the bodies—approximately a year earlier, taking the books and artifacts with him.

- The bodies: There were just over two dozen, mostly women and children, whores and urchins, respectively, judging by the clothes left in small piles throughout the building. Three men.

- The ritual: Each of the bodies had been elaborately prepared, symbols and patterns carved into their flesh. Limbs had been removed and rearranged, body parts mixed and mismatched. None of it was right.

- The faces: There were no heads, but there were faces, flesh cut and peeled away from the bone and carelessly tossed aside, curled with age, littering the ballroom-turned-slaughterhouse floor.

- The victims: Had all been alive while they were being prepared.

Rudyard was not the artist his master had been, and his lack of skill had hindered his progress. His handwriting was rough, a skill learned too late in life to come with unthinking ease, and his understanding of complex magic was grossly flawed. It was obvious to me from what I saw that he would never succeed where Gastonbury failed. He wasn't even close. In times like these, one must be grateful for small mercies, though I suspect it was of little consolation for those who suffered and died under his knife.

I found Karl kneeling by the body of a girl who couldn't have been more than four or five years old. His head was bowed and his shoulders heaved with silent sobs. He held the dried skin of the girl's face in his lap.

"What?" I said. Not unkindly, but not kindly enough. The whole house was a museum of horrors; why was *this* girl's fate somehow worse than any of the others?

"My daughter this age. Now..." Karl's voice cracked.

He didn't need to finish.

Now she gone.

I wrapped the girl's body in a sheet and carried it through the tunnels, past where we'd entered, back toward my neighborhood. Somewhat significantly less posh than where we'd just been; people here actually work for their living. My neighbors are shopkeepers and tailors, clothiers and potters. Occasionally the spawn of some landed gentry living on an "inadequate" stipend whilst endeavoring to drink enough to become the next great Ashburian poet.

The nearest tunnel exit was a block and a half from my home, so we did our best to be unremarkable. Not easy carrying a headless body, with a goblin in tow. But my neighbors are good at looking the other direction when it comes to me, and after a nerve-wracking but uneventful journey, we arrived.

My house: I'd expanded to a modest three rooms that's both more and less than I'd ever dreamt of as a child of the streets, with a thatched roof in which my honey-making friends build their hives. A private outhouse. A small yard in the back with a small pool that Edwin and Laura had bought me. Laura knew a wizard who could make the waters perpetually clean, perpetually hot, and perpetually bubbly.

"We don't have space for it in our house," Laura had said when they surprised me with the gift, which was a blatant lie. She slipped her dress down over her shoulders, stepped out of it, and into pool.

Edwin had looked embarrassed, and nervous, and excited. And nervous. Did I mention that?

Laura had stretched luxuriously, then leaned forward, her breasts buoyed by the bubbling water, and looked at me intensely. "Take off your clothes," she said, "and get in."

Laura was in the pool when Karl and I arrived, and Edwin was pacing my living room. He looked up as I shouldered the front door open.

"Maris, I—"

I handed him the bundle of dead girl. Karl slipped through the door and I closed it behind him.

"—I... What's this?"

The body was dried out, light. Also, she had no arms, and her legs had been removed above the knees, her hands sewn onto the stumps of her legs. Or maybe they were someone else's hands. And of course, she had no head. I let Edwin discover all that on his own.

Probably too cruel, but I was still angry with him for his behavior earlier, more so now that I had seen the results of Rudyard's madness.

When Edwin's stomach let him return to the house, Laura trailed him, wrapped in a towel, dripping on my floor. She saw the body.

"I'll get dressed," she said, her voice small. She picked her clothes from the floor and vanished into my bedroom.

Karl held the girl's face out to Edwin. "Now you see?"

Edwin swallowed, nodded, then went down on one knee. "My behavior earlier was rude and insensitive, and.... It was unforgivable, and I won't ask you to forgive me. But I will say, I am deeply, deeply sorry, both for the suffering you and your people have endured, and for my attitude toward it."

Edwin was raised to be an insufferable ass (you ever wonder why I never mention *his* parents in any of these tales?), and sometimes that upbringing gets the better of him, but he always comes around when he's had time to think it over.

Karl looked at him suspiciously, not quite trusting the change of attitude, I guess. I don't blame him.

"Okay," he said.

Ultimately, Edwin joined the quest. This was not without some debate.

"We last hobgoblins," Karl said. "Knights learn where we live, we die. We die, goblin history die. Goblin culture die. You no come."

Turns out, when human barbarians overran Hob Hill, and most of the goblins scattered into the wilderness, hunted into barbarism themselves, a few small groups did what they could to salvage goblin civilization. Historians, librarians, archivists, and artists, they squirreled caches of books and paintings, historical documents, musical scores, everything they could fit into the deepest, most secret tunnels below Hob Hill. Even as humans began building the first rude hovels of Ashbury atop the ruins of Hob Hill, these goblins prowled the catacombs, using the sounds of construction above to conceal their movement, bringing the most valued cultural pieces of goblin civilization with them, box by box, piece by piece.

There were five groups, each with enough knowledge, they hoped, to rebuild their civilization when they could at last come out of the shadows. The first was destroyed within a year. Over time, news of other massacres came. Karl's group persevered, preserving artwork as best they could, copying books as the pages became brittle with age.

Until now, when my unfinished business stopped murdering Ashbury's most vulnerable members and began murdering goblins. Why goblins? I still don't know. Maybe procuring victims in Ashbury had become too dangerous. Maybe he thought using human children was Gastonbury's mistake. Whatever the reason, in the last year, Karl's tribe had lost a third of their people. Including Karl's daughter.

Edwin's visage was grim. "How many have died?"

Karl counted on his fingers. "Twenty-eight die. Four missing."

"My sworn duty," Edwin said, "is to protect the Duchy from all threats. Your people are not a threat, but the madman that preys on you is. So there is no conflict when I say this: I swear upon my name and upon my fealty to my liege, I shall not betray you."

"No believe," Karl said. "Knight promise to goblin mean nothing.

Knight promise Maris Goselin, then I believe."

Laura raised an eyebrow at that, and Edwin flushed. I may have smirked, just a little. But he did promise. And, for what little it's worth, he kept that promise until the day he died.

"No horse," Karl said, much to Edwin's dismay. Me, my bottom, and my thighs all rejoiced. Yes, I've been on a horse, when I was quite a bit younger than I am now. After Spring and I, well, when his songs started wooing society girls and he no longer needed the dirty little urchin who followed at his heels, I fled Ashbury, ultimately ending up in the support camp of an army. I hadn't cared whose. I cooked some, I washed some, because we all did that. But most of my work was on my back. I thought I was lucky when the captain took a liking to me and wanted to make me his. That was before I had to ride behind him for *hours* on his nasty, flea-infested, shoulder-biting horse, and then *still* cook and clean and all the rest, but now without the pieces of copper to show for it at the end of the night.

That was also before I learned how that particular soldier treated the things he considered "his." I left that camp before his body cooled and joined a band of mercenaries fighting for the opposing side. Infantry, though. No horse.

"No horse," I said, flashing Karl a smile.

"We'd make much better time on horseback," Edwin said. "Or at least a carriage—"

"No horse. We go small paths, tunnels, forest. Horse no fit. Maybe you no fit." Karl gestured with his hands as if sizing out a small passageway, and comparing Edwin to it. "You crawl, that fit okay."

Edwin didn't have to crawl, but there were a few points where both he and I had to stoop almost double, or squeeze through sideways. If we'd taken the road, it would have been a single day's hard ride to get near our destination, with only a treacherous river crossing ahead of us. But the goblin had no intention of taking us on a direct route that might reveal his tribe's location to us, or to anyone watching us. Instead, it took us four days, and describing those four cold, wet days would be as tedious and exhausting as walking them.

Around mid-day of the fourth day, Karl stopped us.

"Wait here. I bring others. Back soon."

He'd been kind enough to leave us by a small brook, so I took the opportunity to wash the grime off my face and the stink from my armpits. Edwin kept watch, in case it was a trap.

Which was both stupid, and quintessentially Edwin.

"So...." Edwin hesitated. "So I have an admission to make. Other than that we're after a bad man who murdered a lot of people, and who is now murdering a bunch of goblins, I'm not quite sure what we're doing here. I mean, I know why I'm here: I'm a knight, and I must bring this man to justice. But you're.... well, you're you."

Dangerous ground.

"Meaning what, exactly?"

"I mean.... I don't mean you don't care, but you're a city girl. That's where you're most comfortable, and where you're strongest. I mean, when I suggested you join Laura and me for a week at the beach, you practically broke out in hives."

"That's different."

"How?"

"I'm Maris Goselin, who called down the sun."

Edwin shook his head. "I keep hearing that, but I don't know what it means."

"Seriously? Even the tabloid press had it half-right."

"I won't read anything those lying bastards write about you. It just makes me angry."

Edwin was the second most infuriating person I knew.

I did not tell him he was a moron. I did not protest that I had personally written an account of the events, mostly accurate and almost unflinching, personal failings and all. I took a deep breath, and gave him the short version.

"It was a few years back. You were probably just about old enough to be a squire, maybe. No, probably not, or you'd already know this."

"That's not fair." Usually, *I'm* the one who doesn't like being reminded of the age difference.

"If you can't be arsed to know who I am, then it's utterly fair. Back to the story. There's this funny thing where some people don't want to die. Life's too short, there were so many things I wanted to do. If only I had more time, I could live without regrets. All that. Well, what if there was a spell to make you live forever?"

"That... is that possible?"

"Of course not. But that doesn't stop people from wanting it. And there *is* a way to abolish death. But that's not the same thing as living forever. Life and death are two sides of the same coin." (Yes, I actually said that. In this case, it's an accurate metaphor. Edwin scowled, likely torn between trying to grasp the concept and dismay at my descent into cliche.) "You abolish death, you abolish life. All that's left is the grey state in between. I've been there, literally. I've seen it."

"That's hideous."

"Then Maris Goselin bring down sun, destroy not-death. Save us all, human, goblin, tree, flower. All." Karl had returned, quietly enough that Edwin hadn't noticed. He walked up to Edwin and poked him in the chest with his finger. "You read, maybe learn. Understand. Maybe you love her better."

I snorted. Edwin blushed.

Karl frowned at me. "Maybe you be easier to love."

There was a short period of time as a little girl that I developed an elaborate fantasy of having a family: a gruff but loving father, a doting mother, and a grandmother who was ancient and wise and saw right through the lies you told others and yourself. She was made of thorns and bristles, and I'm pretty sure she'd have approved of Karl.

I'm not good at being loved, I might have said. Or, *It's more complicated when there's three of us*, or *Trust is hard for me*, or... Instead:

"Fuck you. Let's go kill a necromancer."

The problem was finding him. Karl introduced us to his clan, or tribe, or whatever they called themselves. Lorekeepers. They lived in a cave system under a hill in the most remote part of the Ash forest. Not remote by distance, but by accessibility, and it was only after I caught a glimpse of some of their maps that I realized just how clever the hobgoblins were. Smaller, weaker, and vastly outnumbered by the humans who hunted them, they cultivated the lands around them into inhospitability. The miles of treacherous, mosquito-filled marshes we trudged through? Fed via subterranean irrigation canals from the Ash River.

Once you got past all that, it was actually pleasant.

There was a small altercation when we encountered some of the other goblins, near the entrance to their cavern. Something about not trusting us any further than necessary, not letting us know where the entrance was. On and on it went, until I pointed out that the entrance was probably located where they looked every time they said nobody should tell me where the entrance was.

Irrigation engineers? Yes. Card players? Not so much.

Inside was astounding. Wall after wall of bookshelves, filled to overflowing with ancient tomes, art galleries filled with... well, it wasn't any worse than the crap hanging in the Ducal Palace. I suppose when the barbarians came, the goblins grabbed the portraits of Important People & Events, and left the real art to burn with the city. I'd expect no less of our current aristocratic crop. In one room, a dozen scribes copied disintegrating texts onto fresh parchment. They glanced at us nervously, but kept at their work.

Karl stopped at one of the desks. The woman who looked up at me had green skin and squinty eyes that sparkled with intelligence.

"Maris Goselin," Karl said, "this my wife, Nira."

Nira glanced at Karl.

I crouched next to her chair, so as not to loom. "I've heard of your loss. I'm sorry."

She swallowed. "Thank you." She looked down at her manuscript. "Not your fault."

Though of course, it was.

"Unbelievable," Edwin said. He was paging through an ancient text on architectural theory. "Unbelievable! All this work, saving knowledge and culture and whatnot, and they can't be bothered with simple concepts like grammar."

"Edwin..."

"No, no. Listen to this: '*When things have only name in common and definition different, they homonymous.*' How do they expect anyone to take them seriously?"

"Edwin..."

Edwin chuckled. "'*What contrary to good thing bad; this clear by induction. But what contrary to bad thing sometimes good, sometimes bad.*' What have they got against the verb 'to be'?"

Nira, who had been largely silent, suddenly snapped.

"Life too short for unnecessary words. Verb 'to be' stupid. If is, is.

If is not, why talk about? Maybe humans write great literature about to be or not to be. Goblin time too precious for that."

She snatched the book away from him and put it back on its shelf.

Karl put a hand on her arm. "They here to help. Find our daughter."

"Kala dead," Nira said. "Like rest."

If she was lucky.

We interviewed goblins, some of whom were fearful and some who were hostile, but all of whom had lost someone they had loved. Nira brought out maps, and we plotted where people had been last seen, and where their remains had been found.

Edwin frowned, shook his head, tapped a finger on a blank spot on the map, not far from where Nira told us the first goblin had gone missing. "What's this?"

"Crazy human live there," Karl said. "Many dog. He not bother us, we not bother him."

"A couple years ago," Edwin said, rubbing his forehead thoughtfully, "Baron Fordstaff tried to get the Duke to formally seize neglected properties. He had a map showing all the buildings he called 'national treasures at risk,' including one Gastonbury Manor, to be distributed to loyal supporters who could maintain them properly, such as himself. Obviously, Duke Aramis was having none of it. But that right there is Gastonbury Manor. I don't suppose there's much point thinking that's a coincidence?"

It wasn't a coincidence.

"Crazy human" was the younger of the Gastonbury brothers, who had developed an aversion to other people early in life and claimed the country estate as his own. A recluse, he refused to step foot in Ashbury, even to lay claim to, or dispose of, the property that had come to him, which left Rudyard alone and untethered in Gastonbury Tower.

The gates to the manor grounds were locked, though that presented little by way of impediment. Beyond the walls, the once-cultivated grounds had gone to seed: vine-choked flower beds, knee-high grass that rustled in the breeze and hid the bodies of a dozen or more dogs.

Lord Gastonbury's reclusive cousin fared worse; we found parts of him throughout the house, often in clever artistic arrangements with bits of goblin—a vase of desiccated fingers, a wind chime or mobile of toes suspended from a pelvic bone. He was the first of Rudyard's experiments in his new location. More death on my conscience.

Rudyard himself was nowhere to be found, and as disturbing as the goblin-skin placemats on the dining room table were, this was not where the serious magics were being performed.

"Water," I said.

Edwin handed me his flask.

"No, I mean, the river. I don't think that flowing water is necessary for the spell, but the last time, water was definitely involved. Maybe Rudyard *thinks* that it's part of the spell."

"Ash River one mile west," Karl said. "Three mile walk."

Thanks to the goblin's engineering feats, the waters of the river had infiltrated the forest floor. Rotting tree trunks rose like broken teeth from still, dark waters that teemed with snakes and who knows what else. Newer growth, bushes and trees that could withstand wet roots—like cypress and swamp oak—lined the channels, while atop higher ground the old forest grew thick and dense and dark. Paths dropped away suddenly, or led to deceptive patches of sucking mud.

The winding path Karl led us along was, he claimed, the shortest and quickest way. "If Rudyard go to river, this his path."

"Then we should take pains to move quietly," Edwin said. Which was wise enough, and we walked in silence until we heard the sounds of the river ahead, waves lapping against stone, water birds calling. And cutting through it all, the sound of a small voice, screaming against a gag.

Karl froze, looking at me with a heartrending expression of fear and anguish and hope on his face. This is how I remember him, that last look. Then he drew his sword and ran toward the sound.

"Shit," I muttered, and then Edwin and I followed on his heels.

The first crossbow bolt caught Karl in the chest, throwing him against a tree trunk and pinning him there. The second creased Edwin's thigh as we dove into the underbrush on either side of the path.

Edwin signaled that his injury was insignificant, so I circled as quietly as I could through the brush until I reached Karl. Keeping the tree between me and the crossbowman, I reached until I found Karl's hand.

There was no pulse.

I remember feeling cold, like a lump of ice was lodged in my throat. It spread through my body until it burst from me, a white-cold rage that seized the energy around me and sent it spinning, a twisting whirlwind of power that swept up dirt and leaves and branches and rocks. Nothing could break that barrier, not a blade, not a crossbow bolt, no matter how many crossbows he had pre-loaded and ready to fire. I stepped into the path and moved toward the water's edge, ready to let Rudyard be sucked into my vortex, body ripped piece from piece until all that I could see was red. But he was gone.

All that remained was a goblin child, tied to stakes set in the sandy gravel, screaming against his gag.

If the child had been human, I'd have put his age at eight or nine. I'm not sure what his actual age was. Regardless, he was old enough that he didn't, under any circumstances, want to be carried home. Fortunately, his wounds were superficial enough that we didn't feel compelled to fight him about it.

It took us about an hour to get back to the hobgoblin's lair. Edwin and I took turns carrying Karl's body, and by the time we arrived, the blood had soaked into our clothes.

The goblins rushed to meet us. A goblin man scooped the boy up in his arms. Nira stopped abruptly in the mouth of the cave when she saw us, her hand over her mouth. Then, without a word, she took Karl's body from Edwin and carried him into the darkness of the cave.

We briefed the goblins on what we had discovered, both in Ashbury and at the manor house. We told them what to expect from Rudyard, where he was likely to perform his rituals, where to look for their missing children.

"I am going to find him," I said, "and I am going to kill him. But just in case I fail, this will help you fight him."

"We come, too," one of the goblins said, and the others voiced their agreement. "We all come."

"No."

That's what had been at the tip of my tongue, but it was another that voiced it. It came from the mouth of the cave. Nira stood there, sword in her hand, dagger in her belt.

"Dozen only," she said. "More slow us down. Rest stay, guard children."

Nira rattled off names, and they ran to gather their weapons. She spoke to those who remained.

"Stay, keep children together. Nobody wanders. We not return by morning, you go. Block cave and move tribe. Come back later for books."

"Who avenge you, then?" an older goblin asked.

"Survival more important than vengeance," Nira said. She glanced at Edwin and me. "If we lose with their help, then nothing you can do here but die."

Gastonbury Manor was certain to be a trap, but it was the only place we knew he would go. All his books and notes were there, scattered throughout the manor. Having been discovered, he might seek a new location for his experiments, but he wouldn't leave without his research.

The first proof that we were expected came after we ventured through the gate to the manor grounds. A low, hissing rumble as dark shapes rose up from the grass. The corpses of the dogs moved stiffly as desiccated flesh cracked and crumbled at the joints. Their growls hissed and whistled through their broken throats.

"Maris," Edwin said, as the undead dogs began to lope toward us.

"On it," I said.

The spells used to animate the dogs were clumsy, hastily thrown together, and I was sure that I could unravel them with just a little...

Yes. There. Tug a thread here, twist a thread there, and the corpses loping toward us stumbled and broke apart into clumps of fur and broken bones.

That was the trap.

I'd hardly finished taking the zombies apart when the air crackled and...

...and the world filled with tendrils of magic, millions of them, tangling about our limbs, sapping our strength, our speed. I knew the spell, of course, a standard battlefield tactic to weaken large numbers of opponents, and one of the first I'd learned to take apart. I twisted myself a counter-spell just in time to throw a shield of magical force in front of the crossbow bolt that raced for my heart. I grasped the projectile in one hand and let myself fall backward—at a distance he might be fooled—while slinging a rope of magic around Edwin's legs and pulling him off his feet.

The second bolt passed through the space Edwin had just occupied and shattered against the manor grounds wall.

I let my senses extend, feeling for the flicker of wind that would accompany the next crossbow bolt. With enough concentration, I have snatched arrows in mid-flight. No reason to think I couldn't do that with crossbow bolts. But the next attack wasn't a bolt, and I was almost completely unprepared.

An arc of light flashed and then exploded over where Edwin lay motionless, hidden in the tall grass. Edwin's armor would protect him to some extent, I knew, having woven some of its charms myself.

The goblins nearby were less lucky. I saw only eight still standing, all of them caught motionless in Rudyard's spell. The smell of burning hair filled the air. The bodies smoked under smoldering grass.

Nira was not one of the goblins still standing, that I could see.

Those that were, were targets, their eyes wide with terror even as their bodies refused to move. Rudyard would pick them off one by one, unless something distracted him. He stepped from the manor and stood on the porch, and began loading another bolt into his crossbow.

I stood. Gathered magic around me as I walked toward him. Making myself a target. Rudyard set the crossbow down and cracked his knuckles before beginning his next spell. The power he wielded was mad power, chaos magic that tore at the fabric of the world.

I readied a ball of lightning, pulling its power from the skies, from the subtle friction of blades of grass rubbing against each other. I didn't expect to have enough force in it to kill him before he could do something against me, but it was one of the more visible forms of magic that I could produce. It applied threat, and kept his attention on me rather than Edwin or the goblins, and rushed whatever his next spell was.

The bastard looked me in the eyes and grinned, as if he was confident that I would be incapable of defusing his spell. Perhaps he was right. Perhaps he'd designed this one with me in mind. He raised his arms and began to chant, and power swirled around him.

A small figure launched itself against him from the darkness behind the porch swing. It slashed at Rudyard's head with a sword. Power crackled around him as he flicked his hand at the weapon. It shattered, shards spinning away in a spray of blood.

Then his expression changed to shock as the dagger in Nira's left hand punched through his ribs.

It is beyond my skill to know which of the many wounds Nira inflicted was the one that killed Rudyard. It may have been the first one, the rest simply serving to maximize his pain in departing. Part of me, I realize now, resented that she had been the one to put an end to him, rather than me. As if I had a greater claim to the grief of Karl's death than she had. There was a time when I had been immature enough to have voiced that displeasure. Fortunately, I had grown up enough by then to keep my mouth shut.

Instead, I crouched beside her and said, as gently as I could, "It's over now. You can stop."

While Edwin and the other goblins constructed stretchers for the three dead goblins, I set the bones in Nira's sword hand. There was nothing to be done for the index finger, which had been shorn off, but rest would heal well if set properly and treated with the right spells. That, at least, I could give her.

Nira invited us back to their cave, but Edwin and I felt it more important to spend the time destroying the artifacts of Gastonbury's and Rudyard's work, lest anyone else stumble across them in the future and think to defeat death.

Before they took their leave, Nira rummaged in her pack and produced a leather-bound book. Like the cover, the handwritten pages were neat and functional, though not terribly beautiful. I flipped to the title page.

History of Hob Hill Diaspora, it read. *By Karl and Nira.*

"Two copy exist," Nira said. "I start another tomorrow, with new chapter." She glanced at her hand, splinted and immobile. "I get someone to help."

We hugged. They left. And that, in a better world than this, is where the story would end.

Edwin needed nothing more than to get back into civilization where he could have his burns and wounds tended. Neither of us had slept adequately that night. After taking our leave of the goblins, we returned to the manor, where we gathered and burned every artifact of the horror that had been wrought in the enormous fireplace in the main hall. Everything burned—Gastonbury's books and artifacts, Rudyard's writings, and the hideous products of his work. It had taken us late into the night, but there was no way we would sleep in the scene of that abomination, and instead camped in the forest amidst the mosquitoes and snakes.

It was perhaps noon of the following day when we saw the smoke rising from the forest behind us.

"Something's wrong," Edwin said.

"The goblins are probably burning down the manor," I said. "Nothing we need to be involved with."

Edwin shook his head. "No, something's *wrong*."

We smelled burning flesh long before we arrived back at the goblin's cave. Heard the sounds of voices, human, above the crackling of flames.

Edwin put a hand on my arm, and I realized that I had drawn my blade.

"There is nothing we can do here," he said, "unless some still live. Then maybe we can plead mercy for them."

He stepped out of the bushes.

"Halt! Who goes?" A strong, commanding voice, accompanied by the soft sound of steel being drawn. "Sir Edwin!"

The man laughed, strode forward, clapped Edwin on the shoulder. "You're a long way from home," he said. "I didn't think I'd see you this far from your clinic and your—" I felt the word 'whore' gather on his tongue. "Your *friend*."

"What happened here, Sir Ferryk?" Edwin asked.

"A terrible thing," Ferryk said. "These bastards murdered Lord

Gastonbury, right on the front step of his home. You should see what they did to his dogs. Luckily, we were able to track them back here."

He led Edwin toward the mouth of the cave, and I followed, still hidden in the foliage.

What I saw was worse than I feared. A bonfire roared, fed by books and paintings. Dozens of goblins had been reduced to blackened, cracked bones, while those atop the pile melted and shriveled in the heat. More smoke rose from the depths of the cave. A half-dozen knights and their squires were busy tossing more of the goblin dead on the fire.

"They were having some sort of party," Ferryk said. "No doubt celebrating poor Gastonbury's demise. We took them by surprise. Some of them fled into the cave, but we had a few barrels of oil for just such a contingency." Ferryk let out a good-natured laugh. "Sorry you missed all the fun! But at least you're here for the barbecue."

He snatched the blackened body of a goblin child from the fire and tore its arm off, offered it to Edwin. "No?" He chuckled as he tossed the arm over his shoulder, back into the flames. "Can't blame you. Nasty creatures are nothing but gristle—"

Edwin's hand moved to his hip and then out. Sir Ferryk stopped talking as his head tumbled from his neck and rolled in the dirt. His eyes blinked twice, and then went still. Edwin stared at his bloody sword, and so did the other knights.

There really was no choice then, after all.

If you're reading this, perhaps you are wondering right now about my confession regarding the disappearance of seven knights and their entourage. Should I not be concerned with consequences?

No. None of it matters anymore.

Six weeks after we sank the bodies into the swamp, Duke Aramis was assassinated, with the goblins set up to take the blame. As Ashbury geared up for a full-scale war of extermination, a fledgling knight too wet behind the ears to blindly follow orders unexpectedly brokered a lasting, if uncomfortable, peace with the goblins. Too late for Nira and her tribe, though, or the knowledge they guarded.

I published Karl and Nira's book and what little else Edwin and I were able to salvage from the cave, and sent copies to all the goblin tribes. Little consolation for what was lost and can never be remembered.

Artists moved into the Rail District, and the wealthy followed. Derelict became "quaint," and quaint became upscale. Larissa died of old age before the clinic was shut down for attracting an "undesirable element" into the neighborhood.

Edwin and Laura succumbed to last year's plague. There were no children, no other family. There is no one else to be hurt.

As for me, I'm just the crazy old crone who lives all alone in a house made of bees, selling honey and charms to those who dare buy from me, until the next time Ashbury needs saving.

GOSLING

True value of thing not absolute. It not determined by surplus labour or cost of production. It not determined by use value. It not determined by stupid market. These thing help determine *cost* of thing, but cost not same as value. True value of thing is *personal*. Always personal. Always changing.

> (Toba, from lost manuscript *Das Money*, as quoted in *History of Hob Hill Diaspora*, Karl & Nira, Wikkid Which Press, 437A.A., p. 241.)

My earliest memory is of geese.

Spring says I spent the whole day chasing the goslings as they trailed after their mother, by the reflecting pond in Ashbury Park. He was there begging, near the meat-on-a-stick stand, and it was a beautiful day in April. The way he tells it, I was the funniest thing he'd seen since the winter, when Eric the Grocer came out with a broom to chase off the kids stealing moldy turnips from his trash, and ended up buried under a roof's worth of snow, shaken loose when his broom missed Spring's head and struck the gutter instead. Momma goose would walk, and the goslings would follow, and I would toddle after them, and then they'd move again.

Spring says I was a pretty little girl, with pigtails and ribbons, and a pretty pink dress. Maybe two years old. More or less. Who knows? My parents, he figured, were surely there, on the shore, on one of the benches, maybe, or camped out on a picnic blanket with a bottle of wine. Watching. Protecting. Ready to save me from whatever the world could throw at me.

Spring was old enough to remember all that, just barely. My memory is different, a single, vivid image: a hissing monstrosity, wings spread wide enough to obscure the sky. A hard beak striking snake-swift. And pain.

Spring says he chased her away with a stick, the mother goose. One of the goose's spurs had slashed my arm, deep enough that I still bear the scar. He says he called out for help, asked people to fetch my parents, but nobody could find them. And when night finally came and the weather turned, and we were alone in the park, he took me by the hand and led me back to his home, a box in an alley in the Rail District.

I don't remember any of that, though. I just remember the wings. And I don't wear pink anymore.

I've sometimes dreamt of being a cobbler. Everyone needs shoes, at least in the winter, and the quality of one's shoes can make a huge difference to the quality of one's life. But my talents are elsewhere, and anyone cursed with a pair of shoes crafted with these old hands is in no way better off for it.

Now, if you've been keeping up with these intermittent tales of my scandalously wasted youth, you already know that I've been many non-shoe-related things in my surprisingly long life—thief, sorceress, whore, soldier, beggar, detective, healer, to name but a few—only one of which I'm ashamed of. A job is a job. You do what you need to live, and if you can get some joy out of it, that's a bonus. If someone else's life is a little better for what you've done, even better.

In the end, any job is the sale of a bit of your body, your mind, and what my old friend Brian would call your "soul" (someday I'll finish my *Treatise on Poly-Global Conceptions of the Nature of Self*, but not to-night). It's the sale of a portion of what little time we have in this world, in exchange for something else that we think we value.

When we were children, Spring and I did anything and everything we could, short of violence, to stay fed and alive. By the time I was thirteen, and Spring a few years older, we were both looking for something more than just survival. Spring found his future in his music. I took a different path, and we drifted apart.

Maybe a year later, I stole something shiny to give to the boy I'd loved and lost. The wrong thing, from the wrong man, which, for good and ill, set in motion that which made me what I am today.

But it didn't get me the boy.

It would be wrong to paint this as a story of unrequited love. There was plenty of love, even before we knew what it was we were doing. When you live in the streets, if something makes you feel good, you do it.

And it's not like we had anyone there to tell us it was wrong.

And it wasn't wrong.

Spring was a born musician. He was always humming or singing, tapping out the rhythms of whatever song was going through his head onto any nearby surface. When we got a little older, it was my body he used as his drum. It was infuriating. It's one of my most enduring and beloved memories. I saved up spare pennies and bought him a real drum, hoping he'd get it out of his system, but that just made him look for ways to extract new and different tones from my body. I couldn't afford the lute I gave him, but I was pretty sure the guy I got it from could afford to lose it. It was old and battered, with half the varnish worn off.

"Oh, Gosling, it's beautiful!" he said. I watched his fingers, for the next few hours, plucking broken melodies from the thing.

It was weeks before we discovered that you're supposed to *tune* the strings, and by that time, he'd already written songs to match the strings as they were. That first accidental tuning was his, and is now being taught to bards across Fortannis. But those songs? Those were mine.

Kilanh, his drummer and wife-in-all-but-ring, brought that old lute to me a few months ago. She said Spring never talked about me, never even uttered my name again, after the night we sealed the hole in the world to keep life from leaking out. After he left Ashbury, never to return. But she said he played that lute every day of his life, for all that it was more glue than wood anymore, and he played it the morning of the day he died, and she had to either smash it or give it to me. As she told me this, standing on my front step with the thing held stiffly toward me at arm's length, the morning light dappling her fur the color of my fig tree's spring leaves, I thought she might actually do both and splinter it over my head. But she didn't. She just stood there, a whole opera of emotions in her eyes, until my hand closed around the lute's neck. She froze as my skin touched hers, for just a moment, before she let go. Then she nodded, a weary soldier, and duty fulfilled, walked away without another word.

When we were young, really young, we spent a lot of time hiding, and got quite good at it. There was a group of boys about Spring's age who wandered the streets, looking for victims. If they caught us—and they always could, if they saw us, because my legs were so short—they would take everything we'd managed to gather that day. Coins, begged or borrowed, food, clothing. Whatever we had. But they didn't just rob us. They beat him. Spring. Punched him until he went down, and then kicked him until he was a bloody ball curled up in the dirt.

He could have gotten away, but when he did, they hurt me, and kept hurting me until he came back and let them do what they wanted to him.

I found those boys, later, after I'd returned to Ashbury, with my new name and my self-aggrandizing title. They'd grown older, but not kinder. They carried spiked clubs and knives and extracted "protection fees" from shopkeepers, and anyone else out alone who didn't look like they could protect themselves. The city guard couldn't be arsed, back then, as long as they kept it inside the Rail District.

Lady Maris Goselin wandered one night, seemingly uncertain and possibly a bit drunk, into the dark streets that little Gosling could navigate with her eyes closed, looking as timid and frightened as she could manage with a straight face.

It took those boys all of fifteen minutes to find her and put a blade to her throat. But nobody's ever found *them*. I doubt anyone looked.

He was good. So good. His songs were simple but heartfelt. They were *true* songs. And people noticed.

It started with him making more money busking than begging. And then someone offered to pay him to play at a ball they were putting on. He almost declined, saying he didn't know any waltzes. But it was so much money, and they said if they'd wanted waltzes, they'd have hired a polka band. They wanted something different. They wanted *him*. And after that performance, so did everyone else.

And then, then there was *money*, and we didn't have to live on the street. We had a room. Not just a room, but one with a kitchen, and a bed, a nice big bed that fit us both.

But too often, I slept in it alone, or came home to find no room in it for me.

With the music came money, yes, but also girls. Pretty girls, who smelled of lilac or lavender and wore beautiful clothes that peeled off in layers; I imagined it was like unwrapping presents, for Spring. One day, I knew, he would find one he'd want to keep, and he'd forget all about me.

For as long as I could remember, it had been the two of us, together against the world. But now the world had found a way to lure him, and I knew that from then on, the only person I could depend on was me.

I can't say why the thought of Spring with these girls evoked such jealousy. We had both lain with others, and both of us had traded our bodies for easy cash when the opportunity arose. We'd exchange stories, joking about the men and women pathetic enough to pay street urchins for sex, and the weird shit they wanted to do. But this felt different. This tasted of betrayal.

I moved out, back onto the streets, and avoided his concerts. He didn't try to stop me. Or if he did, I didn't listen. I don't remember which.

In fact, I don't remember much of what followed. I drank a lot. There was a woman who sold bottles of alcohol infused with poppy. I dreamed a lot. I woke up in unfortunate places, with people I didn't know. I found myself wanting more and more to lose myself in those dreams. And I was there one day when the woman received a delivery of that liquor.

The man was handsome, in a roguish way, his clothes clean and crisp, his dashing hat tilted at a rakish angle. He was, I could tell by his demeanor, a man who aspired to aristocracy—every gesture culti-vated elegance, but with an eye toward baser desires. That eye looked at me the way that Spring looked at the pretty girls who crowded the front rows of his concerts. It was an opportunity I couldn't resist.

I learned more about the nature of power over the next few months than I knew existed. More than I could understand at the time. I learned that I was stronger than I had thought. But before too long, I started thinking that I was stronger than I was.

His name was Salidas. He took me home that first night, with an offer of silver—rather than copper—and that was where I stayed, except when running errands for him. If Spring cared that I was gone, or missed me, or even noticed, I couldn't tell you.

In fact, I couldn't tell you a lot of what happened over those months. The potion he offered was more potent than what he sold to the woman I'd been buying from, and I moved from dream to dream. And however nightmarish one dream might be, there would be something more pleasant awaiting me when I returned to him, my task accom-plished.

But not even the poppy's dream could completely overcome the habits a child learns on the streets. One eye out for danger, the other for advantage.

What did I do for Salidas, exactly? Whatever he told me. Made deliv-eries, collected payments. Stole. Spied. Where I had occasionally sold my flesh for my own gain, I now did so for his. I could no longer choose, or decline, a partner, nor decline their wishes. It wasn't that he would hurt me for displeasing him, or for costing him money. He didn't need to. All he needed to do was withhold from me the one pleasure that made the rest bearable.

Time passed, I don't know how much, before the event that set everything else in motion. I'd been tasked with accompanying a delivery to a private residence in Oldtown, on Ashbury Tor. Would you know it? Perhaps you would, though old man Cedrello has been dead thirty years now. There was to be a party that night, with a highly fashionable and exclusive guest list, and Salidas had negotiated the contract to provide refreshments and ancillary entertainment. He had procured a caterer and a barkeep, and every imaginable liquid, poppy-enhanced or not. I was to ensure that everything arrived at its destination and was accounted for at the end of the night.

Sometimes, people mistook youth for inexperience, and thought to take advantage. We wouldn't see them on the job again, after that. It didn't occur to me to think about what happened to them. Knowing what I do now, I suspect I could help resolve a number of missing persons cases. But knowing what I know now, nobody cared enough to look for them to begin with.

It's funny how mature and world-wise you can think yourself, when you aren't old enough to realize how much you're being manipulated. It's funny how much you can think you're the one in control. Well, maybe funny isn't the right word. But I digress.

The delivery boy's name was Artoud. He was big, with hands that could encompass my whole face and eyes that were both kind and wary. The kind of boy who takes a rough job to support his family after his parents die, because he can handle it—and maybe he can, for a while, and maybe he can get out before it changes him and his eyes are no longer kind, or maybe he can't. I don't know what happened to Artoud. He was still alive, and still working, when I fled Ashbury, and he wasn't around when I eventually returned.

As Artoud lifted crates from the cart and brought them into the house, I tallied them on a sheet of paper just like Salidas taught me. Turns out I had a head for numbers—for patterns, really, and what are numbers but patterns?—and Salidas never met a talent he couldn't turn to his advantage. The tally at the end of the night would need to

match, minus sales. And of course, as I would need to stay for the entire duration, as time afforded I was to join the other half-dozen young
women and men who were to provide the guests with, as they say,
ancillary entertainment.

It was only after I had seen Artoud off and entered the mansion
(through the servant's entrance, of course), that I heard the unmistakable sounds of Spring warming up. "Testing the space," he called it, by
which he meant the acoustics, though I didn't know the word at the
time.

It was too late to turn around. It had been too late before I'd left the
warehouse with Artoud, too late as soon as Salidas assigned me this
task. Assignments were non-negotiable, even for me.

So instead, I walked in like I owned the place. Like I didn't feel like
I was about to throw up. Like my heart wasn't pounding in my ears. I
perched on a stool in front of the bartender and ordered something I
shouldn't have.

The bartender poured and slid the glass in front of me.

"He's so good," she sighed. "Don't you think? I mean, if I'd known
he'd be here, I'd have *paid* to get this job."

"If you like that sort of thing." I shrugged. "Loosen that bodice a bit
when he comes by, maybe he'll give you a personal preview before the
party starts."

"Oh, I couldn't... Do you think?"

I turned away from her, maybe because she was beautiful and of
course he would, and I couldn't blame him but I would anyway, and I
didn't need to have her face in front of me while my mind played
through what they might do. Or maybe because he'd started singing
one of my songs.

I turned around when he was halfway through the first chorus, and
his voice caught and his fingers fumbled a chord. Just a second before
he recovered, and I was probably the only person in the room that noticed, but it was there. He continued the song, staring at me.

"He's looking this way. I think he noticed you," I told the bartender.
I swallowed my drink, thumped the glass down in front of her stupid,
fawning face, and ordered another.

Spring made a beeline toward the bar as soon as he finished the
song.

"Oh my, oh my!" the bartender said. She turned around quickly and
when she turned back, her bodice was loosened so much that it might

as well not have been there.

He stopped abruptly in front of me, looking as if he had wanted to catch me up in his arms and spin me around like he used to. And I don't know what would have happened if he had. But he didn't. Instead, he shook his head, like he was trying to break loose a thought that had gotten stuck.

The bartender leaned forward and draped her breasts on the bar, with her long, raven tresses flowing around them. "Can I get you anything, sir?" she breathed.

"Small beer," he said, not even glancing at her. Then, to me, "Where have you been? I looked for you."

"Where you wouldn't look. Obviously."

He reached out to touch my face, reconsidered, touched my shoulder. There. Even just that, the shock of it jolted my heart and woke parts of me I had thought permanently numbed. I was glad for the solid wood beneath my ass, because my knees were rubber.

"So, what? You're working for Salidas now? I mean, I'd heard rumors, but I thought you were smarter than that."

I ran through a half-dozen rejoinders in my head, all of them too embarrassing to recount, and was only saved from having to utter any of them by the arrival of our host, Lord Cedrello himself. One heavy hand reached out to clasp Spring by the shoulder while the other held aloft the most beautiful instrument I've ever seen, a twelve-stringed lute, somewhat larger than the usual. It was carved of some sort of golden wood, very fine-grained (which, incidentally, no woodworker I consulted subsequently was able to name). The lacquer was like velvet to the touch. The magic in it was palpable, and Spring took it with the sort of reverence I have seen only rarely in this world.

"I amuse my household with this on occasion," Lord Cedrello said, his ample cheeks beaming with good-natured self-deprecation. "Even a rank amateur like myself sounds good. I would love to hear how it sounds in the hands of someone as accomplished as yourself."

Spring gazed at it, entranced. "Sure," he said, though I could tell he wasn't even aware he had spoken. He plucked at the strings, already retuning the instrument to his own idiosyncratic tunings. "Of course."

And he wandered away with it. To practice.

Lord Cedrello took Spring's untouched small beer, sniffed it, and put it back, and then ordered something expensive-sounding that turned out to be white wine. "That's a good look for you, Melissa," he said to the bartender as he walked away. "Keep it up and you might find a permanent position here."

Melissa waited until he was out of earshot. "On my back, no doubt. Thank you for the most humiliating moment of my life." She shoved herself angrily back into her shirt.

I stood and leaned over the bar to face her, glaring like it was her fault. "You think that's humiliating? Try living with him."

Spring's performance was, well, magical. I'd never experienced anything like it. Under his fingers, the lute played notes that were more pure than fresh rainwater, when the song called for it, or growled with desire, shouted with exaltation. The sounds displayed themselves as colors, rainbows washing over us, and tastes, mingling with the drinks on our lips. Too many of them tasted of our mingled sweat, his and mine, of salt, of my taste on his lips.

And everyone in the room was tasting me as well.

I did my best to wash it away, and Melissa, strangely understanding given how I'd treated her, did her best to keep up with my orders.

He played far longer than his usual set, longer than he had songs to fill, until his fingers blistered and bled. By that time, I could barely stand. The party should have been over long before, and Artoud had arrived to cart away the leftovers. He sat with me at the bar. I think maybe he kept me upright.

Spring stood on the stage in mixed wonder and exhaustion as the guests applauded. Even the applause, where it resonated in the instrument's body, turned to colors that showered over him. He bowed and took his leave, slipping through a door behind the stage, with a last longing glance at the lute he'd left on a chair in the middle of the stage.

"Can you bartend?" I asked Artoud. I didn't wait for his response. I grabbed Melissa's hand and dragged her after me, following Spring.

We found him alone in a dimly lit room, staring at his bloody fingers. He turned to me and opened his mouth to speak, but there were no words.

"Don't talk," I told Melissa, and guided her into his arms. He looked at me, but I slipped away.

"I love you," I said, "and I'll always get you what you want."

But I was already out the door when I said it, and down the hall. Out of his earshot.

There is clarity in purpose. I knew now what I wanted, and what I needed to do to get it. I also knew that if I continued to indulge in the fruit of the poppy, I would falter, meandering into the same aimless existence I'd been leading since moving out of Spring's apartment. There was only one end to that road, ultimately, and I'd discovered that I no longer wished to hurry my arrival there.

Salidas was unconvinced of my resolve and employed a number of techniques to test it before I extracted myself from his service. None of them were pleasant, but in the end he suffered far worse, so there's no point in going into details. It was easy enough to escape his attentions. I knew the streets better than anyone, and I could vanish into them without a trace when I wanted. I was certainly good enough to out-smart Salidas.

Melissa, I discovered, had moved in with Spring, surprising her fiancé, and lived with him for a couple months before everything went pear-shaped.

The theft took that long to plan. There were, of course, the old tunnels that lace the underbelly of the old city, and I did manage to find the place where I *should* have been able to gain access to the sub-basement of the Cedrello estate. Entrance that way was blocked—sealed magically long before anyone still living had been born. I doubted Cedrello was aware of it, but that hardly mattered. The doors and windows were also guarded: physical locks and bars, as well as magical wards and plain old human guards. I was able to find some old building plans in a shop that catered to aficionados of old maps, architectural drawings, and paintings of dead rich people, which I obtained and memorized. Certainly, there would be some changes in the ensuing centuries, but there's only so much you can modify a building built of granite without bringing the whole thing down on your head, no matter how much magic you had at your disposal.

Breaking into the Cedrello manse would be trivial for me now, or at least, not extraordinarily difficult. But then? That was before I knew that some of what I sometimes saw when I was tired and my eyes wouldn't focus was magic, to be gathered and shaped, and before I'd honed any appreciable skill with a blade. My assets then could be counted on one hand: I was small, quiet, plain, and clever. Also, fast. And when I say clever, I don't mean smart. Because none of this was very smart.

In the end, I had to wait for another party. Salidas, of course, would be providing the entertainment, and though I was no longer in his employ, I knew enough of how his business operated that I was easily able to find purchase in the undercarriage of the ale wagon and slip in through the servants' entrance as Artoud unloaded the shipment.

Melissa was at the bar, wiping already-clean glasses of any potential dust or finger-smudges. She looked up as I passed, her eyes dark and swollen, as if she'd been crying all night, and I knew that whatever had been between her and Spring was over, whether they were aware of that fact yet or not. There were questions in those eyes, but not interest, and she left the questions unuttered as I made my way through the sea of tables in the great room toward the stage. The object of my mission would be there, in a room behind the stage, ready to be produced to delight the crowd and strike yet another bard sick with envy.

Cedrello appeared from behind the curtains just as I was lifting my ass to the stage.

"Hello, lass." His voice was deep, powerful, with undertones of suspicion. I stood, facing him, but with my eyes downturned in the way of servants everywhere. I bowed awkwardly.

"Your lordship."

"I remember you. Goose... no, no, Gosling, it was, if I recall correctly."

"Gosling, sir. Just double-checking everything before the guests arrive."

"There was a boy earlier doing the same thing."

"He's new, Kenny is, your Lordship, still training, and Mr. Salidas, he wanted to ensure everything tonight went smoothly for you. So I'm to go around after and check his work, overseeing-like, but without hovering and making him nervous. Where's he now?" As I spoke, I made a show of checking for loose floorboards, and that the curtains opened and closed smoothly.

"Attending to the pleasure rooms. Nobody would complain directly, of course, but we heard whispers that some of the ladies were displeased with the selection available at prior parties, so it'll be good to add some more lads this time. Salidas says there's a new potion now that'll let a man go for hours. Might need to give that a try myself, some day."

I wouldn't recommend it, if I cared, as the recovery was said to take as many days as the hours of endurance one gained, with no guarantee that full functionality would ever return without further use of the potion. But I didn't actually care.

Behind the curtains, two chairs sat on a fancy wool carpet, facing the audience and angled slightly toward each other. I pointed to where the carpet curled up in one corner.

"Where do the musicians come in? If it's from the back, in this dim light, that over there's a trip hazard. Kenny should'a caught that. Help me turn this around." I caught myself. "I'm sorry, your Lordship, didn't mean no disrespect, sir. I'm sure I can handle it myself."

"Nonsense, my dear. It's much appreciated. It wouldn't do to have Ashbury's second-most-famous bard break his arm before the performance."

We moved the chairs and then turned the rug around. The latter turned out to be much more difficult than I expected; it was surprisingly thick and plush, backed with a material that gripped the floorboards. The sap of a tree from deep forests of the southern continent, Cedrello told me, boiled down to a thick resin and shipped "at great personal expense."

We were both a little out of breath when we finally got the carpet into position. Cedrello dabbed the sweat off my brow with his handkerchief. He hooked his finger under my chin and raised my eyes to meet his.

"Once my guests arrive, I won't be able to get away to enjoy the best attraction of the evening. Perhaps we could inspect the pleasure rooms together?"

Not if Kenny was there. Maybe Melissa wasn't informed enough to know my standing with Salidas, but Kenny certainly was.

"What's wrong with right here?"

"Anyone could walk in and discover us, at any moment!"

"Yes," I said, and gave him my best approximation of a wanton look. And after a moment's hesitation, he nodded.

Cedrello was still buttoning his waistcoat as he slipped through the curtains to greet the first of the arriving guests in the antechamber. He'd pressed a silver coin into my palm, "just for you, don't share a copper of it with that bastard Salidas." Not bad pay for five minutes work.

Once he was gone, it was trivial to find the lute. It was in a room at the back of the stage behind a hidden door with what I'm sure Cedrello thought was an unpickable lock, sitting in a golden stand. Ignoring the countless other treasures that filled the room, I slipped it into a sack and took my leave.

Of course, it was just as trivial for Cedrello to figure out who took it.

Salidas, I learned, bore the brunt of Cedrello's initial anger, which he dutifully transferred to me in short order. Shorter than I expected—turns out that my secret places weren't as secret as I'd thought, and I was dragged down a dank, ill-lit corridor, stripped of anything that might hide a weapon—which is to say, everything—and tossed unceremoniously into a cell.

My hand slid on the damp stone, and I tasted blood when I kissed the floor. I wasn't sure if my cheekbone had cracked with the impact, but I'd been in enough brawls to know my eye would blacken and swell shut in short order. Not that it mattered; the door slammed shut, taking the meager light with it.

I want to tell you that I was strong. That I bravely collected myself, assessed my situation, and began to plan my escape. But I promised myself I wouldn't lie, not in any of these tales. Especially not this one. I didn't do any of those things. I just lay there shivering on the cold stone and cried.

"Gos?"

Spring? What was he doing here?

"What are you doing here?" His voice, not mine.

I didn't have the words to answer him. I knew the minute Salidas burst into my hiding place that I was probably going to die. It wouldn't matter if I returned what I'd stolen; he had a reputation. The only bargain I could make would be whether I died slow or fast. But if Spring had been pulled into my disaster, not even that was simple. I tried to say I was sorry, but all I could do was sob.

"Spring? Where are you going? Don't leave me!" A woman's voice, hoarse with fear.

"Just running out for a cup of coffee. Like I can go very far, for fuck's sake?" Spring snapped in annoyance, and then he sighed. "I'm sorry, Melissa. That was uncalled for."

Fuck. Who else had I marked for death? How wide had Salidas cast his net?

Salidas kept us waiting long enough for hunger and thirst to set in, and for Melissa and I to fully express what we thought of each other. On reflection, I'm pretty sure that my opinions were petty and juvenile, focusing the pain of my whole stupid, pointless life on the one person in the room who was entirely innocent. On the other hand, Melissa's accusations were pretty accurate and entirely unfair, which did nothing to endear her to me. Spring gave up trying to negotiate peace when it became evident that all he could do was make enemies of us both.

Salidas made his entrance as dramatically as I'd expected, the door slamming open and four armed thugs—Marcus and Tarvind and two others I didn't know—sweeping into the room ahead of him. They bore painfully bright lanterns. We stood, blinking against the light.

In the suddenly crowded room, it became painfully clear just how pathetic we were. Children, really, stripped of anything that could give us any dignity, any illusion of maturity or pretense of competency.

One of the thugs, Marcus, grabbed Melissa by the throat and slammed her against the wall, hard enough to elicit a whimper, but not hard enough to crack her head. He pressed a knife against her, angled to slip between her ribs.

"Please don't!" Spring cried. Another guard blocked him. "Don't hurt her! I gave you everything you wanted!" His eyes flicked toward me.

Salidas laughed at that. "Yes, you sang us a pretty song. She was in the first place you suggested we look."

It was like a gut punch, and I stared at Spring, unable to breathe. Things were bad between us—bad enough that I'd done something desperately stupid to try to bring him back—but he'd ratted me out. We'd been together almost our entire lives, and then this.

"Honestly, I didn't expect to find her at any of the locations you gave me—they were the type of hiding place a child would choose." Salidas turned to me. "Really, Gosling, I expected better of you. From the expression on his face, I'm guessing your friend did, as well. No matter. Mr. Spring, you sang so well for us before, perhaps you could sing us another song."

"What do you want to know?" Spring sounded defeated.

Salidas scoffed. "Know? Please, do you really think you have anything else of value to offer? No, I just want to hear you sing. I'm told you have a golden tongue, but alas, I have not had the pleasure of one of your performances. I'd like to hear it for myself." He glanced at Marcus, who twisted the knife enough that Melissa squeaked, and a thin trickle of blood ran down her bare belly. "You *can* sing a cappella, can you not?"

Spring sang.

It was an early song, from before his songs turned to songs of the girls who'd turned his eye. I wondered what he'd written about Melissa. No, I didn't want to hear it. Now he sang a song about the streets, about surviving when everyone around you didn't care if you lived or died.

"It's true," Salidas said to me, as Spring rounded up on the second chorus. "He's got a great voice. I'm glad I got to hear it."

That was apparently a cue to two of the other thugs, one of whom grabbed Spring by the head while Tarvind thrust pincers into his mouth, mid-utterance. Spring screamed and fell to his knees as Tarvind pulled the pincers out and down.

Salidas looked down at Spring's extended tongue. "Pity if it was the last time."

I stared, paralyzed with horror. I couldn't imagine anything worse than taking Spring's music away from him. And Salidas... Salidas had taken me in when I was lost, taught me, given me purpose and direction. Yes, he'd used me, but he used everybody. I hadn't realized it while I still worked for him, but he'd also shown a tenderness toward me that didn't extend to anyone else. Now, he was ordering Spring's maiming as casually as ordering a crate of wine.

"You don't have to do this," I pleaded.

"Oh, little Gosling, that's really all up to you. You understand that I'm going to need to make an example of you, yes?"

I nodded miserably.

"And that grieves me, you have no idea how much. I had such high hopes for you. All this, my business, my small empire, it might have been yours, when it came time for me to retire." He shook his head, and the heaviness in the gesture lent truth to his words. "I can't even promise you a clean death, now that Cedrello is on the war path, but if you return what you stole, I can at least spare these two for you."

I looked up at him, barely daring to hope. But what did he mean by "spare"? Salidas would honor a contract, even one as coerced and informal as this, but I knew him well enough to insist the terms be defined.

"Please be specific."

He sighed. "They'd need to leave the city, of course, and never return, which is a shame. The boy really does have talent. But they'd be alive. And intact."

I nodded, letting myself feel relief rather than dread. "Then let's get this over with."

"Are you *insane*?" Melissa said, as soon as we were once again alone in the dark. "As soon as you give them what they want, they'll kill us all."

"Salidas said he'd let you go."

"You trust that lunatic?" Melissa's voice was close to panic.

Yes, actually, I did, but she was pissing me off. "The other choice is to watch them carve the two of you up, and then have to give it to him anyway. What's the point of that?"

"I not going to let him kill you," Spring said. His words were thick and sluggish, like his tongue was still in shock. Still, he'd recover to sing again, while I would be lucky to get a quick death.

"What are you going to do," I snarled, "sing him to death? Wave your magic penis around and summon a horde of screaming girls to overrun the fortress? Please. You can't save me. Nobody can. We're locked in Cedrello's dungeons, and if Salidas doesn't execute me himself, Cedrello will."

Melissa shifted. It sounded like she'd maybe sat back down. In the darkness, I couldn't tell. "I can't believe Cedrello would hurt anyone. If he knew what Salidas was doing, he'd have him dragged in front of a magistrate."

I was probably five years her junior, and I wished I could be that naive. She'd never been a street kid, that much was certain.

"Sure," I said. "Of course."

Salidas returned with my clothes (picked clean of anything that could be used as a weapon, of course), and a leather collar, which he fastened around my neck.

"You won't be able to remove it," he said, as my fingers explored the clasp. Magic, of course. I could almost *see* the power that emanated from it. Abruptly, he turned and strode away, to the cell door, and out. "Come along, girl."

The collar tightened, and I scrabbled at it for a minute before I realized what was happening. It wasn't that I couldn't breathe, though I couldn't. It was that I suddenly felt lightheaded, as the collar constricted the blood vessels. I ran after him, the collar relaxing as I collapsed at his feet. My vision had narrowed to a tunnel, rimmed with black that pulsed in waves.

He helped me to my feet and gave me that smile, the one that had caught my eye that first day. Gave my shoulders a squeeze that might have been meant to be comforting, or might have been meant to mock, and kissed me on the cheek.

"Best if you stay close."

I was as close as a shadow as Salidas led me out of the dungeons, through Cedrello's reception hall, and out the front gate. I tried to memorize every door, every turn, every hallway, every guard posted. I'm sure Salidas knew what I was doing, but he didn't seem to care. Maybe he was even more sure than I was that there was no way out, for me. That was a depressing thought.

The lute wasn't actually very far away, but it still took a few hours to retrieve it. Most of that time was spent trying get Salidas to let me out of the collar. The tunnels under the city were *my* secret, mine and Spring's, and I wanted to preserve a place to disappear into on the off chance that, after Spring was released, I somehow managed to escape. Or to save that secret for Spring, if he ever needed it.

I swore every oath I could think of, reminding Salidas that he still held the boy I loved more than myself, but he remained unconvinced. Eventually, I had to take him with me into the tunnels. Salidas whistled with appreciation of what I'd revealed.

"Oh, little Gosling, I can't believe you kept this from me for so long."

"Does it buy my life?"

He just sighed.

"I could draw you maps," I offered. Hard to believe I hadn't thought of this before. Salidas's reputation could withstand the hit, if what he got in return was worth it. And this was certainly worth it. "Show you all the places it gives you access to, and the combinations to get in. Almost every mansion in the old city. Even the palace."

He stroked my hair with what might have been affection. When he spoke, his voice was weary. "If only your life was in my hands."

My stomach clenched. If not Salidas, then there was only one other person it could be. I'd known Cedrello wasn't a good man, but I'd assumed him to be a typical rich man—happy to benefit from the misery of others, but not one to get his own hands dirty. But I suddenly realized that Salidas wasn't concerned for his reputation. He was afraid of Cedrello.

I had never seen Salidas afraid before.

Shuddering, I nodded my understanding, and handed Salidas the sack containing the lute.

"Well," I said, as Salidas inspected the sack's contents. "This is it. You'll let Spring go now? Please don't make him watch." At least I could hold him to that.

Unexpectedly, Salidas pulled me into a fierce hug. "Oh, Gosling, of course. Your friends are safe. You have my word." Then he took back the knife I'd liberated from his belt.

Our return was greeted with an obscene theater of power. Cedrello kept us waiting in the foyer for nearly an hour. Salidas suggested I hold the lute. That I return it with my own hands. We took it out of its sack to make the gesture look better.

"Not that I'm concerned," he said, "but little details might make a difference in how things proceed from here."

When Cedrello finally condescended to grace us with his presence, he arrived with a girl on his arm even younger than me.

"That was fast," he said, his expression benevolent and jovial. His eyes sparkled when he saw the lute in my hands.

"Gosling and I came to an agreement," Salidas said. "She cooperates, and her friends go unharmed. As you can see, she has been quite co-operative."

"You're going soft, old friend."

Salidas' eyes narrowed. "You won't think that when I'm through with this one. Besides, those two didn't do anything wrong."

Cedrello smiled, wide and warm and utterly false. "Well, that's good to hear. Let's finish this unpleasant business and get it behind us."

He took the instrument when I handed it to him and made a point of inspecting it for damage (there was none, of course—it was supposed to be a present, after all). Unexpectedly, he handed it back to me. He pinched my cheek affectionately and mussed my hair.

"Come. Let's put this toy back where it belongs."

He had me carry the accursed thing through his house, past guards and servants who watched silently, their faces carefully blank, until we reached the stage. Cedrello made a show of checking to make sure nobody else was in sight before he revealed the secret door. He asked the girl to open it, and showed her the combination on the lock.

Salidas gave me a worried glance, and the girl smirked at me as the door opened to the windowless room, darker and more foreboding than I'd remembered it.

Cedrello lit a match from the lanterns on the stage and inserted it into a cavity in the wall just inside the door. One by one, with a hiss and a poof, sconces set into the wall lit themselves, gradually revealing the treasure room. Before, I'd only had eyes for the lute, which I was able to find just from the light filtering through the door. Now, the treasury's full glory was revealed: armor and weapons, art and jewelry and a hundred other things were carefully arranged on shelves and tables and cabinets. Some pieces hung on the walls while others rested on custom stands. In the center of the room, one stand stood empty.

Cedrello ushered us in and formally invited me to place the lute back into its cradle. As I did, he pointed out some of his other treasures to the girl, telling her what this ancient vase was, and that ancient shield, and this other painting by master artist whatshisname, and, of course, how much all of it was worth. Her eyes glittered. Salidas pasted on a smile.

Once the ceremony was over, Cedrello clapped me on the shoulder, hard enough to knock me off-balance. "Well done. Come on, let's give the other kids the good news."

He sent the girl up to his room to wait for him, and led us down into the dungeon. The guard unlocked the door. I noticed that neither Marcus nor Tarvind were there. Just Cedrello's people. They brought lanterns into the cell. Cedrello swept in after them, gesturing expansively.

Spring and Melissa sat against the far wall, huddled together for warmth. They rose shakily as we entered.

"Well, kids, I've got good news. Seems my dear friend Salidas promised to let you two go if this little bitch returned my property, and she's come through. So, hey, it's your lucky day!"

"It... It is?"

"Yes, Melissa, you won't be dying today. After all, you did nothing wrong, did you?" Cedrello's left arm still gestured, but his right hand had dropped to his belt—to the hilt of his knife—and my stomach dropped.

"No, your Lordship! We didn't! How was I supposed to know Spring's crazy ex was going to do something this stupid?" Melissa went on and on, panic and fear and relief and misery driving her words, and Cedrello just... smiled.

I had a horrible feeling that he was going to draw his dagger and gut poor, naive Melissa like a fish.

But it wasn't Melissa that he stabbed.

Salidas cursed in the darkness, wheezing and gasping for breath. That's how I knew it was bad—Salidas didn't curse, as a rule. It was one affectation I'd stubbornly refused to learn from him. Punctured lung, I realize now, and likely quite a bit more, but at the time, all I knew was that it was bad.

He said my name, and I shuffled toward the sound until I found him. In the darkness, his voice came ragged and quiet, like a whisper. "Lockpicks. In my boot. Left. Too much blood on my hands to use."

I found the tools and started to stand.

"Wait." His hand found my face. His fingers were wet and slick and I bit back a sob. "The collar." His hand trembled as he traced the line of my jaw and throat until he found the thing. An almost imperceptible click at his touch, and it fell away somewhere behind me.

Someone bumped into me and cursed. Melissa, following the sounds of our voices, with Spring behind her.

"We have to help him," she told Spring, who seemed less eager. She knelt down next to Salidas and a moment later, I heard the sound of fabric tearing. Melissa, converting his shirt to bandages. Spring supported his body as Melissa worked. Salidas' breath hissed across his teeth as Melissa tightened the makeshift bandages.

"That's good," Salidas said. Still, he'd need a healer as soon as we could get him to one, and that meant getting out of this cell and past Cedrello's armies of guards and servants.

I chafed with impatience. "You still have your knife?" I didn't want to search him and get my own fingers too gummy to work the lock properly. "Melissa, see if his knife is on him."

"Isn't a knife you need," Salidas grumbled. "Smart girl, you'll figure it out. 'Sides, you're not a killer. Get the lock. I'll handle the guards."

"You can barely stand."

Salidas's hand found my shoulder and squeezed with nearly his customary strength.

"Spring will hold me up," he said. "I don't need legs to cut a throat."

As escape plans went, it had its flaws, which Melissa was quick to point out.

"Even if you *can* take out the guards, how do we get out of the building?"

"Magic," I said, "and music," and told them my idea. Because I had an idea.

The new plan didn't involve a knife at all, at least not initially. I picked the lock, and when nature sent one of the guards in search of a latrine, we tugged the door open and Salidas stumbled out, falling into the other guard's arms.

Spring and Melissa followed Salidas with a dramatic show of concern, helping him off the guard, and so on. Making benign, non-threatening nuisances of themselves. Creating confusion and being a distraction. I suspect Melissa's breasts made a significant contribution to that last bit.

Me? I was small and fast and did what I did best, both literally and figuratively: I ran away.

Cedrello's gracious tour of his property came in useful. I'd oriented the layout of the dungeons relative to the stage and the street—and not coincidentally to the catacombs that lay below the building. From our cell, it wasn't that hard to find the nearest entrance to the tunnels. I needed to evade another guard station on the way, but I found it—an alcove in an inconvenient spot, not useful for anything except maybe storing some broken chairs, not really worth the effort to cover over. After all, who's going to see it?

The question was, would the door work? Entrance *from* the tunnels had been magically locked. My hope was that whoever cast the spell that prevented entrance also understood the benefit of a quick escape. My hope bore fruit, or at least, opened like a flower when I pressed the right places in the ancient stonework. The combinations to the doors from out in the tunnels were all different, but from within, they were almost all the same.

Once the escape route was verified, I moved like a shadow, as quickly as I dared, up to the reception hall, to the stage, and to the hidden secret room. It opened to me once again (more easily than I expected, in fact, since Cedrello hadn't bothered changing the combination yet), and once again, I took the lute from its golden cradle. Oh, and a dagger. I'd noticed it before—an ugly knife that stood out against a much more impressive array of weapons laid out in a glass case. It was half the size of its jewel-encrusted neighbors, the leather of its hilt stained and frayed and its blade blackened and pitted with corrosion, but still razor sharp. Just right for someone like me.

I put an unlit match in the cavity by the door and listened to the sconces hiss. Leaving the door open, I draped one of the stage curtains over a lit lantern before making my way back into the dungeons.

It didn't take long for someone to notice my little distraction.

As expected, only one of the two guards abandoned his post at our cell to see what the commotion was all about, but a thirsty blade against the throat can convince many an otherwise loyal minion to unlock a door.

One of my favorite half-memories is from when I was very, very young. I'd have nightmares (of geese, most often) and wake crying. Spring would sing me back to sleep.

It's time to sleep

GOSLING

You're safe with me
It's time to sleep
It's time to sleep

It was the sort of lullaby only a five-year-old can compose.

Please stop screaming
You're safe with me
Please stop screaming
It's time to sleep

It worked every time.

Sometimes, the simplest songs are the most powerful. I was betting that it'd work again.

Spring took the lute from my hands.

"It's not going to work," he said, as his fingers found the chords.

I stood on tiptoes to find his lips. "It will. Sing loud. Play louder." The magic-enhanced lullaby needed to be heard by the entire household.

The strings sang with power. And so did he.

Spring gently shook me awake. I was lying half-on and half-under the snoring guard. We woke Melissa, and then Salidas, who looked like he'd have been better off left to sleep. His face was grey and lined with pain. He couldn't stand without support, and Spring and Melissa each took one side. Together we helped him down the hall to the tunnels.

"Take him to RaKazn," I said, and Salidas nodded. "He's the closest healer we can trust. I've got one thing to do, and I'll meet you there."

I hugged Spring, and then (very gently) Salidas.

"You stay alive for me, you bastard. I want you to owe me."

"No promises, love."

"Go."

It wasn't too hard to find Cedrello; he was in his bedchamber, snoring vigorously, the girl asleep atop him with her head in his lap and her thighs inconveniently positioned on either side of his face. When I rolled her off him, she slipped off the side of the bed with a loud thump.

She cried out in pain and surprise, and Cedrello started awake.

Stay where you are, you bastard, I thought fiercely. *Don't move a muscle.* I could practically visualize thin bands of colored threads wrapping his body tightly, immobilizing him.

This, I realized many years later, was my first use of magic. I didn't recognize it at the time, since the way I use magic is so different from any of the established schools. I just thought it was an aftereffect of Spring's lullaby. Maybe my life would have been different if I had understood earlier. Or maybe I'd have just gotten myself into more trouble than I could handle, and then I'd never have gotten a chance to grow up to regret my life choices.

I was going to cut Cedrello's throat. He'd hurt Salidas, who, I was surprised to discover, I cared about more deeply than I'd expected, even after everything that had happened between us. And he was planning to murder Spring, who'd never hurt a fly and wasn't even involved. And I knew that as long as he lived, I'd never be safe in Ashbury. But I found I couldn't do it. I just stood there with the ugly, pitted blade pressed against his carotid as the girl gawked at me. And I was out of time—the household had started to stir.

Growing up on the streets, I was no stranger to dead bodies—people's luck ran out in back alleys all the time, whether by violence or illness or winter's cold kiss—but I hadn't ever seen one being made. And even more importantly, I'd never been the one doing the making. Salidas was right; I wasn't a killer.

Ironic, don't you think?

I couldn't just let him go unscathed, though. Cursing, I shifted my focus from his neck to something else he held precious, pulling it taut from the loose flesh at its tip.

"What are you doing?" the girl asked, eyes wide and hand to her mouth. I'd thought it was pretty obvious, and didn't bother answering.

It was a clean cut. Blood sprayed across the silk sheets. And my arm and chest and face. Novice mistake—always point the cock away from you before you give it a trim.

"No, no, no." Eyes darting between Cedrello's groin and my knife, the girl edged away from me. She posed no danger, so I ignored her.

Cedrello whimpered, still too bound in magic to do anything more.

"I just took an inch off the top." I tried to keep my voice calm and matter-of-fact. Like I castrated men and showered in their blood all the time, no big deal. "Come after any of my friends, and I'll take the rest of it."

I reached over and tossed the cowering girl an oversized shirt, the first piece of clothing I saw. "Put this on and let's go."

"I'm not going anywhere with you, you crazy bitch!" On her feet now, she backed away from me, fumbling behind her for something to use as a weapon. What she found was a half-drunk bottle of wine. She gripped it by the neck and held it threateningly between us. Wine spilled over her bare feet.

Shouting echoed from downstairs. Cedrello was starting to thrash around, fighting against his invisible bonds.

I shrugged. "Fine, you stay here, then. Just remember, Cedrello doesn't leave witnesses. And he doesn't give access to his treasure room to anyone he expects to be around to use it."

Footsteps pounded on the stairs. In the hall. Time to go.

I smashed the window and jumped up onto the sill. Below me lay a narrow inner garden encircled by a cast iron fence topped with razor sharp spear tips, and a wider outer garden beyond the fence. Dropping into the inner garden would leave me just as trapped as I already was.

"Wait!"

The girl minced across the broken glass, pulling the shirt over her head. I reached down to help her climb up to my side.

Cedrello's bonds were fraying, and as soon as I noticed that and thought, *they're not going to hold,* of course they didn't. He broke out of the spell with a roar, grabbing between his legs to staunch the bleeding. The door burst open.

Taking hold of the girl, I threw us both backward and out as hard and far as I could, hoping to clear the murderous fence. With desperate screams, we plummeted to the ground.

Not the best-thought-out plan, but all these years later, I still don't see any other option open for young-me. Between my broken ribs and the girl's broken ankle, the only reason we weren't run down in the street was that the gas from the sconces in Cedrello's treasure room chose that moment to reach an open flame. The explosion shook the ground and sprayed us both with shattered glass, knocking us back off our feet. And that's what saved us from being run down like wounded foxes.

We climbed back to our feet, brushing glass from our hair and clothes, and hobbled away.

The girl cursed me the whole way, even as she leaned on me for support. Leaned painfully, I might add. I can't remember her name, for the life of me, but I still remember the way the bones ground in my chest every time she clutched at me. It was my own fault, I told myself. My own fault for trying to save her, and my own fault for having set every bad thing that happened in motion.

It took us almost an hour to get to RaKazn's Infirmary. Spring and Melissa weren't there.

But Salidas was.

He lay on a cot against the wall, cold and still.

What came next is a blur. I remember screaming at RaKazn, accusing him of intentionally letting Salidas die. I remember breaking down and sobbing. I remember dragging the knife's vicious, pitted blade in thin, parallel lines across my arm, wondering why I couldn't feel the pain. Wondering how deep I'd need to cut to feel it.

I didn't get the chance to find out. RaKazn finished healing the girl, and when he found me, backed into the corner behind a desk, bleeding all over his floor, he slapped me hard and snatched my knife away before I could recover from the shock. Then he heaved me up onto his table and got to work.

RaKazn was young (though he seemed old to me at the time) and well built, strong enough to keep me from squirming away from him. He was well-spoken and educated, and I never found out what scandal drove him from his high society practice to minister to the criminal class.

First, he stopped the bleeding, knitting the walls of the veins I'd cut into. The severed tendons were next, before he turned to my original injuries. Having one's bones shift around magically looking for their proper place is no less painful a process than having someone do it manually, but I refused to scream. Just gritted my teeth and stared at Salidas' pale, lifeless face.

"There," RaKazn announced, as my chest stopped crawling. It still hurt when I took a deep breath, but not in an imminent-lung-puncture sort of way. He grabbed my wrist and extended my arm for inspection. "I'm tempted to leave that to scar up, for being such an idiot."

"I deserve it."

"I dare say you do. Lucky for you, I hate leaving a job half-done."

He did, anyway, because Spring and Melissa chose that moment to come back looking for me. They'd obviously argued about it, because Melissa had dark smudges under her eyes, like she'd been crying, and Spring had the tense twitch in his jaw that I knew from experience would be there until he spent a week locked away writing a song about it.

Then Spring saw all the blood, on the floor and all over me, and all that fell away. He ran to me.

"Gos! Are you alright?"

I pushed RaKazn away and sat up. "No. No, I'm not. I trusted you. How could you let Salidas die?"

"Oh Gos. He was dead before the door closed behind you. We almost left him in the tunnels, but... I don't know. We couldn't just...leave him."

I took Spring's hand in mine. Unthinkingly, he leaned toward me. Melissa turned away, scowling. Her eyes widened as she saw Cedrello's girl.

"*Amber?*" *That* was her name. Memory is such a strange thing.

Amber looked up from where she sat huddled into the corner of a sofa with her knees drawn up against her chest.

Melissa took a step toward her. "Amber, what are you *doing* here?"

"I don't know. Probably making the worst mistake of my life. I was scared to stay, after what *she* said, about Cedrello not leaving witnesses. After what she *took*."

"Witnesses? It's not like Cedrello's in any condition..." Melissa glanced at me and faltered. "Oh, no. When you said you had something you had to do, I thought—"

"I couldn't do it." I shook my head. "I *tried*. I had the knife against his throat. But I just couldn't."

Melissa glared at me. "You really can't do *anything* right, can you?"

"We have to leave the city." I said the words, but I couldn't even imagine what it meant. I'd literally never been outside the city. The closest I'd ever seen to wilderness was Ashbury Park, which had a stage and paved paths and groomed gardens and little paddleboats and meat-on-a-stick vendors and musicians and pickpockets and mimes. Yes, and geese. Just thinking of stepping outside the city walls filled me with existential dread.

"But if you didn't kill him, where did the blood come from?" With growing apprehension, Melissa turned to Amber and asked, "What did she take?"

"Oh, just this." I fetched it out of my pocket and tossed it to Melissa. She caught it. Dropped it. It made a tiny, wet noise as it hit the floor.

"Ew." Melissa edged back, vigorously wiping her hands on her skirt.

Okay, maybe it was a little more than an inch. I was sure he wouldn't notice the difference.

RaKazn broke the nervous silence. "You have to leave, all of you. Take that... that..." He gestured. "And Salidas. No charge for my services today as long as none of this traces back to me."

Melissa nudged the thing on the floor with her toe, and giggled. When it became clear that she wasn't able to stop, Spring gathered her in his arms and held her as the giggles became frantic and, ultimately, turned to sobs.

We took Salidas' body back into the tunnels, and then made our plans. First order of business: grab a few necessities from Spring and Melissa's apartment. That included some of Spring's instruments—including the magic lute, strings detuned and packed with socks to keep it from making a sound from within Spring's pack—and some cash, and a change of clothes for each of us. I'd left most of my wardrobe behind when I walked out of Spring's life, and none of his lovers were stupid enough to insist he get rid of them. Or maybe they were, and he chose otherwise. I don't know; we never talked about it. Fortunately Amber was close enough to my size, though she was sullen and ungrateful enough to complain about having to wear anything I had ever touched.

I stood watch, perched uncomfortably on the roof as they packed, a precautionary offer I regretted almost immediately as my body reminded me of all it had been through. I was considering crawling back through the window when I noticed a group of toughs approaching from the direction of Oldtown. It could have been a coincidence. They could have just been the Oldtown Splatball team taking a break from practice to look for a proper pub, or something. Not something I was willing to bet Spring's life on.

We went out the window on the other side of the building and across several adjoining rooftops, down into a neighbor's courtyard, down the alley and into the maze of streets beyond.

After dark, Spring and I took Salidas' body to his office. I wanted to set him into his chair, but his body had stiffened and refused to cooperate, so we cleared the desk and laid him out on it.

I thought we should leave a note, even though neither Spring nor I were well-equipped to do so. Salidas had been teaching me, but we'd focused on what we thought would be useful—numbers and sums and the names of things that could be enumerated and valued. Spring had never even learned that. We were saved from that embarrassment by the arrival of a carriage in the warehouse. Artoud, returning from his rounds.

We waited in the office as he stabled the packhorse and made his way inside with the inventory documents. Standard procedure. It took us a while to calm Artoud down, but he finally accepted that we weren't going to kill him. Eventually, with a bit of financial inducement, he agreed to arrange for our passage with a caravan leaving the North Gate the following morning.

"Thanks, Artoud. You're the best." I squeezed his shoulder. "Be safe. There's no room for mistakes right now."

He tried to smile, but it broke on his face. "You too," he said, unable to hide the guilt in his voice.

The following morning, we attached ourselves to a caravan at the West Gate. If Artoud sold us out like I expected, Cedrello's thugs would be focused on halfway across town. Sure enough, we encountered no trouble once Spring produced enough money to interest the driver in taking on a few more mouths at the last minute.

Leaving the city was just as gut-wrenching as I expected, at least for me. Spring was wide-eyed and cautiously excited, and Melissa seemed to have gotten caught up in his sense of impending adventure. Amber sullenly stomped along with us, casting nasty looks in my direction.

"I don't even have my own clothes," she whined.

"You're better off," I snapped. "Those fell off too easily."

Melissa glared at me, but spoke to Amber. "We'll get you something better at Yegril." Yegril was the closest town big enough to have an actual market.

Spring just sighed, put his head down, and strode on ahead of us. A minute later, Melissa joined him, and then Amber, leaving me alone.

It was a two-day journey to Yegril, for a small group, pushing hard. At a caravan's pace, and with the hills in between, it would take us four or five days.

We didn't make it.

When the caravan watch raised the alarm of riders coming fast, we didn't wait to find out if the approaching riders had come from Cedrello, or even anyone who meant ill. We just ran. Not even Amber put up a fight about it. We didn't stop to hide, just kept moving through the hills, away from the road.

I'd always imagined the world outside of Ashbury as a horrible place, filled with dirt and snakes and more biting insects than I could count. Leaving the road did nothing to disabuse me of that opinion. Quite the contrary. In addition to all that, there were wolves that howled in the not-distant-enough distance, and one night, a bear shuffled through our camp, snuffling us as we lay terrified, as if trying to determine if we were food.

We'd all secreted a little food in our packs, but that ran out quickly, and none of us had the faintest idea what wild fruits and berries might kill us. When we came across a farmhouse, Spring was able to buy us shelter for the night, snug and warm and safe in nests of dry straw in the barn loft, and enough provisions to last a week.

The next morning, we woke with the roosters, less uncomfortable than we'd been for days, and I found that something almost resembling hope had wormed itself into my dreams. We were away, we were safe, we had food. We were going to make it.

The farmers invited us to share their breakfast at the big wooden table out back, scrambled eggs and fresh cheese and still-hot bread. The sun was burning away the morning chill. It was glorious.

After breakfast, the family dispersed to attend to their inexplicable farming tasks, leaving us at the table.

I sighed contentedly. "I almost hate to leave, but I guess we should get back on the road."

Melissa exchanged looks with Spring.

"Yes, *we* should."

I didn't like the way she stressed the 'we.' Spring looked down at his lap.

"I don't care what you do," Melissa continued, "or where you go, but it won't be with us."

"Ooh, harsh," Amber said. Then: "Wait, you're serious?"

Melissa scoffed. "All this is *her* fault. She ruined my life, she ruined Spring's life, she ruined your life. She got Salidas killed. She ruined *everything*. We got out. We're safe now. And I never want to see her again."

I didn't say anything. I couldn't breathe. I couldn't *breathe*.

I have vague memories of Amber, of all people, arguing on my behalf, but I can't tell you what she said. Melissa got up and walked away, Amber trailing after her, still arguing.

Spring still wouldn't look at me.

"Say something," he said.

Didn't he understand I couldn't fucking *breathe*? "I...I *can't*." The words cracked as I spoke them, and nothing else came after.

He reached for my hand, and I pulled away. So we just sat there, in a horrible silence full of guilt and betrayal and recriminations, until Melissa came back with Spring's pack, Amber on her heels.

She shoved it at him, and said, "Let's go."

Spring finally looked at me. He opened his mouth, as if he was going to say something. But he didn't. He just got up, shouldered his pack, and walked away.

Amber stood still, frozen.

"I'm so sorry," she said, at last. And then she ran to catch up.

WISGARTH'S LEGACY

The letter came today, from Amisara. Sergeant Wisgarth is dead. *Lord* Wisgarth now, apparently, with Captain and General in between, somehow moving from mercenary scum to knight of the realm—with the right leverage, I'm sure.

As well respected in the House of Lords as on the field of battle, the letter said, *and beloved by all fortunate enough to have known him.* As if one's so-called legitimacy matters to the person at the business end of the sword.

It's been eight years since I've seen the old bastard, when he came to Ashbury with the Amisaran delegation for trade talks, and thirty-five since I left his company. Still a mercenary then, but he had "plans." We went to dinner. It was tense, starting with me sniping about his life choices—with about as much control of my emotions as the teen-aged girl I'd been when I'd served under him—and ending with his wine in my face. I'd gone home and drunk myself stupid and cried myself to sleep. I'd neither seen nor heard from him since.

Lord Wisgarth's last will and testament was short enough that a notarized copy had been included. A single page, naming me his heir and, for all practical purposes, sole beneficiary of his estate.

Leaving me to clean up his mess, no doubt.

I'm so angry I could kill him.

To say that my feelings surrounding Colin fucking Wisgarth are complicated is an understatement. Without what he taught me, I could never have become the best that I've been. To get there, though, he made me the worst thing possible.

I'm leaving for Amisara first thing in the morning, if I'm not too hung over.

I think it's time. No promises, but if I can't face this now, I never will.

There are parts of that night that evade my memory—whether from time or shock or blunt trauma or lack of sleep or just too much happening at once for one young girl to endure. This part, however, I remember clearly, word for word—or close enough not to matter:

Sword at my throat, gauntleted hands grasping my bare arms. Guards. Soldiers of the enemy camp, the camp I'd just walked right into.

To Sergeant Wisgarth, they'd been told, for questioning before I was given to the men to pass around, for however long I lasted. So they dragged me, despite my protests that my feet worked just fine, to one of the larger tents in the enemy camp. Four of them, for one small girl. Two of them gripped my arms and one carried my few belongings— Dhav's sword, my knife, a small sack of coins and jewels, and a larger sack I'd frantically stuffed with clothes and bread and a couple of sticks of hard sausage, one of which a guard was dutifully tasting for poison. The fourth soldier was there for decoration, it appeared, and good decoration he was: tall and muscular, with dark skin and perfectly sculpted features, clad in black leather armor I'd have ached to peel from his body in other circumstances. Which is to say, circumstances that didn't involve me being dragged through the mud, covered in my dead lover's blood, in the middle of what was rapidly becoming one of my more ill-conceived plans to date.

Given my proclivity for ill-conceived plans, that was saying something.

We stopped in front of the tent. The decoration clapped twice. We waited, until at last the tent flap shifted and a man slipped through.

At first sight, he didn't seem particularly imposing; if his body held any strength, the cut of his clothing worked to obscure it. His face, however, was a different story. Intensely dark eyes—brown that verged on black, flecked with gold and green—were set back behind thick, black eyebrows and a matching beard, bisected by what must have been a horrific scar running horizontally from his left ear to his lip.

"Karos," he said, addressing the decoration, "what do we have here?"

"We caught her sneaking into camp, sir."

I laughed.

One of those thick, black eyebrows raised.

"If I'd been sneaking, you wouldn't have seen me," I said. "There are two ways to get into this camp unseen, but I wasn't really looking hard, so there may be more. I only needed to get close enough to talk to someone that matters. Is that you? I'm here to enlist."

The men chuckled, even Karos, and I remember my face reddening.

Sergeant Wisgarth didn't, though. His eyes narrowed, assessing, and then: "What makes you think a twelve-year old girl—"

"Sixteen," I lied. His face told me he didn't believe me, and he was only off by a couple years.

"What makes you think you have what it takes to gut a man?"

"Look at me," I said, glancing down at my shift and sleeve, but meaning it all—the red-brown stains flaking from my hand and face and neck, my matted hair, still sticky and damp. "None of this is my blood. Well, except for what's between my thighs."

The men exchanged glances, and those on either side of me shifted, almost certainly unconsciously, away from me. Loosened their grip. Just slightly. But if it came to it, *just slightly* might be the difference between escape and whatever other fate might befall me.

"A girl can slit an unarmed man's throat in his sleep. Doesn't make her soldier material."

"He wasn't asleep," I said, "and he wasn't unarmed. He was just stupid, and slow."

Wisgarth stepped closer, and the guards tightened their hold on me. He gripped my chin, thumb on the bruise Dhav's fist had left two nights ago, lifting my head to expose my throat, where the imprints of Dhav's fingers were starting to darken. They bloom to many colors over the next few days, the bruises, I knew from experience, and Dhav would drape my discolored neck with looted jewels and tell me how beautiful I was. Until it was time to sell them. More bruises, if I got too attached to any of them.

Wisgarth pulled a handkerchief from his pocket. He spit on it and wiped blood from my face with the damp cloth, examined my darkened eye, my bruised cheek, my fattened lip. He was still assessing when another man approached at a run.

"Sergeant Wisgarth, sir," he panted. "Sir, news from enemy camp! Captain Tristan is dead!"

The men holding me tightened their grips, enough to leave more bruises. Wisgarth kept his eyes on me.

"Interesting. Murdered in his sleep, was he?"

"No sir. They say he died fighting. Whoever did him carved him like roast venison and ran off with his whore, they say, and his sword."

Wisgarth's eyes narrowed as he glanced over my belongings, especially the sword. He pursed his lips.

"Is that what they say? Very interesting." He stepped back to look me over one more time, and the unscarred side of his face quirked up into half of a wry grin. "Very interesting, indeed. Karos, have a bath drawn in my tent."

Karos's eyes narrowed, the tiniest fraction, before he nodded sharply. With a curt "Yes, sir," he turned on his heel and disappeared into the camp.

Lord Wisgarth's house is small by Lordly standards, palatial in comparison to my humble home. Exquisitely furnished: an austere elegance that was singularly Wisgarth. I suppose as the new owner, I could just walk in (as if a locked door could stop me), but that seemed improper. It certainly didn't *feel* like my property. Instead, I waited for Wisgarth's footman to usher me in.

The door opened silently on well-oiled hinges and the footman scowled out at me.

"My most sincere apologies, Mistress, I was not told you were in town, or I would not have left you waiting like a commoner. Please, come inside."

"Mistress? Seriously, Karos, never call me that again."

Karos had aged, his hair and beard white and his face creased with deep crags, but the decoration that had first escorted me to meet Sgt. Wisgarth so many decades before had maintained his breathtaking beauty. I reached to pull him into a hug, but he stiffened, and emotions that I didn't understand flashed across his face. I stepped back.

"Allow me to take your bags, Mistress. Unless what you are telling me is that my service to this household is no longer required."

Something was off. But I wasn't going to discover what it was by standing on the steps and further antagonizing Karos. I dropped my luggage at his feet and brushed past him, as if I deserved to be there.

I'd fallen in with Dhav Tristan's Shadow Reavers Regiment the same way any woman might. Displaced and lost and desperate, I'd wandered right into the mercenary camp, and they put me straight to work. No questions asked of a girl, as long as her hands could cook and scrub, and her legs could spread. Banished from Ashbury and betrayed by the person I loved more than my own life, I'd wandered far north and west, nearly starving to death, and now I travelled with the camp I knew not where. I didn't really care—I was surviving. After being abandoned in the wilderness by my ex-lover and his girlfriend, I was surviving, and maybe some day, when that certain someone heard what I'd endured because of him, he'd be overcome with guilt and... well, it varied. I fell asleep each night playing through the scenarios. It was all very pathetic.

We moved from skirmish to skirmish, sometimes just ahead of the enemy, sometimes the other way around. I didn't know who the enemy was, and I didn't care. Sometimes our numbers grew smaller, and some of the men would visit a local village to recruit, returning with boys who either learned to fit in—and fight—or disappeared in a few weeks.

That was my life, for months: cooking, washing, fucking, then walking to a new place to do it all over again. Until one day, Captain Dhav Tristan noticed me, and suddenly I wasn't some anonymous girl there to provide services to any man in the company who needed servicing. I no longer had to take the shit jobs that the older women didn't want. I'd been elevated. Now the other women had to do what *I* told them, and none of the other men dared touch me.

Dhav welcomed me into his tent like he was entreating a princess, and rewarded me with luxuries—fine clothes, jewelry, an actual mattress to sleep on.

Nobody warned me of what was to come. Not that I'd have listened to them if they had. I had finally found someone who appreciated me for what I was. And not just *someone*, but someone important. A great man who would make a mark on the world. And I would be there, making that mark with him.

And when Spring realized the mistake he'd made, what he'd thrown away, I could inform him that he was being invited to my wedding—as the entertainment.

Karos showed me to Wisgarth's bedroom, against my protests, insisting that it was the only room fit to house the Mistress of the House. Capitalization pronounced. He'd made it clear that while he was employed in Service (also capitalized) that he would be referring to me as Mistress, as was proper. I told him that in that case, I would forthwith call him "Sir" in all our communications. He offered his resignation, and I almost accepted it. But that would leave me alone and rudderless in a strange city in a strange land, facing what I was sure was going to be an unexpectedly challenging task, by which I mean setting Wisgarth's affairs in order and figuring out how to dispose of the assets as quickly as possible so I could get back to Ashbury where I belonged. It would have been nice to have a friend to help me through it, but it appeared that I would have to settle with just the household help.

While I unpacked, Karos drew me a bath. After two weeks on the road, I could surely use one, even more than food and sleep. I soaked in the tub until the water grew tepid, trying, and failing, to relax. Although we were well into autumn, the weather had not yet turned, but the house still felt chill to me. Wisgarth's wardrobe contributed a padded silk robe to my comfort, but I still felt compelled to add a few logs to warm the hearth.

The scent of sautéing onions filtered under the door. Karos announced that dinner would be ready in half an hour, if it pleased his

Mistress. I bit my tongue again and thanked him. Half an hour to kill.

Going through Wisgarth's dresser seemed both morbid and tacky. The nightstand on one side of the bed was conspicuously empty, the drawer left open, and not even a lamp on top. The other nightstand held a book and a lamp. The drawer was locked.

The book was a cheap novel, not even warranting a leather cover. The bookmark indicated that Wisgarth had gotten a little over halfway through before he died. The protagonist was a young woman named Talia who set out from her impoverished village to journey to the distant city of Ashbury to apprentice to the famous wizard Ellinon Floreshat. So, a historical fantasy. Historical since Ellinon was dead these last ten years. Fantasy since his criterion for apprentices had been more their family's wealth than their magical potential. Still, it was competently written, and despite myself, I found myself drawn in....

I woke, still sitting propped against the headboard. Morning light was filtering through the window. Someone had draped me with blankets and set the book on the nightstand with a bookmark inserted where I had drifted off. A new bookmark; Wisgarth's remained where he had left it. It had felt only respectful to leave it in place, and I was glad Karos shared that feeling. He had emptied the bath, and the chamber pot, as well. Good thing.

Karos swept in while I was refilling it.

"Excellent, Mistress, you're awake." He carried black fabric that looked suspiciously like it would billow draped over his shoulder, and what appeared to be a sewing kit in his other hand. "Are we ready for a big day?"

"I'm *pissing*, Karos."

"Indeed, Mistress. That is an excellent start to the day. Please, can you put this on?"

"It's a dress."

"Yes, Mistress." Karos laid the thing out on the bed. I was right. It *would* billow.

"When have you ever seen me in a dress? I don't even *own* a dress."

"I gathered as much, Mistress, which is why I took the liberty of having one made for you. We used your laundry to size it, so we should be able to finish it with a single fitting."

"I'm not going to wear a dress, Karos."

"Ah, but you're in Amisara now, Mistress. There are customs and laws here that you would do well to honor."

Laws? It's true, I hadn't seen any women wearing trousers since I'd crossed the border, and I'd received a fair share of odd looks, but my appearance garners odd looks in any company—people just don't know what to do with a woman whose hair ranges from a short fuzz to non-existent, and who doesn't try to hide or remove her scars. "There are customs in Ashbury, too, and I've made a career of thumbing my nose at them."

"You are very far from your base of power, Mistress. From a strategic and tactical perspective, it would be wise to remain inconspicuous while you assess your circumstances."

Which is exactly what Wisgarth drummed into the head of every soldier under his command, every time we broke camp for a new location.

And it's not like I hadn't stooped to wearing a peasant skirt and a wig when I was reduced to picking pockets in Ashbury Park to pay my bills.

"Fine."

The dress actually fit, insofar as every button intended to button actually did, and every clasp clasped, and every strap tied and every belt buckled. Despite ample fabric that successfully obscured my admittedly subtle curves, the collar laced uncomfortably tight against my throat, and layers of black lace and ruffles and frill conspired to hide any exposed flesh with a depressing burst of ostentation. I doubted even Laura would have been able to pull off this *bubo-en-regalia* look.

Karos took a step back to assess, nodding and frowning simultaneously. Then he came at me with a fist full of pins and a placid demeanor that belied malicious intent.

Eventually, after much invective and many tiny wounds, I was ordered out of the horrible thing. Karos draped it carefully over his arm and swept from the room. He paused in the doorway, almost as an afterthought.

"Master Wisgarth's tailor is waiting downstairs. He will make the alterations. Please take the time to freshen up, Mistress. You're due at the courthouse in an hour, and it wouldn't do to exhale anywhere near the court clerk in your current state."

"Courthouse?" I asked. But he was already gone.

I'd grown used to it: the company men sniggering as I walked past; the women shaking their heads with mock pity that I knew was truly envy. Dhav was a strong man, a man the others all feared. All he wanted, I thought, was a girl who could not be broken. But they knew better. What he truly wanted was a girl strong enough make the breaking last. To watch me break, fully and utterly. Until there was nothing left to be broken. Then he'd have no more use for me, and he'd throw me to the men like raw meat to the dogs, as he had all the others before.

What Dhav didn't realize was that I was already broken. Nothing he could do actually mattered, when the only person I had ever cared about had literally walked away from me and left me utterly alone. There was nothing left for Dhav to break.

The one thing Dhav hated was failure. He hated it from his troops, and he hated it from those others of us who served him, and punished it severely. At first I had misunderstood the special punishments he reserved for me as a means to mold me, *to make me perfect for him*. But he saw my refusal to break as his own failure. And that was something he could not tolerate, especially in front of his men.

It was when his fingers closed on my throat that last night—not in anger, and not with the detachment of punishment that I'd come to expect, but with the same calculated coldness employed in cutting the throat of a distracted sentry—that I finally saw the truth. If he couldn't break me, he'd kill me. I meant nothing to Dhav. I wasn't even worth feeling bad, or good, about killing.

As he squeezed my windpipe with his left hand, he fondled my breast with the other and calmly explained what a disappointment I was to him. How I had failed him. How sad and pathetic and useless I was. How I wasn't even worth giving to the men to pass around before dumping my body in the road.

And that's when I realized that maybe I cared about living, after all.

He cursed when I put my knee in his groin and broke one of the fingers on the hand he was using to choke the life out of me. Pulling my knife from my skirts as I twisted out of his grasp, I jammed the ugly, pitted, and razor-sharp blade into his bicep. I felt it scrape across bone, and he pulled back abruptly, cursing. His fist met my face then, and the world spun. I found myself face-down on the floor, unsure of how I got there, and the knife was no longer in my hand but over a foot away.

I don't remember reaching for it, but apparently, I did, because when he lifted me by my hair with his dagger drawn and poised to gut me, I found the knife clutched in my hand. I twisted my body away from his thrust and scooped with my arm, narrowly diverting his blade from my belly, while my shorter blade found the side of his neck.

Even spraying blood from a mortal wound, he didn't go down easily. He tried to slash at me again, but I'd wrapped my arm around his wrist and held it tight to my body, while I sliced and stabbed at anything I could reach. When he finally fell, I followed, still gripping his blade arm, stabbing at him again and again until I realized that he was no longer bleeding.

Nobody interrupted. Nobody *ever* interrupted. Everyone at camp was used to the sounds of someone being hit—or worse—coming from Dhav's tent, and for once it worked in my favor. But I couldn't risk being caught.

I packed quickly, taking only what was mine, and what I felt I'd earned in my months of service, and slipped quietly from the camp as only a child of the streets can.

Sergeant Wisgarth wisely but unnecessarily had me strip-searched before dismissing the guards. I was expecting that my continued well-being would depend upon my giving to Wisgarth what I'd learned any man in a position of power might demand, but instead, he focused on my injuries while grilling me about the gaps in the camp's security. I'd been less successful at avoiding Dhav's blade than I had thought; there was a nasty gash on my left side across my ribs, deep enough to expose bone, and in our struggles, he'd managed to punch the cross-guard into my back and under my shoulder blade. I hadn't noticed the injuries until Wisgarth started tending them and they suddenly became excruciating.

Karos entered, carrying the first pot of hot water for the bath. Wisgarth caught his arm and described what I'd revealed to him about their own camp's security.

"Find out if what she says about our defenses is true and report back immediately."

When Karos returned, Wisgarth had finished cleaning my wounds, and I had managed to get the worst of the blood off the rest of me.

"She's right, sir," Karos said. "I've posted additional guards."

Wisgarth watched me from the corner of his eye. "Good. Still, it's embarrassing that we've left such holes in our security."

"Don't feel too bad," I said. "Dhav is even more crap at it than you are. Was."

"Oh?" Wisgarth raised an eyebrow. "Do go on."

Despite the second fitting, the finished dress felt like an oversized potato sack hanging from the still-overly-tight collar, caught in the middle by a wide belt that cinched around my waist. And then, yes, it billowed around my ankles. To my surprise and annoyance, the costume came with a ridiculous pillbox hat and a matching black lace veil. As soon as it was placed on my head, Karos announced that it was time to go and ushered me out the door.

"Did we actually pay this tailor?" I asked as I followed him. "Because this is the ugliest dress I've ever seen." If anything, it looked—and felt—even worse *after* the alterations.

"Perhaps Mistress would be more comfortable in her armor."

"There'd be space enough for it in this glorified coal sack."

Karos offered yet another unreadable expression before nodding his head curtly. "Indeed, Mistress."

The courthouse was six blocks away. Within a block we came across a cafe offering coffee and pastries, and my path naturally strayed.

Karos intercepted me. "There's no time, Mistress. Besides, you don't want to risk dripping raspberry jelly or somesuch on your new dress."

I grumbled, and so did my stomach. "I missed dinner last night."

"Yes, Mistress, I'm quite aware." Karos sounded put out. I suppose he had every right to, but I was feeling put out as well.

"And I still don't understand the point of this stupid costume."

Karos spun to face me, unveiled emotion showing on his face for the first time since I arrived. Raw anger. And raw grief. I took a step back.

"*Pretend* you're in mourning. Pretend you *care*." He turned and stormed off toward the courthouse.

He didn't look back to see if I followed. He didn't need to.

Dressed in a pair of Wisgarth's trousers and an oversized shirt, I led a small squad of men into the Shadow Reavers camp. Though Wisgarth was trusting enough to give me back my knife, he and Karos kept close to me with swords drawn, while the other men followed behind. The plan was simple: with Captain Tristan dead, his lieutenants would be locked in a struggle for control of the company. A single major blow to morale could fracture the company permanently.

A major blow like the complete destruction of their supply chain.

It was hours before dawn, early enough that the cooks hadn't yet emerged to start prepping breakfast, late enough that those who'd stayed up late drinking were in no condition to be an issue. Each man carried casks of oil and sulfur matches. The campfires had burned down to embers, but that would be enough to ignite a match.

As I was leading Wisgarth and Karos to the supply tent, the flap at its entrance shifted and a figure emerged.

Her name was Nita. She was one of the older women in the camp, maybe twenty-five, maybe even older. Her daughter was perched on her hip, holding a shriveled carrot between her grubby hands, chewing on the end of it.

"Oh! Gosling! You gave me a start. What are..." Nita's voice trailed off when she saw Wisgarth behind me. She opened her mouth to scream.

Nita had always been kind to me—kind to everybody, unless they had crossed her. She was generous with advice for the younger girls, how to get on in the camp, how to negotiate sticky situations with the men, or that men got them into. She had warned me against Dhav, and I'd laughed in her face.

I put my knife in her throat.

Karos moved quickly to catch her as she fell, and Wisgarth took the child as her arms went limp. Karos dragged the body into the tent and we followed.

"Take her." Wisgarth held the girl out to me.

I stared at him in horror. There was no way I was going to touch the thing.

"Okay, fine. Take the oil and spread it around."

That I could do.

It was dawn when we got back to our camp, minus one man who took a crossbow bolt in the chest, plus one toddler that screamed our location out to our pursuers as we fled. On the other hand, the Shadow Reavers lost a dozen men, all their food and supply wagons, and half their horses. And one of their women.

And I cemented my place in the Kilted Skullcrackers.

My appointment with the court clerk took us deep into the bowels of the courthouse. Several lamps burned on the single desk in the center of the small, windowless office, and the ceiling was darkened with what might have been hundreds of years of soot. Cabinets lined the walls, presumably stuffed with documents. Wooden crates filled with yet more papers and scrolls were stacked haphazardly throughout the room.

The clerk was a harried-looking woman in an efficiently simple grey dress. A placard on her desk identified her as C. Alion. Her hair was piled on top of her head, held in place by two pins that could be deadly in a fight. I wondered if she knew that.

She took a folder from one of the stacks on the left side of her desk, glanced inside, and said, "Lady Wisgarth. I'm so sorry for your loss. Especially coming so suddenly while you were traveling."

I was suddenly very, very thankful for the stupid lace veil. What kind of con was Karos pulling?

"Thank you," I said, when I could find my voice. "Yes, it has been difficult. Wi... Lord Wisgarth and I maintain interests in both Asimara and Ashbury, and we haven't been able to spend as much time with each other as we should..."

"...And then this." With a wry smile, the clerk finished my thought. She reached across the desk to pat my hand. "I'm not going to say that it'll be okay, and I expect the next few days will be hard, but Mr. Tarunog has been diligent in filing the necessary paperwork, so at least this small part of it can go painlessly. Do you have—?"

Karos cleared his throat and presented documents from his satchel. The clerk looked them over and compared them to the papers on her desk. They included identification papers, an extremely fanciful family lineage, and a Certificate of Marriage, all containing a more-than-passable forgery of my signature. The marriage certificate also contained Wisgarth's, with Karos and two others I didn't recognize as witnesses, and the stamp of the judge who officiated. It was dated only a few months after his visit to Ashbury. We'd been "married" almost eight years.

It wouldn't have been hard for Wisgarth to have my signature forged, I supposed. After all, he was the one who taught me how to write. I mean, I wasn't entirely illiterate when I came to him, but my education had been circumscribed by my former employer's needs—lists of goods, numbers, sums. Spelling was unimportant, as long as it was understandable. "Ayl — 23 botals, Wiskee — 3 botals," and so on. Grammar, even less so. Wisgarth insisted that everyone under his command could read and write properly. "If you don't retire in a box," he said, "you'll need a job when you're tired of fighting. This'll give you a foot up, wherever you go."

But by that time, I'd already seen my first battle, a retaliatory raid by the most imposing of Dhav's former lieutenants, Franq Abillo. They were trying to steal our own supply wagons and had managed to kill two sentries before the men could raise the alarm. I heard the call to arms and launched myself out of Wisgarth's tent, barefoot, in only the shirt and hose I wore to sleep, Dhav's sword in my hand. Abillo saw me, declared that I was a female sexual organ, and charged me. I charged back, blocked his strike long enough to drop my sword and slide between his legs. My knife found the artery in his unprotected inner thigh, and I also stabbed him in the ass while I was down there. Then all I had to do was stay out of his reach until he collapsed from blood loss.

It was my first combat kill. It was exhilarating. There was no way I was ever going back to anything else.

Karos cleared his throat again. The clerk was looking at me expectantly.

"I'm sorry. Memories." I waved a gloved hand.

The clerk nodded indulgently and repeated herself. All I needed to do was confirm that I was who the papers said I was. The clerk gave me a paper to sign, which I did. *Lady Maris Goselin*. A hesitation I couldn't help. I hoped it wasn't revealing. *Lady Maris Goselin-Wisgarth*.

With a pitying smile, the clerk collected the document and blotted it dry. She countersigned as witness—it was the same signature that had appeared on the marriage certificate. Camilla Alion, ASW. Just how had Wisgarth managed this scam? She sorted the papers swiftly and efficiently—Karos's pile and her own—and told us where to go to claim the body.

Karos took the papers, bowed, and exited the office. The clerk caught my arm as I stood to leave.

"He's very good, your man. I hope you'll afford him some consideration when you remarry. It will be terribly hard for a man of his age to find a new position."

Which were a string of words that clearly implied that I was lacking vital information necessary to make any sense of.

"I'm not planning on remarrying."

Her shoulders dropped. "Oh dear, you really *have* been out of Amisara for a long time, haven't you?"

Karos was in a foul mood for some reason, and it took all my energy just to keep up with him as his long strides bore us to the morgue.

"What's the rush? He'll be just as dead now or after lunch, which I'll remind you comes after two other meals that I missed."

Karos spun on me, fist raised. He took a deep breath and lowered his fist, but seemed to have trouble unclenching it. "It's been over a month. Over a month that I've been waiting to see him since the health department took him away and said they would only release him to you. To *you*, not to the person that's been at his side for forty years! So please forgive me, *Lady Maris Goselin-Wisgarth*, if I care fuck-all about your breakfast."

Something about spending time with Karos, with Karos and Wisgarth, had me reverting to the hormonal teenager I'd been when we'd first met, quick to fly into a rage at any provocation, and ready to climb on top of anyone I felt like to either fuck or kill. It's funny how company can erase the years. Either that or the sudden rages of my second change, which I thought had finished with me, had come back for one last hurrah. I resisted the completely-rational-at-the-time urge to storm off to the nearest restaurant, and just nodded, not trusting my mouth not to say something stupid if I opened it.

Together, we entered the morgue, presented my totally genuine papers, and were escorted to "Long Storage"—a large room filled with caskets, arrayed four high in a heavy-duty rack. Each casket was labeled with a number. The mortician consulted a chart and then extracted one of the caskets using an ingenious adjustable gurney.

The caskets, I could see, were sealed both physically and with magic that radiated from a wax seal at the head of the casket. The mortician saw me examining it.

"The seal is a preserving spell, for people who are in a situation like yours. It preserves the beloved's remains outside of time, so that the bereaved have the opportunity to gather and still bury the body within the internment period."

"The what?"

"Lady Wisgarth is only recently come to Amisara, and is not fully familiar with our laws," Karos said.

"Ah." The mortician looked relieved at such a simple explanation. "The deceased must be laid to rest by an authorized priest within three days—seventy-two hours—of death. Punishment for failure to comply is... strict. But just, I suppose. According to our records, once we open the casket you will have sixty-eight hours to bury the body."

"The funeral is scheduled for tomorrow," Karos said, and the mortician beamed gloomily with approval.

I nodded, and the mortician gave me a tool that looked like an extra-wide chisel. I used it to chip the wax seal from the casket, breaking the spell, and then the mortician popped the lid off with a pry bar.

My stomach lurched, and I staggered back from the casket, hands pressed against my mouth. The mortician's hand steadied me.

"It's always a shock. Take your time."

"May we..." I glanced at the door. I didn't trust myself to speak. Fortunately, the mortician was sympathetic.

"Of course. However long you need. Our porters will be available after lunch to bring Lord Wisgarth's mortal remains to your home." With a bow, he took his leave.

And I dared another glance at Wisgarth's corpse, and the writhing tendrils of magic that permeated it.

When we returned from our raid, my first night under Wisgarth's unofficial command, he called Karos to him. Rocking Nita's screaming baby, he ordered Karos to finish filling the bath. Karos frowned at him unhappily, but saluted with a "Yes, sir," and vanished into the camp.

I felt oddly disconnected. It had been a long time since I had gotten any sleep, and in that time I had killed Dhav, fled my camp, joined a rival mercenary troop, led a raid on my old camp, and killed Nita. And now I was staring at Nita's baby, bouncing in Wisgarth's arms. He'd given her his little finger to suckle.

"Why are you so fixated on that bath?"

He scoffed. "You're not getting in my bed the way you are."

It's not like I actually expected anything else, though I was starting to really feel the beating Dhav had given me and could have used a rest. But Wisgarth left me to bathe myself as he went in search of a woman in the camp who could take the child. "There's always *someone* willing, in a camp like this." When he returned, he stitched the wound across my ribs ("Not worth bothering Sohu"—Sohu being the healer), gave me a fresh shirt to sleep in and checked to make sure there were no weapons hidden in or around the bedding. Then he crawled in after me, draped one arm over me, and promptly started to snore in my ear.

When I woke, I was alone.

The second night, when he started to snore, I shook him awake.

"Why are you bringing me to your bed if you aren't going to take me?"

He sighed. "Don't worry, it's only until the men get used to you. They're good men, by which I mean, they're good at killing whoever they're paid to kill. But they're not *good* men. You'll fit right in, if we don't drive you away."

He turned, putting his back to me, and resumed snoring.

Wisgarth did not look peaceful in death. He looked like he'd died gasping for breath.

Karos was wringing his hands. There were tears in his eyes.

"Tell me what happened."

"He got sick." Karos sniffled. Wiped a hand across his face. "It was just a little cough, the first day. Like little puffs of air. The next day it was worse. He grew feverish. I gave him all the remedies I knew, but nothing helped. I sent out for a healer, but there..." He cleared his throat. "There was a delay, and by the time the healer arrived, Colin was...."

He didn't seem to be able to say the next word, so I offered an alternative.

"Murdered. He wasn't sick. This was necromancy. The remnants of the spell are still in his body, though they're fading fast, now that the time spell is broken. Give me some paper; I need to take notes."

All we had were official government-issued documents. I scribbled and sketched all over the back of my marriage certificate, and the even-more-fabricated family lineage document. Once I'd learned all I could like this, I pulled my knife and punched it down into the center of Wisgarth's chest. Karos gasped and pulled me away.

I brushed him off. "Didn't you hear me? He was *murdered*. For a spell this complex, you'd need an accomplished necromancer, and anyone who gets good enough at magic to do something like this develops a personal style. It's like handwriting. Unique, and difficult to imitate. If I can see enough of this spell, I might be able to identify the murderer if I see their work again. And for that, *I need to see inside his chest*."

A second strike cracked the breastbone, and I was able to convince a stricken-looking Karos to help me spread the ribs.

I was right. The spell had attacked the lungs, blackening them, and turning them into something more akin to badly set pudding than a functional organ.

There was no way to avoid it. I plunged my hands into the liquifying mass that had been Wisgarth's lungs, catching at threads of magic. It took me perhaps ten minutes to tease the retreating threads back, to reassume their active form—the one that killed Wisgarth—without altering them by my own efforts. I described what I learned to Karos. Karos transcribed what I told him and sketched out the pattern well enough that I knew that I could replicate it if wanted. Not that I would ever want to. I'd sooner cut off my hands.

But I'd learned what I'd set out to learn: if I came across *any* magic by the same spellcaster, I'd recognize it.

I extracted my hands from Wisgarth's lungs. A viscous black sludge dripped from my fingers. I looked up at Karos.

"Help?"

I grew up on the streets of Ashbury, one of the many lost children who huddled together for warmth in back alleys and abandoned buildings, who ran underfoot in the marketplaces, begging and stealing to live, taking pleasure where and when we could, whether it was alcohol or drugs or sex. We didn't have plans for our future, because most of us didn't live long enough to have one, and when my friend Spring's music launched us out of poverty, I managed to completely screw that up by still thinking like a street kid.

I was determined to leave that world behind, to kill the person I'd been and reinvent her as something new. The Kilted Skullcrackers was the crucible in which she died and the person I was to become was forged.

I quickly learned that I was actually very good at killing. What I lacked in upper body strength compared to the men, I made up for in speed and accuracy. The men started calling me Eyehunter, for my ability to sidestep a sword or spear and put a dagger through my enemy's visor. And the skills I'd honed in the streets of Ashbury, being small and quiet and generally beneath notice, made me a good scout. Sergeant Wisgarth started sending me out regularly to eliminate sentries, even without a related action, or to sneak into the enemy's camp and execute some key person or otherwise reduce their effectiveness on the field of battle.

I remember a small part of myself suggesting that I should be disturbed by my newly-found cavalier attitude toward ending another human being, but I couldn't care enough to interrogate it, and that voice rapidly learned to shut up. If Wisgarth was concerned, he kept it to himself; I was too useful as I was.

Wisgarth kept me in his bed for a month before he trusted me enough to be out of his grasp overnight. It took Karos longer to trust me, and he never really warmed up to me, no matter how much I threw myself at him. I had made a decision not to bed any of the men in the company, no matter how bored or drunk I got. I knew how men got with women when jealousy reared its head, and it wouldn't look good if I had to kill one or more of them.

Karos was different. He was beautiful. Stunningly so, and he held himself so aloof and unattainable that I couldn't help fall deeply and desperately in lust with him.

Talia, in the novel Wisgarth had left on his nightstand, was two days on the road when someone at an inn where she stops for the night steals her pack from her room, leaving her with only the clothes on her back and her (extremely light) purse. During the day, she departs the road to avoid the travelers she suspects of robbing her, and loses her way in the woods. As nightfall descends, she comes upon a small cabin. The woman who lives there is old—by Talia's estimation perhaps as old as thirty (that made me laugh, in a vaguely self-pitying way)—but still very beautiful. In a not-terribly-subtle bit of foreshadowing, the woman says it's not yet the full moon, so Talia can stay one night, but must leave first thing in the morning. There is only one bed, of course. The author went to great effort to detail the beauty of the woman, of her intoxicating, almost animal scent, of the strange tingling that the innocent Talia feels betwixt her thighs as their naked flesh brushes up against each other under the covers.

The next morning, the woman ushers her out the door, bidding her make good distance. Alas, it is not to be, for around midday, she is set upon, yes, by the same men she'd avoided the previous day, who turn out to be not just robbers, but slavers (of course). After some initial unpleasantries that involve the removal of Talia's clothing, the slavers discover that she has never had sex before, which makes her especially valuable to a particular flavor of buyer, and this prevents the unpleasantries from becoming even more intrusive.

That night, after the full moon rises, there's a howl in the distance. Surprise. The werewolf tears through the slavers camp, killing them all. It approaches Talia, vicious and snarling, and then shoves its head under the blanket to sniff deeply between her legs. Conveniently, the slavers left Talia naked, even though they'd decided not to partake of her themselves. The scene shifted from graphic carnage to even-more-graphic sex with a single paragraph of transition.

The scene brought back memories of Kilanh, Spring's drummer and lover, a Sarr, whose feline and feminine charms had dragged me back from despair one very dark day. Whatever the motivation for writing the scene, the author captured with accuracy the hazards of such a coupling, from coming up for air with a mouthful of fur, to having unexpectedly sharp teeth pressed against sensitive bits while your lover's tongue does its work. Of course, a wolf's tongue wouldn't have the same rough, sandpaper texture as a Sarr's, so presumably could be applied more vigorously.

It was the first time I'd become aroused since Laura and Edwin died in the plague that swept through Ashbury, two years earlier. But it felt wrong to masturbate in poor murdered Wisgarth's bed, while reading his smut, so instead, I marked my page and forced myself to sleep.

One of the grim realities of the world is that the powerful can, and usually do, take whatever they want from the powerless. Sometimes this is disguised as trade, simple economics. In war, that illusion is stripped away.

In the ordinary course of business, soldiers have little to no power over their own circumstances. Someone else tells them where to be, who to fight. A single command could lead to their deaths. Personal power appears in brief windows—the taking of enemy prisoners, the sacking of a city. And then, that power is nearly absolute.

With the Shadow Reavers, I had never witnessed first-hand the sacking of a city. I'd heard the men boasting, but the words were meaningless, lacking context. The first time the Kilted Skullcrackers sacked a city, I watched with dispassionate disgust as the soldiers, mercenary and regular soldier alike, prowled the streets, dragging women from their homes and raping them. It seemed grossly unfair, even if it was "normal, expected behavior," that the *women* of a fallen city should bear the weight of its men's failures. So I did my best to even things out.

I had the most attractive men brought out into the street, stripped and bound, and took them, one after another. My fellow soldiers would take bets on how many men I could drain before sun-up. I was young; I could go all night. I'd go until my legs gave out, or I'd sur-passed the highest bet, and take the pot myself.

I was proud of how many times I won. *Proud.* Can you imagine?

I don't know how to stop being the person who did these things. And no matter how much I drink, those men's faces still ambush my dreams.

The funeral was sparsely attended. A priest. A journalist. Karos. Me. And a representative of the government to witness that the event took place, within the boundaries proscribed by law, and all rites and rituals dutifully performed. Invitations had gone out to a select few acquaintances, but none of them seemed inclined to pay their last respects.

As the "widow," there were certain rituals that I had to perform—the washing of the face, the hands, the feet. A kiss on each eye, and on the lips. Karos had warned me against breakfast, probably not for my sake (he'd grown even more chilly toward me since the impromptu autopsy), but in order to not spoil Wisgarth's ceremony with an untimely revisit of sausage and eggs.

I tried to look properly grave and sorrowful through the festivities, and I suppose I succeeded, as the government witness seemed satisfied with my performance. But it was Wisgarth's fault. He's the one who turned me into the callous monster I'd become under his command. I'd killed a man, yes, in self-defense, but it wasn't until I'd met Wisgarth that I became a murderer. He could have thrown me to his men and let that be an end to it. Taken me as a spoil of war. Sent me packing. Instead, he trusted me and let me have what I wanted.

How do you forgive someone for that?

Karos was quiet in the carriage, riding back from the graveyard. Tense. Sorrow and anger in conflict. I thought I knew how he felt.

Once back at Wisgarth's house, he let out a long, slow exhale.

"At least it's over now," he said, as he stripped off his formal footman's dress and threw it to the floor. "I've fulfilled my promise. You've got your inheritance. I hope you choke on it."

"What?" I followed as Karos stormed up the stairs and into the footman's chambers in his undergarments. "No, no, no, you don't get to quit."

He tried to slam the door in my face, but I blocked it with my foot. There was a disconcerting crunch. I hopped in after him. "Do you really think I want any of Wisgarth's shit? And what's it to you, anyway?"

His back was to me, and I grabbed his shoulder, half to force his attention, half for balance. Karos spun with a backhand that sent me back against the door.

"It should have been *me*."

I tasted blood, and my left ear rang. "You don't want to die like that. Nobody should die like that."

"No." Deflated, he sagged onto his bed. "*I* should have been the one to wash him and kiss him goodbye. Not you. You don't love him. You don't even *like* him."

I learned fairly quickly that Wisgarth had no interest in women, at least, physically. It took significantly longer for me to learn of his interest in men. He was understandably circumspect, as the culture within the military, or at least in its mercenary incarnation, was profoundly intolerant of such behavior. Not because it was "wrong," but because any man who was capable of loving another man was seen as somehow less. Less physically capable, less brave, less analytical. More apt to let his emotions cloud his judgment. Not the sort of man you could trust if things went pear-shaped. Not the sort of man other men would follow.

Sometimes, when we were on leave, Wisgarth would use me as cover for covert meetings with other men. I'd cool my heels while he had his wick tended and come up with a cover story in case we needed one.

It never occurred to me that Karos was similarly inclined, or that anything other than a professional relationship existed between the two of them. Was this something new? I mean new as in within the last thirty years. Or did I just live my life as a soldier encased in a bubble of my own self-interest? It didn't matter.

I hobbled to the bed and sat beside him. "Oh, Karos, I had no idea. I'm so sorry. I'm sorry for your loss, and I'm sorry for anything I've done that increased your pain."

"Easy for you to say."

"Please. When was the last time you heard me apologize?"

He chuckled, then sniffed, wiping tears from the tip of his nose, and lay back on the bed.

"What do I do now?"

My fingers found his, squeezed. "First, you get dressed. Second, you explain all this inheritance bullshit to me. Third, we solve Wisgarth's murder. Fourth, you buy this place from me for a copper."

"You make it sound easy."

"The hard part is done, I think. Oh, also, you move back to the master bedroom."

He shook his head. "I can't sleep there alone."

"You won't need to. Not until you're ready."

176

But we didn't get a chance to talk until that evening. There was a summons to the courthouse to attend to additional paperwork. I won't bore you with the details. I had to attest to all sorts of crazy things, like not being an agent of a foreign power, and so on. They asked me if I had settled on a new husband yet (still grieving, thank you very much), and reminded me to register my suitors and so on. They gave me a handbook full of rules. From Karos's expression, I suspect that I failed to hide how ridiculous all this was, but I did try.

As we walked back to the house, Karos gave me a brief overview of Amisaran sexual politics. Amisara was governed under the so-called principles of natural law by two leaders, the Archfather and the Archmother, ostensibly equal, but historically, priority has been given to the Archmother, as the instantiation of the so-called "creative force." All the laws were geared toward advancing somebody's idea of what was natural, and discouraging what was unnatural.

Same-sex relationships were not considered, in Amisara, natural, and the best way to become a social pariah was to let it be known that you engaged in such activities.

"Why would you choose to settle here?" I asked Karos in disbelief.

"We were engaged as additional security for a diplomatic mission—the Archfather felt that the Amisaran forces were too insular and might not recognize all the threats." Karos shrugged. "He and Colin got on... well."

It took me a moment. But yes, Wisgarth had started a torrid affair with the leader of a country that despised his kind.

"This didn't bother you?"

"Colin has always had several beds to warm. They come and go, but I was always here. This one was different. This time, it was Colin who got played."

We were coming up on the house, where two women in professionally subdued dress waited. The first of the suitors, or rather, their representatives. One was here on behalf of her brother, the other her cousin, and both had issued invitations for dinner that evening.

"You have to accept," Karos whispered in my ear.

"Both of them?" I didn't bother whispering.

Karos nodded. "It's assumed you've already researched likely suitors and will schedule them in order of preference."

"Indeed. Ladies, please come in, have a seat in the foyer, we'll be right back."

As soon as I got Karos alone and out of earshot, I growled, "This is morbid. They don't even wait for the body to get cold."

"A woman isn't considered competent to manage her money. If she doesn't have a husband or a responsible male relative to manage financial transactions, the transactions are not considered valid. If a widow doesn't marry before taxes are due, she loses everything and may be imprisoned for tax evasion."

"I thought women held power in Amisara."

"Well, things change." Karos let out a slow breath. "About seven years ago." He sounded embarrassed. I'd interrogate that later. First I had to deal with these ridiculous suitors.

I wrote a time on two slips of paper, folded them, and marched back into the foyer. I handed one of the notes to the closest of the two women.

"I expect your brother to pick me up here, at this time. Thank you for coming. Karos will show you out," which he did with polite efficiency before she could register a complaint. Once she was safely gone, I handed the second note to the other woman.

"Let me guess," she said, with a wry smile.

"I'm new to the city. I'd hate to get lost in the dark trying to find my suitor's home."

She nodded, amused. "I like your style, Lady Wisgarth, but be careful. You're not in Ashbury anymore. Frankly, you're hardly in Amisara anymore."

It seemed that the only person surprised that I got pregnant was me. I was lucky for almost two years, and when my luck ran out, I refused to believe it. My blood had never been terribly regular, anyway, and if I couldn't hold down my food, well, had you *tried* the food?

Still, there's only so far you can let your armor out before it leaves you dangerously exposed. I went to the company's medic, Sohu, to find out what was wrong with me. He scowled at me.

"If you'd wanted to be rid of it, you should have come to me a month ago. Or earlier. The longer a parasite like this has to establish itself, the harder it is to get rid of it, with or without magic."

I still didn't understand. Willfully ignorant, I think is the right phrase.

He brewed me a tea made of bitter herbs and bade me return when the time came. I threw it back up about an hour later and went to bed. Sharp cramps woke me in the night. Nothing I couldn't handle, I thought, until I realized I really couldn't, by which time I also couldn't walk, or even stand. It was Karos who came in response to my cries of pain and carried me back to Sohu's tent. But it wasn't until I was on my back on his operating table with him digging between my legs that I realized what kind of parasite he had been talking about.

Not that I'd have made a different decision. I can't imagine anyone who'd be a worse mother than me. That's what I told Laura when she told me that she wouldn't mind if Edwin and I made a little Edwin or Maris of our own.

Despite the drugs Sohu gave me, I was still in desperate pain when he finished. He was unsympathetic.

"If you didn't want to get pregnant, you should have come to me *before* you started having sex." Before I could say something smart-ass about sewing me closed, he continued. "There's a spell that—"

"Do it."

"It's nearly always reversible, when you decide to start—"

"It doesn't need to be reversible."

"Don't you want to know how—?"

"I just want to never, ever, *ever* have this happen again."

It was likely the opium that left me open enough to see what he was actually doing as he spoke an incantation while he gestured over my abdomen, watching his every move with my eyes slightly defocused. As he chanted, threads of many colors rose up around us, and his fingers caught them and wove them into a complex pattern that he then pressed into my body. I found myself mimicking his motions, watching with delight as the threads clung to my fingers, spinning into a new form, the threads twining into each other, pulsing as if with power.

I cried out in sudden pain; Sohu had slapped at my hands and then punched me hard in the gut, and was backing out of the tent, eyes wide. I reached for the pain, intense enough to cut through the opioid haze, and the colors fell apart and faded away.

"What were you doing?" he said, shock and fear in his voice.

"Just making pretty colors, like you did."

And that was how I first learned I had a talent for weaving magic.

As soon as the suitors' representatives left and we were alone, I turned on Karos. "Okay, explain."

General Wisgarth (he'd moved up the ranks since I'd left, purely symbolic since there was only a single company to command) took a job helping the Amisarans settle a small border dispute. He and the Archfather had wrangled late into the night nailing down the contract, which, if you're slow at this sort of thing, meant that the contract wasn't the only thing getting nailed.

After the conflict was profitably resolved, the Kilted Skullcrackers stayed on payroll, helping the Amisarans with a host of minor issues, while Wisgarth groomed the Archfather into offering him a title and some land that pulled in enough in revenue to sustain their modest townhouse. (So, there *was* other property, and presumably peasants tied to it to work the land; it's just that nobody thought it necessary to mention it to his (ahem) widow, who, lacking a penis, could not conceivably know how to manage it.)

But what was actually happening was that the Archfather was grooming Wisgarth to help him carry out a coup. Wisgarth had hinted something to this effect to me when we'd met, years ago, and without knowing any details, I managed to offend him into wasting perfectly good wine instead of giving me the details that would be useful to me now. It hadn't occurred to me that they'd do it *here*.

Wisgarth was looking for a place to settle down, a place where he could drop the facades, drop all the lies, and live the life he wanted, with whom he wanted. The Archfather offered him a title, a guaranteed income, and a promise that as soon as the Archmother was no longer a power, laws regarding the equal treatment of homosexuals would be swiftly enacted.

Which they were. But as far they regarded said equal treatment, they came down distinctly against, rather than for. The Archmother, it seemed, had also taken lovers of her own sex, and this, after the coup, was the reason given for her "temporary" sabbatical for "reeducation." Homosexuality was made even more strictly illegal, punishable by imprisonment or death. Women were stripped of property rights—prohibited not from owning property, but from managing it—and long-forgotten customs that predated the matriarchal rule of the Archmother suddenly returned with the force of law. The subjugation was so complete that a woman was even prohibited from bringing any of her former household with her when she remarried, making her wholly dependent on her new husband. Which explained the courthouse clerk's odd statement about taking care of Karos.

These temporary measures would ease, the Archfather promised, once the crisis was past. A year, maybe two at most. That stretched to three, then four, and over that time, as life became ever more restrictive, at least for women, those expectations faded.

Further complicating things, once a year, on the solstice, the Archfather would march the Archmother out to review and approve the changes proposed for the coming year—it was a big all-day ceremony held in the Colosseum—before disappearing from public view again.

If Wisgarth was murdered, Karos said, it was because he had been working to free the Archmother. To correct the mistake he had made.

Before he could tell me more, there was a knock on the door, and the sound of raised voices on the other side of it. I hadn't had time to freshen up or change from my funeral clothes. But then, I didn't have another dress to my name, and apparently trousers were illegal. For women.

Karos moved to the door, but I intercepted. Throwing it open, I announced, "You're early! Not the best way to make a good impression, but I suppose there's nothing to do about it now."

Both of my actually-quite-punctual suitors broke off arguing with each other to stare at me. Their escorts, consisting of the women who had brought me the invitations in the first place, seemed similarly taken aback, though less affronted and more simply shocked.

"You gave them both the same time slot?" Karos seemed equally at a loss.

"Yes, it halves the amount of wasted time."

There was, of course, an immediate argument over whose table I should attend first. Which was pointless, as I had no interest in touring either residence. The argument grew heated enough that violence seemed a real possibility.

"Oh, if only someone clever could think of an alternative that would prevent this needless bloodshed," I said, the back of my hand pressed melodramatically to my forehead. "Like a restaurant."

The cousin laughed out loud, much to the boys' annoyance, and made a suggestion. Not good enough, of course, and for the next twenty minutes, the competitors recommended ever-more-expensive venues until they finally both agreed that Trg Lepa was the best restaurant in the city, and they would split the bill. Never mind that Trg Lepa was the first restaurant suggested. The cousin who'd made the suggestion and I glanced at each other and rolled our eyes.

It was a bristly affair at first, but after the wine had gone around a couple times, everyone relaxed and a good time was had by all.

One of the boys—Boris, I think—leaned over at one point. "I don't suppose there's any chance we're getting married." Which was ridiculous. He was barely a third my age, which can be exceptionally nice for an evening, but I imagine the novelty would wear off the first time we tried to discuss anything substantial. Or anything at all.

"You, sir, are not even getting a goodnight kiss. Any more of this *really* good wine, though, and I might drag you both home to remind me what youth is good for."

"As the Lady Wisgarth's chaperone," Karos said, "I must inform these fine gentlemen that I would deeply regret their unfortunate castrations."

"Subsequent castrations?" I asked.

"Of course, Mistress."

Actually, they both looked a little relieved. I suppose when you're in your early twenties and your family sends you out to seduce a woman in her mid-fifties whom you've never met, just to increase the family fortune, maybe failing isn't such a bad thing.

Ultimately, we all got along well. The boys started telling each other boarding school stories, and soon enough it was apparent that a lasting friendship had been forged. The one I got along with best was Darialth, the cousin who'd first warned me against being too clever. She was the oldest of the four, still unmarried at thirty-one, "protected" by her much younger cousin, Rofexho. (Hearing his name, he gave me a gap-toothed grin and raised his glass, then went back to some improbable tale of manly prowess.)

"Well done, Lady Wisgarth," she said. "But you may not be as successful when the stakes are higher."

The following evening proved her right, and Karos put one of the men on his back while I held the other two off at knifepoint. The owner of Trg Lepa suggested that I find a different venue for my future antics. We called on Darialth that evening, and I hired her to research my future suitors.

But that was the following evening. This evening, we drunkenly stumbled back to Wisgarth's home, argued about propriety over another bottle of wine, and ended up in bed.

Karos lay stiff and nervous next to me on his side of the bed, very consciously maintaining a gap between us.

"I can sleep in the footman's chambers, if you'd be more comfortable," I said.

"I'm extremely comfortable, Mistress."

I was unconvinced.

"What do you think of Wisgarth's taste in literature?"

"I never gave it any thought, Mistress." He shrugged. "I never really read much."

I lifted the book and held it up for him to see. "It's... Well, it's almost the complete opposite of what I'd have expected to see on his nightstand." I opened to my marked page and began to read aloud.

Talia wakes curled up with the woman from the cabin in the woods, who of course has no memory of the prior night's activities. They proceed to make new memories, which I take as an indication that the author had never seen battle, or its aftermath. I can attest that *eau de carnage* is an unlikely aphrodisiac, especially the day after. Karos agreed.

Nevertheless.

Afterward, Talia recovers her belongings and continues her journey.

She keeps off the road and avoids inns, and manages to get herself entirely lost. Escaping the forest, she finds herself in endless rolling hills of heather. Several days later, food is running low, and she starts to worry. Then the weather turns. First, a cold wind from the north, strong enough to flatten the stiff, sharp grasses that rise to her waist in the endless, flat meadow that she'd been in since she left the forest (I was going to have to have a talk with the editor), followed by a driving rain. Drenched, chilled to the bone, she pushes herself on, searching for shelter. Mud sucks at her feet. She's afraid that if she lay down to rest, she'll drown. After hours, exhausted, she sees a light in the distance. Soon, she comes to a small, one-room cabin. Cautious after her experience with the slavers, she peeks through the window to get a sense of what she might be walking into.

Inside, a couple lay under covers by the fire, engaged (of course) in an amorous endeavor that seems so idyllic that Talia is loath to interrupt. When they're done, she staggers to the door, and is surprised when it's opened by two men. They grab her as she falls, and when she awakes, she's been stripped naked and cocooned in blankets, with her hands and feet bound, lying on the bed. The two men share the bed with her, again engaged with pleasuring each other, this time orally. The author described the festivities in graphic detail, along with Talia's feelings and inner commentary (*'Wait. Where did it all...go? How did he fit all that in his mouth?'* and so on).

By the time we reached the climax of the scene, Karos had relaxed beside me.

"Colin was quite good at that." He gave me a half-smile. "Always bringing home new tricks he'd learned. Oh, Gosling, what am I going to do?"

I squeezed his hand. I wanted to say, "Find his murderer and take vengeance," and of course that was what we were going to do, but it didn't seem to touch the heart of his question: when the person who holds your heart is gone, how do you find meaning in a suddenly hollow world? I'd been trying to solve that question myself for a couple of years now, since the plague had left me abruptly alone, and I still didn't have an answer.

Once news of what I'd done—how I'd somehow manipulated magical forces—reached Wisgarth, I was immediately reassigned to train with Sohu. Sohu seemed as thrilled with the arrangement as I was, but Wisgarth was adamant.

"We fight for a living. The more people we have who can heal, the better off we'll be."

It was perfectly reasonable, and I raged against it. That may have contributed to my utter failure to grasp the basics of magic. But really, it didn't make much sense to me, and I didn't have the patience to try. Sohu had me memorizing words in some ancient language and was never satisfied with my pronunciation. I didn't roll my R's right. My Ů's were wrong. I kept mixing up the order of the glottal stop and the tongue click. Wisgarth had been insistent that all the soldiers in his regiment could read and write with some degree of fluency, and had singled some of us (me) out for 'enhanced cultural education,' which stole valuable hours which would have been better spent drinking and fighting and fucking. Still, none of that prepared me for the mind-numbing repetition required to learn the simplest of spells.

In the end, it didn't matter how hard I tried to learn magic, I couldn't. Months went by. I couldn't light a candle. I couldn't heal a paper cut. A year went by, and I gave up. Sohu gave up. Another year went by, and even Wisgarth gave up.

That all changed one day, as we were marching toward what would become the siege of Taramalo. The first hint that we might have a problem came as a massive explosion tore apart a dozen men and flung me hard against a tree trunk. When I came to, the column was in chaos as fire and lightning rained down on the company. Crossbowmen hidden in the forest on either side of the road fired into the confusion.

The back of my head was bloody, and I was seeing double. Everything took on a strange aura, and as I tried to focus and refocus my eyes to clear my vision, I saw the colored threads again. This time, they were centered in the midst of our men, and wherever the spells *seemed* to erupt from, this appeared to be the real source.

The enemy mage had hidden himself with magic, and shielded himself as well. I could deduce his outline from the contours of the power that he'd gathered around him. As I watched, he raised threads of force from the ground and the trees and shaped it into spells of devastating effect. After a moment I came to a sudden pragmatic understanding of something that philosophers in this world and others have debated theoretically for thousands of years: *everything is connected*. The threads of power that the mage was drawing on to kill us were the same threads that ran through the soil beneath my ass and in the roots of the tree I still lay propped against. And I found, when I picked them up myself, that with the right motions, I could interfere with his casting, twitching key threads out of his grasp as he reached for them. Lacking experience, I didn't know what action would do what, and my efforts had mixed results. Even so, I could imagine the enemy mage's rising sense of panic as his spells suddenly became unreliable.

I had to guess what he was doing, of course, but it appeared the spells that hid him from sight also protected him from harm, both directed and incidental.

Offensive spells are inherently unstable; they are hastily thrown together and only need to maintain coherence for a brief moment before the energy is released. It's like throwing a knife. You need to get the throw right, but once the blade leaves your hand, it's, well, it's out of your hands. Spells that need to last, on the other hand, are more intricate workings, elaborate knots and knittings. A spell of hiding, for instance, is more akin to crocheting a lace doily than throwing a knife.

I don't know if I'm the only person out there who can see the doily, but for those us who can, all we need to do is identify the right thread to unravel the whole thing, and then pull it.

Wisgarth had found his way to me. Bruised and singed and bloody, he'd been watching me work for longer than I'd noticed his presence.

"Where is the bastard?" he asked.

I didn't answer right away, not until I'd directed a spray of fire up into the air instead of into the trees where we crouched. I gestured with my head. "Over there, by Gareth's body. Three feet to the left, one back. Give me a minute. He's protected."

I don't think the mage noticed when his shield spell fell.

"Go now."

Wisgarth rushed the mage just as I unraveled the invisibility spell. The mage realized his vulnerability fast enough to throw a desperate blast of raw power at Wisgarth that would have shredded Wisgarth's body, and mine, and probably cleared the forest for a hundred feet behind me.

Just as panicked, I grabbed up everything I could and twisted. I realized quickly that in this struggle, the mage's experience was sure to win, and I'd almost lost my grasp on the writhing mass of magic when Wisgarth's blade took his head off his shoulders. For a terrifying few seconds, the magic became completely unstable, its growth magnified by the mage's panic and subsequent death, threatening to engulf us all before I managed a haphazard containment. Wisgarth had caught the edge of it and lay still, a half-dozen feet from the mage's quickly-incinerating body. I remember Karos shouting for everyone to fall back, even as he ran the other direction to drag Wisgarth away.

The ball of power was a dilemma. Unlike earlier spells, I couldn't just point it at the sky and let it go. It was too powerful; any relaxation of the net I'd thrown around it would release enough power to shred the net, and nobody was far enough away to survive it, especially not me.

In the end, I pushed it down, into the road, as deep into the soil and rock as I could, and ran as far as I could before I let it go.

I woke in Wisgarth's ridiculously comfortable bed, Karos snoring in my ear. His arm was draped over my hip, his hand on my belly, and his erection nestled in the crack of my ass. Which, I must admit, had been part of a recurring fantasy of mine the entire time I'd taken contract with the Kilted Skullcrackers, and for some years afterwards. And I must also admit to being tempted to find said erection a warmer home. But it had been a few years since I'd had sex, and I honestly wasn't sure how well things would work. And, even if he *was* interested, against all evidence to the contrary, was there any scenario that wouldn't be awkward?

It might not be my decision, though. Karos's breathing changed, and he pressed himself harder against me. His hand reached lower, between my legs, searching...

"Colin, I've missed...." Suddenly, he pushed himself away from me. "Mistress! I'm so sorry!" One hand covered the tented blankets, the other his mouth.

"Karos."

"I *knew* this was a bad idea. But the cursed thing hasn't worked since Colin died, and you're not even..."

"Not even what you're interested in, in a lover. I understand, Karos. Trauma writes itself on our bodies, whether we know how to read it or not." Grief was like wearing a coat made of nails. Sometimes it was unbearable, other times, you might not even notice it, until you bump up against something that drives the nails home again. And when you're always on the edge of being scraped raw, the body finds its own ways to compensate.

When I was younger, I would throw myself into sex, mindless, meaningless sex with anyone I could draw between my legs, and blackout alcoholic binges, often in combination. It was different when Edwin and Laura died. Then I just withdrew. Shut myself into my home. Tended my garden and my bees. Went hungry when the food ran out, rather than leave my house to go to the market. Of course I understood.

"You know, Karos, I spent almost a decade with you and Wisgarth, and I never realized you were together until now. Were you together that whole time?"

Karos nodded. "He's why I became a mercenary."

"Now, that sounds like a story I should hear."

He looked sidelong at me. "You know I'm originally from Amisara?" I shook my head. "Colin was just a simple soldier in the company when they took a contract with us. There had been an uprising in the north that we were to put down, with a little help. The mercenaries mocked us when they saw us training. I was young, a hothead, and of course I responded. We were an elite force, I was the best of our class, and they were rubbish. Their uniforms where old, their armor mismatched, and they *slouched*. There was no way they could stand against the discipline of a proper soldier.

"The mercenaries chose the smallest of their ranks to face me. I took a training sword for myself and threw another to him. He let it bounce off his chest and fall to the training grounds floor. He stepped over the blade and into range, grinning. I swung at him, and he put me on the ground with my own dagger against my throat. Humiliated, I watched as he bested another three of our company with no more difficulty than he had with me. The mercenaries' mocking laughter rang in my ears long after they left for the pub."

"So you like being humiliated?"

"Hardly. For two days I stewed over it, and when I thought I understood how Colin had bested us, I sought him out to challenge him. Of course, after our disgrace on the training grounds, our commanders had prohibited us from further challenges, so we met late at night. I lasted longer, nearly a minute, before he disarmed me in a move that took me to my knees. I was determined not to lose, though. Before he could bring his blade to my throat, I caught hold of his crossguard with my left hand, and with my right, I reached under his tunic. I managed to pull him free of his codpiece and planned to crush his balls in my fist, but he was too fast."

I couldn't help notice that the blankets had tented up again. Neither could he.

"I'm sorry, Mistress. Perhaps this is a story best left unspoken."

"If you don't stop calling me Mistress in private, Karos, I'm going to stab you. I'm sure you didn't call Wisgarth 'Master' when you weren't creating appearances."

"No, but...."

"No buts. Those are parts we have to play, for now. That's all."

His smile flickered between pained and genuine. "I suppose you'll insist on hearing the rest?"

"Oh, yes. And...." I drew the covers back, exposing him. "I'd also suggest *that* that seems like a terrible thing to waste. What with it rising from the dead and all."

"Mis...."

"Maris. Or Gosling. And no, I'm not expecting you to use it on me. But I suspect Wisgarth would approve if you were to take things into your own hands."

Karos laughed. "That he would, dirty bastard."

He took the thing into his own hands, then, and proceeded with the tale. I lay my head on his shoulder to watch. I felt something long lost within myself start to stir.

"Oh, *that's* the game you want to play, is it?" Karos affected a reasonably good facsimile of Wisgarth's gruff voice. As he continued, it was clear that this particular piece of the memory merited frequent revisits. Wisgarth had dropped his sword and seized Karos' wrist instead, and with a sudden twist, dropped Karos onto his back. I knew the move well, at least the first part. The technique I'd learned ended with drawing a dagger and putting it anywhere it would end a fight, or taking the opportunity to run away. This variation was new to me.

Wisgarth dropped a knee onto Karos's gut, driving the wind out of him, and then set a boot against Karos's throat. He unbuckled Karos' tassets and lifted away his fauld to reveal his drawers, which he tore away with astonishingly strong fingers. Karos found himself unexpectedly stiff in Wisgarth's hand, in a way that had eluded his few abortive attempts with women, and when Wisgarth took him in his mouth, he came in just a few short strokes, fingers of his free hand curled into Wisgarth's hair.

After a month of depravation, Karos needed little more to spill himself across his belly and chest and, from the feel of it, my forehead.

With a long, shuddering sigh, Karos finished his tale.

"Colin slid off me and rolled to his feet. He adjusted his codpiece and wiped his mouth. He looked down at me, sprawled on the ground, shook his head, and said, 'Looks like you're going to need a lot more training.'"

"A lot?"

"Oh yes. So much training that by the time we finished putting down the rebellion and Colin's company was moving on, I went with them. I couldn't imagine training with anyone else. I still can't."

We had a lot to do, if we were going to find Wisgarth's killer, and if that day was any indication of what the future held, we would have no time to do it. Wisgarth's holdings were apparently more strategic than I'd realized, because suitors came out of the woodwork. These were, by and large, older than the first set, ranging from only a decade my junior to several decades my senior, all of them far more *serious* in their demeanor. Most of them were widowers, while a couple of them struck me as being willing to *become* widowers if the right opportunity appeared. Apparently, by law, I was required to entertain these offers, even knowing what it entailed.

One of them even made his wife deliver his suit. She was my age, though she looked older, broken. This one came to us after I had hired Darialth, who clued me in on what was going on. I brought the woman inside and took her hand.

"You don't have anything to fear from me," I told her.

She patted me, as if she were the one comforting me. "He'll be rid of me one way or another. If it's not you, well, he'd probably prefer someone younger and prettier, anyway."

What is it about people that makes them so awful? It's not power that does it, is it? No, it's something inside that just waits, waits for its opportunity. Power just multiplies the opportunities. I'm not immune. I wonder, sometimes, how often I've been awful to people, without even knowing.

That first week was so hectic, I get it mixed up in my head. Let's see. Day 1: paperwork, funeral, more paperwork, suitors. Day 2: more paperwork, more suitors, get permanently barred from the best restaurant in Amisara. Day 3: Darialth starts work, even more suitors. Lunch and brunch and dinner and tea, and we still had to defer two. Did I mention more paperwork? Because what would we do without paperwork? Day 4: Darialth has my schedule booked through the end of the week. She moves into the footman's room, because invitations are arriving at all hours of the day and night. She says she's never seen anything like it. (Also, more paperwork.) Day 5: well, let's talk about it.

On the fifth day, I was finally unable to convince one of my suitors that a restaurant would be appropriate. No, the only thing that would do was for me to come to see what he was *certain* would be my new home. And by insane Amisaran law, I could not refuse.

His name was Jon Lord Torsbad, and he'd been married five times in the last three years. Women just seemed to find him irresistible, so irresistible that they could overlook his many flaws, like his arrogant, domineering attitude, his misogyny, or his astronomical marital death rate. I couldn't see it, myself.

He didn't bother greeting us at the door. Instead, we were brought directly to the dining room, where Karos and I were seated separately—I to the left of the head of the ostentatiously large table, and Karos on the opposite side, further down.

Two of what I assumed were Torsbad's daughters or hired stand-ins bracketed Karos, fawning ineffectually. Lovely girls. I'm sure previous male chaperones had been suitably engaged with their long, mostly-bare legs and plunging necklines. Torsbad's chaperone took the seat to my left. She was an imposing woman who stood a full head and a half taller than me, and was likely twice my weight in muscle.

None of this was suspicious at all.

Torsbad swept in with maids in tow. Took his seat. He was nothing to speak of, an average man about my age, a bit flaccid around the middle. Starting to bald, and trying to make up for it with facial hair and a combover. When he deigned to look at me, all I saw was greed. The maids, even more revealingly garbed than the daughters, poured wine and distributed small plates of nondescript food. Torsbad raised his glass, speaking for the first time.

"To the lovely and elegant Lady Wisgarth, who has chosen to grace us with her presence this evening."

Everyone raised their glasses.

I turned, frowning at the far end of the table. "Karos, what have I said about your drinking? No, I will not accept an apology. No wine for you." I turned to Torsbad. "Punishing someone by making them do what they were supposed to do in the first place seems a bit weak, don't you think? Karos, you are to neither drink nor eat anything for the remainder of the day, or I shall have you whipped."

Anger flashed across Torsbad's face, almost instantly controlled. He nodded his approval. "It's important for the help to know their place. Fortunately, once you've joined my household, you'll be rid of him." He raised his glass again.

While I was confident that Karos would be able to defend me effectively if I were drugged—and I was certain my wine was drugged—I wasn't sure I wanted the hangover that would inevitably entail. I set my glass down. Torsbad's chaperone glowered her disapproval at me.

"You're being rude," she said. Her hand found my knee and squeezed.

Not gently.

I suppose this was where most of Torsbad's future dead wives made the mistake of drinking the drugged wine. I chose to break a finger instead, and then punched her in the throat.

The drug was interesting. It put its victim into a dazed, suggestible state that would last at least long enough for a hasty wedding. Or for a hasty confession to the constabulary. I'd have preferred to just stab him a lot, but Karos suggested that this might be misinterpreted. In general, killing one's male suitors was frowned upon in Amisara in a way that killing one's wife was not.

Even so, Karos and I spent several hours under interrogation, missing an appointment for evening drinks with yet another suitor. When we finally returned home, I told a distraught Darialth that as much as I enjoy ridding Amisara of evil, there's far too much of it, and I wouldn't accept another such invitation under any circumstances.

Day 6: Darialth quit.

I know what you're all thinking: stop talking about yourself, already, and tell us what happens in the novel. Alright, I'll tell you.

Talia stays three days in the small hut with the two men, who spend much of the time having sex. With each other, not with her. "Our wives would kill us," one of them says. Turns out, every year, these two spend a couple weeks together in this cabin deep in the woods on the edge of a lake (which, if we'll remember even though the author did not, only pages ago was in a meadow, not to be confused with rolling hills of heather), away from their families, while their wives take care of the farms and the kids. They hope it doesn't bother her, but they aren't giving up any of their time together. Oh, did I mention they untied her when they were convinced she wasn't trying to kill or rob them? That's okay, the author forgot to mention that, too. It's assumed, I guess, because she's tied up in one scene and not in the next, with no indication that the author (or the editor) remembered that not three sentences ago Talia was worried that the ropes would chafe her skin. When the men return home, their wives get their own vacations. One of the wives is friendly with the blacksmith. The other is friendly with the blacksmith's wife. While the men are happy to show her how to please a man, she doesn't get any practical experience.

When the sun comes back out, they give her directions to their village, where the men's wives take her in. She replenishes her supplies and sets off down the road toward Ashbury.

In the course of her adventures, she meets:

- A knight (Kira), who Talia unrealistically saves from bandits and who rewards Talia with her feminine charms;
- A rogue-with-a-heart-of-gold ("Eric") who rings Talia's bell like it's never been rung, but runs off with her purse;
- A barmaid (Elle), and a variety of patrons who are eager to provide Talia gainful employment since the local whore is out on maternity leave;
- A band of goblins who capture her for reasons unclear, but have to be convinced to have their way with her ("No, no, it's just, all this rope, and being helpless and all, well, it's very exciting, so if it wouldn't be any trouble, *I* certainly wouldn't mind..." and so on.);
- A traveling carnival, including musicians, clowns, contortionists and acrobats, a strong man, and an animal trainer who turns out to be quite skilled with a whip.

In her travels, she learns bits and pieces of magic. A healing spell here, a light spell there. A bit of shielding and telekinesis. Some of it she gets from scrolls and books she comes across, some is taught to her. The rogue (possibly not really named Eric) is a repeating character (of course), whom she repeatedly trusts, and who repeatedly disappoints her.

While the story clearly had Karos's interest, we didn't have a repeat of the first morning's adventure. Which was fine. It was fun the first time. I'm sure it would have just gotten progressively more frustrating over time.

Darialth, of course, was *scandalized* (titter), by our sleeping arrangements. It took several days for her to realize that we were telling the truth.

"So what do you do in there with Karos, if you're not, well...?"

"Reading."

"Reading?" Disbelief.

I nodded. How to broach this? "I know that in Amisara, some things are considered, well, unnatural. But the natural world is a lot wider and more diverse than—"

Darialth's eyes widened as I spoke, and her mouth opened in shock. I shouldn't have said anything, but now there was nothing but to go forward and hope to minimize the damage. And then...

Then, she leaned forward, bent her head down toward mine, and kissed me on the lips.

When I awoke, after the ambush, I wished I hadn't. The explosion had torn and burned my flesh, thrown me through the air, and tumbled me across the ground. There were broken bones, I discovered over time: cheekbone, several ribs, left femur and right ankle, just to make hobbling around extra fun.

"She's awake," someone said. "Go fetch the captain."

Captain Tomlinson had never warmed to me, no matter how much value I brought to the team. It just didn't do to have girls running around with swords; other girls might start getting ideas, and then where would we be? To tell the truth, I never warmed to him, either. At that moment, though, I didn't have the strength to have emotions about what it meant that he wanted to see me. Which was just as well, because he wasn't the one who walked through the door. (There was a door, I realized. I wasn't in a tent. I had no idea where I was.)

It was Wisgarth. *Captain* Wisgarth, now, apparently, since while the mage was sowing chaos and death, his crossbowmen were targeting officers with brutal precision. Wisgarth knelt beside my bedroll. (I was on the floor, I realized. More details were filtering through the haze of pain. The room was crowded with bedrolls, each containing a patient. The air was thick with the stench of rotting flesh and pus, and the hum of background noise started resolving into moans and cries of pain.)

"They tell me you'll live," he said.

"Not all it's cracked up to be." My mouth was dry, and someone dripped water from a cloth onto my lips.

It had been two days. Wisgarth filled in the salient details. Over half our company had been killed or wounded badly enough to take us out of action, and we were holed up in a village an hour's march from the ambush site. We had too many wounded to go further, so here we stayed, which was a problem, since the village had no healer, and Sohu had lost an arm, crippling his spell-casting ability. So people either recovered, or slowly and painfully died of their wounds. Wisgarth had sent runners looking for healers, but with the war now in full swing, it seemed all the healers had been sent to the front.

My wounds were debilitating, but not mortal. My long spell of unconsciousness seemed more connected to exhaustion than the injuries I'd sustained.

Three other companies had been attacked as we had been, Wisgarth had learned, and had taken far more casualties—no more than a ten percent survival rate—and the war had settled into what promised to be a long and grueling siege.

"We need to get you on your feet as quickly as possible," now-Captain Wisgarth said. "With your power, you can change the shape of the war."

My power? I couldn't light a candle. All I could do was grab what others constructed and make it not work the way they intended. That wasn't a lot of use against a hail of arrows or a cauldron-full of boiling oil. I tried explaining that to Wisgarth, but he didn't understand. His eyes went cold.

"That sounds a lot like insubordination."

"Sir?"

"You have your orders."

I cursed him roundly long after he left, and then I sent for Sohu.

Darialth was not the sort of woman that I'd imagine most Amisaran men coveted (that being: petite and willowy and desperate to please because being insufficiently pleasing wasn't a viable option). She was tall, strong of both body and will, though still soft around the middle in a way I had never been, with a clever wit and a biting tongue that didn't suffer fools.

For all that her family had enabled her to avoid men, she was an experienced kisser, and after what Karos and Wisgarth's smutty novel had wakened in me, I yearned to just fall into that embrace and lose myself there. Instead, I broke contact and pushed her away.

"Darialth. I can't..."

She closed the space between us. "Oh, I think you can. I think you want to. I think you know exactly what to do."

Things were too precarious to throw out of balance right now. "I don't sleep with my employees." Unless they're contracted specifically for that purpose. That seemed to be an unnecessary level of detail, under the circumstances.

That was something else I'd learned from Wisgarth. Though what his and Karos's relationship meant for that lesson was a question I didn't want to dig too deeply into.

"Oh," Darliath said. Her eyes narrowed. "I see."

"It's not.... Look, you're beautiful, yes, and under other circumstances..."

"'Other circumstances.' Fine," she said, lips pressed together. And she turned on her heel, sweeping up the stairs, and into her room.

Shit.

This is why I work alone. The obligations of a power relationship are just too confusing.

The only thing to do was to go to bed and hope it had all blown over by morning. I needed Darialth's calm expertise to get through this madness, and I valued her friendship, and I hoped I hadn't destroyed all of it with my incoherence.

Karos and I were undressing for bed when the door swung open. Darialth hesitated, then strode forward and stuck a folded sheet of paper in front of my face.

"What is it?" Of course, I knew what it was, but I didn't want to take it from her hands. That would make it official. As long as she was talking, I could talk her into staying.

She stepped closer. "My resignation. I quit."

I shifted to create more space. "You can't. I need you. I'm not—"

"I don't *need* your money. I took the job as an excuse to spend time with you. Now it's in the *way* of spending time with you. So I quit. So, are you coming quietly, or am I going to have to throw you over my shoulder and carry you to bed?"

"That, I'd like to see." Karos laughed.

Darialth jumped, as if she'd only just now realized that there was a naked man in the room. Her face reddened. "It seems I've misunderstood, and miscalculated badly."

How to explain? Fortunately, Karos spared me trouble.

"Gos has become less certain of herself in her dotage," he said. "She'll be weighing the pros and cons until you give up on her, so carrying her to bed might just be your only hope for success."

Darialth shrugged. "Oh. Okay." And with that, she ducked down, threw me over her shoulder, and marched me out of the room.

When we were done (no, this isn't Wisgarth's novel, so I won't go into details, except that I cried afterward, and I don't want to talk about that either), I told Darialth that I needed to go back to read to Karos. Reading together had somehow broken through the walls that had existed between us since we'd first met, so many years ago, and I wasn't willing to risk that.

"Reading," she said. Still skeptical.

"Come with. It's a big enough bed." Wisgarth's tailor must have made the sheets, because the mattress itself had to have been custom built. Wisgarth, Karos had told me, was compensating for decades of sleeping on a bedroll.

Karos was still awake, sitting up in bed going over accounts. He smiled when we came in (was it relief on his face?), setting aside his papers and shifting to make space.

Darialth: "This feels weird."

Me: "Everything in this whole country is weird."

I settled in the bed between Karos and Darialth, propped up against the pillows, and reached for the book. I gave a brief summary of what had come before (Talia sets off to find her fortune, gets sidetracked over and over, meets lots of interesting people—I didn't mention that she sleeps with them all; let the next sex scene surprise her.) And then I started to read.

197

The first thing I needed to do was figure out how to make myself see the magic threads again. The first time, I was drugged; the second was after a concussion. Neither of those seemed like good options for a long-term strategy. But I was pretty sure that I understood something unknown to most mages: the basic mechanics of traditional spellcraft. The incantation serves to pull the appropriately colored strands into the correct place in front of the caster for the rote hand motions to be generally successful in weaving them into the pattern needed to affect the spell.

Sohu only had one hand, now, so of course, his spells were failing—half the weaving would be left undone. But the incantation should still bring up the threads. And if I could see them, I could use them.

We worked for hours the first day, and only at the end of the day, when I'd become too exhausted to focus right, did I catch a glimpse of them. But in my excitement, I couldn't repeat the experience. The following day, we tried again, with somewhat better results. On the third day, I was able to see them consistently. I asked Sohu to show me the gestures that accompanied his healing spell. We practiced for an hour before Sohu proclaimed it "close enough."

We rearranged our positions so that I could sit in a chair, with Sohu kneeling behind me. He'd cast the incantation, and I would be his hands. We tested it on my broken leg. Then on my broken ankle.

I stood up, finally mobile, though not yet out of pain. But my ribs and face could wait. Sohu was grinning. I grinned back through the pain.

"Let's go save some lives."

Storytime: Against all odds, Talia finally makes it to Ashbury. There had been a tearful goodbye orgy; the carnival would not be crossing into the city limits. Some sort of scandal a few years back had resulted in them being banned from the city, so the carnival would continue on to the next town before setting up.

Darialth's fingers wandered my body, and her own, as I read the orgy scene, teasing me into arousal. Karos managed his own arousal without assistance.

Talia enters Ashbury alone and wanders the streets for a while. She's never seen so many people! It's exciting! It's overwhelming! The author used exclamation points liberally to make sure we understand just how exciting it is!

Darialth's head disappeared under the covers, following her fingers. I don't think she was as invested in the plot as Karos and I were. And I can't say that I minded. Her tongue was experienced in more than kissing.

Eventually, Talia ends up in an inn with a bowl of stew, a mug of ale, and, when it comes time to pay for her meal and an evening's lodgings, an unexpectedly empty purse. The barmaid starts raising a fuss, something about calling the city guard, when some coins drop on the table. The barmaid glances up, blanches, pockets the coins, and leaves without another word.

The person who'd covered Talia's tab shifts a chair around and straddles it, leaning forward over the table. "This is where you say, 'Thank you,' and introduce yourself. Unless maybe introductions haven't been invented yet wherever you're from? Here, I'll start. My name is Maris Go—"

"What the fuck am I doing in this book?"

Darialth's head popped up from under the covers between my legs. Her eyes were wide.

"Wait. You're *that* Maris? Maris *Goselin*? The Maris Goselin who called down the sun? Who defeated the False Duke of Ashbury? Who..." She suddenly realized that she still had three fingers inside me, and pulled them out abruptly.

"Put those back," I snapped.

She fumbled dangerously until I told her to stop. Seems she was literally terrified of me. Karos was no help. Just kept chuckling. "Your reputation precedes you."

"Shut up."

"I didn't think you were real. I mean, the you in the stories."

"What stories?" It's hard to sound menacing when you're on your back and a gorgeous woman is looking up at you from between your thighs, but I did my best. Karos's laughter persisted in being unhelpful.

She pointed at the novel with glistening fingers. "There's a whole subgenre? I mean, the character isn't *always* named Maris, but it's pretty clear who she's meant to be. They're very popular with a certain demographic in Amisara."

"Colin has a whole bookcase dedicated to Maris Goselin novels," Karos managed to say, between giggles. "I assumed this was one of them."

"You didn't think to mention this?"

"And ruin this moment?"

"The woman in my bed is afraid to touch me. I think the moment is officially ruined."

"I'm not afraid."

"Yeah? Prove it." But there was no salvaging the moment. Not Darialth's fault; if anything, once the initial shock subsided, she'd become even more eager. I just couldn't relax enough to enjoy it.

In the meantime, Karos had been reading ahead. Out loud. Which did *not* help with the relaxation bit. Novel-Maris, by the physical description, was me about ten years ago. She doesn't have to work hard to extract the guileless Talia's purpose in coming to Ashbury.

"Problem with that," she tells Talia, "is that Ellinon died two years ago." Talia looks stricken, when she should have looked relieved, given how Ellinon treated his apprentices. No wonder one of them stuck a knife between his ribs. Novel-Maris makes the same comment.

Would it surprise you to find out that novel-Maris and Talia end up in bed? It didn't surprise me. What *did* surprise me was just how accurately the author described my body, and how I explore the body of a new lover.

Who *wrote* this thing?

Turns out there were literally dozens of people writing Maris Goselin books. Thrillers, adventure, romance, mystery, true-detective, horror, and, yes, erotica. There was even a genre called NPF—Natural Philosophical Fiction—which involved imaginary Maris Goselins in the far future where normal, everyday objects possessed powers properly reserved for magic—horseless carriages and self-opening doors and such. Apparently my own narratives were also highly popular, though I don't recall ever receiving a royalty payment from any Amisaran publishers. I'd have to have a talk with my agent.

But before that, we had a mystery to solve, and suitors to dispose of (and quite a bit more, though I didn't know it yet.)

I slept fitfully, nestled between Karos and Darliath, too angry and frustrated to get any real rest. The night was interminable, and yet ended too soon. When light began to filter through the curtains, I crawled out over Darialth, not wanting to wake Karos, who'd feel compelled to start the kettle for tea. I put on Wisgarth's robe and shoved my feet into his oversized slippers and made my way downstairs to the kitchens.

Bright light shone through the window. It had snowed overnight, and everything was covered in a thick blanket of white. Winter had come early to Amisara.

Wisgarth had five lovers in Amisara, not counting Karos or the Archfather, who seemed only to call on him now when he needed a covert favor. These were the same men who'd skipped the funeral. He had spent the evening with one of them—Karos didn't know which—the night he fell ill. It seemed reasonable to start the investigation there.

Darialth had sent invitations to them all to meet for a "private memorial," which we'd set for a cautiously distant date. We received four responses, all positive. I wasn't properly sure what we'd do for that, but that was a fear to be faced at a later date. We decided to pay an unannounced visit on the gentleman who failed to respond.

That meant trudging through a foot of snow, in skirts. If I hadn't already hated Amisara, I would have started. Karos was right, though, that my mourning dress was roomy enough to hide my leather armor. If anyone noticed anything, they'd likely assume it was a corset. Karos wore armor as well, and a sword: half footman, half bodyguard.

Dragging the dress through the snow proved impractical, so I girded it about my loins. The wind blew unpleasantly against my bare legs. We'd gone far enough that it didn't make sense to go back for trousers. Darialth grinned at me and followed my example. She had insisted on joining the expedition, despite the danger. Or perhaps because of it. But she'd been smart enough to wear leggings beneath her skirt.

His name was Tomás Tomič, and he didn't have a noble title. He lived in a "modest" house only slightly larger than Wisgarth's, with his wife and their three children. He was, Darialth told me, the publisher and senior editor of one of the two major broadsheets in the city, the one that wasn't in the pocket of the government. *The Timely Courante* published daily, and while a significant portion of it was dedicated to gossip about the rich and powerful, it also was known to take the government to task for abuses, even coming perilously close to advocating for women's financial independence.

"Their offices have been raided on several occasions," Karos said.

"What's been odd," Darialth added, "is that coverage of Lord and Lady Wisgarth has been so sparse. I'd have thought your... unique... handling of your suitors would have sustained a special issue dedicated to your antics."

"I have ice in my boots," I growled. "Are we there yet?"

The door was answered by one of the children, a boy of ten or eleven. He looked us over and then ran off, shouting, "Papa, there are some people here to see you!"

He left the door wide open. It seemed bad form to let all the heat out, so we entered and closed the door behind us.

I had divested myself of boots and was trying to break the crusted snow off my socks when the boy reappeared, Tomás on his heels. Tomás stared at my bare legs for a moment.

"This is all very irregular, ma'am. Can I ask—" His voice choked off when he noticed Karos. "Ben, get your sisters and mother and take them upstairs. No questions, please."

Ben seemed about to argue, but changed his mind and ran off. Maybe it was the look on my face, or Karos's.

Tomás invited us into the drawing room, where a fire blazed cheerfully. A single lamp was lit in the room, illuminating a desk, which boasted of several stacks of papers. Additional light came through the window. "I was just reviewing tomorrow's edition." He sighed. "I don't suppose I'll be making deadline."

Karos closed the curtains. Whatever happened here was best not witnessed. Tomás swallowed nervously as Karos drew his blade.

"It's dark in here," I said. "Maybe you could light the other lamps?"

"What? Oh, yes, yes, of course." He fetched a box of matches from his desk. "I know I don't have much right to ask favors, but can we leave my family out of this? We could go somewhere? Private? I promise I won't resist."

He struck the match, and I extinguished it with a subtle wave of my hand.

"Light them without matches, please."

Karos stepped forward and placed the tip of his sword against Tomás' throat.

"I don't understand." The charred match shook in his hand.

"It should be obvious," Karos said, backing Tomás up against a bookcase. "You murdered my husband. I want to know why." His face was hard, and he gripped his sword so fiercely that the veins and tendons of his hand protruded. I was afraid he was going to simply gut the man right then and there.

Abruptly, Karos was lifted off his feet and thrown down to the floor. Nobody else could see, but bands of power wrapped around him, trapping his arms and legs. He cried out, and the bands covered his mouth, gagging him.

I knew this magic. I'd know that signature anywhere. I turned my face toward the woman at the bottom of the stairs. Threads of power twisted around her fingers, extending to Karos' motionless form.

"I don't think we've met," I said to Tomás. "Care to introduce us?"

"This... this is my wife, Ellinor. Ellinor, this is Lady Wisgarth, I think you may—"

"Shut up!" the woman snarled, and Tomás complied. She glared at me. "Why did you have to come here? Why couldn't you just leave things be? Isn't one death bad enough? Does it have to be all of us?"

I took a step toward Ellinor. "Perhaps my introduction was a little misleading. I prefer my maiden name, Maris Goselin. Perhaps you've heard of me?"

Her eyes widened and she made a valiant attempt to try to redirect her spell at me, but I already owned it, entangling her arms in her own magic and bringing her to her knees.

"Much better," I said.

Darialth waved at Karos, who still writhed on the floor. "She's still got him."

I shook my head. "No. I've got him, because he's too angry right now to trust not to start killing people."

I was moving Ellinor to a chair when I caught movement out of the corner of my eye. I was throwing my knife before I knew I'd drawn it, and it was only as the blade was leaving my hand that I realized what my target was.

Heart in my throat, I lunged forward, twitching my fingers against the haft as it slipped out of my grasp. It wasn't enough to miss the boy completely, but spoiled the throw enough to hit his chest more-or-less flat and drop to the floor as he charged me.

Ben swung at my arm with a kitchen knife, cutting across my wrist, and then slashed across my belly. I'd need to thank Karos later for designing the dress for this contingency. Fortunately, Ben's swings were wild, leaving him wide open to a foot planted in his solar plexus. He went down hard and the knife skittered across the floor. Darialth pounced on him, pinning his arms behind his back before he could recover enough to struggle.

I sank to my knees and burst into tears.

Trauma is an unpredictable mistress. The things people have done to you raise their heads when you least expect. Maybe they throw you into a rage, maybe into the bottom of a bottle. The things you've done to other people, on the other hand? That's a whole different level of inescapable. And it comes back to hit you at the most unexpected times.

I know what happened next thanks to Darialth.

My attempt to stop my own knife disrupted my control over the binding spell. Ellinor, who'd been suspended in the air en route to the chair I was going to interrogate her in, dropped suddenly, pitching face-forward onto the floor. She started picking herself up using that chair for support. Karos, recovering with the reflexes of an old soldier as soon as the spell fell away, grabbed his sword as he rolled to his feet and launched himself at Ellinor. With a cry of rage and frustration, he stabbed downward, piercing the chair cushion and punching through the wooden slats below, right in front of her face and between her hands.

"Don't fucking move," he growled.

And then he turned his back on her, knelt in front of me, and pulled me into an embrace.

"It's okay," he said. "The boy's fine, you didn't hurt him. You didn't hurt him." Over and over as he gently rocked me. I felt so stupid, but I just couldn't stop.

By the time I'd gotten control of myself, Tomás had sent Ben back upstairs to take care of his sisters, and Ellinor had separated the sword and the chair—taking extreme care to be entirely non-threatening with it—and was healing the chair, so none of us would have to sit on the floor. Everybody politely ignored my breakdown, for which I was grateful. Tomás looked like he'd also had a good cry while I was otherwise distracted.

A brief summary of Tomás and Ellinor's story: they'd known each other since they were young, the best of friends, and when the pressure came for him to "man up" and get married, Ellinor offered. In love but not in lust. Karos said something snide about her being his skirt, and I hushed him, but Ellinor nodded. He was a good and loving father to all the children, not just the one he was personally responsible for.

"If nobody was betraying anyone, why did you murder Colin?" I asked.

"I didn't mean to!" Ellinor looked like she'd already exhausted her tears. "*He* made me do it."

"Made *us*," Tomás corrected. "We're both responsible. But you have to understand. He was going to destroy us, and, and send our children to the mines. And I accept our guilt. Just... protect the children when we're gone."

"What mines?"

Tomás and Ellinor stared at me. Darialth answered.

"*Your* mines, Lady Wisgarth."

Karos covered his mouth. "Colin, what did you do?"

And I thought back to Wisgarth's comment, so long ago. *Good men, but not* good *men.*

And also: *You'll fit right in.*

"Next question: who is 'he'?"

Which turned out to be a stupid question that everyone answered in a sort of haphazard unison. The Archfather had visited with Tomás and Ellinor. Wisgarth was forgetting his proper loyalties and needed a reminder. The spell he gave Ellinor was supposed to make him sick, yes, but just enough to scare him back into line. Or at least, that's the line that the Archfather sold them.

"I've been dreading every day since we heard Colin died," she said. "Did I cast the spell wrong? Are we being set up? There are so many ways for us to disappear; it's just a matter of time before we become too much of a liability to let live."

"And that explains why *the Timely Courante* has been so tame lately." Darialth shook her head. "It's brilliant, in a sick way, taking out two threats in one move, and pinning the blame elsewhere."

Tomás put his head in his hands. "I've doomed us all."

I made some sort of unladylike noise that might have been a bitter laugh, if my nose wasn't still full of snot. "Please. Wisgarth was always the best strategist on the field. This is no exception."

The book on Wisgarth's bedside had been a clue; he'd left the book-mark on the page where I first appear. The only people who had been "in" on the scam of my alleged marriage had been Karos, and the woman who performed my part of the marriage ritual. She was a shape-shifter, and a self-styled "student of sentient nature." Which is to say, an aspiring writer. If I refused to take up my part, Karos could at least salvage the inheritance by finding and marrying this shapeshifter, simply by tracking down the author and offering to cut her in.

Which means, right after the fraught dinner date where Wisgarth had tried—and failed—to draw me into his scheme, oh, so many years ago, he'd hired the shapeshifter to come to Ashbury and study me well enough to fool the courts in Amisara. And the shapeshifter had done so by seducing me. I wondered if the name she'd given me was Talia. It was useless; I'd spent the months following the meeting with Wisgarth blind drunk, and remembered very little of it.

Of course, if Karos had just told me this straight off, I'd have just walked back out the door. Or, more likely, been even more petty, and simply gone to the courthouse and announced that Wisgarth had no legal heir. So we'd played this game, and if Wisgarth hadn't been murdered, I'd have quickly tired of it and told him to fuck right off with his inheritance, I was doing just fine, and plan B with "Talia" would have fallen into place once I left.

As for the property granted by the Archfather for his services, Wisgarth had visited it once, without Karos, and refused to talk about it. There was a monthly income statement and subsequent deposit into the accounts; other than that, Wisgarth exerted no administrative control. Who did? That was obvious.

The Archfather.

Turns out Wisgarth wasn't alone in working against the Archfather. He had built a network, which included Tomás and some of the other Amisaran power brokers, working diligently to sow political discontent while trying to identify the Archmother's location.

Darialth and her cousin were both involved in a different network, which moved in the underground music scene—or at least, what young people today call music.

The latter were ready to take to the streets in what they hoped would be massive protests; the former, having experienced war in some context or another, were more inclined to clandestine action.

On the other side were the Amisaran military, who ostensibly owed loyalty to both Arches, and might share sympathies with those who felt seven years' imprisonment was excessive for the crime of liking other girls, and the Kilted Skullcrackers, now under the direct control of the Archfather. Unlike the regular military, my old company would not hesitate to cut down anyone the Archfather pointed them at.

The focus of previous protests was the palace, where the Archmother was assumed to be held in a tower or dungeon or something. Those protests had been small, and had been graciously permitted to continue until they lost momentum and disbanded naturally. It was rumored that the leaders of those protests were picked up later and sent to the mines, though there was always a paper trail that pointed to a sudden move to Ashbury to care for an ailing aunt or whatnot.

I felt certain that the Archmother was nowhere near the palace.

"If your group can muster a sufficiently strong team to ride to the mines," Darialth offered, "we can create a distraction that they can't ignore at the palace."

"It'll be dangerous," I said. "If the protest is big enough to appear a threat, they'll just slaughter you. What you'll need to do is spread the secret that you're there as a distraction while another group works to free the Archmother."

Tomás shook his head. "You don't think the Archfather has ears amongst them? Young people are too naive, too trusting—"

"I'm counting on it. Darialth, timing will be everything. We need enough time to get far enough ahead that they can't catch us when they give chase, but not so much time that the spies won't hear the news before the massacre starts. Err on the side of safety, because I need you alive. And Tomás, don't be so sure about your own ranks."

Karos nodded. "I know who'll be riding with us."

I looked at Darialth, who nodded.

"I understand," she said.

Good.

The first magic I learned was how to perform Sohu's healing spells. At first, I used him for the incantation, until I understood what threads were used in what order, and then by myself, plucking the strands from wherever they were, without relying on an incantation to pull them into an expected location and order. Once I understood that, I started learning how to perform Sohu's healing spells one-handed. The sooner I could figure that out and teach it to Sohu, the sooner I could leave the healing to him and move on to actually learning *useful* spells.

You know, the kind of spells that turned enemies into non-combatants.

Sohu was delighted to discover that his contract wouldn't be terminated. I, on the other hand, discovered a whole new world of frustration. Without examples to work from, I was weaving blind.

Over time, I came to recognize that each color thread represented what I eventually chose to call a "Becoming," although I'm sure that's an inadequate metaphor. Each represented potential energy generated by the interactions of things in the world, energy that could be actualized. They included Becoming Well, Becoming Cold, Becoming Hot, Becoming Ill, Becoming Light, Becoming Fast, Becoming Liquid, and so on. Casting a spell was taking a selection of these Becomings and weaving them in a way that enhanced the properties of some while reducing the properties of others. For a spell to treat fever due to an influenza, one needed a strand of Becoming Ill (a sickly yellow-green color), and then other color strands that could stand as its opposite, twisted around the Becoming-Ill strand and obscuring it, neutralizing it. To make someone sick, you'd do the opposite.

Ordinary spellcasting tends to be overly complex and highly inefficient, consuming much more power than needed (and by extension, requiring more of the caster's strength to control), and producing a much weaker effect. In general, I had little interest in teaching my potential enemies to become more effective at killing me. And let's face it, mages don't really need more power. They cause enough problems as it is.

Once I stopped being *entirely* self-absorbed—which is to say, years after I had left the Kilted Skullcrackers and the soldiering life behind—

I did realize the importance of enabling people like Sohu, whose skills were erased by their disabilities. I wrote a series of manuals, including *The Right Hand Path: A One-Handed Guide, Vol. I*, etc. (and subsequently, also *The Left Hand Path*), providing one-handed versions of common useful spells—healing, illumination, protection, and so on. All under a pseudonym, of course. The last thing I wanted was people showing up on my doorstep wanting to learn how to convert their flesh-melting spell to a one-handed version. I suppose I shouldn't have been surprised that two-handed mages were just as eager for each edition. Turns out two-handed mages aren't keen on letting go of the reins of their horse to cast a protection spell, or lay down their shield in battle to heal their dying friends.

That was later, though, after I'd left the company and returned to Ashbury. The royalties provided me a solid basic income until black market copies overtook the market.

In my time with the company, I concentrated on the nastier powers. I convinced a combat mage to show me how to throw fireballs. It was wildly inefficient, half of the power dissipating in transit, and then much of the rest spent without ever touching a target. A strong fireball could take out maybe a dozen targets. It was far more efficient to focus the Becoming Hot more narrowly. Helmets, for instance, were good. I could take out twenty or thirty men who weren't able to get out of their headgear in time, and leave the rest of the enemy without head protection for the coming battle. That was fun. More fun was when I could narrow the effects to a smaller set of targets, and affect all of their armor, not just their helmets. When I did that, none of them survived. That was my favorite.

Until I discovered how to exploit Becoming Dead.

By the time the plans were set, the weather had thankfully changed again. The snow had melted under a bright sun, leaving the roads muddy but passable. We left in the night, heading north toward Wisgarth's/my/the Archfather's holdings. It was five hours ride before the road ended, turning into a narrow, winding path up the side of the mountain. The horses would be a liability now, and besides, they needed the rest.

So did my ass. I ride so infrequently, I somehow manage to forget just how painful it is. Every time. It doesn't get easier with age.

As expected, plans for the protest leaked, and both the regular military and a strong contingent of the Kilted Skullcrackers had been deployed. Right about now, Darialth and her team would be spreading the rumor that the protest was just a diversion while a team frees the Archmother from the infamous totally secret mines. Hopefully before the troops moved in on the protestors and the slaughter began.

Our company was small, designed to be agile, inconspicuous, and dangerous. Karos had selected a handful of soldiers whom he trusted, as well as Ellinor, whom he didn't want to let out of his sight. Darialth's cousin Rofexho was eager for more direct action, and after a brief argument, I agreed to bring him along. It was a mistake, I was certain; either he'd be useless, in which case he'd feel like I'd sidelined him from glory and make things difficult for me with Darialth, or he'd get himself killed (and make things difficult for me with Darialth). But refusing to bring him would make things difficult for me with Darialth, so my options were limited.

Tomás was staying behind, printing manifestos, lists of demands, collections of pithy chants and lyrics to resistance songs of his own composition. If there'd been more time, I'd have pointed out that songs are more memorable when they have a consistent rhyme and meter, but, hey, it wasn't *my* revolution. All I wanted to do was avenge Wisgarth's murder and solve my inheritance problems so I could go back home to Ashbury, where I belonged. Why did that have to be so complicated?

There were four guards at the entrance to the mines. Two held crossbows, which they aimed at Karos and Ellinor, both of whom, I suppose, looked more dangerous than I did. Karos and Wisgarth's tailor had done a masterful job redesigning the mourning dress for this expedition; in addition to hiding armor and protective leather trousers beneath its billowing—what's the word for the part of the dress that billows? that part—it also provided easy access to several hidden blades of varying lengths and other tools of the trade. I just didn't *look* dangerous. I ignored the crossbows and the drawn steel and stepped forward to present my papers.

"Lady... Wisgarth?" The guard seemed confused.

"Lady Maris Wisgarth, yes." I'd almost given my real name, but then I remembered all the ridiculous novels. I was supposed to be a grieving widow, not a terrifyingly powerful, sex-crazed mage. "I've come to inspect my holdings."

"I don't think that would be possible, ma'am."

"These lands were granted to my husband by the Archfather, is that not correct? No, you don't need to guess, we have notarized copies of the documents here. Karos?" Karos produced the documents with his customary efficiency.

The next line was hard to say with a straight face. "With Lord Wisgarth's untimely demise, the Archfather expects me to select a husband who can faithfully administer the trust which he has bestowed my family." I tapped the guard on the forehead with my index finger. "I do not take this commission lightly, young man."

There are *some* benefits to age. The guard blinked, glanced at the guard to his left, and then nodded. "Yes 'm. Of course." He dropped his gaze. "I'm sorry for your loss, ma'am."

"Thank you."

He stopped at the door, a thick iron door built into the rock face, barred and locked. "Are you sure, ma'am? It's not for the faint of heart."

"Son, I've survived one of the Duchess of Ashbury's tea parties."

He laughed nervously, and reached for his key ring.

So it turns out, Novel-Maris didn't actually sleep with Talia that night. Novel-Maris paid for Talia's room and board for a week to give her a chance to get her feet back under her, and went her way, leaving Talia all alone in a big city, and the sex scene was Talia's fantasy. Which actually sounds like something I might have done at the time: help someone out when they were in trouble, with no expectation of anything in return. I'd actually found my way to a more-or-less good place. I was secure, and I was happy (when ghosts of my past weren't screwing with me), and I was loved in a way I scarcely believed possible. And I honored the debts I could never hope to pay by paying debts I didn't owe.

After all she's been through, Novel-Talia becomes obsessed with Novel-Maris, and begins researching her. Real-Talia, of course, had been paid by Wisgarth to do just that, and even though I didn't remember the events in the inn, the more I read, the more I was starting to feel well and thoroughly played.

Talia discovers where Novel-Maris lives and watches her comings and goings. One evening, a couple comes to visit. By the description it's Edwin and Laura. My mouth was suddenly dry, and I needed a sip of wine.

"Keep reading," Darialth said. "This sounds like it's about to get interesting."

She had no idea.

As evening turns to night, Novel-Maris escorts her guests to her back yard, where they undress and climb into a small pool of water, which some magic keeps hot and bubbling, yet not boiling. Talia climbs a tree to get a closer look at what's going on (do I need to tell you what's going on?), and suddenly, with a loud crack, the branch breaks.

With a shriek of terror, Talia drops...

"Fuck! I remember this!"

"What?"

"She called herself 'Lydia'. She fell right into the hot tub. She probably would have broken her neck if I hadn't... well, I threw a spell up to keep the branch from killing anyone, and she got caught in it."

I skimmed ahead on the page.

Darialth kissed my nose. "That accurate, huh? Go on, read it to us. Oh, come on. It's not like we're not going to read it anyway."

Talia/Lydia flounders in the water, her clothes tangled in the branch. She's drowning. Oak, it turns out, is *really heavy*. Edwin, being Edwin, is trying to single-handedly lift half-a-ton of oak. Novel-Maris, being me, frees Talia by dissolving her clothes. (I didn't actually do that; I ripped them to shreds no larger than a finger-length. I should have dissolved them; it would have saved me hours of cleanup.)

"This isn't another one of those Cheom-sent demons, is it?" Edwin says, as he eyes the beauty that climbs out of water.

"No such luck," Novel-Maris says. "Laura, Edwin, this is Talia. She's new in town, and, what, got lost on the way to the pub?"

"No," Talia says, her eyes falling to Novel-Maris's breasts. "I just got lonely."

Novel-Maris doesn't push Talia away as she closes the space between them. "Do you make a habit of dropping into people's hot tubs every time you want to have sex?"

"Hot tubs? No." Talia's fingers follow the line of Novel-Maris's hip, along the crease of her thigh, and find a sensitive spot. "No, that's a new one even for me. But really, it's all about getting in the door."

The mines were well guarded, both magically and physically. Archers held the narrow pass that was the only approach—concealed behind narrow crevices within the rock face itself, only the most experienced of attackers would recognize the danger before being subjected to a hail of arrows. And that was only the most obvious of the defenses. Karos had been assessing since before we'd arrived; a well-supplied force of a few dozen could hold off an army of thousands for a week, at least. Plenty of time for reinforcements to arrive.

The guard said only I could enter the mines. But my manservant, Karos! Surely a Lady cannot be stripped of her closest servant. *Who will carry my bags?*

Really, it's all about getting in the door.

The best thing I can say about the mines is that they were dismal. The guard, who claimed his name was Corporal Semphor Semphorsen, wouldn't allow Karos past the guard's station and shook his head when I tried to insist.

"It's not allowed, ma'am."

"Surely you can make an exception, Semphor, dear." I made a point of touching him gently every time I spoke to him, in the non-threatening way of a kindly aunt: a squeeze of the hand, a pat on the shoulder, that sort of thing.

He hung his head. "Can't, mum. There's not much more down you can go in Amisara than to be guarding the mines, except to be working them."

"Oh, dear. Well, there's nothing to be done about it, then. Never you worry, I'll put in a good word with your superiors. We'll have you out of here in no time."

It was better to leave Karos in the guard station, anyway. He'd be well positioned to intervene if things went sideways, and hopefully get our companions out of the killing field before the killing started. We'd even worked up an unnecessary bad knee scenario to give us an excuse to leave him in this position.

Two hard-faced guards with crossbows escorted us as Corporal Semphorsen gave me the tour. Semphorsen was demonstrably uncomfortable with their presence. We started with the top level—the guard's barracks, the mess, the kitchens, various storerooms. Semphorsen was clearly stalling, perhaps hoping to wear the old lady out before she insisted on seeing the mines themselves. That was fine by me. The more time we spent, the more space there would be between the Archfather's troops and the protestors in the city before things got ugly.

"These conditions are appalling, Semphor. The people defending our realm deserve so much more."

"It's not that bad, mum. If you've never been on the front lines in the rainy season, you wouldn't understand."

Of course I understood. Still. "At least you'd have fresh air. When was the last time the maid was in?" I didn't have a white glove, but there was enough grime on the bed frames for that to be unnecessary.

Eventually, when we started revisiting rooms, I had to intervene. Reluctantly, Semphorsen led me to a large chamber containing a platform suspended over a deep pit. Another two guards manned the capstan that raised and lowered the platform. As we climbed aboard the platform, another guard ran into the chamber and whispered something to one of the crossbow-bearers.

They looked at each other and raised their crossbows.

"What are you doing?" Corporal Semphorsen stepped between me and the crossbows.

"Step aside, Semphorsen. Got word from the Archfather. Bitch isn't leaving."

"There's got to be a mistake, she's just an old lady." Arms raised, Semphorsen took a single step forward.

A crossbow bolt punched through Semphorsen's chest and he staggered back against me. I used his weight to spin me out of the trajectory of the second bolt, and killed those guards before they could either reload or draw their blades. The runner had time to draw, but it didn't help him. The two guards manning the capstan raised their hands; their swords and spears were leaning against the far wall. I told them to lie down on their bellies, facing away from me, with their hands on their heads.

Semphorsen hadn't bled out yet, but he wasn't looking good.

"Hush, dear, I've got you." I wrapped him in some healing to staunch the immediate bleeding. While the spell kept his remaining blood inside the artery the bolt had nicked, I'd need to remove the bolt itself before affecting a more permanent cure. And that meant cutting him out of his armor first.

He struggled when he saw the knife, stained with the blood of the guards I'd put down.

"Hold still, Corporal," I snapped, channeling Wisgarth. Eyes wide, he did.

Karos and the others arrived while I was pushing the bolt out Semphorsen's back. They quickly bound the two remaining guards.

"Archfather's troops are climbing the hill," Karos said, kneeling beside me. "What's with this one?"

"Stepped in front of a crossbow for me, seems only fair to put him back together. The guards watching the gate?"

Karos glanced around. "Neutralized. About the same mortality rate as yours, assuming this lad lives."

"He'll live."

"I will?"

I caught myself before I said, "I promise." The day wasn't done yet. I couldn't assess our own team until I was done with Semphorsen's injuries. "Any casualties on our side?"

"Superficial, except for Tweeds, but Ellinor was able to patch him up."

"Good. Ellinor, take the troops and guard the gates. We only need to hold them a couple of hours. Karos, use these two guards to run the lift. Semphorsen'll take me downstairs."

Karos glanced at Ellinor. "Use Rohexo. I'd be more use at the gate." By which he meant, he'd be more use countering Ellinor if she turned on us.

"Rohexo's a puppy. He isn't brutal enough to put those two down if they decide not play nice. I have faith in your ability to cause pain." Also, if Ellinor *did* turn on us, she'd kill Karos first, and I needed him alive.

The bolt came free in a gush of blood, and for a few moments I didn't have the time to deal with Karos or the others. When Semphorsen was healed, Ellinor and the others were gone, and Karos had gotten the two guards hooked up to the capstan with their hands still bound behind their backs. I looked back at Karos.

"Take us down."

I've seen a lot of bad things in my life. I mean, I've seen—and done—worse than what I saw in the mines. But the sense of grueling hopelessness was palpable. The people were emaciated, dressed in tattered rags, chipping feebly at the walls with picks, their hands and feet shackled together. They didn't seem to be mining for anything in particular; there was no ore or coal, and no buckets, nothing to collect what was found.

When we drew near, the miners would lay down their tools and lie face down on top of them. They were of all ages, from children to people well beyond my years, though those were noticeably scarcer. It didn't seem the sort of existence that promoted longevity.

"How many are there?"

Semphorsen swallowed. "On the books, mum? Fourteen thousand two hundred ninety-one. Alive? Less than a thousand. Nobody's keeping track of that."

"I came here to free one person."

"The Archmother."

"Yes."

"You can't help her. It's not chains that bind her."

And I suppose he was right. But not for the reasons he thought.

When I was still experimenting with such things, I'd discovered that, while all spells needed to contain their opposite to be at all efficient, truly terrifying things happened when you entangled those opposite forces in significant-but-equal measures. For example, Becoming Alive threads, a sort of shimmery silver color, were good for aiding childbirth and conception and increasing crop yield and so on. Those spells of necessity included some measure of Becoming Dead (a dull grey that leaves its shadow on any threads it touches), because death and birth are opposites and parts of a cycle in which one side or the other is in ascendance. But if you hold those forces in a static, unchanging equilibrium?

Well, then you get what we had here.

The Archmother had been too powerful for the Archfather to control, so he'd killed her. (To be precise, Wisgarth had killed her.) Once she was safely dead, the Archfather constructed an elaborate web of power that controlled her body, her actions, her words—even, to some extent, her thoughts. Then he brought her back to life. But by then she'd been dead too long, and Becoming Dead had become an integral part of her essence.

Now, with enough perfume and makeup, and a wig, she could be trotted out once a year to make some pronouncements. And the rest of the time?

Well, here she was, dressed in the same tattered rags as every other prisoner, but without the shackles. Her skin was pale and grey, bloodless, and her head was shorn. Unlike me, no new growth was likely. Her fingernails were cracked and torn, or gone, and she stank of meat just turning to rot.

The second-most disturbing thing about her was the fact that she didn't breathe.

The most disturbing thing? When I addressed her and told her it was time to leave, she looked at me with despair, inhaled, and said, "I can't. I have to dig."

"See what I mean?" Semphorsen said.

"She does what the Archfather tells her?"

"Yes."

"And he comes down here personally to collect her when he needs her?"

"No, mum. He sends a guard to fetch her upstairs."

"So she'll respond to a guard in the Archfather's employ?"

"Yes'm. But... You don't mean...?"

"I don't recall you tendering your resignation."

"I suppose I'm already doomed." Semphorsen took a deep breath. Exhaled. "Archmother, you are to accompany the Lady Wisgarth to the surface."

The Archmother hissed at the name, but stopped scratching at the wall.

"The Archfather is coming," Semphorsen went on. "Lady Wisgarth will prepare you for his arrival. You are to follow her instructions, please."

The Archmother straightened to her full height and looked down at me with imperious contempt. "What does my loving husband want now?"

I ignored her, afraid that any wrong statement might trigger some failsafe in the Archfather's spells. Instead, I turned to Semphorsen. "Corporal, I assume you have keys to these shackles?" He nodded.

"Good. Free everyone and get them to the lift. Tell them to bring anything that can be used as a weapon."

Semphorsen smiled for the first time since I'd met him. "Yes'm!"

Ellinor hadn't turned on us. She and a small crew of archers were holding off the Archfather's troops. Dozens of dead and wounded littered the killing field, and the rest of the forces held back. Two of the Archfather's mages were trading potshots with Ellinor. Each of them individually was more than a match for her, but the mine's defenses protected her.

Of course, everything would change when the Archfather arrived. His carriage had been spotted approaching the mountain. In the further distance was the haze of dust kicked up by thousands of feet. From what I'd learned of the Archfather's abilities while Karos, Darialth, and Tomás planned today's actions, I was dubious about trying to take him on face-to-face, especially with his combat mages backing him up. What I could do was prevent large-scale bloodshed in advance of the final confrontation. Hopefully.

None of the miners had expected to get out of the mines alive. Armed with pickaxes and shovels, we offered them a chance at least to see the sun one last time. Most of them took that offer. Good thing it was a nice day. Around seven hundred miners filed out to face off against the Archfather's significantly larger and better-armed forces, gathered downhill just out of our archer's reach. The regular troops weren't as disrespectful to the miners as the mercenaries, but they weren't exactly respectful. The Kilted Skullcrackers, my old unit, shouted insults and obscene threats, while the regular troops simply called the miners criminals and traitors. On the mountainside, gravity gave our archers greater reach, protecting the miners, at least until more magical resources came to provide them cover.

So now it was my turn.

Karos and I worked our way to the front of the massed... well, I wouldn't go so far as to call them warriors. Ignoring the regular troops, I waved to the members of my old company.

"Hello, boys!" I called, my voice amplified through a simple spell. "It's me, Gos. I know, I know, it's been a few years, and I should have written. Maybe the new kids don't know me, but I'm sure there's a few old-timers left. Maybe you've heard stories?"

The Kilted Skullcrackers gradually fell into a nervous silence.

"Guess you have. Good. I'd have felt guilty if I didn't give you a chance. For old time's sake."

One of the men stepped forward. He was a hulking brute with scars crisscrossing his face, maybe in his mid-forties.

"Captain Hanson," Karos informed me. "You remember young Ariq?"

I did. He was a cute kid. Joined my last year. He was there when Wisgarth terminated my contract.

I was twenty years old, more or less. The Kilted Skullcrackers were the most sought-after and highly paid company of mercenaries in the north, maybe in the world. It had gotten to the point where wars were being lost or won in the bidding process—whichever side won our contract won the war. We rarely even got to fight, that last year. The enemy would simply surrender.

It left me grumpy and frustrated. All this power and no release for it.

Sometimes between contracts, Wisgarth would bring us to camp outside an unremarkable small town in eastern Icenia. There was someone he'd visit with there, spending a day, sometimes more. Whatever, he wanted to play house for a weekend or three, that was his business. I didn't care.

What pissed me off was that, while passes were given to small groups of men to go into town for a few hours, I didn't get one. I never got one. Everyone got a turn, but it was never *my* turn. One day, I decided to *make* it my turn. What was Wisgarth going to do, fire me?

I'd been in town for a few hours when Wisgarth found me. He was furious, angrier than I'd ever seen. Orders, insubordination, absent without leave. Blah, blah, whatever.

"Go on, fire me," I said. "You think I can't take a contract with someone else?"

"Just go back to camp, Gos. I'll explain it all later."

But it was too late. There was a girl in the street, maybe nine or ten years old, staring at me. We hadn't seen her approach.

"That's her, innit?" I can still remember her voice. Her accent.

"No," Wisgarth said. He was going to say more, but he didn't get a chance.

"Liar!" She pulled a knife and started to take a step toward me, and then fell on her face, her life-thread dangling between my fingers.

"Nita!" Wisgarth cried out and threw himself at her. It was too late; she was dead before she started to fall. I am nothing if not efficient. Cradling the girl's already-rotting body, Wisgarth looked up at me with tears in his eyes. "Get out of my sight."

It didn't make sense. "You have a daughter?" How could he have a daughter?

"*We* have a daughter, ever since you murdered her mother."

By this time, a crowd had gathered, including some of the men.

How was this my fault? It was *his* fault. He should have told me. I said as much.

"You're a murderous fucking bitch."

"I'm what you made me." Murderous bitch? I could empty this town, how'd he like that?

He held the girl to his chest. "I know. Go back to camp now. Gather your gear. Karos will pay you out. Be gone before I return. Because if I ever see you again, I'll kill you."

I was an hour on the road, with no destination in mind, just walking in any direction that counted as "away," when I put it all together, what Wisgarth had really been telling me. To say that the magnitude of what I had done, that day, and years earlier, when I killed Nita, who had always been kind to me, hit me that day would be a gross exaggeration. That would take many months of hard drinking. But that's where it started.

Ariq had seen me on my worst day. The day that changed how I approached my magic, and my life. I spent years in hiding, looking for ways to make sure I never did anything like that again. To not, by reflex, or anger, or fear, or mere convenience, simply snuff out people's lives. I found it, finally. It took another year and a return to Ashbury to find a tattoo artist with the right skills to write the disruption spell into my flesh. And doing so, I hobbled myself, permanently. I couldn't cast the kind of mass-casualty spells I used to casually dispense if my life depended on it.

Didn't mean I had to mention that fact to Ariq.

"Ariq? You're all grown up! Doing well for yourself, I see."

"You too, lass." He had to shout to be heard across the distance. "Lovely as ever, though don't tell my wife I said that, she'll have my balls." He shook his head. "Damn, I'd love to fight at your side one more time, but you know we've got a contract. Bad for business if we switch sides mid-battle."

"I can respect that."

"On the other hand," he said, waggling the corresponding appendage, "a reputation's no good if you're not around to cash in on it."

"There is a certain pragmatic wisdom to your words, young Ariq."

"On the third hand..." Ariq glanced at his two hands, then lifted his kilt, looked down, and shrugged. "On the third appendage, I've been thinking of retiring, anyway. Took up learning carpentry in my off hours. Wife's been on me about it for a couple years now."

"Well, your wife sounds even wiser than you. I'd love to meet her. Maybe when this unpleasantness is over, we can get together for drinks."

"I'll hold you to that. She's a big fan of yours, she's read all the books."

Of course. Who hadn't?

With that, he saluted me, then Karos, and then strolled down the trail, sword slung casually over his shoulder. The older Skullcrackers were close on his heels, while the younger ones lingered uncertainly for a few minutes before following. Some non-trivial number of regular troops left their colors on the field and fell in step behind them.

Karos grinned in approval. "Boy's always had a good head on his shoulders. Now, what are we going to do with this lot?" He gestured with his thumb at the remaining troops, who shuffled nervously. Though much reduced, they still held an advantage simply by their numbers over our hunger-weakened miners.

"Go back to Ellinor. Tell her to throw a protection over me. I'm going to try something."

Not that I was going to trust Ellinor's abilities, but it was better to have two impenetrable shields than one.

Once my shield was in place, I began improvising. I needed something impressive. Something with lots of flashing lights and the sounds of crackling energy. And big. It needed to look like it could grow to encompass their whole army. While it was building, Ellinor threw spells at the enemy mages—distractions, but it kept them from disrupting my work. Glad she was showing initiative.

I'd been thinking an ominous dark cloud full of flashes of lightning, but ended up with the opposite—flashes of absolute black in a blindingly bright cloud. There was no way they could see through it to target me, but the same was true for me. I began to walk forward, pushing the display before me.

It would have been embarrassing to walk right into their front lines, but a sudden cheer behind me told me my gambit had worked—the enemy had been put to rout.

I let the spell dissolve and watched the retreat, and then returned to the mines, and the Archmother. The troops would be back soon enough, with the Archfather, and there was a lot more I needed to learn before then.

The Archmother was less than cooperative. I was trying to find weaknesses in the spell that controlled her, but it was mostly hidden. Every time I tried to circle her to get a full sense of the patterns, she'd just turn to keep her face to me. And she talked. Oh, how she talked.

She was full of questions, ranging from the critically sensitive to the trivially mundane. What were our plans for her? What designers were the men wearing to the Winter Ball this year? Did Lady Rivaldi have a boy or a girl? What was the Archfather going to say to her when he arrived? I ignored them all, except one.

"Where's your husband? *Lord* Wisgarth. Shouldn't *he* be doing this?"

"He's dead."

"I'm so sorry for your loss." No she wasn't. She was just sorry she wasn't the one to kill him.

"You'd have enjoyed the way he died."

"*It's not enough!*" she hissed, and power crackled around her edges.

I flinched away, instinctively. I knew that power, only too well. Unleashed, she could kill everyone and everything on and in this mountain with a wave of her hand. Except for the Archfather. He was a bit tougher than we were. He'd require her full attention, at least for a few minutes.

But the surge of energy had one benefit; it showed me how the Archfather's control spell contained her. And the key to unraveling it would start with him.

We tried to get the miners back inside for their protection before the Archfather arrived, but more than half of them refused. Why do I keep calling them miners? Prisoners. They'd rather face their deaths in the open air than go back in there. Can't say I blame them, but it was still a senseless waste.

As the Archfather trudged up the path, his troops fell away on either side in obsequious fear. Reasonable, given how grumpy he looked. At the bottom of the hill, hundreds of protestors who had followed from the city chanted slogans. That didn't seem to improve his mood.

"It's time," I said, and Semphor ordered the Archmother out the door. I stayed close by her side.

The Archfather stopped about a dozen paces from us.

"What's this nonsense about, Helen?"

The Archmother—Helen—shrugged. "The Lady Wisgarth claims you have something to say to me."

"The *Lady*...." The Archfather laughed. "*There's* a phrase I never thought I'd hear. And you are said 'Lady'?"

I curtseyed, keeping my eyes on him. Everything now depended on timing.

"And this Lady, her plan is to, what? Trot you out and expect you to raise a hand against your beloved?"

The Archmother smoldered beside me.

"Nothing to say, dear? Perhaps you should demonstrate to the 'Lady Wisgarth' your dedication to your vows."

That was it. That was the trigger, and lines of control flashed into existence.

I cut them.

The Archmother looked at me and raised her hands to strike me down. Power crackled across her fingers. She turned her head slightly and smiled. She almost seemed to expand as she realized her freedom.

The Archfather smirked as he awaited my destruction. But not for long. The Archmother's spell threw him backward; he lashed out wildly, missing her entirely. Over a dozen prisoners died, sliced to fist-sized pieces, caught by the edge of the misdirected spell. The others screamed and ran.

For a time, Ellinor and I worked to protect them from stray energy from the duel. Then it was just me. I didn't see how Ellinor died. I think one of the enemy mages got her, because for a short while, I was defending against both of them. And then, one after the other, their spells stopped, and we got the surviving prisoners to safety inside. After that, there was nothing else to do but to wait, and watch.

There was a cry of triumph from the field. The Archmother stood above the cowering Archfather, holding his severed arm above her head.

"Please," the Archfather whimpered. "Beloved."

And then there wasn't enough of him to say anything else.

Into the silence that followed, a thousand voices raised up in joy. "Archmother! The Archmother is free!" And then, as the news spread throughout the realm at the speed of magic, many thousands more.

And wouldn't it be nice if we could end the story here? But the Archparents had reigned unchallenged for centuries, which, frankly, was not the best way to ground a ruler to reality in the first place. The Archfather's betrayal, and the Archmother's subsequent murder and banishment to eternal torment hadn't improved her state of mind.

"Seven years." Her voice carried down the mountain and across the plains and, we learned later, through the streets and alleys of the city of Amisara.

I stepped up to her side and looked up at her with what I hoped was a guileless smile that didn't give away that I knew there was a problem.

She sneered at me. "Wisgarth." Not broadcast. She turned her attention back to the assembled troops and protestors.

"Call me Maris," I said, but she ignored me.

"Seven *years* you left me to rot. And you expect what now? To be praised? To be *forgiven*?"

Energy crackled across her body, no longer constrained by the Archfather's control spell. But that wasn't the only spell he'd placed on her. I couldn't counter the Becoming-Dead energy that she was gathering, not at this scale and without preparation, but I could un-ravel another spell that nobody else was now maintaining.

"Maris Goselin," I said.

And she looked at me in sudden recognition before the spell that animated her unspooled, and her lifeless body dropped to the ground.

I don't really want to talk about what happened next.

Karos found me, sitting on the ground upwind of the Archparents' remains, whose decomposition had proceeded with unusual gusto.

"I tried," he said. "I couldn't get to them before they killed Ellinor." The enemy mages. He'd killed them. Trying to save Ellinor. Who'd murdered the man he loved. Whenever I start thinking the world has started to make sense, it veers into chaos and contradiction.

It was about to get worse.

The prisoners, the protestors, the surviving guards, and the former Archfather's suddenly-leaderless troops had conferred, and ap-proached me with their decision. They hoisted me up off the ground and lifted me over their heads.

"All hail the Archmother! All hail Maris Goselin!"

In the novel, Talia spends the next three days and nights in a sordid foursome betwixt her, Novel-Edwin, Novel-Laura, and Novel-me.

Lies.

It was only one night, and Real-Laura told Real-Edwin, "Don't even think it."

(I'm pretty sure he thought it.)

Real-Talia, or Lydia, or whatever her name really is, came to visit me at the palace. She went by Lydia, and claimed Karos told her I wanted to see her. I'd said no such thing, but he didn't seem to have the same awe and deference to his new Archmother that afflicted most of the populace.

I recognized her instantly, probably because she hadn't changed (other than having intact clothes). And if I hadn't recognized her looks, I'd have recognized her scent. It made my knees weak. Darialth, standing next to my—alright, I have to say it—my throne, flinched suddenly; I'd reached for her arm and dug my fingernails into her skin.

"What's wrong?"

"This is Talia. Or Lydia. Or F.L. Dagonné." The author's pseudonym. "What's your real name?"

"Lydia will do." She quirked a grin, and I thought I'd melt. "I haven't used the real one for so long it doesn't matter anymore. Karos tells me you're a fan."

I felt myself blushing. "I've only read the one. It's been..." What was the word I wanted?

"I have lots more. I could bring copies up to your chambers? I mean, if you wanted them signed?"

"You could?" Could this really be happening?

My face stung suddenly. Darialth was staring at me. "What is *wrong* with you?" She spun on Lydia. "What are you doing to her?"

Lydia laughed and made a gesture, and suddenly I could think again. "Aphrodisiac spell. I learned it from a werewolf."

"It's.... very powerful."

"Also very targeted. I could teach you. Karos thinks you might find it useful."

"You used this on me in Ashbury."

She nodded. "Wisgarth was furious. But if we wanted the wedding to go unchallenged, my performance had to be perfect."

Darialth frowned. "For the witnesses."

What witnesses?

"Exactly. And after that stupid tree limb broke, I knew I wouldn't have another chance."

"And you think I want this spell because...?"

"Karos said you'd want it. Now, I don't sell this spell—it's really...personal—but there is something you can do for me that could change my life."

"Like arrest you?" Darialth's arms were crossed.

"Or stab you in the face," I suggested.

Lydia laughed, shaking her head. She leaned in close. "Blurb my books."

Blurb my books.

Meaning: "Give me a sentence or phrase praising my books that I can print on the cover to help sell more books."

Very explicit books.

About *me*.

Stabbing her in the face sounded like a better option.

"Fine," I growled.

The problem with adulation is how hard it is to convince people to stop adulating.

Darialth and I had been in talks with Tomás, who hadn't faced his wife's death yet. He'd put her body in Long Storage and thrown himself into his work. We were all in agreement that it didn't matter how good an Archmother I tried to be. Too much power concentrated in one person was bound to create horrible abuses. In fact, I'd made a point of refusing to see supplicants, hearing court cases, or making any decisions or pronouncements at all. I was afraid that anything I said might have disastrous ripples of unanticipated consequences, or, even worse, that people might actually *like* what I decreed, and then I'd never escape this nightmare.

Tomás had some theories about what a government might look like if responsibilities and powers were split up and balanced, if the people selected their rulers.

"Well, they selected me, so maybe that's not the best idea."

"But if they selected new rulers every few years, and we placed limits on how long those people could rule?"

Darialth nodded her agreement. "That would ensure that even bad mistakes could be corrected."

"It would also remove competent rulers," Tomás said. "These are the people we want in power, the people who deserve to rule."

"No. Nobody *deserves* to rule." This was the hill I would die on. "Maybe that's a word we need to abolish. No more rulers. Get rid of the difference between the people and the government. The people rule, the government does what the people want done. How do we make that happen?"

"First thing," Darialth said, kissing my cheek, "is we get you fired."

227

Karos is the one who came up with the plan.

"You're really good at pissing people off. All of a sudden you're treading on eggshells. So just, you know, be yourself."

Okay, maybe not much of a plan in itself, but Tomás and Darialth helped flesh it out.

My first decree came on the ninth day of the reign of Archmother Maris Goselin-Wisgarth. I gathered the people to the palace court, which had a convenient system of spells built into the podium to project my voice throughout not just the city, but the entire country.

It was my first speech, and I thanked my supporters with a shaky voice. Fortunately, I had a script in front of me, or the sound of my own voice booming all around me would have rendered me speechless. I thanked the former Archfather for turning the former Archmother into an undead abomination, and the former Archmother for dismembering her husband and being convenient to kill. "I wouldn't be standing here," I said, "if it weren't for my predecessor's self-sacrifice or whatever."

The massed population laughed.

Change was never easy, my speech continued, and while the revolution had succeeded, and they had a new, benevolent ruler, the hard work of change still lay ahead of us. Amisara had for too long stifled under boot of my predecessors. It was a cultural backwater. We were going to change all that with a new cultural aesthetic.

Toenail clippings.

Henceforth, all toenail clippings would be collected, placed in glass boxes (which could be purchased for a nominal fee from the newly formed Ministry of Cultural Enforcement), and displayed prominently in the front window of every home.

Tomás immediately published a scathing condemnation of the speech, and the new law. Gossip disappeared from *The Timely Courante*, replaced with articles and public commentary, only some of which had been seeded by us.

Every day, there was a new decree. All horse manes must be dyed pink. Laundry was to be scheduled by color. That sort of thing.

Nothing that someone might come across and think, "Actually, that's a good idea."

Which is harder than you might think. I was actually surprised how popular the laundry color schedule was. I hear there are some neighborhoods that kept that one, even to this day.

It took two weeks of ever-weirder decrees before I started getting booed off the stage. I was offered the opportunity to abdicate three days after that.

Turns out creating a whole new form of government doesn't happen overnight. As former ultimate dictator, I had to recuse myself from the proceedings. The most I could do was write anonymous letters to the editors of both broadsheets, which had begun actually competing to see who could provide the better content as they helped shape the form of the new government.

But the wheels of bureaucracy wait for no government, and the laws that caused all my headaches at the beginning of this adventure were still in place. The suitors that came to call were more respectful than they'd been the first time around, obsequious, even fearful, but with my tax deadline looming, I needed to make a decision.

"Don't be an idiot," Darialth said. "The right choice has been in front of you the whole time."

When I posed the question to Karos, he looked at me gravely. "Did you meet with Tesmir?"

"Who?"

"Talia. Lydia."

"Oh, yes."

"And she showed you the aphrodisiac spell?"

I pushed air through closed lips. "She did. I was less good at actually learning it." Which nowadays was unusual for me. "We'll make it work."

On the fateful day, we met at the courthouse for (surprise) more paperwork, before being escorted through underground passages to the Wedding Chamber, buried somewhere deep beneath the city. Darialth, my maid of honor, awaited me there, as did her cousin Rohexo, who had been more than happy to volunteer to be man of honor, after Karos admitted to having not made any friends he could call on in Amisara.

"Seems Karos has made *quite* an impression on the lad," Darialth said.

The Wedding Chamber was a domed, circular room, in which the primary fixture was a very large bed. Darialth and Rohexo would be our two independent witnesses; the government had assigned a judge to administer the ceremony, and an official witness. I was surprised to find that the witness was Camilla Alion, the courthouse clerk I'd met my first day. The same one who had witnessed "my" marriage to Wisgarth, eight years previous. She smiled warmly at me.

"It's about time you figured it out," she said, with a glance at Karos. "The man's clearly mad about you."

I bit my tongue.

This was going to be weird. Darialth had given me the basics of the Amisaran wedding ceremony. There was a ritual, an exchange of vows before a judge. Then there was a consummation, before witnesses. And I mean, it's not like I had never had sex in front of other people before. But I would be having sex with *Karos*, who wasn't attracted to women, in front of the woman I *was* sleeping with, *and* her younger cousin. And a judge. And the lady from the file room in the courthouse who *thought* she'd watched me have sex before.

When I expressed my reservations to Darialth, she laughed. "You are Maris Goselin, who called down the sun, and, if I recall correctly, tentacles. In a public park. You'll be fine."

So I calmed my nerves, squeezed Karos's hand—Karos looked more nervous than I did, and I suppose he had cause for it—and told the judge we were ready.

Ready. That was laughable. But Darialth had said that the job of the maid and man of honor was to make sure the ritual was a success. So, we were as ready as we could reasonably expect to be, until the judge announced, somewhat more loudly than I'd expected, that the ceremony was about to begin.

The dome above our head split, and with a bone-shivering grinding of stone against stone, the walls retracted into the floor, as the floor lifted upward into the open air.

Ten thousand voices cheered.

The Wedding Chamber had converted itself into a stage, rising up into the center of the amphitheater.

Next to me, Darialth's eyes shone. "The last time they raised the

Wedding Chamber was for the Archparents wedding, over two hundred years ago. I'm so proud of you!"

I thought I was going to be sick.

A lot of what happened next is still shrouded in a haze of shock and embarrassment. I remember saying something like, "I thought your job was to prepare me," to Darialth.

To which she grinned and replied, "No, my job is to prepare you now. You're acting like you've never been married before."

I'm going to set the stage, so to speak, because trying to weave these details into an explicit narrative of what happened next would be impossible (see: "haze" above).

The rainy season in Amisara—an awkward month of chilly, violent storms shoehorned in between winter and spring—had set in with a vengeance, and today brought no reprieve. This did nothing to dampen the spirits of the ravening hordes that had squeezed into every available seat in the amphitheater. From where I stood, they were fields upon fields of rain hats and oil-coats, faces obscured with magnifying lenses. Street wizards moved among the seats, selling hand-warming and boot-drying charms. Other vendors hawked less magical warming beverages, three of which I could have used right about then.

The cold and the drenching rain did not penetrate the Wedding Chamber. A diffuse glow illuminated the stage for better visibility. The Marriage Bed was designed to optimize one thing, and modified itself to provide support where it was most needed—lower back, knees, so on—while simultaneously not getting in the way. Sadly, the secrets of its creation were lost a millennium ago.

I suppose I can't put this off any further.

The judge said some words. Darialth put a meaningful elbow in my ribs, and I said some words. Karos said some words. The court witness wrote a document and passed it to all of us to sign. There was a cheer. Then a hush came over the crowd. They all leaned forward in their chairs.

Darialth disrobed me, and then, uh, prepared me. Good thing she was familiar with my buttons, because it was really hard to relax with thousands of eyes watching every move of my poor, middle-aged body. I mean, it's one thing to trust one person not to be judgmental about the droopy bits, but ten thousand strangers? On the other side of the bed, Rohexo seemed to be having far less difficulty preparing Karos.

And can I interject here? I mean, I guess I can. It's my story, after all. Okay. So, as weird as this whole ritual was, doesn't it seem doubly so in a land that outlawed exactly what was happening? How does that even make sense?

Consummation was less straightforward; all Rohexo's good work came undone when Karos knelt between my legs. Despite my faithful casting, "Lydia's" aphrodisiac spell failed spectacularly. What followed was a comedy of false starts and awkward teamwork that I'm not going to go into, other than to suggest "You can do it!" is maybe not the best thing for ten thousand people to chant at a time like this. F.L. Dagonné's latest trashy novel goes into agonizing detail from Talia's front-row point-of-view. I forget the title, but it's the one with my blurb splashed in big letters across the front and back covers:

Don't you fucking dare publish this book.
At least cut Chapter 19, or I'll fucking hunt you down.
—Maris Goselin.

No, I didn't hunt her down.

When it was finally finished, and Karos rolled off me, it still wasn't finished. Camilla Alion, the clerk, approached, offering one final humiliation.

"As the official witness," Darialth explained, "she needs evidence of completion."

"Best part of my job," Camilla said, with a grin and a wink. "You think I like paperwork?"

I should have just stayed Archmother. I closed my eyes and imagined ordering everyone in Amisara executed. Or at least the people in the audience, who had begun chanting. The chant turned into a cheer, and I opened my eyes to see Camilla consulting with the judge.

The judge turned to us and smiled for the first time. "I hereby pronounce you Wife and Husband."

The crowd went wild, and I wanted to crawl into a hole.

Beside me, Karos started snoring.

Of course, it *still* wasn't over. Why, why, why couldn't it be over?

Because everyone had to sign the Witness Book. And the Witness Book was in the Wedding Chamber. It went on for hours. Everyone was compelled to congratulate Karos and wish me good fortune with the start of my new family. I bit my tongue and thanked them. Some of them commended Darialth and Rohexo for a job well done, and it's true, none of this would have been successful without their timely and vigorous intervention.

At last, the line eased to a trickle and came to an end. The last figure to enter the Wedding Chamber removed the wide-brimmed hat that obscured her face. Of course.

"Lydia, is it?"

"Lady Tarunog." She affected a mocking bow. "Can I ask why you didn't use that little trick I showed you?"

If only. "It didn't work. I mean, I couldn't get it to work for me."

"Ah. Well, it was always a personal spell. At least it made for a very entertaining evening. "

"Don't you dare write anything about this. Not a word."

"I wouldn't dream it."

She kissed Karos on the cheek, and me on the lips, and didn't even try to hide the notebook protruding from her jacket pocket.

And then it was time for Karos and me to get dressed, go home, get back undressed, and reward Darialth and Rohexo for their services.

Darialth's bodyguards preceded her, insisting that they search my Ashbury home in advance of her visit. Of course, my bees disabused them of this idea fairly quickly, but fortunately, I managed to keep both the guards and the bees calm enough that nobody got hurt as I ushered them back out the door.

It had been four months since the wedding, three-and-a-half since I'd left Amisara. I'd ached to get away, to be *alone*, at long last. To have a bed to myself. To not have to coordinate meals with other people. Or talk. I'd grown so sick of there always, *always* being someone within earshot who could, at any second, demand my attention.

I got some seeds started in the windows, for spring's plantings. I cleaned the house. I went to restaurants and ate and drank what I wanted. I hired a man for an evening, but sent him away halfway through. It just seemed pointless.

I was not going to admit that I was lonely. I wrote it down.

"I am not lonely."

As a self-affirming statement, it seemed pretty weak, even at the time.

When I got Darialth's letter that she would be in Ashbury to establish formal diplomatic relations between the Duchy and the newly elected government of the Free People's Republic of Amisara, my heart soared, and not just because she said that she would be bringing the divorce papers for me to sign. Soon, Karos would have the inheritance that should have never been mine, and I would be able to put Sergeant Wisgarth, and Karos, and the Kilted Skullcrackers and the rest of that whole chapter of my life forever behind me.

But even that wasn't why.

When the knock came, I flung the door open magically, pulled Darialth through, also magically, and swung the door shut to keep out the annoying bodyguards. I stopped it just before it slammed, closing it with a soft click. Another spell silenced the sound the guards would surely make trying to break down my door. Darialth fell forward into my arms with a squeak, quickly muffled as our lips met.

The bees came out to greet her, buzzing happily in front of her eyes, landing on her arms and nose to taste her, dodging deftly as we reacquainted ourselves with the feel of each other's bodies. Something was different, though. She just felt *different* in my arms. I'd warned her of the bees, so she didn't panic. That wasn't it. I couldn't put my finger on it.

The portfolio she carried had fallen from her hand and spilled on the floor. A bunch of legal papers, it looked like, plus an autographed copy of the latest in the Talia series.

"The divorce papers are, uh, in there," she said, a little breathless, when our lips separated. "My wife is, uh..."

She looked around, and then at down at our bodies, shirts pulled open. She'd been as eager as me from the looks of it.

But also: wife?

"My wife, uh, is an official witness, and a notary," she said. "For the divorce. And, uh, she's still outside."

I started to apologize, but she shut me up with a kiss. I started to button her shirt, and she stopped me there, as well. Together, we opened my front door.

Two guards were at my door, one with a broken dagger he'd clearly been using as a pry bar, while another stood back in the street, assessing the building. A fourth had gotten stuck on my garden fence. Behind the guards, a woman stood with worry engraved on her face.

Camilla Alion.

They gaped at us—bare-chested and covered in bees—and I gaped at Camilla. *Wife?*

Darialth addressed one of the guards by name (no, I don't remember her name). "Wait out here, please. We'll leave the door unlocked, but we don't want to be disturbed, unless there's a war or something."

The guard grinned. "Yes, councilor."

"And don't go starting a war so you can walk in on us."

"We'll do our best, mum. But we'd be remiss in our duty if we didn't walk in just a little bit."

Dariath sighed. "This is my life." She reached out a hand to Camilla and escorted her in. The door closed behind them.

The bees encased Camilla and found her acceptable. Once she was relatively bee-free, Darialth draped an arm over her shoulders.

"When Camilla found out I'd be meeting with you, she insisted on coming." She kissed Camilla on the cheek. "Do you want to tell her why?"

Camilla gave me a nervous smile. She placed one on hand on the bump of Darialth's bare belly, which... wait, was *that* what felt different?

"I wanted to be here when you found out."

"Wait." I blinked. "Who?"

"Karos," Darialth said. "And you."

I didn't understand.

"The Marriage Bed is very persuasive," Camilla said. "*Someone's* going to get pregnant. If the bride has some charm against it, it'll be someone else. That's why there's always a maid of honor; if the groom gets pregnant, things don't usually go very well."

"That's not..." I drew a much-needed breath. "*Sex doesn't work like that!*"

Darialth laughed. "In Amisara, sex works however we want it to. And, now it's legal, too."

I was trying to wrap my head around the Marriage Bed logistics of two men, or, in Darialth and Camilla's case, two women, when Darialth interrupted my thoughts.

"But that's not the real reason Camilla wanted to come." She nudged her wife gently. "It's okay, love, go ahead."

"Well, you know, I mean, of course you know, you were there, but we have a new country and a new government. And nobody disappears into the mines anymore, and people can love who they want, and nobody is forced into marriages they don't want just to survive. It's a whole new world for us, a whole new life. And I wanted to see where it all started."

I didn't understand what she meant. Darialth nudged her again.

"The... the hot tub? With Talia?" She blushed fiercely.

Which would have been adorable, if it wasn't such a punch in the chest. The hot tub had sat unused since Edwin and Laura died. It had gone stagnant, my state of mind overcoming the spell that kept it fresh and hot and clean, and filled with mosquito larvae until I drained it. Then it just filled with autumn leaves, composting slowly year after year.

"I'm so sorry!" Camilla's voice was edged with panic. "I take it back. Pretend I didn't ask."

Darialth pulled me close and held me tight, and I lost myself there for a moment, but then pushed her away. I don't know what my face looked like. Not pretty, I'd guess, since Camilla took a step back when I turned to her.

But when I reached for her hand, she let me take it. Darialth took my other hand, and together, I walked them to the back yard.

"It's been a few years since it's been used," I said, "but maybe it's time."

Darialth squeezed my hand and kissed my forehead.

"That is, Madam Councilor," I added, "if you don't mind getting your hands dirty."

SLIPKNOT

It has been a year, now, since she's been gone, and I have to face the fact that she isn't coming back. I mean, of course she isn't; I saw her step into the maelstrom with my own eyes. I *felt* her essence ripped from this world. Alia and Levras have been encouraging me to write it down, while the memories are still relatively clear. I've been looking at the diary I'd been keeping at the time, up until I was suddenly too busy to keep a diary, and I'm having a more difficult time remembering *who I was*, then, than what happened. Who exactly was that timid, fearful boy? Who was Sollaman, son of Jonthan, squire to Sir Tanyrr? The type of person who keeps diaries, I suppose, and wept every night over his fractured idealism. Not much else, if I'm honest. I will try to tell this tale as faithfully to the person I was then as I can manage.

Perhaps, then, I will be able to move on.

Where to start?

Alia says with Tanyrr, and that seems as good, or as bad, a place as any.

Sir Tanyrr was furious.

More than that, he was humiliated. For the second time.

The first time, the old crone had patted him on the arm, thanked him for his service, handed around a plate of fresh-baked oatmeal-and-raisin cookies, and closed the door in his face. She'd had bees in her hair, and one perched on the tip of her nose.

The next time Sir Tanyrr pounded on her door, the bees had buzzed ominously about her head as she told him to go fuck himself sideways with a rusty pitchfork, since he couldn't take a polite hint. When Sir Tanyrr informed her that he was there on the Duke's business, she'd issued a hoarse, dry cackle.

"Oh, the *Duke*, you say. Well, that's different. You can have *him* fuck you sideways. Tell the bastard I'll be checking up to make sure he does you right."

It would have been hilarious if I didn't know what would be in store for any of us who dared laugh. In fact, the moment the most eminent Lady Maris Goselin, self-proclaimed Whore-Witch of Ashbury, slammed the door in his face and the cloud of bees that had gathered above her head retreated back into the thatch roof of her hovel, Sir Tanyrr spun about, growled something incoherent, and then back-handed Levras, who had the misfortune to be closest, so hard Levras sprawled backward into the street and was nearly trampled by a passing carriage-horse. Alia and I rushed to pull him from under the thrashing hooves while Sir Tanyrr stormed off.

Sometimes it's hard to remember what an honor it is to be chosen as a squire, especially for a knight so accomplished as Sir Tanyrr. He sat at the right hand of the Duke, and was trusted with the Duchy's most critical missions, of which this was no exception. Except that this particular mission hinged on the cooperation of a senile old hag who had, by all reports, forgotten what the word cooperation meant decades ago.

My journal entry dated 04.23.482 was brief, and I will let it stand on its own:

> *Levras's face is a massive bruise, and he's having difficulty eating. Or talking. I think his jaw is broken, but Sir Tanyrr won't hear of it, and I know better than to mention it twice. We're to take our bruises as part of our training. It's all part of getting tough.*

SLIPKNOT

Sir Tanyrr's face was grim after his meeting with the Duke, and we all stayed well out of reach. From where Alia, Levras, and I had been waiting on the far side of the throne room, we'd been unable to hear what transpired between Sir Tanyrr and Duke Farlow, until the Duke raised his voice.

"She's just a little old lady, Tanyrr. If she's confused, unconfuse her. If she's uncooperative, make her cooperate. Get the information we need, Tanyrr. Today. We don't have much time, and I won't accept any more excuses. *Everything rides on this*, Tanyrr. Do whatever needs to be done."

This time, when the old woman answered the door, Sir Tanyrr pushed his way in, shoving her with a mailed fist. She fell backward, arms and legs and cane flailing, and he strode in. The door slammed decisively in our faces and refused our attempts to open it.

About five minutes later, the door opened again. The crone stared out at us, blood dripping from her nose and mouth, bees swarming in an angry cloud around her. She wiped her face with the back of her hand, scowled at the blood, and said, "I'm getting slow in my dotage. You three, make yourselves useful and drag that trash out of here."

We entered the witch's house with some trepidation. Bees landed on my arms and face and neck, and also on Alia and Levras, and I was careful to move very slowly to avoid getting stung. Sir Tanyrr was sprawled unnaturally on the floor, whimpering and only half-conscious. It looked like he'd developed several extra joints in his arms and legs, and a number of his teeth lay strewn about the floor.

Alia picked one up, wide-eyed.

"Genuine knight's-teeth," the old woman told her. "Freshly harvested. Good money from the right buyer. Go ahead, take them all. I already have a jar-full." She waved vaguely at the shelves that covered half of her walls, crowded with more things than my eyes could make sense of. "Somewhere in there."

Then she noticed Levras's face.

She made a noise like a horse clearing its throat. "Sit." She pointed to a hard chair. "Now."

Wide-eyed, Levras hastened to comply, though he looked to Alia and me for support. The witch ground a few pinches of different herbs in a mortar, mixed them into a glass of water, and ordered him to drink. He cast a fearful glance at me, and I shrugged, so he drank it.

She patted him on the shoulder. "Go on, run along now and play with your friends."

We used two sturdy poles from the witch's garden and a bed sheet to fashion a makeshift stretcher and carefully eased Sir Tanyrr onto it. It wasn't easy—Sir Tanyrr was a monster of a man, taller than me and built like Levras—and as we tipped him up to position the stretcher, Levras stumbled and nearly fell.

"Good, good," the witch cackled. "He's ready. Help him back into the chair."

I did as I was told. Levras said something incoherent about ducks. I'm pretty sure he said ducks. He said he couldn't feel his lips.

Alia, who had been inspecting Sir Tanyrr, cried out suddenly. "Solly! I think he's dying!"

Sir Tanyrr had started wheezing, and his face was turning blue.

"Turn his head to the side and clear his throat," the witch said. "Probably just swallowed his tongue. Meant to cut it out earlier, but I forgot. Now hold still, dear."

That last was directed at Levras, who cried out, apparently in sudden pain, as the crone did something sudden and violent to his jaw, then said, surprise in his voice, "Oh. That didn't hurt at all."

"That's the drug. Kept you from passing out while I put your dislocated jaw right. But never you worry, dear, you'll have plenty of pain in a few hours. Soft foods for the next week, and no blowjobs. Now get out, the lot of you."

We took Sir Tanyrr home, Alia and I carrying the stretcher as Levras stumbled behind us. We rolled Sir Tanyrr into his bed and left him there to recover. He was a knight, after all. The toughest in the Duchy, he claimed. He'd be fine.

We found Levras asleep at the kitchen table, where he had eaten the entire inside of a loaf of bread, leaving only the hollowed out crust.

When Sir Tanyrr failed to report back to the Duke, the Duke came to him. The guards entered first, then the Duke and his entourage, and then more guards.

To say Duke Farlow was displeased would be an understatement.

I have never seen anyone so upset, not even Sir Tanyrr, though the Duke was less physical about the expression of his displeasure.

No, not *Sir* Tanyrr. Just Tanyrr. Tanyrr Gustavson. *Former* knight of the realm. The Duke spent nearly an hour deriding him most cruelly, ultimately stripping him of his titles. "I'd strip you of your properties, as well, but I don't suppose there's much point to *that*, now, is there?"

Alia and I had been there, attending to Tanyrr's needs, helping him sit up and whatnot, witness to his unmaking, while Levras made tea and his signature blueberry mini-scones. He walked in with a massive tray just as the Duke's vituperation ground into silence.

"Tea, Your Grace?" Levras asked.

Duke Farlow slapped the tray from his hands; tiny pastries flew, and scalding tea splashed across the rest of us. "Out of my way, idiot, or I'll have you thrashed." He pushed his way past a flinching Levras, his entourage following in his wake.

"Kill me now," Tanyrr moaned.

The three of us discussed it, but ultimately decided to just drink several bottles of Tanyrr's best wine, instead.

Lady Maris Goselin, the Whore-Witch of Ashbury, scowled suspiciously at me from the darkness of her doorway.

"That's it, then?" she asked. "Just come to return my bean poles and sheet? No ulterior motive?"

"No, mum. Lady. And sorry about the sheet. We weren't able to get all the blood stains out."

"Sir Tanyrr put you up to this." She waved her hand in dismissal and started to close the door.

"There is no Sir Tanyrr," I said. "The Duke was very upset. Stripped him of his titles."

"About time," she muttered. "I suppose the miserable coward will have to come talk to me himself, after all. Least he could do if he expects me to risk my life again for his stupid Duchy."

She couldn't have been speaking of Tanyrr, so she must have meant the Duke. But I'd never heard Duke Farlow called a coward. He vanquished the trolls at the Battle of Trellheim, and faced the grim Archlich Ravino in a duel to the death. Duke Farlow embodied all that was brave and noble in Ashbury. But of course, he *must* have already spoken with the witch and received her guidance in facing the horrors that now threatened Icenia, for he had left Ashbury hurriedly that very morning, accompanied by his guard and a select few of his household. I said as much.

"Really." She pulled the door back open. "Why don't you bring those poles in? Might as well set them back up in the garden, while you're here."

She gave me tea and cookies and made me recite everything the Duke said to Tanyrr, and vice versa. Tanyrr had been uncharacteristically taciturn, however. Usually he was happy to either boast or castigate, but I suppose he had excuse for neither at the Duke's latest visit.

"I did tell Farlow that I'd take his balls if he ever dared darken my doorstep," the witch said, "but fleeing his own city to avoid me? That's even more chickenshit than I expected of him."

What concerned me most wasn't that the Duke didn't want to talk to this crazy old bat, but one of the things he said to Tanyrr. That there wasn't much point in stripping him of his lands.

As if those lands weren't going to exist for long.

How she got in, I don't know. The first indication we had that Lady Goselin was in Tanyrr's house was when she stormed out of the master's private chambers. She stomped right up to me and hooked her cane around my neck, pulling me close so she could slap the back of my head.

"Three days and you haven't gotten him medical help?"

"He refused," Alia said. "He said he'd be better off dead, with what's coming."

"And what's that?"

Alia shrugged. "We don't get paid to ask those kinds of questions." Alia had wasted no time regaining the wry insolence that had both frightened and excited me, when we first met. Before Tanyrr had beaten it out of her.

"I don't think we're actually getting paid anymore," Levras added, helpfully.

"Doesn't matter," the witch said. "He's beyond talking now."

"He's.... dead?" I think all three of us shared the mixed emotions that were clear in Levras's voice.

"No. Will be soon, though."

"We did bring in a healer, but Tanyrr drove him away." Another shrug. "He said to just let him die in peace."

The witch shook her head. "No, he doesn't get away that easily. You'll need to bring him back to my house." She glared at each of us in turn. "*Now!*"

It was easier this time. Levras is easily the strongest of the three of us, and now he wasn't too intoxicated to pull his own weight. I have nearly a foot on him, but Levras is built like a fortress, and I, well, I'm rather the opposite. More like one of Lady Goselin's bean poles, to tell the truth. It's strange how we both managed to be envious of each other, though on my part, I'm sure that the way Alia looked at him when she thought no one was looking played some small part. All Alia and I had to do was support Tanyrr's legs to keep him from dragging on the cobbles.

The witch had us lay Tanyrr out on her kitchen table. She took a pair of gardening shears to his clothes. He hadn't allowed us near him long enough to change him since our disastrous last visit (and we hadn't bothered offering twice), and they'd as a result become grievously soiled.

Once he'd been stripped naked, she set us to bathing him, while she fed his clothing, armor and all, into her stove. We offered the rags we'd used to clean him to the fire, as well, when we had finished that task. The leather and wool stank like burning hair, but some magic the witch called Proper Ventilation kept the smell from permeating the house. The metal plates glowed red in the embers.

That was only the first task of many. We worked on Tanyrr for hours, grinding herbs, making poultices, pulling limbs into shape and splinting them, cutting away rotting tissue. The witch supervised, correcting us as needed with a sharp crack of her cane, or a sharper word. When at last the preparations were complete, the three of us collapsed in a crowded heap onto the loveseat, exhausted. Putting a blade to a man with intent to harm takes a toll, I've heard, but I think when the intent is to heal, the toll is perhaps greater. More fraught. Still, it was nice to have us all crushed together, Levras and I squeezed into the seat side-by-side, with Alia's weight distributed between us.

She has a most entrancing scent. It was almost nice enough to ignore the way she leaned into Levras. And I also couldn't help notice how excited and nervous Levras had become, casting agitated glances at me across the halo of Alia's hair, as if to beg forgiveness for what was developing between the two of them. After all, if Tanyrr was really no longer a knight, then we were really no longer squires bound together in common service. Physical affection between any of us was only one of the many things that were no longer prohibited.

But the time had come for actual magic. I extracted my face from the fragrant cocoon of Alia's hair to watch. I've always loved magic shows.

And this one was exceptional. Lady Maris Goselin was always spoken of in hushed tones, with an odd mixture of reverence, fear, and distaste, whether the speaker used her formal name or a cruder epithet. It was clear that her reputation was not overstated; even as an octogenarian, the woman commanded magic in a way unsurpassed by any other Ashburian mage, living or dead. I'd never seen anything like it.

Halfway through, the witch stopped, mid-spell, magic dripping from her fingers. "What are you staring at?" She was talking to me.

"I..." My face grew hot. "I just like to watch magic being done."

"He says it's pretty," Alia said, touching her index finger to her temple.

The witch snorted derisively and went back to work. When she was done, Tanyrr looked a good deal healthier than he had for days.

"Well, that was fun. Lad won't wake up for a long bit. You can come pick him tomorrow. You, girl. You still have those teeth? Good, bring them tomorrow."

"But you said they'd fetch a good price."

"With the right buyer." The witch glanced meaningfully at Tanyrr, lying stretched out on her kitchen table.

"Oh," Alia said, and I could feel the smile grow on her face through the posture of her body, still half on my lap. "Of course. The right buyer."

Tanyrr was glad that Alia brought his teeth, less happy that he had to pay for them, and furious that we hadn't thought to bring clothes for him. He couldn't very well order any of us out of our clothing. Well, he could, but what would be the point? He was taller than me, and built proportionally like Levras. We had nothing that would fit him.

Where Tanyrr was more verbose than he'd been in days, Lady Goselin was even less gregarious than she'd been the day before.

"She's looking awfully grim," Levras muttered, hopefully enough under his breath that only the three of us heard. "I hope she doesn't turn us into frogs. I'd be a terrible frog."

"I've heard frogs have remarkable tongues," Alia said, and Levras flushed bright red.

The witch spent fifteen minutes getting Tanyrr's teeth back in his head, after which she told him to "get the fuck out of my house, and take these useless lumps with you." Meaning us. But she stopped me. "Leave this one. He's tall, and it's been ages since I've been able to dust above the cupboards."

When Tanyrr started to object, she told him to take a sheet to cover himself and go. "Wouldn't want to commit unsanctioned comedy in this city," she said, waggling a single dangling finger, and soon enough I was left alone—horribly, terrifyingly alone—with her.

As soon as the door closed behind Alia, the tip of the witch's cane struck my chest, prodding me backward until my calves encountered the loveseat. Another prod had me seated.

"Now. You. Explain your behavior."

"What behavior?"

"While I was healing that oaf. What were you doing?"

"I... I just love watching people do magic. I wish I could do it myself, but I've never had the knack for it."

Her eyes narrowed. "Watching?"

"Yes." I shook my head. "You'll think I'm crazy."

"Already know you're crazy. You took up with Tanyrr."

I tried to swallow the lump in my throat. Alia and Levras had both laughed at me when I told them. Everyone had, when I was a child, laughed, or worse, until I learned not to say anything. I'd only told my fellow squires in the spirit of sharing our strengths and weaknesses. We would be putting our lives in each other's hands, after all.

"If I let my eyes go a little fuzzy, it's like I see colors. Colored lines in the air, on the ground, in the trees. Everywhere. And when people cast spells, the lines turn into these amazing patterns! Don't look at me like that. You asked."

"How long have you been seeing these.... these colors?"

I shrugged. "Forever. I just learned not to say anything."

The witch crossed her arms and frowned at me. "Two golden threads. Pick up one in each hand, between your thumb and forefinger."

"What?"

"From the floor. Any two will do."

There were more than two. They covered the floor, ran down the walls. The thatched roof where the beehives lived was full of them. Gingerly, I plucked up two at random. They felt sweet and warm, like a field of clover on a sunny summer day, and weightless as a strand of spiderweb.

Elation mingled with dread, catching my breath. I'd never dared to touch them, *to hold them*, before.

"Good," she said. Could she see what I had just done? "Now weave the right-hand thread through your left-hand fingers, like so, and then, yes, like that, and then twist it three times widdershins around the other thread."

I did as I was told. My heart was beating through my gambeson, and I was certain that the old lady would comment about the stench wafting from my suddenly-damp armpits.

"Now. There's a dull grey thread lurking in the shadows under the bed. Tie the end of it to the right-hand golden thread. Yes, that one. Now, twist those two threads together as you wrap it three more times widdershins."

It took a bit to get my fingers to manage this motion, but on the third turn, suddenly, a light flared up in my hand. It was weak, barely half the strength of a candle flame. Warm, but not hot, to the touch. But it was *magic*! Magic that *I* had performed!

The witch exhaled slowly, as if she had been holding her breath as much as I had been.

"If you had any idea what's in store for you, child, you'd lose that stupid, shit-eating grin. Might as well enjoy it while you can. Your first assignment: figure out how to turn it off."

She waved a hand, the gesture that meant the day was done, don't let the door hit me on the ass on the way out.

I practically skipped home, cupping my tiny ball of light protectively in my hands. Only when I'd arrived home did I realize that she'd totally forgotten to have me dust her cupboards.

I didn't sleep that night, and dragged my ragged self to her cottage at first light.

The door opened at my knock. Lady Goselin was at her desk, looking like she hadn't slept either.

"See you didn't figure it out."

"No, Lady, in fact—"

"Maris," she said. I was at a loss. "No more of this Lady bullshit, unless we're somewhere where we need to make an impression. And I'll call you Solly, if that's acceptable, or Sollaman, if it's not. We have some big decisions to make today, and we need to deal with each other directly and honestly, without rank or age or status or duty to Duke and Duchy or *anything else* that might influence the decisions."

I nodded my assent, afraid my tongue would betray me.

"Good. Then, your spell. It's, uh, different."

"Yes, L—." Stupid tongue. "Maris. Nothing I tried worked. I tried unwinding it. I tried winding in a reverse pattern. I tried increasing the amount of the grey thread in the mix. I tried using other colors. I even tried pulling the center strand out. Nothing worked."

"Instead you have a light that is both brighter than before and also radiates darkness, which is a really interesting effect, if it was what you were trying to achieve. Well, at least you didn't set anything on fire."

"I almost did! I was trying a pattern of perpendicular coils, and luckily I noticed how hot it got before I secured it in place."

"Yes, there's a lesson there. Imagine a pool of water, perfectly still. If you drop a pebble in, it creates ripples. If you drop two pebbles in, both create ripples. What happens where the ripples intersect?"

"They interfere with each other?"

Maris nodded. "And that means what, exactly?"

"Some of the effects will magnify, and others will be negated?"

"Smart kid. If you'd coiled the cross pattern a little differently, you could eliminate the heat instead, or focus it. The differences are subtle, and when you're casting anything of substance, a miscalculation can be catastrophic. So make your mistakes with small things until you learn how to fix them on the fly to get the effects you want. Getting a few blisters is better than burning down a village."

That was a sobering thought. How close had I come to destroying the building, and killing everyone I cared about, and Tanyrr as well?

"The good news," she continued, "is that one of your attempts was closer than you thought. The world is sticky. It likes to stay in the state it's in, and once you change that magically, it gets even more stubborn with the bit you've changed. It's just a matter of overcoming inertia. You were probably just a little too timid. It also helps to take hold in exactly the right spot to maximize leverage."

She slipped into what I called the Sight. She was much better at moving between ways of seeing than I was; I wouldn't have noticed if I hadn't known to look for it.

"The strand that makes the center loop of the knot of the spell, there are two ends hanging. One end goes into the Earth, the other diffuses into the air. That's the one you want to tug on. Take hold about one palm's-breadth below the center of the spell, these three fingers, like so. Yes. Then tug like so. Harder."

The strand pulled free. The spell unraveled, both the original spell and all my accidental supplements. The light fizzled into nothingness.

She nodded her approval. "Very few spells are a simple slipknot like this one. More often, they're a collection of knots that you'd need to unravel, and you have to know where to start. What order to pull at the threads. Again, start small. Enlist fellow mages to practice with. Learn to recognize the patterns and you'll be able to take apart other people's spells, or take control of them."

She had me put together and unravel the light spell a few more times. It was more tiring than seemed reasonable, given that the threads I was manipulating weighed literally nothing at all. Still, she had one final lesson for me.

She took me out into her yard, where vegetables and herbs and flowers grew in seemingly chaotic garden beds. Bees flitted between the flowers, while chickens hunted crawling insects. In a pasture fenced off from the gardens, several goats grazed contentedly. Maris brought me to the closest of the goats. She bent down and kissed its forehead, then knelt beside it, beckoning me to join her.

"This is Toby," she said, rubbing between her horns affectionately. "She's a good girl, aren't you, Toby?"

Toby just looked at me and chewed whatever was in her mouth.

"The threads of magic that come from living things are more subtle than what's generated by the world at large, partly because whoever is generating them is using them, whether they know it or not. You have to look carefully."

It was true. If I tried hard, I could. The threads were small, tightly bundled to the beast, and almost infinitely variable in shade and texture and intensity.

"I see them." I breathed out.

Maris nodded. "For this next spell, we're going to draw directly on the magic that lives inside Toby. Do you see a thread, sometimes when you look at it it's pale and a little silvery, but other times it's a deep blood red? That's what we'll start with. It may take a little time to find because it appears to change in front of you, but when you find it, take hold of it and draw it a couple inches from her. There may be some resistance, like when you dismantled the light spell. A sharp tug should do it."

I searched the goat for almost half an hour before I found it, hidden away behind a curtain of brown and amber threads.

"I found it!" I announced triumphantly, as my fingers took hold of it. Toby's eyes grew wide, but I didn't recognize what I was seeing until I had already pulled: abject, paralyzing terror.

The thread came loose in my hand, and Toby collapsed, lifeless. Already starting to spoil.

"That's what you can do, Solly," Maris said. "To anything. To anyone. That's the power you hold in your hands. I can teach you. I can show you how to do this at a distance. How to eviscerate entire armies in a heartbeat. You can rule Ashbury. You can rule the world."

I realized I'd been backing away from her, and from Toby's rotting corpse, shifting backward on my knees.

"No," I managed to say. "You stay away—"

My stomach betrayed me, then, and when I'd finished emptying myself, I was alone. Maris had returned to her cottage, taking the surviving animals with her. Even the bees had retreated inside. Just a single worker hovering near me, as if watching. And Toby, who would never go anywhere again.

I backed away from Toby, to the garden gate, and through it. And then I ran all the way home.

Breathless and exhausted, I stopped with my hand on the door-knob, frozen by a sudden realization. How could I be sure I'd never use this? What if Tanyrr struck one of us again? What if I walked in on Alia and Levras and was overcome by a fit of jealousy? What if?

How could I be sure that, no matter what, I never used this power against anyone, ever?

There was only one solution, of course.

The question was whether I had the strength to go through with it.

The sun was getting low on the horizon when I reached Ashbury Park. If I was going to kill myself, I wanted to be somewhere where I felt at home. But I couldn't put Alia and Levras through the horror of finding me, and that was doubly true of my parents and younger sisters. Ashbury Park was at least pretty.

I found a secluded spot overlooking the river. The grass was thick and lush, spotted with dandelions and buttercups and red clover and violets. Butterflies fluttered between them, competing with a variety of bees.

I wished I had thought to bring something with which to write a note. But maybe it wouldn't be an obvious suicide. Maybe my death would look like a murder, or just an unfortunate accident that went unnoticed for too long. Maybe I could spare the people who cared about me at least that guilt.

There was nothing to do about it now. I studied myself with the same unfocused detachment I had afforded Toby, until I found what I was looking for. I reached for it. Stopped. Maybe it would be best to wait until dark. One last sunset.

A bee landed on my nose.

"Hard to do it yourself, isn't it?" Maris Goselin groaned to a seat beside me. "At least, I couldn't do it. There, there, don't cry." She patted me on the arm.

"Do you have any idea how long I've yearned to be able to do magic? And then to find out that I... that I have a power so horrific, and so *easy*? All I'd have to do is lose my temper *once*, just once, and I'd become the worst kind of monster."

"Second worst," she said, and sighed. "If you can't live with it, I understand. But you shouldn't have to kill yourself over it. I can do that for you."

"Would you?" It is a testament to the power of despair when an offer like that sounds like mercy.

"Of course."

She reached out to me, finding my lifethread effortlessly, and I understood then what Toby had felt in her last moment—all-encompassing terror. The horror of utter extinction.

"Are you ready?" Maris asked, her voice kind, gentle. "Any last words or final wishes?"

I could barely speak, and what I wanted to do was to scream for her to stop. Instead, I said, "Finish it."

She gave my lifethread a sharp tug.

I didn't die.

Instead, her body went rigid, wracked with pain, until with a gasp she fell back into the grass. She trembled as I helped her sit up.

"I don't understand. Why aren't I dead?"

"Suppose you had a clever young girl who was too powerful to live but too much of an asshole to die? She did the only thing she could think of, and found another way." She smiled at me. "There's another way, but there isn't enough time to take you all the way through it. I can show you the path, and then you'll have to find your way to the end on your own. But I had to be sure you'd go through with it."

She used her cane to help herself to her feet.

"Go on home, child. Be at my door at daybreak. And bring your friends, this time." She sighed deeply. "Stop smiling. Tomorrow's going to suck."

Tanyrr insisted on joining us. He made a point of taking the lead as we made our way through the pre-dawn streets toward Maris's front door. The door opened as he raised a hand toward the knocker.

"Oh, for fuck's sake." Maris looked like she still hadn't slept, haggard and fragile.

"Lady Goselin, please accept my most heartfelt and sin—"

"Shut up."

"And most sincere apologies for my prior conduct. I place myself at your servi— ow!"

Maris cracked him on the forehead with her cane, hard enough to draw blood. "You three, inside. You, good Sir Ex-knight, can wait here for instructions. If you're feeling useful, that is."

We sat around her small table. Levras took one look at her, the state of her hair and her trembling hands, and realizing the lack of refreshments, set about familiarizing himself with her kitchen, at least enough to set a pot of water to boil for tea. After a moment's hesitation, he steeled his nerve and sent Tanyrr off to the market for a dozen hard rolls and some fresh cream. To my surprise, Tanyrr didn't argue. Just nodded once, and set off purposefully down the road.

I didn't feel right mentioning that Maris's remaining goats likely could supply plenty of cream.

Once Levras settled down, Maris filled us in on what was happening.

The problem with struggles for power, she told us, is that among those who are already powerful the one who wins is usually the most capable one. The one most capable of brutality, that is. The problem Ashbury has is very different—generations of peaceful succession within a single family had led to the rule of someone who was singularly *in*capable, so much so that he'd invented adventures out of whole cloth to boost his image, and paid to have those stories repeated as fact.

"Your taxes at work," Alia grumbled, and Maris nodded.

"A weak man who fears others might discover his weakness is dangerous," she said. "And your Duke is no exception. Falkirk in the north went through some troubles recently... feh, it was before any of you were born. The new duke there has not been a good neighbor. He's made a fiefdom of Dwarrenagor, and has been arming the trolls of Trellheim. He's annexed parts of Brittington, and there have been whispers of troops massing on our northern border. When I was younger, I could have settled all that, but my bladder isn't up to that kind of travel anymore."

"What's any of this have to do with Duke Farlow?" Alia asked.

"What has Solly told you about yesterday?"

I shook my head. "Nothing."

Maris looked at me, eyebrow raised, and I felt myself deflating. "How much should I tell them?"

"Their lives are as much on the line as yours and mine, but it's up to you."

So I told them everything. Tanyrr returned from the market in the meantime, and Levras set out to putting together a tray of breads and jams and fresh whipped butter. Tanyrr waited outside, face pressed to the window. I turned away from him, just in case he had a hidden talent for reading lips. Levras and Alia stared at me when I finished.

"So you can just..." Levras made a pulling motion. "And it's like blowing out a candle? That's...."

"Brilliant," Alia finished, just as I said, "Awful."

"You don't understand," Alia continued. "That kind of power hasn't been seen in a lifetime. There was once a mercenary queen they say could slay entire armies with a single wave of her arm. Fortunately, one of her generals recognized how dangerous she'd become, and had her murdered in her sleep."

"Hadn't heard that one," Maris said. "What'd you say her name was?"

"Queen Gos, they called her, and...." Alia trailed off, suddenly pale.

"Go on, then," Maris said. "What was that short for?"

Alia's voice was smaller than I'd ever heard it. "Gosling... Please don't kill me."

"So your brave Duke Farlow," Maris continued, casually spreading strawberry jam on her toast as if Alia hadn't just put her foot in her mouth so deep it had lodged in her esophagus, "when he couldn't convince this 'Queen Gos' woman to lay waste to Falkirk, decided to bring the greatest magical artificers in Ashbury together to construct such a weapon to wield himself. Fortunately, they miscalculated, and instead created an uncontrollable death maelstrom that will keep growing until it envelops the whole world."

Levras, who had just refilled Maris's tea, slapped the toast out of her hand.

"*Fortunately?*"

He looked like he was about to say more when a cloud of bees descended from rafters. Instead he backed away, staring aghast at red smeared across the palm of his hand.

Maris laughed and reached for another piece of toast, and the ominous buzzing lessened as the bees returned to their homes. A few settled on Levras's hand, investigating. Others settled on the toast, which had landed face-down, of course.

"Yes, *fortunately*," she said. She handed Levras a napkin. "As long as we attend to it in a timely manner. Solly, you have first-hand experience. Tell me, how much damage do you think 'Queen Gos' could have done in her lifetime if she'd had the imagination to think big? The biggest she could dream was to become someone important people valued. It never occurred to her to become an important person herself. Now imagine if, when she died, that power didn't die with her, but went to someone who didn't even have the most rudimentary understanding of how to control it. There's no telling how much damage Farlow would do, and how much more damage would be done by whichever asshole killed him for it. As it stands, the spell is undirected, so we have a better chance to defuse it."

"Do you know how to do that?" I asked.

"I have some ideas." She looked over the three of us critically. "But we'll need to train you first. We'll start immediately. You two," she said to Alia and Levras, "and Tanyrr... Actually, why don't you bring him in? Just show some discretion in what you say around him."

"Okay, what's the plan?" Tanyrr said, after Maris filled him in on the situation at the palace. He crouched by the table, since there were no more chairs and leaned forward eagerly. I think he thought there was a chance to redeem himself with his belov'd Duke.

Maris rolled her eyes. "Solly will be helping me prepare the counter to the spell that is currently raging uncontrolled inside the palace. You three, and anyone you can draft into the effort, need to evacuate Hob Hill. I mean, Oldtown, at the crest of Ashbury Tor," she said, when she realized she'd lost us. "Start with the buildings closest to the palace, but don't stop there. Once the spell breaks free of the palace walls, it will expand quickly."

"What of the palace itself?" Levras said. "The Duke left with only a small retinue. The word is the doors are locked, and none have entered or left since his departure."

Maris shook her head. "There's nothing you can do for them."

"Leah?" Tanyrr called the duchess by name, with such a note of concern I had never before heard from his lungs. "She didn't travel with Farlow."

Maris's jaw tightened, and she looked away. "I'm sorry. Maybe if I'd listened when you first came—"

"*Maybe?*" Tanyrr roared, flipping the table as he rose to his full height. His fists clenched. Bees swarmed him. "If she's dead because of you, and if we live through this, I *will* make you pay. For the Duchess, and for my Duke."

"Be very careful, Tanyrr." Maris's voice was calm, conversational, and full of hidden danger. "I don't want any of the bees to lose their lives frivolously."

"There is nothing frivolous in my promise."

Maris sighed. "I know, dear. But I'm not the reason she died."

"If you had—"

"I went to the palace after Solly told me Farlow had fled."

"You did?" He took a step back. "You got in?"

She nodded. "Everyone inside is dead, but it wasn't magic that killed them. I mean, other than the mages who loosed this spell—and they died instantly. It hasn't spread that far yet, and I've been maintaining a containment spell these last few days. No, those left in the building died before Farlow departed. By steel."

"I.... I don't understand."

"I don't, either. My only guess is the craven bastard didn't want to leave witnesses to his failure, and his cowardice."

"But..." Tanyrr fell to his knees, grief etched upon his features. "His own wife?"

"Perhaps she was less discreet than she thought," Alia said. Which was only slightly less cruel than to say that Tanyrr himself had been indiscreet. I had never even suspected. Perhaps that was naivety on my part.

"He's not a good man, your precious Duke," Maris said. "There's a reason beyond mere cussedness that I've distanced myself from his court."

Tanyrr clenched his teeth. "I'll hunt him down."

"I know."

"But first we have to save the people who *can* be saved."

Which sounded more like what I'd expected to hear when I signed up to squire for a knight than anything I'd ever heard while he was one.

Once we were alone, Maris let out a long breath. She brought her teacup to her face and breathed deep of its floral scents. "He's a keeper, that one."

"What?"

"Levras. Don't let him slip between your fingers."

"It's not like that. We're just friends." Besides, he was with Alia, or Alia was with him, or would be soon. It was too depressing to try to explain, and Maris wouldn't understand, anyway.

She reached out and patted my shoulder. "Let's get to work."

She led me out into the garden. The chickens and goats edged away from me. I noticed fresh-dug dirt in one corner, and Maris nodded. "I gave her a proper burial. Don't worry, we won't be adding to the graveyard today."

That was a bigger relief than I had expected, though I wasn't happy with the qualifier.

"Glad it's a nice day," she said, pulling her shirt over her head. She wore no underthings, and stood bare-breasted in front of me. "On a morning like this, you'd never suspect the end of the world was festering in the shadows." She unbuckled her belt.

"What are you doing?"

"Sunlight will make it easier to see."

I looked around at the surrounding buildings, at the crowded street on the other side of the waist-high garden fence. "But..."

"Nothing the neighbors haven't seen before. And if they have a problem, fuck 'em."

She wore nothing under her trousers, either. I averted my eyes.

"You're missing the point." She stepped close to me and gripped my jaw with surprisingly strong fingers. "I'm like you, only worse. Your friend was half right when she said Gosling was dead. You're looking at her corpse. The reason the person she used to be stayed dead is written on her flesh. Today, you'll need to understand what that means. You'll need to use your eyes—both your regular vision and your magical vision—and your sense of touch."

She stepped back and spread her arms.

"So what do you see?"

It took me an embarrassingly long time to see it. We spent the entire morning, broke for lunch, and returned to the garden after noon. I learned to ignore the people who gathered at the fence to watch. The shadows had started to grow long when I realized that a pale line that curled from her clavicle down under her breast was not one of her many scars. It was part of a design.

"Is this what you're talking about?" I traced the line with my finger.

It was rough, as though torn by a needle.

"Very good. Walk away, close your eyes. Turn around three times and come back. Still see it?"

"Yes."

Maris gave a curt nod—resounding approval from her, I would quickly discover. "Good. That's enough for today. Tomorrow we'll explore more."

Alia, Levras, and Tanyrr joined us shortly after dusk. Tanyrr and Alia were furious, Levras despondent.

"Idiots, the lot of them!" Tanyrr fumed.

"They wouldn't even send their children to safety," Levras lamented.

"Of course not, since this is all an obvious hoax at best, but more likely a transparent attempt to trick them into leaving their treasures unguarded." Alia spat on the floor, glanced fearfully at Maris, and knelt to mop it up with her sleeve.

"News of my disgrace is widespread," Tanyrr said. "I have been judged unworthy."

Alia snorted a laugh. "You've *never* been worthy, until today."

"I *failed* today."

"Today, you tried your best to help people who would rather humiliate you," Alia said, and Levras nodded his agreement. "I've *never* been proud to stand at your side before, but I was today."

Tears welled up in Tanyrr's eyes, as unexpected to him as to any of us; he brushed them away angrily. "But what do we do?"

"I don't know about you," Maris said, "but I'm going to bed. I haven't slept for three days, and I'm too old to sustain that. The containment spell I put up won't hold for more than another day. I don't have the strength to renew it again. There'll be a sudden expansion as it breaks free of my spell, then steady growth, gradually increasing in speed."

"Broadsheets," Levras said. "We need to take this to the broadsheets. Get the news into every hand in the city."

"You think they'll believe us any more than anyone else?"

Maris afforded Levras an approving glance. "No, it's a great idea, and I'm embarrassed that I didn't think of it myself." She struggled to her feet, shuffled to her desk and began digging through the drawers. "I'm so tired I'm not thinking straight anymore. Ah, here it is."

Tanyrr took what she held out to him. A rock. He frowned.

"Give that to Melkin at the *Daily Ashburian*, so he knows I'm involved. Tell him what's happening, and the concrete steps citizens can take, and he'll get it printed. Give him dirt on the Duke, and he'll even be happy about it." She handed Tanyrr a slip of paper. "His home address. This late, he'll be there if he isn't at the Pink Pony on Alrovado Street. Once Melkin's on board, all the others will follow. Tomorrow, get out there and try again. Solly, I'll expect you at daybreak. Now get out of my house."

Exhaustion hit me hard as we set out to find Melkin, and I stumbled over cobbles. Levras caught me.

"Let's get you home, Solly."

Alia nodded. "We've got this. Levras, take him to bed."

For some reason, Levras blushed. But he got me home safe.

We were at the market before dawn.

"You and Lady Goselin will starve yourselves if we don't force you to eat," Levras said, which may not have been too far from the truth.

Maris was still asleep when we arrived, but the door opened to my touch. She looked older and frailer lying there than anyone I had ever seen. It was hard to imagine she was the same person who had handily dispatched an overbearing Sir Tanyrr a week earlier. I hated to wake her, but she'd be angry if we let her sleep. Still, I waited until Levras had tea ready and breakfast scones in the oven. Alia and Tanyrr set the table.

Maris was groggy when she woke, disoriented. She blinked at me without recognition for a minute before giving me a pale smile and patting my hand. I'd brought her tea, but she waved it away.

"Don't get between an old lady and her outhouse."

The first of the broadsheet reporters, Tali Petradottr of the *Evening Bulletin*, arrived as we were finishing breakfast. She carried a pad of paper and a self-inking quill.

"These three speak for me," Maris said, indicating Alia and Levras and, yes, Tanyrr. "They're headed to Oldtown to lead the evacuation. Perhaps if you ask nicely, they'll allow you to go along." Petradottr was wise enough not to press.

After they were gone, Maris wrote a note directing all questions to Tanyrr, Alia, and Levras, and tacked it to her front door. We went back out to the garden, where she stripped again, and we resumed our investigation.

Now that I knew what to look for, I found it again easily. Even better, I was able to trace the entire nigh-invisible pattern of lines and whorls that covered her body. She gave me a stick of charcoal and had me draw the outline on her flesh. When I was done, she inspected my work with approval, and then she washed it off with soapy water. The pattern, she said, she'd discovered and painted onto her body, weaving a binding spell into the paint. A tattooist then scribed it into her flesh with a dry needle, with Maris feeding the binding spell through the needle's movement. The result was a pattern made of the faintest scarring, nearly imperceptible, unless you knew exactly what you were looking for, and how to see it. The myriad other scars carved into her body were far more obvious.

"Now, do the same thing, but, without any crutches."

She wrapped my hands in burlap, making improvised mittens of the coarse fabric, and then blindfolded me with a strip of black silk. She placed the charcoal back in my hand.

"I don't know how to do this," I said.

"If you knew, you wouldn't need to learn."

I can't describe what it was like, searching for patterns in the dark. I couldn't depend on Maris; I couldn't depend on anything external. It was only by looking within that I found my way. And when I did, it *hurt*. I can't tell you what I did, but eventually, Maris said, "That's enough."

I sat back in the dirt and drew a shuddering breath. My whole body was trembling. I couldn't make my hands work.

Maris removed my blindfold. It was night. I had no idea how late it was. She took the charcoal from my numb fingers and pulled the burlap from my useless hands.

"You did well, Solly. Come on, it's been a long day, and tomorrow will be longer. I think we could both use some sleep."

But it was not to be. Maris's cottage was well lit when we entered, candles and lanterns casting erratic shadows. Tanyrr and Levras sat on the floor; Alia, Tali Petradottr, and two others I'd never seen before gathered around the table. All of them stared as we entered.

Maris dropped her clothes by the door and pulled a mug from a cupboard, seemingly unconcerned about her nakedness in front of unexpected houseguests. Levras leapt to his feet.

"Let me get that for you. You two must be famished!"

My stomach growled in response. We'd neglected to break for lunch, or for anything, really. My lips and tongue were sticky.

"Ale first," Maris said. "Everything else is optional."

"We hope you don't mind," Tali said, "but with the palace gone, and the Duke 'missing,' the people are looking for guidance. We're trying to determine what that should look like."

Maris drained her mug (I did the same—it seemed impossible that I'd ever not be thirsty again) and handed it to Levras for a refill. "So you're using my home to stage a coup?"

"You can hardly call it a coup when the government has abdicated!" Tali slapped the table. "We're filling a gap, until something more permanent can be put in place."

"Like Duke Farlow returning." Maris held up a finger. "Do not underestimate the masses' tendency toward inertia."

"He's welcome to try," Tanyrr said, his hand curling into a fist.

"Wait," I said. "You said 'the palace gone'?"

"Yes." Alia sounded grim. "You were right about the rapid expansion. We almost lost Tanyrr."

"He was brilliant!" Tali said. "He threw himself into a building as it was being overcome, and ran out with two children and their mother in his arms just as it was collapsing!"

Tanyrr lowered his head. "Her husband and oldest son were lost."

Who was this new Tanyrr? Had Maris done something to his mind when she tended his injuries? Was he feigning modesty in front of the press? Had Duke Farlow's betrayal really led him to reevaluate his life? Or was it simply that absent the Duke's influence, absent the demands of power, some "real" Tanyrr was emerging from the shadows? I wish I could say. When I mentioned it to Maris, later, she shrugged.

"Even the worst of us can change, if they want to. Not everyone takes as long as I did."

But that was later. Right then, Maris said, "Well, kids, you're welcome to plot your revolution, but I need to get to bed. Solly, you'll want to check your work before I wash it off."

So I did, acutely aware of Alia and Levras's eyes as I inspected the old woman's naked body. Maris remained oblivious, allowing me to turn and position her limbs, to lift her breasts away from her ribs to view the charcoaled lines there.

"Are they...? Is it right?"

She ruffled my hair. "It is. You're a fast learner. Go on, go plot with your friends."

I did as she said, but it was useless. My mind was still visualizing patterns and threads and colors, and could make no sense of talk of rank and fiefdoms and command structures. Maris had been listening, though, as she washed the charcoal from her skin.

"Not that I'd know the first thing about politics," she said, drying herself with a towel, "but it all sounds very complicated from here. If *I* were plotting a coup, I'd keep it as simple as possible. You're creating a provisional council at best, to give structure to society. For anything permanent, you need either overwhelming force, or the overwhelming support of the people. And you'll only get the latter by involving them in the process."

She pulled a selection of volumes from one of her many bookshelves and dropped them on the table.

Tali picked up one at random. "*The Amisaran Experiment: Explorations in Self-Governance.*" Her eyes widened. "How do you have this? These books were all banned. I remember the burnings, when I was little."

I had never heard of book burnings. Or of Amisara, for that matter.

Tanyrr looked as confused as me. "What do they mean by 'self-governance'? There can be only one duke over a territory."

"Shush," Tali said. "I'll explain it later."

Alia and Levras were looking at one another, their heads touching as they pored over the book. *Minutes of the Provisional Council of Amisara, Vol. 1.*

"They published everything?" Alia asked. "All their arguments? Even their mistakes?"

"Daily, in the broadsheets. And citizens were encouraged to comment publicly on the decisions. But never you mind, I'm sure you weren't thinking of going that far. You can put those back on the shelf with the others. I'm going to bed. Try to keep your voices down."

I found my head nodding shortly afterward, and ended up crawling onto the bed beside her. I don't remember falling asleep, but when I awoke, Levras was snoring in my ear and the body that was tucked closely into mine wasn't Maris's. Not nearly bony enough.

I lay there, luxuriating in the scent and warmth of Alia's body, until she became aware of just how awake I was.

"Hope you kept that in your pants," she murmured.

Of course, I had. It's just that pants have limited ability to hide certain things. "I'm sorry," I said, shifting my hips away from her, only to realize that Levras was similarly awake. He'd stopped snoring at some point, and I hadn't noticed.

"I'm sorry," he said, rolling away from me, and out of the bed.

All this might have led to an awkward conversation if Tanyrr and Tali hadn't made an entrance through the back door at that moment. Tali wore nothing but a towel wrapped around her waist; Tanyrr didn't have a towel. Their hair was wet, and their skins bright and pink.

"You're awake!" Tanyrr proclaimed. "Good. You've just got to see what the old woman has back here! Never mind the kettle, I'll bring tea out to you."

What "the old woman" kept in her back yard was a small pool, set into the ground. Hot, but bearably so. Some hidden magic caused the water to swirl and bubble.

We looked at each other in awkward indecision, until Alia pulled her shirt over her head.

"What?" she said. "It didn't kill Tanyrr."

"What about...." I glanced down at the front of my pants.

"Fine, you can let it out. Just don't try sticking it anywhere uninvited."

Though the water was relaxing, once we acclimatized to the temperature, the situation was still awkward enough that none of us seemed able to *actually* relax. Fortunately, the pool was large enough that we could sit without touching each other, except where our feet came together in the center. I used the time to describe what the previous day's studies had entailed, and the discoveries I'd made, my story cut short when Tanyrr and Tali returned with a hot kettle and a tray of teacups. Tanyrr poured, and Tali passed around the cups. Then the two of them climbed into the tub with us, fitting themselves between Levras and me.

And suddenly there was no room to maintain our awkward distance anymore.

"Where's Maris?" I asked, trying to ignore Alia's hand on my thigh, and trying to figure out where to put my own hands. I was certain that neither Tali nor Alia would welcome them. A quick glance at Levras was enough to know that he was struggling with the same concerns.

"Errands, she said." Tanyrr shrugged massive shoulders. "Said we should get back to our 'adorable little coup and saving lives and whatnot,' and that you should introduce yourself to the bees." His attempt to imitate Maris's voice was only marginally successful.

"The bees? How?"

Another shrug. Tali used the opportunity to duck her head under his arm and press her cheek against his chest.

We talked about what the city guard had been doing, both to evacuate those at risk, and to find the displaced temporary shelter. The guard had placed themselves under Tanyrr's—and by extension, Alia and Levras's—direction, as the upper echelons of their command structure had either fled with the Duke, or never escaped the palace. Another effort was underway by the scholars and students of the University of Ashbury to preserve artwork and rare texts. The art museum and the university library were being emptied, and teams were searching abandoned homes for anything "of historical, educational, or cultural significance" which could be salvaged.

"Who decides what's significant?" I asked.

"That's highly subjective." Tali looked at me with an oddly sly expression on her face. "In a crisis situation, you just have to address things as they, ahem, arise."

And with that, she ducked her head under the water, into Tanyrr's lap. Tanyrr's face went bright red, and his fingers tangled in her hair. One or more of us gasped out loud, and Alia's hand shifted from my thigh to the one thing that had stubbornly refused to relax, squeezing gently.

Levras and I both looked at Alia, wide-eyed, at the same time, and Alia stood suddenly, slipping and almost falling as she scrambled out of the bubbling pool.

"Time to get to work!" she announced, and ran, still dripping wet, into the cottage.

Levras and I climbed out more circumspectly, both of us acutely aware of our own states. By the time we'd struggled into our trousers,

Tali had climbed onto Tanyrr's lap. We gathered up the rest of our clothes and followed Alia inside.

Alia flushed red when she saw us. She'd dressed, though her hair was a wet, tangled mess, and she was poring over the labels of the hundreds of small bottles of herbs and extracts. "I don't know what they put in the tea. You're the magician. What'd they use?"

"I've only been a magician for four days! You think I've had time to learn all this?" Levras was more likely than me to know what any of this stuff was.

"Fine! Whatever! Just... don't start thinking that meant anything."

We fell into an uncomfortable silence, none of us daring to look at each other. I claimed a place on the loveseat with a pillow propped behind my back—the most comfortable place in the cottage, outside of the bed or the hot tub, neither of which seemed like a good idea at the moment—and tried to think of bees. Despite the fact that my thoughts were swarming, I didn't have much luck.

Alia and Levras didn't say goodbye when they left.

Not long after, Tanyrr and Tali came in, happy and laughing and nude, toweling each other off. I tried to ignore them, concentrating on bees, to little avail. They dressed, ate a hurried breakfast, and left to continue the evacuation effort.

Before they left, Tanyrr stopped to clap me on the shoulder. "Don't give up, lad. She's already starting to see you with new eyes."

"No, she's not," I said.

Tanyrr laughed, deep and hearty and thoroughly humiliating. "The three of you were made for each other. I've never seen anything so obvious. You all need to start thinking about what you can give instead of what you can get, and all of you can get what you need." He tapped me on the forehead. "You love each other. So love each other. It's not complicated."

Tali linked her fingers into his and pulled him toward the door.

And that's the last time I saw him.

Sometime in the night, the sound of the maelstrom had started being audible as far out as Maris's cottage, a soft susurration like dry autumn leaves in the wind, somewhere in the distance. Barely noticeable. Besides, I was distracted.

I remained distracted throughout the day, what with one thing or the other, and the sound grew so slowly, it was just like any other sound in the city: background noise.

Until it became suddenly, horribly, unignorable.

I don't know what happened, exactly. I'd ignored my hunger, and had even stopped thinking about bees. To be honest, it was hard to think about the bees when all I could think about was all the crazy emotions that were tangled up in the odd relationships between me and Alia and Levras. And this new Tanyrr, the happy, caring one... I still hadn't managed to wrap my head around it.

I'd managed to let these thoughts shift into a constant background noise, while the foreground went blank.

"Not bad," Maris said. I hadn't heard her come in. "I'm sure the other two hives will come around eventually."

I only realized I was covered in bees when they took to the air. They made a beeline across the cottage to bump off her body, and then flew back up into the rafters.

"All right," she said. "Off your ass. We've got a lot of work ahead of us."

This time it was my turn to strip naked in the garden and be gawked at by passersby on the street, and Maris's turn to wield the charcoal.

The distant rustle was noticeably louder outside the cottage, now, and I said something about it. I don't remember what. She cracked me across the shins with her cane.

"Focus on the task at hand, or you'll never learn."

So we repeated yesterday's exercise, but this time, I guided her hand on my body. The pattern had some similarities to Maris's, but the shape of it was different, contoured not only to the differences in our bodies, but also to other differences. In our essences, or our energies, or something. I really don't know. There were differences. I suppose each of us is unique, and that any pattern to bind a person's power would have to be unique to them.

I was really happy with my progress. The second time we did it with both of us blindfolded, me so that I couldn't cheat by seeing, her so that she wasn't tempted to interpret what I told her through what she saw herself. I had to guide her verbally, and through touch. It was the most difficult thing I had ever done, but I seemed to have developed an ability to push through and find hidden stores of strength behind the exhaustion.

We had nearly completed the pattern when a low rumbling started.

"What's...?"

"Fuck!"

The rumbling grew louder, punctuated by sharp cracks. The blindfold came away from my eyes, and what I saw terrified me like nothing I'd ever seen before: Maris Goselin, wide-eyed with worry.

A tremendous crash shook the ground under our feet.

"Hob Hill's collapsing," she said.

Hob Hill was what Maris called Ashbury Tor, I recalled. What the goblins called it, when they lived here, Alia told me, much later. "The tunnels must go down farther than I know. The maelstrom must have destabilized the whole hill."

But... Alia and Levras were there.

"Go," she said. "I'll just slow you down." And then, "Wait! Pants, first."

The streets were chaotic and full, half of the people fleeing the center of Ashbury, the other half rushing inward to see the devastation for themselves. I ran barefoot, struggling with my belt and my shirt. What I'd do when I got there, I had no idea.

I broke out of the crowd and into Oldtown at the edge of Ashbury Tor. The center of the hill had become a massive crater that extended beyond the maelstrom. Fires raged in some of the buildings that remained on the edge of the chasm, already starting to spread to adjacent buildings.

Something bumped my nose, and I almost jumped out of my skin. It bumped my nose again, and this time my eyes focused on the tiny yellow creature hovering in front of my face. Once it realized that I'd noticed it, it flew away. I followed.

The bee led me deeper into Oldtown. I climbed the cracked and broken streets, past ancient, shattered buildings that had once housed the richest of the rich, the noblest of the noble. I followed the bee to a waterline, dozens of people passing buckets to quench a fire that was already beyond their control, perilously close to the crumbling edge that dropped away into the jagged teeth of a freshly revealed ravine.

Alia and Levras were in that line. I ran to them.

"Stop! There aren't enough buckets in Ashbury to put out this fire."

"Shut up and help," Alia snapped.

"We have to try," Levras said. "Or the fire will consume the whole city."

More of the street crumbled away; one of the water-bearers nearly tumbled to his death. Still, Alia and Levras refused to abandon the fool's errand.

It was infuriating. They were too stubborn to recognize a lost cause, and they and everyone else in this line might die as a result. And here I was, a mage who was so powerful he could make a tiny light glow, and draw charcoal lines on an old woman's skin. If I knew what I was doing, I could simply snuff out the fire, or summon water from the air to drown it. I could...

And then suddenly, I could see the energy being generated by the fire, and by the heated stone, hungry and feeding. And I knew how to help.

I found the cold of the earth in the ravine, deep blue and black threads, and the cool pale blue threads of the sky, wrapping it around the overheated rock. I used the energy of the fire itself to feed the smoke back into it, starving it of the air it needed to breathe. It wasn't enough to put the fire out, but enough to bank the flames and give the others the chance to douse it. I made some mistakes, yes—unexpected bursts of flame where I brought in the wrong mix of threads, or wove them improperly, but I noticed the effects as they were happening and adapted.

Honestly, I was pretty proud of what I'd done, even though by the time we'd controlled this one blaze, Maris had arrived and had extinguished all the other fires that had started. Her bees had also arrived en masse, flying through the rubble, finding survivors trapped in the wreckage.

I'm not sure how it was that I realized what they were doing, or how I understood what they were telling me, but I did, and I helped Maris direct the rescuers. By the time the bees left just before dusk, they had given us enough information that we were able to save hundreds of lives. But not all of them. Too many had been crushed under the rubble or fallen to their deaths into the pit that had been exposed.

Others died as more of Oldtown collapsed under the stresses that the maelstrom exerted. We worked through the night, until Alia and Levras forced me to stop. We'd done what could be done. Oldtown had been evacuated.

It was too dangerous now for anyone from Ashbury Tor to return to their homes, whether it was to save priceless artworks or irreplaceable heirlooms. The only people braving the ruined streets of Oldtown were looters. Alia was one of those who took umbrage. She drew steel to confront the thieves, but Maris called her back.

"Do you know who those people are?"

Alia scowled. "Does it matter?"

"Exactly my point. Everything out there will be lost, one way or another. Does it matter how it's lost? Come on, let's go home. We've got a lot to get done today."

I've avoided talking about the maelstrom. There's a reason for that.

I couldn't look at it.

I'd expected it to be loud, but it wasn't. In itself, it was quiet—silent as the tomb, as they say. The sound, that crackling rustling that seemed to permeate all of existence, of dry leaves, of fields of golden wheat in the wind, was the sound of the world losing coherence at the maelstrom's touch.

I didn't need to look at it to know what I'd see.

Toby the goat's corpse, writ large in the center of Ashbury. Not just death. Life, being ripped away as if it had never belonged.

The city slowly resolved from shadow as we walked back to Maris's cottage, oddly peaceful in the pre-dawn light, as if the world wasn't being ripped apart.

There were nearly a dozen people in the cottage, asleep in Maris's bed, on the loveseat, on the floor. Some had been here the day before; others were new. I saw no sign of Tanyrr or Tali; I assumed they had decided to spend the night camping in the back again, in or near the hot tub. The table was covered in notes—rough drafts of declarations, manifestos, skeletons of government structures.

"Oof, look at these louts," Levras said. "We can clear them off your bed, Lady Goselin."

"Eh, let them sleep. We've no time for it." She shuffled to the stove and set a kettle to boil. "Levras, if you'd be so kind, the tea is in that cupboard. No, no, there's a tin on the top shelf. Yes, that's the one. Use those leaves. They have a bit more kick to them."

"We've been up all night," I whined. "I was exhausted *before* we were interrupted. I couldn't possibly do another round of training right now."

Maris breathed out through her nose slowly. "You've seen that thing. It's growing too fast. We don't have a lot of time to get you ready before facing it. We don't have time to sleep."

Levras made us biscuits with gravy, and sausages. The tea did, indeed, have a kick, one unlike anything I'd experienced before. It pushed away sleep, yes, but left me anxious and jittery. It made my teeth hurt.

There was a knock on the door. Maris waved her hand and it swung open.

Tali entered, her face blank.

"Oh," Alia said. "I thought you and Tanyrr were in back." She spoke just a bit too quickly; she'd had two cups of the tea.

Tali walked past Alia, silently handing a copy of the morning broadsheet to her as she made her way to the table to review the papers generated overnight. Alia watched her quizzically, shrugged, and looked at the broadsheet.

"Fuck," she said, her hand covering her mouth.

"What?"

She held the broadsheet out to us.

Ashbury Hero Falls, the headline said. There was a hasty etching of Tanyrr's face. Tali had written the copy.

"You can read it later," Maris said. "Right now, we have work to do. Yes, all three of you."

She led us out into the garden and told me to strip again. This time, I had to guide Alia and Levras in drawing the charcoal lines on my flesh. Maris had us do it over and over, washing off with soapy water between attempts, until it felt like we could reproduce the patterns in our sleep. We didn't break for lunch; Maris just brought out some bread and cold meats, and more of that awful tea, and after that, she had us all put on blindfolds. I was so tired, and the job of finding the pattern and guiding my friends so exhausting, and Tanyrr was *dead*; my body didn't even react to Alia's hands on my naked flesh.

It didn't even occur to me until later, the next morning, when we woke tangled in each other's limbs in Maris's bed, when my body remembered how to react. Levras, as well, though he at least had trousers on to disguise his discomfort. He and Alia extracted themselves quickly and set about putting together some breakfast, while I gathered bedding around my waist and set about trying to remember where I'd left my clothing.

It was well after dawn. Ashbury's budding revolutionaries had camped on the floor in the library portion of Maris's one-room cottage, or had gone home, or camped in the back—with the exception of Tali, who was writing feverishly at the kitchen table, barely acknowledging the rest of us. Maris had claimed the loveseat for herself. She looked tiny and frail, curled up in one corner; her skin was grey, and for a moment I was afraid that she wasn't breathing.

She jerked awake when I touched her, wrapping her hand claw-like around my wrist. With visible effort, she pushed the panicked confusion out of her eyes. Relaxed her hand. Turned the death-grip into a kindly pat. Tried to say something, but coughed instead.

She really didn't look well.

"It's late," she rasped. "You should be training."

"Breakfast first," I said. "Or we won't get anywhere. And *regular* tea this morning."

"S'pose you're right. You're wise to watch out for the other stuff. It can be a hard habit to break."

I did finally find my clothes, outside where we'd been working. The goats had been at them, and it would take more than a few stitches to make them functional again.

"Well," Maris said, "you won't be needing them today anyway."

This day we actually wove what Maris called the hobbling spell. Alia and Levras took turns drawing on me, while I pulled power out of the earth and tied each line to my flesh, as if I was stitching a wound.

If I thought it hurt before, I was wrong. This was like driving a hot needle into my flesh and using it to pull coarse twine through the wound.

But worse than that: with every stitch, I felt as if some of my newly discovered and barely-explored power was being stripped away. As if I were tying weights to my limbs. Hobbling spell was right.

Maris guided me on the first attempt, but had taken a seat on a bench after that and just watched. She seemed to be wilting as the day went by, but when any of us expressed concern for her, she waved it off.

"Made it eighty-five years. I'll survive another day. You just worry about yourselves."

Four times, we went through the process, before we got it right. My skin felt raw, my whole body did, but we'd done it. We'd succeeded.

Maris struggled to her feet and approached.

"Nice work," she said. "Took me months to get this far. Don't get a fat head. I was working blind. How're you feeling?"

"Good," I said. "But I'm glad we're done."

"You have confidence in your work, then?

I did. I could *feel* it, the spell, wrapped around me. "*Our* work," I said, including Alia and Levras. "Absolutely."

She patted my arm. "Good. Time to test it, then. Pick one of them."

"What?"

"Your confidence is absolute, isn't it? Shouldn't be any danger." She pushed Alia toward me.

Levras stepped forward, interposing himself. "I trust you."

I didn't. I couldn't imagine either of them lifeless, rotting corpses like poor Toby. No, actually, the problem was that I *could*.

Maris laughed. "Get one of the chickens, girl. I'll not be sacrificing another goat."

Alia didn't hold the chicken tight enough. When I found the lifethread, the hen panicked, flapping her wings and scratching for release. And then she went still.

With an uncharacteristic squeal, Alia let the corpse fall to the ground with a wet splat, and jumped back as the body burst and splashed on her shoes. Blood welled up from a long gash the hen had gouged in Alia's arm; Maris's chickens were apparently of a breed where both roosters and hens grew spurs.

I took a step backward, tripped and fell on my ass. I barely managed to turn my head to the side before emptying my stomach.

"Self-confidence is good, until it gets someone killed." Maris loomed over me, her face haloed by the noon sun. In that lighting, and with that angle, she looked sinister. "Keep at it until you get it right, and try not to run out of chickens. Do not stop, no matter how tired you get. We don't have enough time left to be kind. You need to get to the point where you really can trust the life of someone you love to what you've wrought, because at some point, the lives of everyone and everything you love will depend on it. And I know pressure doesn't help, but you have to get it right today."

I killed three more chickens before we got it right.

But when we finally did, the relief was so overwhelming that I hugged Alia, and the chicken (who pecked my forehead hard enough to draw blood), and Levras. Then I looked for Maris. She wasn't out in the garden. I ran into the cottage to tell her the news.

"Maris, I did it!" I announced, throwing open the door.

"Shhh!"

There were even more people in the cottage than had been there before. They'd dragged the loveseat over to the kitchen table, and someone had brought an additional table and more chairs. I recognized a couple of them by sight, but only Tali by name. Several of them shushed me angrily.

"Quiet, you'll wake her. Why are you naked?"

Tali ignored me; she was writing feverishly again, or perhaps still, listening intently as the others argued, quietly but intensely, around her, and capturing key elements of the conversation for the ages.

Maris was a small lump under the covers of her giant bed. No, I wasn't going to disturb her. I went back out to Alia and Levras to tell them.

"So, what do we do now?" Levras asked.

"Wash him off and do it again," Alia said. She tossed a soapy rag to Levras. "Unless you want to trust that this wasn't just blind luck. Personally, I like my flesh the way it is."

Levras washed me off while Alia watched. Now that the anxiety of persistent failure had eased, the fact that I stood wet and naked before my two closest friends, one of whom was scrubbing my buttocks while the other watched with a smirk on her face, came suddenly to the fore of my mind. To my embarrassment, my body responded. It turned out to be significantly harder to wash away the charcoal when the spell was woven through it correctly, which just extended my mortification.

My body remained a distraction, both to myself and to my companions, as we continued our exercises, but we succeeded in not murdering any more poultry. We worked late into the evening, stopping only when my stomach growled, and we realized that we had missed both lunch and supper.

Maris was still asleep when we went in, though I had no idea how she could sleep through the cacophony of over two-dozen people arguing over what structures would need to be put in place to provide the people the ability to form a new government. One gentleman suggested that only the people as a whole had the right to create those structures, and that the whole concept of a provisional government was illegitimate.

His point seemed moot, though, as runners from the city guard came regularly to report news and request orders.

Alia listened carefully as Levras and I put together a meal—originally designed for the three of us, until it became clear that the gathered revolutionaries had been too busy arguing amongst themselves to pay attention to the time, or their stomachs.

"The way I see it," Alia said, "with Falkirk massing troops at our northern border, you'll need to get consensus from the people as soon as possible on whether to ratify the provisional council or to bring back Duke Farlow. If he's fallen in with Falkirk, as I think I heard someone say, Falkirk will use his 'cause' as a reason to invade. So the first thing we need to do is demand his immediate release. Ashbury will not stand for any of our citizens being used as hostages."

Tali nodded, scribbling furiously on a fresh sheet of paper. She stopped and looked up. "That might swing opinion in Farlow's favor."

"You're right. First thing would be a vote, and *then* the announcement."

"Third thing," Levras said, heaping his aromatic improvisations into serving bowls, "is to hold a second set of elections to bring more people into the council. I'm sure you're all good and smart people, but look at you lot. You're hardly representative of the people of Ashbury. If you're going to create a just society, you need the poor and working classes to hold as much power as the wealthy." He paused as the others fell silent. "That *is* your goal, right?"

Tali looked over about a dozen pages of tiny script, drew a line through several of them, and across a few other scattered paragraphs. Started a new sheet. *On the Formation of a Just Society*. The characters were not as steady as I'd come to expect from her. Her hands trembled when they weren't pressed against the table.

She reached for her cup of tea, but I reached it first.

"How long have you been awake?" I took a sip. The tea was bitter with the unmistakable flavor of the leaf that Maris had given us, and it seemed that Tali was brewing it stronger than Maris advised.

"Give that back," Tali protested. "I'll sleep when there's time."

"You mean, you'll sleep when you're dead. You're already halfway there. There's nothing you can do for Tanyrr, and there's nothing you'll be able to do for anyone else if you kill yourself with this stuff."

"For Tanyrr? You think I'm doing this for Tanyrr? I barely knew him."

"I think we all barely knew him," Levras said. He brought her a fresh cup of tea, this one smelling of chamomile and lavender. I suspected valerian root, and learned later that he had also found skullcap and lemon balm extracts in Maris's cupboard, and used them liberally, with a generous dollop of honey to mask the taste of the soporifics. "A few days from now you'll be needed more than ever, but if you don't stop now, you won't be able to help when it matters most. You've already laid down a solid foundation. Trust that it'll hold overnight."

After eating, we relaxed for a little in the hot tub, and then, overcome with exhaustion, we slept under the stars on a blanket spread on the ground, huddled together for warmth.

I don't know where Levras hid the unusually strong tea leaves, but he hid them well; Tali was asleep face-down on the table when Maris kicked us awake at dawn the next morning.

"Well?" she demanded, once we'd had enough tea to be coherent. She'd had it brewed before she woke us. "Did you get it working? I still have some hens left, so either you got the spell working or you gave up. Which is it?"

"We got it working."

"Just once, I bet. Kids today have no work ethic."

"Six times, successfully."

"Really. You, girl, you'd trust your life to it?"

"Yes, mum," Alia said, without hesitation.

Maris attempted her best harrumph (a hacking cough spoiled the effect). "Good, you're ready for the next step. Clean him up, then. You, Levras, you're with me. Fetch that mortar over there. Oh, and send all these idiots away. They'll need to find somewhere else for their plotting today."

Being scrubbed and inspected by Alia alone was even more mortifying than when Levras did it. *He* actually enjoyed the task. Alia just complained the whole time, and when my body ignored my desperate pleas and responded to her touch, she slapped it away (which, I have to say, did *nothing* to resolve the issue).

"Save it for Levras," she said. A little bitterly, which just punctuated the problem: I was in love with Alia, who was in love with Levras, who was in love with me. That last part was new, at least to me. If he'd had feelings for me before, he'd hidden them, as far as I was aware. Then again, I hadn't gone to any great effort to advertise my affection for Alia. Quite the opposite, actually.

Freshly scrubbed, we sought out Maris and Levras. We found them seated at the kitchen table, where Levras was organizing stacks of papers. The cottage had been cleared out of revolutionaries. Only Tali remained, still face-down on the table.

"They left her behind?" Alia said with just a tinge of the contempt and annoyance that I felt.

"Seemed kinder than waking her," Maris said.

"Besides, you had to see this," Levras added. He gripped Tali by the hair and raised her head. One side of her face was covered in ink, mirror image of one of the political missives she'd penned.

"That, too," Maris said. "Well, we've got six hours to kill. Fancy learning some magic?"

The next six hours were a crash course on magical improvisation: how to identify the nature of a thread, how to combine threads to achieve an outcome, how to knot threads to achieve results outside of their nature.

"It's possible," Maris told me, "to achieve any result you want with any type of thread at all. The spell just becomes more difficult to weave. Remember when I was telling you about ripples in a pool of water?"

"Yes."

"You have to figure out how to manage the interference patterns— that's what creates your effects. By creating oppositional patterns and knots that open or restrict the flow of power, you can control the effects. The more you restrict the type of threads, the colors you use to create a spell, the more complicated it gets."

"How complicated? What I've seen is already more complicated than I'll ever be able to understand. If I didn't have you, I'd be completely lost."

She patted me on the hand. "Eh, you're a clever boy. You'll muddle through."

She had me practice the light spell using only the light green thread born of the new growth of spring plants. It was hideously complex. What had been a simple slipknot using threads of light and darkness turned into a massive undertaking, a twisted and convoluted mess that refused to behave, no matter how much I tried to make it work. Eventually, Maris cast it, to show me it could be done. It worked. But it wasn't pretty.

"It would be unwise to try this with anything more complicated than this spell, until you understand this one inside and out. And the pattern you build will be different depending on what type of power you're working with."

It was more than I could make sense of. If I'd felt any sense of accomplishment after the last few days, this exercise stripped it away. Watching an old woman effortlessly pull together a spell I had no hope of ever understanding did wonders for my self-esteem. Still, time passed, and eventually Maris declared that the henna she and Levras had prepared was ready for application.

This involved me getting naked again, and Alia and Levras painstakingly painting the hobbling pattern onto my flesh with henna, while I cast the spell that bound it into my flesh. If it had felt binding when we'd done it with charcoal, this was many times worse—possibly because the henna tattoo would last for weeks, rather than hours or, at best, a day. When it was done, I was exhausted and miserable and wanted nothing more than to crawl into a corner and cry. But nobody asked what I wanted.

"Ready to test your work?"

I glared at Maris. "Sure. Why not?"

"Go fetch a chicken," Maris told Alia.

"No."

We all stared at Alia.

She raised an eyebrow at me. "You said you felt a difference when you did it right. You feel it now?" I nodded, afraid of what she'd say next. "Then we don't need a chicken. I trust you."

I have to say: those are the three most terrifying words in any language. Even more terrifying than "I love you." The worst "I love you" can do is break your heart. Not stop it forever.

I looked beseechingly at Levras and Maris. Levras seemed terrified, but he just looked to Alia and said nothing. Maris just shrugged as if she couldn't bother to care.

"Standing around with your thumb up your ass isn't going to change the result any," she said.

Even so, I argued, but Alia was insistent. So I found her lifethread—it was becoming easier with practice—and pulled it.

The pain was excruciating, blinding, far worse than when I failed to kill the chickens, and it was the happiest pain of my life, because it meant that the hobbling spell had done *something*, and Alia was *probably* still alive. When I could see again, I realized that I'd collapsed to my knees. Alia was sitting on the garden bench, looking a bit green about the gills, but definitely alive.

"I'm fine," she said, angrily. "Thanks for asking."

"Lucky," Maris said. "Solly, you need to keep the henna paste on for at least two hours. I'm famished. Is anyone else hungry?"

Alia brought her hand to her mouth. "I'll never eat again."

But by the time Levras pulled together a late lunch from the dwindling food supplies—somehow without sacrificing any of the chickens—Alia was as ravenous as the rest of us. We passed the food around Tali, who remained unconscious for the entire meal.

"Not bad for a last meal," Maris said, when we had finished. "Wouldn't you say, Solly? Still, I think what this evening really needs to top it off is some simple beauty."

"We're not beautiful enough for you?" Levras said.

Maris chuckled. "Almost, but no. Actually, I was thinking, well, you know that old saying, remember to stop and smell the flowers? Or was that before your time?"

I had assumed from the start that Maris had been training me to take on the maelstrom of destruction—that everything we had done was to prepare me, to inscribe a pattern onto my flesh that the maelstrom would crash against, and collapse into. I'd been dubious about my ability to absorb that level of energy, and this afternoon's experience with Alia did nothing to dispel that doubt, but it was unquestionably true that what I had bound into my flesh over the last few days was the counter to what we faced now. Duke Farlow had sought the power to do what Maris had once done, and what I could now do—to pull the lifethreads of anyone he wanted, and instead created something that pulled the lifethreads—and whatever the equivalent was for non-living things like palaces and city streets—of everything it touched. That is what Maris had taught me to block. I'd understood that for several days now, and had accepted the responsibility, and the cost. Not for the Duke—*never* for *that* Duke—or for Tanyrr (even the new, *good* Tanyrr), but for Alia, and Levras, and for Maris, and Tali, and everyone else in Ashbury, and the world.

And after all, why not send the plucky sidekick to face certain death in your stead, if you had one handy? Especially if he wasn't even *your* plucky sidekick, but the hapless squire of a bullying knight who was too dead to seek vengeance?

But what Maris had said over dinner made me think that hadn't been her intention at all.

I told Alia and Levras my theory as the three of us made our way to the Rail District, where Rose's Floral Arrangements was located. Surely there were closer florists? There surely were, "but Rose knows what I like." Maris had given us an envelope, heavy with coin, to present to Rose. It seemed excessive for a bouquet.

Some say you take your life in your hands when you enter the Rail District, but it wasn't nearly as rough as I'd expected. Sure, I might not walk alone at night, but it wasn't a neighborhood falling into ruin, rather one crawling out of it.

Rose's Floral Arrangements seemed to be unusually low on actual flowers, for a florist; there was a single display containing but a single bloom of each type. Even more oddly, there was a padded chair on which a topless woman reclined, while another, an older woman, was gently tapping ink into her chest with mallet and needles. The older woman wore a short-sleeved off-the-shoulder dress; her arms and shoulders were covered in intricate patterns of roses and thorns. A highly detailed rose was tattooed on her chest, similar in style and placement to the dahlia she was giving shape on the younger woman.

"Are you Rose?" Alia asked.

"What gives you that idea?"

The younger woman snickered, but quieted quickly at Rose's sharp glance.

"Maris Goselin sent us to fetch her flowers," I said, handing Rose the envelope. "She said you know what she likes."

That elicited a curious smile. Rose tore the envelope open and emptied entirely too many gold coins into Dahlia's lap. The enclosed letter was longer than I'd expect for simply ordering flowers. Rose read it through with a sigh.

"A bouquet it is, then. Let's see, she's been quite fond of snapdragons, lately." She plucked the snapdragon from the display. A lotus flower followed quickly. "Mmm, but I should surprise her."

Her fingers lingered on an odd, angular blossom, with colors ranging from orange and pink to purple and indigo. It looked more like a brightly crested bird than a flower.

"The bird of paradise is a relatively new addition to my offerings. I don't believe Maris has ever had the pleasure... Yes, I think that's the one. Here, take these around back to get them ready for delivery." She indicated the door behind her.

"I think the three of us can manage three flowers on our own."

Rose laughed. "I sincerely doubt that, especially these three. Besides, it's part of the service. Go on. Oh, and while you're back there, think of what you might want for yourselves." She tapped the letter. "Maris's treat."

I took the three flowers into the back room, Alia and Levras in tow. I suppose you could say this was where the flowers lived. Strictly speaking, they likely lived upstairs, or had their own homes. In the back room of Rose's Floral Arrangements, the flowers arranged themselves on sofas and loveseats, lounging by the fire, reading books or magazines. Seven of them were gathered around a table and seemed to be engaged in a game that involved tome-like rule books, dice of many shapes and colors, and a great deal of arguing.

A woman approached us with a smile. "Hi, I haven't seen you three before. First time? Let's see what you've got." She took the flowers from my hand. "Snapdragon!"

One of the game players looked up and grinned. He was a wiry man of medium height, with long, dark hair pulled back into a ponytail, and a fairly impressive mustache. He stood and approached me.

"Perfect timing," complained one of the other game-players.

"Sorry, folks. You'll just have to get by without your favorite smuggler." He leaned close. "Am I for you, or one of them?"

"Um. Snapdragon?"

"That's right!" He pulled his shirt open with a mischievous grin. A snapdragon was tattooed on his chest. "The one and only!"

"Actually, we're picking up for someone else."

"Oh, well, then, no thanks."

"We don't go with people we haven't met, or who Rose hasn't vetted," said the woman who'd greeted us—from the edge of the pattern that peeked from her beneath her dress, I think I'm safe calling her Daisy. She held the flowers out to me with an air of finality.

"I thought Maris Goselin was known here."

"Why didn't you *say* so?" With a twirl and a flourish, Snapdragon snatched the blossoms out of Daisy's outstretched hand and raised one of them over his head. "Lotus!"

"That tears it," said the complaining game-player, as Lotus pushed away from the table. "We can get by without a smuggler, but we won't last long without our field medic."

Lotus was a tall woman, nearly my height, with broad shoulders and arms and hands that looked like she'd spent time working as a mason. She looked like she could crush poor Maris between her thighs.

Bird of Paradise matched his name. He'd been reading by the fire, and when he stood, the flames cast red and orange across the crest of his golden hair.

"Oh, my," said Alia. Or maybe it was Levras.

"So, do you see anything you like?" I asked.

"Don't be an idiot," Alia snapped. She glanced at Levras. Who looked at me. What a trio we were. What if Tanyrr was right?

"Let's go."

Rose asked the same question I had, when we returned to the lobby, flowers in tow.

"I don't see any roses in your display," I said.

"Careful, roses have thorns. Besides, this one's busy for the next..." She looked at Dalia's chest, assessing. "Four hours. And has another engagement afterward. But the three of you have a credit here, when you want."

"Four *hours*?" Dahlia sagged in the chair, and Rose laughed.

"Are you *serious*?" Alia hissed under her breath at me, as we led the flowers back to Maris's cottage. "*She's* the one you'd pick?"

"She's a tattooist. If we live through the next few days, I'm going to need one. All things considered."

"Oh. Of course." She turned away, dismissing me. Instead: "Hey, Snapdragon, what kind of game were you playing back there?"

"What? Oh, it's called *Tanks & Transistors*. Each player plays a character in a world where there there's no magic at all, but there are machines that act almost like magic. I'm surprised you haven't heard of it, if you're friends with Maris."

Maris, it turned out, owned a publishing company that specialized in lost histories, the literature of fringe cultures, subversive politics, and, apparently, games. She was actually the primary author of the T&T rulebooks, under a pseudonym. Rose and, to a lesser extent, the other flowers, contributed to the ever-growing compendium of interrelated publications.

In *Tanks & Transistors*, you could play a soldier, a medic, a journalist, a technician, or a hacker, whatever that was. A series of die rolls determined your character's strength, agility, vitality, and so on, while skills were gained based on game experience and "backstory." It was the most ridiculous thing I'd ever heard of. I had a hard enough time managing being myself, much less some other character.

Fortunately, before Snapdragon and Lotus were able to get too deep into some adventure or other that their "characters" had had, we arrived at Maris's cottage.

"Told you Rose knows what I like," Maris said, as Snapdragon bowed deeply into a kiss on her hand. She tilted her face into Lotus's kiss. "And who is this?"

"Bird of Paradise, m'lady."

Maris raised an eyebrow. "I'll be the judge of that."

Alia, Levras, and I exchanged nervous glances as the three flowers began to strip the clothing from Maris's body, something that would have scandalized and horrified me only days earlier. Now I was just vaguely uncomfortable. Seemingly oblivious, Maris called my name.

"Solly, what did you think of Rose?"

I was at a loss. "She seemed... nice?"

"You know what I'm asking," she snapped, though the edge got lost in the hint of a moan as Lotus's strong fingers kneaded her shoulders. "Don't ever stop, that's better than sex."

"Oh, the gauntlet has been cast," Snapdragon said. "Challenge accepted."

"She seemed competent. I don't feel qualified to judge whether she's good enough for what we'd need." Though by that time, I was even less sure that I'd be in any position to take advantage of her talents.

"Smart boy. Question everything, especially yourself. It'll save you from making some of the mistakes I made. Oh!" Lotus and Snapdragon had picked her up, carrying her to the bed.

Alia leaned into me. "I think it's time to go." Under her breath.

"Where?" We'd sent the revolutionaries to Tanyrr's house.

"We can camp in the back again," Levras said, as he watched Bird of Paradise disrobe.

We ended up, of course, in the bubbling waters of Maris's magical pool, once again awkwardly distant from each other. The only consolation was that there was no way Tanyrr would be jumping in to make things even more awkward. Alia, of course, was the one who was crass enough to mention it, in her typically sarcastic tone. But her voice caught halfway through, and she had to swallow before finishing the sentiment.

I wasn't sure how to bring up what Tanyrr had said to me, or even if I should. But at the time, I also thought that by this time the following day I'd be dead. It wasn't like there'd be a better time.

"The last time I saw him, he said that the three of us were made for each other. 'You love each other,' he said, 'So love each other.'"

Alia tilted her head skeptically. "Yeah? Go on, then. You two."

Levras and I looked at each other. Then, I leaned in toward him. His mouth opened to mine, and his beard and mustache tickled my nose. His chest shivered where my hand pressed against it. I hadn't known what to expect—this was literally my first kiss, which I'd never expected to be with another man—but it wasn't awful. Rather the opposite.

A hard shoulder knocked me aside, and then Alia was there, her fingers knotted into Levras's hair, pulling him to her. A moment later, she released him and attacked me with equal fervor.

I had no idea what to do with a boy's body, but then, I was even more clueless about how to pleasure a girl. It was no less awkward than it had been before we kissed, as it turned out that none of us knew what we were doing. Even Alia, for all her sarcastic, street-smart quips, was a little fuzzy on the particulars.

But we figured out enough to make do.

Maris's garden gate, I'd discovered earlier, had a magical chime, which alerted her to potential customers who were looking for fresh herbs or eggs. That meant my only way out without waking the household was through the cottage itself. I left Levras and Alia snoring on the blanket and crept into the house to put on my clothing.

I was surprised to see all three flowers asleep on the loveseat, Snapdragon sprawled across Lotus and Bird of Paradise (who, from what we'd heard from Maris through the closed door, had lived up to his name). The bed held two forms, clutched closely together, and the kitchen table held a vase that was full of roses. And Tali, still facedown in a pile of papers, snoring.

I was able to slip out the front door without waking anyone, and then, shivering in the early morning chill, I headed off in the direction of Oldtown.

I'd barely gone two blocks when Alia and Levras caught up with me.

"Did you think we were going to let you do this alone?" Levras said.

"But... You were asleep."

"We slept in shifts," Alia said. "We planned it out."

"What do you mean, planned? You couldn't know I was going to do this."

"Please. I knew the second you kissed Levras. Otherwise, it would have been another ten years before you gathered the courage."

Which, granted, probably wasn't far from the truth.

"Anyway, we're with you, to the end."

I waited for the arguments—this was Maris's responsibility, this was too big for us, we weren't even squires anymore. But I knew what I needed to do, even if the effort was likely to kill me. I'd gladly trade my life for theirs. Well, not *gladly*. But I would. But the arguments never came. They didn't try to dissuade me.

Instead, we walked, hand-in-hand, toward my fate.

The maelstrom of death had grown. Oldtown—most of Ashbury

Tor—was gone. I stumbled to a halt. It was too big. I'd never succeed. Nobody could. I was just throwing my life away, and everyone would die anyway.

My friends kissed me, and held me tight. "You've got this." Tears glistened in Alia's eyes. Which was impossible; Alia never cried. She hadn't cried when she'd been assigned to Tanyrr's service, or any of the times Tanyrr had beaten her bloody. As far as I'd known, she didn't even possess tear ducts.

I steeled my nerve, and walked toward the maelstrom. It was more difficult than I'd expected, like I was walking through mud. And then I realized that I was actually sinking into the street, the cobblestones splashing under my feet, until I was ankle-deep in them. Then they solidified.

"That's close enough," came a voice behind me. Maris Goselin's voice.

"What are you doing here?"

"Freezing my tits off," she said. "You couldn't have waited until the sun was out?"

"No, I mean, you should be home, safe. This is what you trained me for, after all."

Maris sighed. She put a hand on my shoulder. It was ice cold. "This is too big for you, though I can't tell you how much it warms my heart that you thought you could spare me this burden. No. You aren't strong enough, yet, for something like this." She traced some of the henna pattern on my flesh. "Never will be, until you make this a permanent part of your body."

I clutched at her hand. She extracted herself with a circular twist.

"Doesn't mean you're off the hook. Might be more than I can handle, too. But I think I can at least reduce its power to something you can manage."

"I can do that."

She scoffed. "We'll see about that." She stepped away from me, standing between the maelstrom and me. Facing me, she said, "One last lesson, Solly. Watch this carefully, because I won't be able to show you twice. This is a spell that attracts power. It doesn't matter what that power is; that would be determined by the threads you choose. It will drag that specific power into your body until you tell it to stop. Or until you die. If I'm not able to eliminate all of this, you'll need to act quickly, before it grows again to more than you can absorb."

She reached out and pinched my cheeks. "So watch carefully, and don't dally."

"It'll kill me," I said. "If I do this."

"Yes."

And then she reached out, and took hold of her death.

It took nearly an hour. When she completed the drawing spell, the maelstrom surged toward her. Into her. I can't say when she died. I hope it was early, but I suspect she held on to the end, even after her flesh had been torn away and all that remained was her silhouette, a shell that pulled at the maelstrom and shattered its force. A silhouette fallen to its knees and curled in on itself in pain.

And then it was gone. *She* was gone, and the maelstrom with her.

A year.

That's how long someone has to be missing in Ashbury to have them legally declared dead, with no body, and no witnesses who wouldn't potentially benefit from the declaration. And apparently, according to the lawyers handling her affairs, I was due to benefit, and my friends with me.

I didn't want to do it, but Rose insisted, and Alia and Levras supported her. From a practical perspective, it didn't much matter. We'd been living in the cottage since her death; without Maris there to complain nobody was going to kick us out. Besides, someone needed to feed the goats and the chickens.

Levras and Rose had been running the publishing company, while Alia made it her mission to preserve the goblin ruins that had been uncovered by the maelstrom. She had set up an organization for outreach to the goblin tribes, and to lobby for goblin rights.

The Republic of Ashbury won its first war, a decisive victory against Falkirk with support from the Free People's Republic of Amisara and the Duchy of Brittington. Amisaran president Darialth Lanisdottr had arrived at the cottage just hours after Maris's death; apparently Maris had written to her early in the crisis, and Darialth had ridden hard for five days, only to arrive too late. She and Rose had grieved together briefly, and then she sought out the provisional council to establish formal diplomatic relations. Duke Farlow had been ransomed as part of the armistice agreement, whereupon he was tried and exiled, the provisional government having abolished the death penalty, and the dungeons having been reduced to dust. The new government still operated out of the home that Tanyrr had bequeathed the three of us, while they argued about what architectural style would properly reflect the new republic's values.

Me? I didn't do much of anything. I got my tattoo; Rose had trained under the man who had done Maris's tattoos, and was more than adequate for the task. I became more acquainted with the bees. Sometimes, I tended the garden. Once in a while, I studied magic, but I was never able to sustain any particular effort for more than a few days at a time.

The funeral was held in Hob Park, where Ashbury Tor used to be, before it was stripped away. Where Maris had died, along with Tanyrr and so many others. They had wanted to put up a statue, like they had with Tanyrr, first hero of the Republic. Maris would have hated it. Instead, we planted an acre of clover and erected some trellis for morning glory. Something for the bees.

Everyone who was anyone in Ashbury had come out for the event. The entire government, of course, many of whom I knew because they'd practically lived in the cottage for weeks. Rose and the other flowers. Tali, holding her daughter, Tanili Tanyrrskid, to her breast. President Darialth of Amisara, with her wife, Camilla, and their daughter, Frida Marisdottr ("ask my moms, they *love* telling that story, especially the first time they meet my friends"), who, as the youngest of the out-of-town guests, was still ten years my senior. Frida was beautiful. Dark-skinned and high-cheek-boned, her hair in long, matted locks that should have looked messy, but looked regal instead. She bore almost no resemblance to Maris, except for the sharp intelligence in her eyes. She had Maris's eyes.

They'd wanted me to give the eulogy, but I couldn't. I could barely bring myself to attend. But there was no shortage of people willing to speak for the ornery crone who'd lived by herself, including Darialth and Rose and Tali. A contingent of goblins had come to pay respects, and both Alia and Levras rose to say some words.

Frida stood next to me, conflicting emotions on her face. She shook her head when I asked if she was going to be speaking.

"We were never close. I only met her a few times, and it was always awkward. I mean, I think she wanted to love me? But I think she was scared to."

Later, when the will was read, she didn't seem surprised—or hurt—that Maris had left the bulk of her estate to me. The publishing company would be shared between Rose, Frida, and me. Other than that, the only things bequeathed to Frida were an old, broken lute, an even older dagger, a wedding ring, and a thick binder full of letters and manuscripts. Frida read the note clipped to the first document, and then held them close to her chest and burst into tears. I didn't ask her what the note said.

Ultimately, we ended up back at the cottage, all a bit drunk, with the exception of Tali, who claimed the baby didn't like wine. She was in deep-and-somewhat-starstruck interview mode with President Darialth and her wife. Frida joined as we three former squires escaped to the hot tub.

Alia started explaining the concept of the hot tub, but Frida interrupted.

"I know what it is," she said, half a smile on her face.

It didn't take long after climbing into the tub for Alia to settle herself in front of Levras; dutifully, Levras set himself to kneading the tension from her back and neck.

"Don't suppose I could get in the queue?" Frida stretched her neck demonstrably.

"Solly's good with his hands," Alia said. "I mean, for back rubs, too."

Frida glanced at Alia, then at me, and I shrugged, hopefully nonchalantly, though it felt like my face was burning.

She wasn't lying; her shoulders and neck were like rocks.

"I agonized for a year whether I should come or not," she admitted. "I think I'm glad I did, but it hasn't been easy. I wish I'd had the opportunity to get to know her like you did. Oh! What are you doing? And don't ever stop."

I'd followed the tension to a spot on the inside of her shoulder blade, a hard knot of muscle that screamed for release, and set about releasing it.

"Sixteen days," I said.

"What?"

"That's how long I knew her. Thirteen if you start counting from the first time we spoke."

"It's not how long, but how the time was spent. She and I spent our time together avoiding talking about what mattered. I think it was different for you. She couldn't afford to push you away."

I was saved from having to formulate a response as the back door opened. President Darialth led Tali and Camilla into the back yard.

"Frida, there you are! I was hoping to show you where the Republic of Amisara was first conceived, but you've already found it." She turned to Tali as she began to disrobe. "Have you heard this story? No? Well, it started right here, when a young shapeshifter fell into this pool..."

I'd actually read Maris's account of the story; one of her many unpublished manuscripts. Darialth deftly skipped large parts of the less pleasant sections, and Tali dutifully wrote it all down, her feet dangling in the pool next to me.

By the time Darialth got around to Maris's wedding, Frida and I had switched places, and I was discovering just how much tension I'd been collecting, myself. Levras and Camilla had kept our wine goblets filled for a bit, then switched us to brandy, so by that time, we were all well relaxed.

Frida rolled her eyes as if she'd endured this dozens of times, as Darialth launched into the wedding story, her wife interjecting embarrassing details. "It can't possibly have been this farcical," Frida said in my ear as the story wrapped up, "or I'd never have been conceived, don't you think?" I wondered what she'd think after reading Maris's manuscript.

"I think she'd have taken a perverse pleasure in having that recited during her memorial," I said.

"You're likely correct," President Darialth said. "What about you three? It's been a year you've been together. I'd have thought you'd have made it official by now."

"Which pair of us?" Alia asked. "Who gets left out?"

"It's fairer this way," Levras added.

"Come to Amisara," Camilla said. "Our marriages respect all families."

"And are recognized by all nations we have diplomatic relations with," Darialth said.

Alia, Levras, and I looked at each other. We had never talked about marriage; it had never seemed a possibility. I'm sure as many emotions flashed across my face as I saw in the others—fear and hope, trepidation, nervousness, embarrassment, among the most obvious.

"We'll consider it," I said, and Levras lifted an eyebrow. "We'll *seriously* consider it."

"Consider it considered," Levras said, his toes seeking mine in the depths of the pool, as he turned his head to kiss Alia.

Alia grinned. "If the ceremony is as grueling as I've heard, we'd better get a lot of practice in," and both Darialth and Camilla laughed.

Tali, to my horror, was taking notes.

Freda leaned forward, her body pressed against my back, and whispered in my ear.

"Let me know if you need a maid of honor."

She was a fantastic maid of honor.

AFTERWORD: BAD PUNS AND MANGLED GENRES

Once upon a time, as they say in these sorts of tales, my friend Mike Ventrella asked if I'd be willing to write story for a shared-world anthology he was putting together. It was for a little-known publisher, with expected pay being a share of royalties on approximately nothing. Enticing, but really, I was more interested in getting my work out in front of eyeballs that could help my career. Still, Mike's a friend. Give me the relevant details, and if an idea pops up, maybe I'll write something. No promises.

Fortannis, it turns out, is the game-world of a Live Action Role Playing (LARP) gaming system, for which Mike wrote the rulebook (the *Alliance LARP Rule Book*). I've played plenty of role-playing games in my day (one of which was with my friend Bob Norwicke, whose D&D character, Brian, was just too much fun not to interject into this world), but I've never LARPed in my life. Mike had written several novels set in and around the Duchy of Ashbury, in the Kingdom of Icenia, on the world of Fortannis, to promote the LARP. And his anthology was supposed to do the same.

Even more enticing.

He sent me a copy of the rulebook, and his first novel. It's High Fantasy stuff. You know, knights and elves and dwarves and wizards.

(Mostly) Noble People performing (mostly) Great Deeds. The battle between Good and Evil. It's what I'd imagined myself writing since the first time (and each of many additional times) I read *The Lord of the Rings* before escaping high school. But it's been a long time, and I've grown away from epic tales of noble deeds by the pure of heart. There's often a right and a wrong, but the details get messy on the ground.

But.

What if there was a park in Ashbury? Named Ashbury Park? Growing up in the Philly area in the '80s, there was no way to escape Bruce Springsteen's iconic and oft-misunderstood anthem, and pretty soon, *Born in Icenia* was playing on a loop in my head. (Which was weird and annoying, because I'm not even a Springsteen fan, y'know?)

I still had no interest in writing High Fantasy, though. Well, fuck it. Genre's just a construct. And thus we find "Lady" Maris Goselin, a paranormal investigator/professional fixer whose whole life has been shaped by bad luck and worse decisions, trying to carve out a place for herself in a society that would never respect someone of her origins. Creating a new identity for herself out of skill and cunning and sheer cussed obstinance. With an estranged rock star ex-boyfriend (see above-mentioned pun). Plus evil nobles and child sacrifice. And tentacles. All wrapped up in a High Fantasy setting.

Wait, what? It's supposed to be Young Adult, too? Oops. Too late, the tentacles are already there.

What a fun character to write! I'm so glad she let me into her life, even if it's just for this one little story that hardly anyone will ever read.

What's that, Mike? There'll be more anthologies? For *even more lack of pay?*

Count me in!

And thus the original formulations of the first five stories in this collection came into being (they've since seen some revision, hopefully for the better).

When Dragonwell Publishing expressed interest in putting out this collection, it gave me an opportunity to explore the parts of Maris's life that I had previously only alluded to. They're not *easy* tales, and it took me longer than I expected to find the courage to dig into them.

THE FORTANNIS SHARED WORLD GROUND RULES

The world of Fortannis, and the Duchy of Ashbury, had certain basic rules that underlay the "shared world" aspect of it. Not being part of the LARPing community that built this world, I didn't quite manage to be as faithful as some might have wanted.

- The nobility is merit-based, not hereditary, and by and large are good people of good intentions. (I mostly ignored this, because nobility doesn't work like that. Even if it starts that way, it doesn't stay that way. Want an example? Just look at the history of legacy admissions in elite colleges.)

- Goblins are inherently stupid and barbaric, and are presumed evil and cunning. They're the butt of many a joke, and have no redeeming qualities. (No. I refuse to assign moral or intellectual qualities to things like race or class.)

- Ashbury was somehow "imported" into the world of Fortannis about 80 years before the start of the first story in this book. (I was unaware of this until much later, after I'd written all sorts of things that contradicted that timeline. So what you hold here is an alternate timeline from the Fortannis/Ashbury canon.)

- The concept of religion doesn't exist in Fortannis. There are no gods and no priests. Ethics and morality are decoupled from adherence to religious teachings. (This is challenging in unexpected ways. Not the ethics part, because if you need a god to scare you into being good, I've got some bad news for you, but the language; it's damned surprising how much of our everyday language refers to religion.)

- Magic is divided into order and chaos. Order magic works with the natural world to create its effects. Chaos magic, on the other hand, is disruptive. It gives access to more power, but at a high cost to the spell caster, and to the world. For Maris, I carved out a different mode of magic use. Her experience of magic is akin to synesthesia, and she's unique in this, she thinks. I think of traditional magic spells as being like classical compositions, effective to the degree that they can be faithfully and precisely reproduced, while what Maris is doing is more like jazz improvisation, playing with the basic elements of power to pull together ad hoc spells.

AFTERWORD

With the amount of deviation from the Fortannis canon, I'll just have to claim that Maris Goselin's Ashbury is on a timeline that vaguely intersects the main timeline during the reign of Duke Aramis, up through Terin Ostler's negotiation of a peace treaty with the goblins. And if you want to know who Terin Ostler is, you'll need to read Michael Ventrella's *Arch Enemies*. 'Cause Maris isn't going to give you any spoilers.

THE BEES

Bees play many roles in myth and folklore throughout our world, notably as symbols of life, birth, death, and resurrection. In some cultures, they were seen as creatures that could navigate between the realms of life and death. In parts of Europe and elsewhere there is an old custom called "telling the bees," where the beekeeper would inform the bees of significant events, particularly of marriages, births, and deaths. Failing to do so would result in either bad luck or in the death or abandonment of the hive.

I'm not certain how Maris came to her relationship with her bees. I expect it started sometime while she was trying to kill who she was, to not be the sort of person who drives everyone she cares about away. That it was part of her personal rebirth and a lasting influence on her ongoing voyage of growth and self-discovery.

Also, like Maris, they pack a sharp sting if you upset them.

One thing is certain—learning to communicate with the bees, and subsequently learning to better control her emotions to keep them calm, has likely saved many lives, including her own.

BRIAN

Ah, Brian.
        There's a joke where a farmer takes her husband to a psychologist because he thinks he's a chicken. Psychologist says, with hypnosis, I can fix that. By the time you leave here, your husband will no longer think he's a chicken. Farmer says, "Don't you dare. We need the eggs."

Bob Norwicke's Brian was a fanatical (and clearly mad) cleric in our

Dungeons & Dragons campaign who believed in a god nobody had ever heard of: Cheom. If I recall correctly, Brian would distribute pamphlets about Cheom everywhere our party traveled. Cheom was pictured on these as a bandoliered Che Guevara sitting in lotus position, purple flying hippos fluttering around his head, and Brian's speech was a word salad of mixed metaphors ("No one escapes the long tongue of Cheom!" and the like.) Did Cheom exist only in Brian's fevered imagination? It didn't matter, we needed the healing spells.

I wanted to explore what would happen if you took a character like this and interjected him into a world with literally no concept of religion. I also wanted to write a story where people of radically different worldviews worked together to solve a problem. I reached out to Bob to ask permission to use his character and discovered that he had been developing stories of his own starring the mad cleric. Oh? And how'd you like to co-write this one with me?

It really was as much fun to write that one as I'd imagined.

FORTANNIS BIBLIOGRAPHY

1. *Arch Enemies* by Michael Ventrella (Reissued in two volumes as *Terin Ostler and the Arch Enemies* and *Terin Ostler and the War of the Words*)

    https://www.fantasticbooks.biz/product-page/terin-ostler-and-the-arch-enemies-by-michael-a-ventrella

    https://www.fantasticbooks.biz/product-page/copy-of-terin-ostler-and-the-war-of-the-words-by-michael-a-ventrella

2. *The Axes of Evil* by Michael Ventrella (Reissued as *Terin Ostler and the Axes of Evil*)

    https://www.fantasticbooks.biz/product-page/terin-ostler-and-the-axes-of-evil-by-michael-a-ventrella

3. *Terin Ostler and the Zombie King (and Other Stories)* by Michael Ventrella

    https://www.fantasticbooks.biz/product-page/terin-ostler-and-the-zombie-king-and-other-stories-by-michael-a-ventrella

4. *Tales of Fortannis: A Bard's Eye View* by Michael Ventrella (ed.) (out of print)

5. *Tales of Fortannis: A Bard in the Hand* by Michael Ventrella (ed.) (out of print)

6. *Tales of Fortannis: A Bard Day's Knight* by Michael Ventrella (ed.) (out of print)

7. *Tales of Fortannis: A Bard Act to Follow* by Michael Ventrella (ed.) (out of print)

8. *Tales of Fortannis: No Holds Bard* **by Michael Ventrella (ed.)** (out of print)

9. *Tales of Fortannis* by Michael Ventrella (ed.) (The Best of Fortannis collection)

   https://www.fantasticbooks.biz/product-page/tales-of-fortannis-edited-by-michael-a-ventrella

10. *It's a Wonderful Death: A Fortannis Novel* by Derek Beebe

    https://www.amazon.com/dp/B0DMWDMQR4

11. *The Doomsayer: A Fortannis Short Story* by Derek Beebe

    https://www.amazon.com/dp/B0D45Q54DV

12. *Alliance Rule Book* **by** Michael Ventrella (ed.)

13. *Alliance Player's Guide* by Michael Ventrella (ed.)

Publication credits for the earlier version of some chapters in this book:

"**Bad Debts**" © 2011, first appeared in *Tales of Fortannis: A Bard's Eye View*, Double Dragon Publishing

"**Embarrassing Relations**" © 2013, first appeared in *Tales of Fortannis: A Bard in the Hand*, Double Dragon Publishing

"**The Mystery of the Dead Cat in the Darkness**" © 2015, first appeared in *Tales of Fortannis: A Bard Day's Knight*, Double Dragon Publishing

"**The Consistency of Small Minds**" © 2016, first appeared in *Tales of Fortannis: A Bard Act to Follow*, Double Dragon Publishing

"**The Hole in Vorak's Peak**" © 2018, first appeared in *Tales of Fortannis: No Holds Bard*, Double Dragon Publishing

BIBLIOGRAPHY

Alliance LARP

For more information about the Fortannis game world and the immersive live-action role-playing experiences it offers, please visit https://alliancelarp.com.

ACKNOWLEDGEMENTS

The stories in this book that give shape to Maris Goselin's life developed over many years, between 2010 and 2024, and it's impossible to acknowledge all the people who supported this effort. The more detailed I get, the more people will feel left out, so... we'll go with the obvious:

Thanks to: Mike Ventrella, who introduced me to Fortannis back in 2010 and invited me to write a story set therein; Anna Kashina, who asked me to flesh out the parts of Maris' life that I'd neglected in the original short stories (and for helping me sharpen the early stories written when I had no idea what I was doing); Bob Norwicke, who contributed the inimitable Brian to Maris's narrative; my spousal unit, Linda, who puts up with me locking myself away to "write"; the Gryphon Cafe for the liquid sustenance without which this book would not exist; and to everyone else who has been in my life in the intervening time, all of whom have contributed in one way or another to what ended up in the manuscript.

ABOUT THE AUTHORS

Much to his embarrassment, **Bernie Mojzes** has outlived Lord Byron, Percy Shelley, Janice Joplin and the Red Baron, without even once having been shot down over Morlancourt Ridge. Having failed to achieve a glorious martyrdom, he has instead turned his hand to the penning of prose, an example of which you currently hold in your hands. Or is perhaps being projected from an electronic device perched atop your stationary bicycle or treadmill as a distraction from mundane tasks. Since undertaking this labor, he has had some three dozen short stories published in anthologies and various online venues, and has himself published the now-defunct online zine, *Unlikely Story*, and has edited two anthologies: *Clowns: The Unlikely Coulrophobia Remix*, and *The Flesh Made Word*. He tries and fails to maintain a long out-of-date website at www.kappamaki.com. Maybe someday that will change.

Bob Norwicke, the voice of Brian in "Embarrassing Relations", makes up stories of people real and imagined, some familiar, some fantastic. He is currently working on an overly ambitious science fiction/fantasy epic as well as a series of short stories called *Tales from the 40*, based on a bus route in Philadelphia. Bob's "A Dog of the Wrong Color," the first story from *Tales from the 40*, won third place in the 22nd Annual Taproot Writing Contest.

ASSASSINS' CODE BOOK TWO

THE GUILD OF ASSASSINS

ANNA KASHINA

ASSASSINS' CODE BOOK THREE

ASSASSIN QUEEN

ANNA KASHINA

ASSASSINS' CODE ORIGIN

SHADOW BLADE

ANNA KASHINA

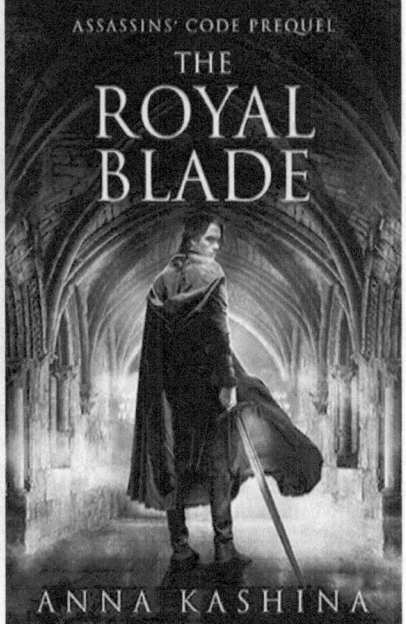

ASSASSINS' CODE PREQUEL

THE ROYAL BLADE

ANNA KASHINA

"A vivid, well-written tale that moves along at an entertaining pace"
The British Fantasy Society

Ashamet Desert Born

Terry Jackman

"A solid mystical adventure that will interest readers from start to finish"
—*Publishers Weekly*

THE GARDEN
AT THE ROOF OF THE WORLD

W. B. J. WILLIAMS

John Lawson

The Loathly Lady

THE BLACKWELL FAMILY SECRET
THE GUARDIANS OF SIN

JONATHAN L. FERRARA